ALSO BY KATHLEEN WEST

Minor Dramas & Other Catastrophes

Are We There Yet?

Kathleen West

Berkley
New York

BERKLEY
An imprint of Penguin Random House LLC
penguinrandomhouse.com

Copyright © 2021 by Kathleen West
Penguin Random House supports copyright. Copyright fuels creativity, encourages diverse
voices, promotes free speech, and creates a vibrant culture. Thank you for buying an
authorized edition of this book and for complying with copyright laws by not reproducing,
scanning, or distributing any part of it in any form without permission. You are supporting
writers and allowing Penguin Random House to continue to publish books for every reader.

BERKLEY and the BERKLEY & B colophon
are registered trademarks of Penguin Random House LLC.

Library of Congress Cataloging-in-Publication Data

Names: West, Kathleen, 1978– author.
Title: Are we there yet? / Kathleen West.
Description: First edition. | New York: Berkley, 2021.
Identifiers: LCCN 2020035702 (print) | LCCN 2020035703 (ebook) |
ISBN 9780593098431 (hardcover) | ISBN 9780593098455 (ebook)
Subjects: LCSH: Domestic fiction.
Classification: LCC PS3623.E8448 A89 2021 (print) |
LCC PS3623.E8448 (ebook) | DDC 813/.6—dc23
LC record available at https://lccn.loc.gov/2020035702
LC ebook record available at https://lccn.loc.gov/2020035703

Printed in Canada
1   3   5   7   9   10   8   6   4   2

Cover art by Jacky Winter / Ka-Boom Pty
Cover design by Emily Osborne
Book design by Ashley Tucker

This is a work of fiction. Names, characters, places, and incidents either are the product
of the author's imagination or are used fictitiously, and any resemblance to actual persons,
living or dead, business establishments, events, or locales is entirely coincidental.

To my family, the people who were there in the beginning,
and to all of you I've found along the way

Alice Sullivan

Alice scrolled through the latest posts on the NextDoor app as she waited for Nadia, who was, as usual, several minutes late for their twice-monthly coffee. Meredith used to join them, but she'd announced a year ago that she'd rather see them on Sundays for power walks than lounge in a Starbucks.

"Two birds, you know?" Meredith had said, thinking of her workout.

Alice and Nadia had agreed to the walks but still kept the coffee dates, a tradition since the kids had been in kindergarten seven years before. Now, Alice's son, Teddy, could wear his dad's shoes, and Nadia's Donovan knew how to code in three languages. All three moms had been nervous to leave the safety of Elm Creek Elementary when their kids started junior high that fall, but it had been a smooth transition so far to "the big school," as they called it. Well, smooth for Alice's and Meredith's children. Donovan continued on his "behavior plan."

The neighbors on NextDoor complained that local kids were "tagging," a term Alice hadn't heard in ages. Shirley MacIntosh, a frequent contributor to the app and one whose posts Alice, Meredith, and Nadia routinely mocked during their walks, had photographed a rudimentary drawing of a penis in some kind of pink paint on a porta-potty at Elm Creek Park. "Who would draw a rocket ship in permanent ink?" Shirley had written. "Haven't today's parents heard of chalk?!"

Alice snorted with laughter—the drawing was definitely not a

rocket ship. She took a screenshot of the post, which she texted to her husband, Patrick, along with a reminder about their daughter's imminent school conference.

Nadia finally pushed through the front door of the coffee shop, her fleece jacket zipped against the mid-October chill. Alice pulled the scarf she'd layered over a silk blouse tighter against her neck. As Nadia placed her coffee order, Alice checked her earlobes for her lucky pearl drops. Patrick had splurged on them for their first Christmas together, and they'd become a talisman for the days she had important client meetings, like today with the Kerrigans. The Kerrigans' midcentury home would require a complete remodel, she hoped by her design firm.

At the counter, Nadia held up a finger, indicating that she'd be at the table in a minute. They'd have to talk fast, and Alice would then beeline to meet with Adrian's second-grade teacher. It'd be tight, but Alice would make it in time to hear that, as usual, Adrian was doing just fine.

Nadia looked casual in her joggers, and Alice felt jealous of her work-from-home lifestyle. It wasn't that Nadia, a software engineer, wasn't busy, but she always seemed so relaxed with no in-person clients to impress. Of course, she did have Donovan to worry about. Alice would try not to mention Adrian's conference to Nadia. When his third-grade teacher had suggested that Donovan had legitimate behavioral problems—anxiety and perhaps oppositional defiant disorder— she and Meredith had basically scraped Nadia off the floor and fielded her hysterical calls and texts for days afterward.

Alice had googled oppositional defiant disorder then. One of the main causes, at least according to the Internet, was a lack of engaged parenting. Alice secretly thought her friend had only half addressed that root cause in the years since the initial evaluation. She wasn't surprised that seventh grade had been a struggle so far. It had been tricky to talk about with Nadia, given how well Teddy had fared.

"Sorry I'm late," Nadia said as she sat. "Did you take the whole morning off for Aidy's conference?"

Alice winced. She must have already mentioned the appointment in a text. "No," she said lightly. "I have a client meeting at nine thirty. Think I'll make it?"

Nadia raised an eyebrow. "Assuming a teacher will run on time at conferences? Bold move."

Maybe your *conferences run long*, Alice thought. *Adrian's should be a snap.* "I think I've got a handle on her, and I'm only Miss Miller's second appointment. How late could it be?"

"I'm sure it'll be fine." Nadia pulled her arm out of her jacket, and Alice knew this was the time to ask about Donovan, but she didn't have the energy.

"How's your mom?" Alice ventured instead.

"The same. But can I ask you about Teddy?" Nadia looked nervous, and Alice braced herself. Sometimes these queries from Nadia—"Has Teddy ever, like, stolen anything at school?" or "How worried would you be if Teddy couldn't find a partner for the robotics fair?"—required an inordinate amount of sidestepping. While she hadn't yet heard the story from Nadia, Teddy had told her at dinner the other night that Donovan had called their science teacher a "fuckhead" in front of the class the previous week.

"Sure?" Alice flipped her phone over, ignoring an incoming text message from her boss, no doubt a pep talk about the Kerrigan appointment.

"So, this might be awkward," Nadia said gently. *At* least she's self-*aware.* "Donovan told me something about Teddy."

Alice touched the base of her throat, feeling the ridges of her collarbones beneath her fingers. "About Teddy?"

Nadia squinted. "Donovan says Teddy has some sort of a feud going with Tane Lagerhead." She shook her head. "'Feud' sounds so dramatic; it's probably the wrong word. But apparently they're not getting along? Donovan didn't know the origin, but I guess there's been some stuff happening on Snapchat." Nadia took the lid off her drink and blew into it. "Have I mentioned how much I hate that app?"

Alice remembered the day she'd allowed Teddy to download it. She'd paused in their negotiation, just as her *How to Talk to Teens* book had advised. She had told Teddy she wasn't sure he was ready for the responsibility of Snapchat. But as they'd reflected on his behavior "honestly and openly," as the psychologist authors of the manual advised, she had to admit he hadn't yet done anything stupid on social media. Alice monitored his Instagram, of course, and the one time Teddy had posted that vaping meme, she'd caught it and made him delete it within minutes. She was pretty sure neither Meredith nor Nadia had seen it, though they all followed each other's kids.

But Snapchat loomed beyond Alice's parental control in a way that made her leery. Still, "everyone had it," as Teddy argued, and without it he might lose out on formative friendship interactions. This last part was Alice's rationalization. But Alice thought she was right. Since he'd downloaded the app, he'd told her about his "streaks" with friends and giggled with her and Adrian about the filter that gave them all flower crowns. It seemed harmless.

"I haven't heard anything from Teddy about Tane," Alice said.

"I guess they're in a pretty public skirmish." Nadia put her head in her hand, clearly uncomfortable. "'Skirmish' isn't the right word, either, but there are hashtags and kids are taking sides. Apparently, Teddy threatened to do something 'major' to Tane." Nadia put air quotes around "major." "Anyway, Donovan's worried."

Donovan's worried? Alice stifled an eye roll. Donovan might want to look in the mirror.

"Thanks so much for the heads-up." Alice sipped her Americano and pushed her dark curls behind her ears. "I'll check in with him tonight." She hoped her tone closed the subject. Alice loved Nadia but wasn't prepared to accept advice from the mother of the most notorious problem child in the class of 2025.

"It's just that, if Donovan—you know Donovan. He's no stranger to drama." Nadia reached out and touched Alice's forearm. "If Donovan

gives me a warning about something? I just feel like it's got to be serious."

Alice blinked hard and fought the impulse to shake off her friend's touch. "Okay." *Don't say anything you can't take back*, she warned herself. "I appreciate it, but I don't really want to talk about it." She slid her arm away. "Can we change the subject? Any interesting projects coming down the pike?"

Nadia picked up her drink and took a long sip. Alice snuck a glance at her watch.

Meredith Yoshida

- - - - -

Meredith clicked out of the NextDoor app as she lit the burner under the oats she'd prepared the night before. Shirley MacIntosh had documented a spray-painting incident at Elm Creek Park, a penis on a porta-potty that Shirley inexplicably misidentified as a rocket ship. Did she think the ball hairs were flames? Meredith screenshotted the post. She'd send it to her group text with Nadia and Alice later.

Meredith lowered her nose to the saucepan and sniffed. She'd snuck in a little protein powder, hopeful that Sadie wouldn't detect it. It had been so hard lately to make sure her nearly-thirteen-year-old had a balanced diet, especially since Sadie had forbidden Meredith from volunteering in the lunchroom at the junior high. With the demands of her daughter's synchronized skating program, Meredith wasn't sure Sadie had the nutrient balance to effectively support her growing body. But if she said "growing body" to Sadie, her daughter retreated to her bedroom and closed the door.

Meredith stirred the oats and took a tiny bite. She flattened her tongue against the roof of her mouth, searching for evidence of the powder. She knew from experience that if Sadie detected anything except honey or brown sugar, she'd have to trash the whole batch. Sometimes, she could get her daughter to stir in banana slices or nuts, but usually not.

Clean, Meredith thought as she swallowed. Breakfast settled, she whipped her phone out of her pocket to check the portal. That was one thing Meredith liked about junior high—the teachers were required to post grades and behavioral feedback online. At back-to-school night, the assistant principal had suggested logging in to the portal no more than once per week, but Meredith reasoned that more was better. She refreshed it in the mornings so she could remind Sadie about any upcoming tests or quizzes, again at lunchtime to gauge the homework volume, and then usually over Sadie's shoulder when her daughter finished assignments either before or after skating practice.

Meredith wasn't checking up on Sadie because she thought she had anything to worry about. Sadie had always been an excellent student with test scores above the 95th percentile. But Meredith had read plenty of articles about the precarious junior high transition. Her favorite magazine, *Thinking Mother*, had had an entire issue on it. The experts seemed to agree on one word to describe the stage: flux.

Flux capacitor, Meredith thought every time she reread the fraying copy. She pictured Doc Brown's haywire hair from *Back to the Future*. She and Bill had introduced Sadie to the classic movie but only made it a few minutes in before Meredith remembered the jokes reinforced rape culture. Sadie had rolled her eyes as Meredith suggested *Moana* for the millionth time instead.

Sadie not liking her favorite movies anymore was just one more indicator of the capriciousness of junior high. At least Meredith had the portal to help her monitor the chaos. As the landing screen loaded in front of her, Meredith raised two fingers to the permanent wrinkle in the center of her forehead. She'd told Alice and Nadia she didn't believe in Botox, which was true. But lately, her eyebrow crease deepened by the day.

This time, the worrying was because of Sadie's science grade. It had been a 93 the night before, and this morning it was an 84. Meredith clicked for a more detailed report just as Sadie arrived in the

kitchen, her stockinged feet shuffling on the wood floor Meredith and Bill had installed the previous spring. Alice had overseen the refurbishment and sourced the reclaimed boards from barns in outstate Minnesota. Alice had also helped Meredith choose her dining room table, place mats, and napkins. Soon, Meredith hoped, her friend could advise on new countertops and cabinetry. Bill would have a bonus coming in December.

"Can I have coffee?" Sadie asked, a smile fluttering. Her daughter had already combed her hair, a heart-shaped barrette holding her growing-out bangs near her right temple.

Meredith laughed. "If you want something hot, you could have herbal tea."

Sadie sat at the table and ran her fingers over the steel-blue place mat. "But Chloe and Mikaela both drink lattes."

Meredith put her phone on the counter and ladled a scoop of oatmeal into a bowl. "Maybe their parents don't know about the negative side effects of caffeine," Meredith said. "That's what you get for having a mom who's up to date on medical research." She winked at Sadie.

When Meredith herself had been a seventh grader, she'd poured gritty coffee into a perma-stained travel mug and taken the city bus to school most mornings. Her mom worked the earliest shifts at the nursing home, sometimes catching a double to cover groceries and gas. With the basics to worry about, she hadn't had time to think about what it meant to start drinking coffee at twelve, even though she'd been a nurse.

But Meredith did consider caffeine. Even though she worked thirty hours per week as a physical therapist, she also made time to think about both Sadie's protein consumption and her science grade. Meredith grabbed her phone again and felt her jaw drop as she looked at Sadie's most recent test score.

"Sadie!" she shouted before she could decide whether it would traumatize her daughter.

Sadie dropped her spoon, the metal clanking against the side of her bowl. "What?"

"What the hell happened on the unicellular and multicellular organism test?" Meredith felt her forehead again, stretching the wrinkle. "Fifty-six?" *Probably*, Meredith thought, *Mr. Robinson had made an error in reporting. And also, why did I say "hell"?*

Sadie picked up her spoon again. "Yeah," she said calmly. "I just totally bricked that." She pushed an overflowing spoonful of oatmeal in her mouth and chewed, her cheeks puffed.

"Sorry for saying 'hell.'" Meredith and Bill had agreed ages ago to watch their language, but the shock of the 56 overwhelmed her. "Fifty-six?" she said again to Sadie. "That's the lowest grade you've ever gotten in your life. Is it a mistake?"

Once she'd swallowed, Sadie lifted her napkin to her face and dabbed at her eyes, though Meredith couldn't see any tears. "Sorry, Mom," Sadie said. "I'm not quite sure what happened. I saw it last night before I went to bed."

Meredith blinked. So, Sadie had known about the failing grade and not mentioned it. "Why didn't you tell me?" Meredith sat next to her at the table and put her hand over her daughter's wrist.

Sadie sniffled again, but her eyes were definitely dry. "I guess I was hoping it would just go away overnight. You wouldn't have to know."

Meredith squeezed. "Sadie, that's silly. It's right here." She waved her phone over the oatmeal bowl. "In this day and age, it's impossible to keep a secret."

Alice Sullivan

———

Alice peeked into the second-grade classroom again and tried not to frown at Miss Miller. She looked at the time on her phone, 8:52, and finally admitted to herself that it had been foolhardy to schedule a conference just ahead of her walk-through at the Kerrigans' new house. She had precisely twenty-five minutes to catch up on Adrian's social and academic development. Meanwhile, it didn't look like the teacher was even close to wrapping up with Eloise and Jean-Luc Bisset, who were already over their time by seven critical minutes.

Alice texted Patrick. "Not going to make it?" She'd known his absence had been a possibility, and he hadn't replied to her reminder.

"I've been Sachman'd," he wrote back. Senior partner Alan Sachman's whims had shaped Alice and Patrick's life for a full nine years since Patrick had joined his law firm. She sighed. They both knew there was no way around a Sachman directive. Many a missed appointment and even one canceled family vacation to Naples, Florida had taught them that. Patrick was about to start spending weeks at a time in Cincinnati because of Sachman, handling a trial for a case he'd been working on for years. He'd only be home on weekends. It annoyed her, sure, but they agreed Patrick's partnership at Sachman Feldstone was a solid investment in the future, a future in which they'd pay two rounds of college tuition and slowly remodel their 1925 two-story. Alice peeked

into Adrian's classroom again, this time achieving meaningful, but she hoped friendly, eye contact with Miss Miller, who held up a finger, making her wait just as Nadia had in the coffee shop.

Alice perused the student work hanging in the hallway. She found Adrian's stilted seven-year-old handwriting on a detailed drawing of a spider, its hairs sticking out wildly from its body. Alice smiled and raised her phone to take a photo. Adrian had always loved insects. *Arachnids*, she corrected herself, in the case of this black widow. Adrian had lectured her just the previous week on people's too-common miscategorization of spiders. Alice scanned some other drawings and saw similarly wobbly lines and eraser marks on the labels for the body parts.

But as she stepped to the right to check out another row of drawings, her smile fell. Were the other kids spelling better than Adrian was? Adrian had skipped the "c" in "black," and replaced an "e" for an "a" in "fangs." Harriet McMillan, who always looked like she belonged in the Crew Cuts catalog, had managed "cephalothorax" on her drawing of a crayfish with nary an erase mark. Alice frowned at a cross section of a sea urchin by Esme Bisset with "cortical granules" written in neat, straight printing. She walked back to Adrian's picture, her letters angling up and to the right, the tails of each "s" trailing off in wispy pencil snakes.

Alice touched her daughter's writing as the Bissets finally exited the classroom, all beatific smiles and apologies for running over. At the same time, her phone buzzed with an incoming text message. Maybe, she hoped, Bea Kerrigan was running late.

"It's okay." Alice rushed by the Bissets and glanced at her phone. The message was not from the Kerrigans, but rather from a number she didn't recognize. "Sorry to be awkward," it began, "but Teddy"—Alice bristled as she slid the message open—"has got to lay off at school. Can't you do something about this?"

"Sorry to keep you waiting," Miss Miller said as Alice gaped at her phone. *Can Teddy lay off what?* And who'd sent this? She'd forward it

to Meredith as soon as she made it back to the car, she decided. Meredith would know. Nadia's warning flashed into her head then, the way she'd repeated "feud" over coffee. Miss Miller cleared her throat, and Alice plopped the phone down on the miniature table.

"Sorry," she mumbled. "I got a little ambitious with my own schedule this morning. I've got about twenty minutes." She winced then, wishing she could redo her whole entrance. If she were a second grader herself, Miss Miller would certainly correct her distracted behavior.

Alice awkwardly crossed her ankles as she shifted in the tiny chair. "Then we'll talk fast," Miss Miller said, smiling now. "First of all, I just want to tell you what a delight it's been to get to know Adrian." She looked up from her folder, eyes sparkling. For a second-year teacher, Miss Miller projected a comforting confidence. Alice settled in for another round of accolades. "Adrian is warm and hilarious, and many of the children seek her out as a playmate and work partner."

A familiar swell of pride grew in Alice's chest. Of course Miss Miller loved Adrian. Everyone did. In fact, none of the kids' teachers had ever reported anything but that the Sullivans were pleasant and capable.

That was why Alice startled so visibly when the fresh-faced teacher uttered her next word: "But." Either that word or the sudden vibration of her cell phone on the tabletop beside her made her jump.

"I'm sorry." Alice quickly moved to decline the call and noticed that the ID read "Elm Creek Junior High." "Shit," she said.

"Excuse me?" Miss Miller's smooth cheeks took on a blush.

"I'm so sorry," Alice blurted. "It's my son's school." She stared at the phone case and repeated that mystery text to herself. *"Can't you do something about this?"* She rubbed her collarbone again. "I'll call them when we're finished. Go on." Alice pointed to the manila folder under Miss Miller's hands, the evidence behind the teacher's disconcerting "but."

Miss Miller seemed flustered now. She tapped her French mani-

cure on the file. "I was just about to say that although I adore Adrian, I'm developing some concerns about her academic skills."

"Concerns about her academic skills?" Alice repeated vacantly, a faint hum in her ears. She reached for a piece of paper from the stack the teacher had in the middle of the table. "Can I have one of these?" she asked, not waiting for an answer. Along with the paper, she grabbed a black felt-tip from Miss Miller's wire mesh cup. Alice wrote, "Academic skills." "What are your concerns?" She realized her tone was brusque, but she didn't have time to correct it.

"I'm primarily concerned with Adrian's reading." Alice wrote "Reading" on her paper and put a little bullet point beneath the heading. She couldn't bring herself to make eye contact with the teacher. "We'd like kids to be at level M by the end of the year, and I most recently tested Adrian at an E."

"E," Alice wrote. Then she counted across her fingers. "That's eight levels," she said, her breath shallow. "Adrian is eight levels behind?"

Miss Miller shook her head. "No. By the *end* of the year, we'd like her at M. But by now? I'd feel better if she were at least an I or a J."

"*You'd* feel better?" Alice repeated. Miss Miller's face turned a darker shade of pink. "I'm sorry." The teacher looked like she was dressed for brunch at the Alpha Phi house, a pink cardigan over a pin-striped button-down. It was hardly this girl's fault that she had to deliver the bad news. *Unless it is her fault*, Alice thought. *None of Adrian's other teachers have found her deficient.* "But are you sure?"

"I'm sure about her reading level," Miss Miller said. "Can you tell me how homework is going? Are you doing the twenty minutes of reading per night?"

Now, Alice flushed. The words "She reads fine" had risen to her lips automatically, but she realized she couldn't remember the last time she and her daughter had actually practiced out-loud reading together. Alice knew very well this was part of the nightly homework in second grade. She had done it religiously with Teddy.

The teacher worried a paper inside her manila folder. Alice couldn't quite read it upside down. "What level books is she reading with you?"

"Actually." Alice backtracked, guilty. It was bad enough that Adrian was behind. Lying about it wasn't going to improve things. She tried to imagine what Patrick, perpetually calm, would do if he were here. Certainly, he wouldn't try to cover their parental negligence. What kind of example would that be for the children? "We've gotten a bit lax about practicing." Alice glanced over Miss Miller's shoulder at the white-potted plants the young woman had placed at precise intervals on the windowsill. "I can see now it's necessary, what with the E." She gestured at Miss Miller's notes, and her phone rang again at her fingertips. "I'm so sorry." Alice flipped it over to decline the call. Elm Creek Junior High again, she saw, and this time a cold stab of worry pinched her chest. "It's my son's school." Alice stood, grabbed her notes, and moved toward the door. "It might be an emergency. I'll have to reschedule?" She pressed the green answer button as she walked toward the hall.

IT WASN'T AN emergency at school, but rather an "incident that requires your immediate attention."

"Can it wait an hour?" Alice asked, desperate.

"No," the assistant principal said. She could picture the face that went with the voice—a young guy with doughy cheeks and a full head of reddish hair—but she couldn't remember his name. She'd heard only "assistant principal" as she hustled out of Adrian's classroom. "Unfortunately," he said, "the severity of the incident doesn't permit any delay."

Alice thought about calling Patrick and making him go, but they both knew the consequences of crossing Sachman. "I'm on my way." She stabbed the button to end the call.

"Siri, call the office on speaker," she barked. The Kerrigans would

be irritated. They'd probably already fought traffic to get to their new home, and as the daughter of Minnesota's governor, Bea Kerrigan wasn't used to waiting or compromising. She'd famously convinced her husband to take her family name, "to preserve the legacy," Alice had read in the *Star Tribune* archives as she'd tried to woo the couple. Ramona would also be irate. The Kerrigans would elevate the prestige of the firm, and they'd been a key piece in Alice's pitch to get the *Elle Decor* photo shoot. She'd already begun playing with Easter table arrangements and wall colors in her own home, preparing for her "about the designer" section, which they'd document three months in advance.

As she raced toward the junior high's reflective front doors, Alice told their assistant to "apologize profusely." She'd have called Bea herself, but there wasn't time. The elementary and junior high were only a half mile apart. Once inside, Alice could see Teddy sitting against the glass wall of the office, his head tipped back, honey-blond hair smushed against the pane. Were his eyes closed? Was he crying? As she rushed toward her son, one of his friends, Landon, tapped on the glass next to his head. "Dude," Landon said, wonder in his tone. Alice stopped, mouth open. "How much trouble are you in?"

Alice watched as Teddy turned toward Landon, an impish smile on his face. He raised a hand to his ear, indicating that he couldn't hear through the glass.

"You clown!" Landon bellowed, shaking his head. Teddy bent in giggles. "Classic." Landon sauntered away, and Alice froze with trepidation. For the first time since she'd seen the school's number light up her iPhone, she considered the possibility that Teddy had really done something wrong. *My Teddy?* She tried to remember if he'd ever been in trouble at school. There was that time in first grade when he'd refused to do the teacher's lesson on jazz music, opting instead to sit in the office. But that was something they'd since joked about. He'd been six! And, of course, there was the block-throwing incident with Sadie

Yoshida at kindergarten round-up. But since those early days? She couldn't recall a single reprimand beyond being too chatty in class.

Alice pushed away the memories of Nadia's warning and the anonymous text that morning, but then, the comment from Teddy's band teacher on his midterm report crowded into her memory. Alice tried to recall the wording as she approached the reception desk. Something about being a follower and not a leader. When she'd asked him about it, Teddy had said that Mr. Petschl was extra strict. Alice did remember the teacher's gruff demeanor at back-to-school night. He probably *was* strict. She'd signed the midterm and handed it back to her son.

When Alice made eye contact with Teddy in the office, she watched his face transform. The lighthearted smile she'd seen for Landon morphed into a bewildered sadness.

"What happened?" Alice rushed to him as Teddy slumped further in his chair.

"It was an accident," Teddy said. The lanky assistant principal exited his office opposite the chairs where her son waited. The hair near the man's temples appeared damp with sweat.

"Mrs. Sullivan." He wrinkled his nose. "Why don't you and I talk first?" Alice tugged at the end of her scarf and wished again that Patrick could be here. She glanced back at Teddy, wary, as she followed the administrator into his brightly lit office. The placard on the desk read JASON WHITTAKER.

Before she was ready, her left arm only halfway out of her jacket, he launched in. "As you may know, Mrs. Sullivan, it's been a difficult start to seventh grade for Teddy."

"Difficult start?" Alice pulled her arms free and shoved the down-filled jacket behind her. She blinked at the smaller letters engraved on the nameplate: ASSISTANT PRINCIPAL. "Is this about the midterm comment from the band teacher?"

Jason clicked his mouse and read off his monitor. "This is actually my third interaction with your son. His third disciplinary infraction," he clarified, "in the last four weeks."

The note Alice had written herself at Adrian's conference just fifteen minutes before flashed into her consciousness. "Level E," she'd scrawled, fear and embarrassment seizing her. And now there were three disciplinary infractions at middle school? And there'd been that aggressive text, too. Alice blinked rapidly and hot tears welled. Mr. Whittaker pushed a box of Kleenex toward her without making eye contact. "I had no idea," she said, her voice breathy.

"Don't you check the portal?"

"Portal?" Alice felt like a malfunctioning robot. All she could do was inanely repeat his words. Meredith had mentioned the portal, but Alice had chalked her friend's vigilance up to overprotectiveness. After all, Meredith had cut Sadie's grapes in half until she was in second grade. She religiously read the teachers' Friday newsletters top to bottom. Alice and Nadia lightly mocked these behaviors. Skimming those weekly newsletters, after all, had always served Alice just fine. "Teddy has always been a great student—always As and Bs," she said now. "I haven't really had to track his homework."

Jason rubbed his chin. "Well," he said, "sometimes things look smooth on the outside, but there's a lot happening under the surface."

That might be true for other kids, Alice thought, *but not for Teddy.* He'd always been completely transparent. "Guileless," her mother had said more than once. As Alice's mom had a PhD in child psychology, Alice trusted her implicitly. "He's never had any behavioral problems before," Alice insisted.

Mr. Whittaker frowned at his computer. "He's got both lunchroom and hallway infractions now. You can see them on the portal. That's why we have it, so you can have an up-to-date picture of what's happening at school."

Alice narrowed her eyes. Her initial shock at being called into the office had given way to the steeliness she inhabited during hard-nosed conversations with contractors and suppliers. "I'm here now. Why don't you tell me what I need to know."

Mr. Whittaker cocked an eyebrow. "Well, the other incidents pro-

vide context," he said, matching her change in tone, "so we'll review those first before I get into what happened today." He glanced back at his monitor and clicked something. "First, in the lunchroom, Teddy dumped his spaghetti in someone's lap."

"What?" Alice felt knocked off balance again. "Who?"

"I usually don't share students' names, but Teddy and this other boy did seem to have a history. It was Tane Lagerhead." Mr. Whittaker tilted his head, waiting for her reaction.

Alice didn't know of any history other than Nadia's comment from that morning. "Tane has been in Teddy's class since third grade with no issues." She closed her eyes for a moment, searching her memory. She could see Tane's too-short pants at sixth-grade graduation, but neither she nor Teddy had commented on them. "That doesn't sound like Teddy," she said about the lunchroom. "Certainly it was an accident?"

"I interviewed several witnesses, Mrs. Sullivan. And then last week's altercation in the hallway suggests a pattern."

"A pattern?" Alice's bravado ebbed just as she'd summoned it.

"Teddy crossed the hallway and knocked Tane's books from his arms." Alice tried to imagine it. She shook her head. "And then he tripped him," Whittaker said.

"What?" She knew Teddy to throw an elbow on the soccer field, but pushing kids in school hallways? No way. Whittaker must have her son confused with someone else.

"Yes," Mr. Whittaker said, certain. "And then he threw Tane's math book in the third-floor compost bin."

"In the compost bin?" Alice couldn't stop her echo. The whole situation seemed outlandish.

"Before you ask"—he held a hand up—"the security footage confirms it was Teddy."

Alice looked over her shoulder, as if she could see through the closed door to the seating area where Teddy waited. She felt as if she were watching a television show. *This poor mother*, she'd say if she were.

How could she be so clueless? Although her tears had dissipated, she dabbed her eyes with her Kleenex. "Shouldn't someone have called me about these behaviors?" Alice asked, finally. "They seem sort of serious for just a portal."

Whittaker's shoulders stiffened. "I'm in charge of discipline for more than one thousand students. I have to rely on the systems set in place." Alice felt herself melting into the back of her chair. Mr. Whittaker stood then, and as he moved Alice noticed a familiar sandalwood smell. *He uses the same shampoo as Patrick.* "I think we should get Teddy in here to explain what happened today."

Alice shuddered. Behind her, the assistant principal opened the door. Alice turned to see Teddy shuffle in. He looked smaller than he had that morning, and despite Alice's attempts, he wouldn't make eye contact with her.

"Teddy," Whittaker said once they'd both sat. "Perhaps you can explain what happened this afternoon."

"Perhaps," Teddy said, snide.

Alice jerked upright. "Teddy!" An image of him dropping Tane's math book into a garbage can flashed in her mind's eye, and then another vision of spaghetti on Tane's lap.

She stared at her son, and pale pink splotches appeared on Teddy's cheekbones. "It was supposed to be a joke," he mumbled. Teddy looked at Mr. Whittaker. The assistant principal turned his palm up, an indication that he should continue. Alice felt her throat closing. "After the band played the theme from *Jurassic Park*—you know that song, right, Mom?"

She nodded. Despite the tension of the moment, she heard a few bars of the piece in her head, and as Teddy continued, she pictured Laura Dern running in cargo shorts next to a brontosaurus. "Well, as we were leaving the stage," Teddy said, "I just grabbed Tane's pants. Like, as a joke."

Alice blinked away the CGI dinosaur. "What?"

"It was a *joke*," Teddy said, a tinge of desperation in his tone. He reached out and rubbed a leaf of the plant on the edge of the assistant principal's desk. Alice swatted at his arm, then immediately worried Mr. Whittaker would report her for some kind of abuse. "Tane always wears shorts under his sweat pants," Teddy rushed on. His nail beds turned white against the armrests of the chair. "I know because we're in the same PE class and soccer. It's those sweat pants that always hang down in back. You've seen them, right, Mom? So yeah, I, like, pulled them, but I didn't think they'd come all the way down."

"So what happened next?" She heard the chill in her voice, anger replacing the confusion and disbelief she'd withstood during the first minutes of this meeting.

Mr. Whittaker jumped in. "Tane's buttocks were exposed to the audience."

Teddy spasmed, an inappropriate laugh bubbling out of him. Alice squeezed his hand. "Stop," she said, and then she looked pleadingly at the assistant principal.

He continued. "And the left-hand side of the auditorium also saw his—"

Before he could finish, Alice interrupted. "I'm so sorry," she said. "We'll find a way to fix this." She stood, jerking Teddy upright. She'd had enough.

"I'm going to suspend him for four days," Mr. Whittaker said flatly, "as this is his third offense and detention has clearly had no impact." Alice felt saliva pooling near her molars. *Suspension?* She'd only heard of Nadia's Donovan getting suspended. No one else she knew had even mentioned the assistant principal.

Mr. Whittaker put a finger on his calendar. "We'll see him back here next Thursday. No school or soccer until then."

Teddy fell back into his chair, his hand slipping from Alice's. "Four days?" he blurted. "But I can't miss practice."

Whittaker seemed on the verge of a smirk, and Alice felt again as if

she were living in a movie, seated in Ed Rooney's office looking at Ferris Bueller's attendance record. "You're not playing soccer," Mr. Whittaker said to Teddy. Alice could see in his straight spine, the tilt of his chin, that the man had begun to enjoy himself. "In addition to the academic suspension, I'm instituting a two-game athletic penalty. I believe that takes us to the end of the regular season."

Teddy's eyes filled. "But—" he said.

Mr. Whittaker cut him off. "We have a zero-tolerance policy for bullying, Mr. Sullivan. You can try soccer again next year."

"We'll be in touch," Alice mumbled. She needed to talk to Patrick. She needed to get out of this office. She pushed Teddy toward the exit.

Teddy Sullivan

Teddy had expected his mom to begin her inevitable lecture the second he buckled his seat belt. Instead, she cranked the classical music station and clenched her jaw. As they rolled out of the school parking lot, Teddy looked over his shoulder at the second-floor classroom where Sadie and Tane were currently in math. Had Sadie commented on his Finsta post? he wondered, thinking of his fake Instagram. Had she doubled down on #TeamTane?

No Elm Creek soccer until next year. Teddy remembered Whittaker's punishment. Ordinarily, Teddy wouldn't care that much because club travel soccer was way more important. But everything had been worse on the premier team since Tane had joined.

It had all started when Tane showed up at tryouts even though he'd been down two levels the year before. Teddy's dad had looked nervous when Tane walked over to the group. "Kid's tall," he had said, just before the drills began. "Strong legs."

Teddy evaluated his dad's statement, measuring Tane against the other kids he'd been playing soccer with for years. "But I'm better." Teddy had squeezed his water bottle over his head in the August heat. His dad hadn't answered for a few seconds. A familiar, uncomfortable sensation had traveled up Teddy's sternum. This type of nerves, he knew, never helped his play. The last time he'd felt like this, he'd shanked a penalty kick in the previous year's playoffs. His dad had pulled his ball

cap down over his eyes as the clock ticked away on the Elks' loss, a game Teddy could have saved if he'd just been a tiny bit better.

"Don't you think I'm better?" Teddy had prompted at tryouts. He had glanced down the sidelines at Tane, who had jogged over to check in with his own father, a white-blond dude who had to be at least six feet five.

Teddy's dad had put a hand on his shoulder. "His size is an asset, but you've got great skills. They'd be crazy not to take you at striker."

As they'd started, Teddy had thought of the nail polish Tane had worn on his index fingers to sixth-grade graduation last spring along with his too-short pants. Totally weird. He had also remembered Tane telling him in fourth grade that he'd played rec league, where everyone was happy just to get a participation trophy. That wasn't how Teddy had ever played soccer. But at premier tryouts, Tane seemed so confident, sure he belonged there even though every other kid in the group had been on a premier or a C1 team the previous season. Teddy had seen flecks of purple polish near the cuticles of Tane's nails as he gripped a ball during Coach's instructions.

The team didn't need anyone new.

When the roster had come out a week later, Teddy's eyes had bulged when he found Tane's name ahead of his own on the alphabetical list. On his Insta, he'd posted a screenshot of the email. His caption read, "Can't wait to ball with this sick crew." On his Finsta, he'd enlarged the middle of the alphabetical list where "Lagerhead" appeared and wrote, "This should be interesting." Landon and McCoy had added surprised emojis.

On the day he was suspended, Teddy had posted on his Finsta again in the bathroom between the time Mr. Whittaker, the total ween, had force-marched him to the office and when his mom had arrived to pick him up. He used a *Napoleon Dynamite* still as the photo, but it was the caption that really sealed it. "The end of the #battle," he'd written. "Hope all you #TeamTane haters enjoyed the show at the 7th grade assembly. #micdrop or #pantsdrop, I should say."

The comments had already accumulated by the time he'd washed his hands and dropped the phone in his backpack. At the last second, when his mom was in the office with Mr. Whittaker, he'd remembered to delete the Finsta profile from his phone. He might never, depending on the level of his mother's rage, see the device again. He stared at the Elm Creek soccer field as they turned in to their neighborhood, and laughed at the pink penis painted on the side of the porta-potty.

"Nothing's funny," his mom said, her voice low.

Evelyn Brown

S*uspended?"* Evelyn felt shocked. "My Teddy?"

"I know," Alice whispered. "I'm so confused about what's going on with him. He's not himself. Or"—she paused—"he's not who I thought he was. Does that happen in junior high? Kids just mutate into some totally different person? Why didn't you warn me?"

"Junior high is hard," Evelyn said automatically. She had warned her, of course. And Evelyn had spent her career researching the jarring transformation from childhood to adolescence. She'd studied Alice's development, obviously, and wondered at each phase how much of her daughter's personality and decision making came from her innate qualities—baked into the DNA she inherited from her birth parents— and how much Evelyn had managed to sprinkle on top with the "nurture" part of the equation as her adoptive mom.

But Teddy? In Evelyn's mind, Teddy was a still a cherubic three-year-old, golden curls swirling around his perfect little ears. Obviously, she knew he'd gotten bigger. In fact, his physical growth stunned her every time she saw him these days.

Evelyn could hear Alice rummaging on the other end of the line, probably digging in her junk drawer. For someone who kept the other ninety-nine percent of her house perfectly spotless, Alice had a knack for misplacing her keys or a roll of Scotch tape. Evelyn often thought that Alice's obsessive cleanliness might be a reaction to Evelyn's own

laxity as a housekeeper. She glanced over at her dirty lunch dishes languishing on the side of the sink. "What are you looking for?" she asked.

"What? Oh." The rummaging stopped. "I was hoping I had a safety pin in here."

Evelyn smiled to herself. Although her condo was on the messy side, she knew exactly where she kept her spare safety pins—in a plastic box in her sock drawer. They'd been there for years.

"Well, in any case," Alice said, "I'm afraid to even leave him in the house alone. I'm not sure I can trust him, even if I take his phone. Do you think that's irrational?"

Evelyn was proud of herself for limiting her parenting advice to the moments when Alice actually asked for it. "I think you're right to be cautious." She kept her tone light.

Alice sighed. "Can you come over? Maybe pick Adrian up from school at three? I hate to ask at the last minute."

Evelyn smiled. She was used to these requests. She enjoyed them. As much as Alice wanted to be all things to all people, there were so many times Patrick was traveling or working late. Her daughter got stuck between car pools and client meetings. As Evelyn had cut back on her teaching schedule in the last couple of years, she'd been happy to help out. Thrilled, even. What a gift to be so close to her grandchildren. She'd have to get back to her work later, an article she'd agreed to review for the *Journal of Applied Adolescent Psychology*. But she could do that in the evening if she drank black tea that afternoon, instead of her usual chamomile. Maybe she could make a cup for Teddy, too. Get to the bottom of things with him. Or try.

"I'll be there in thirty." Evelyn logged out of her laptop and added her mug to her dish pile. She pictured Alice pacing her kitchen, stopping to google phrases on her phone like "my seventh grader is a bully" and "I don't know my child anymore."

Evelyn hoped she'd also have time to reassure Alice that afternoon.

She wanted to put in some face time with her before she dropped her own bomb. She hated to think of Julienne this way, as a violent explosion, but Evelyn knew that was exactly how Alice would receive her, even though Evelyn had always before made Alice her priority. She winced, imagining what Alice might google after Evelyn finally told her the news.

Sadie Yoshida

Tane arrived back in math class just as Sadie watched Alice's car leave the parking lot. Teddy had looked up at the classroom from the front seat. *He's looking for me,* she thought, and she felt both flattered and irritated. She had wanted him to pay attention to her at the homecoming game, and he'd totally ignored her. But *now* her opinion mattered? Now that she was legit friends with Tane?

As Tane handed Mr. Sadler his hall pass, most of the kids glued their eyes to their worksheets. McCoy Blumenfeld, though, started laughing, little barks escaping his lips as his shoulders shook. *He's an infant,* Sadie thought. *No wonder he's best friends with Teddy.*

"McCoy," Mr. Sadler said, annoyed, "why don't you go to the drinking fountain and compose yourself." A couple of other kids snickered then, but Sadie gave Tane a half smile. She was surprised he hadn't just vacated the building after assembly. *She* would have gone home, she thought, if it had happened to her. And she probably never would have come back. Nudity in front of the entire seventh grade? This was the kind of story people would be telling their grandchildren at Thanksgiving in fifty years.

"Did they make you go to the counselor?" Sadie whispered as Tane took his seat next to hers. Maybe if she'd seen *everything* in assembly, she would have felt shy about speaking to him, but she'd closed her eyes as his pants went down, holding her breath just as Mikaela had grabbed her arm and screamed.

Tane nodded. Mr. Sadler turned back to the rectangular prism he'd drawn with a dying purple marker on the whiteboard. "Teddy's mom just drove out of the parking lot." Sadie pointed at the window. "I'm guessing he got suspended." Tane didn't say anything. Sadie squinted at the parked cars. She zeroed in on their PE teacher's Honda, which Sadie knew by the 26.2 sticker on the back windshield.

This whole thing—the #TeamTane/#TeamTeddy fight—had started when they'd had a sub in PE class who let them play dodgeball. Sadie remembered her elementary PE teacher saying the game was banned. These days, phys ed was all about the cooperative activities, not the competitive ones. In fact, they'd used the brightly colored dodgeballs just the other week to play some stupid thing called Star Wars Battle. The object had been to push one of those inflatable exercise balls over the other team's home line by pelting it from behind their own barrier. Some of the boys had abandoned the task and started chucking their dodgeballs at each other from across the gym. Even Tane had joined in. Sadie had watched him pick up a red ball, smile at Teddy on the opposite team, and fling the orb at his head. Everyone had laughed— Sadie, too. It was funny—not really a big deal.

But then Teddy had mentioned it in car pool. Tane Lagerhead had been such a "douchebucket" about the game, he'd said.

"Language," Sadie's mom had scolded, her eyes never leaving the road as the two kids sat in the back seat. Even though Sadie had topped one hundred pounds, her mother insisted she sit in the back, claiming it was safer, though it made Sadie look like a baby. While they drove, Sadie had changed the subject to their math test, but then that night Alexandra Hunt had posted "#TeamTayne" on her Snapchat story with a picture she'd found of a random kid, not Teddy, with his head thrown back, a ball smashing into his nose. Alexandra hadn't gone to Elm Creek Elementary with them. She didn't know that before seventh grade, Tane was always the one with the too-small shirts, the brightly colored socks, the nail polish that he used to wear on all ten fingers before switching to just the index ones sometime last year. Alexandra

also didn't know how to spell his name. "#TeamTain," Mikaela Heffernan had posted the next day with a picture of Tane bent over an assignment in study hall, his adorably floppy brown hair hanging into his eyes. "#TeemTane," Chloe Cushing added with a pic of Tane in the lunch line. The intentional spelling errors were almost as funny as Alexandra's original photo. Teddy stood in the background of Chloe's pic, mostly hidden behind Tane's shoulder. Teddy had been one of the tallest kids in their elementary class, but Tane had definitely caught up over the summer.

So when they'd had that sub in PE, a guy who seemed like he was about two seconds out of college and super into being "cool," everyone had already posted tons of Tane pics. Apparently, Sadie wasn't the only one who'd noticed Tane's new middle school look, and yet she felt like she'd gotten in on the ground floor of the Tane craze. The two had been friends since the first day of Quiz Bowl practice. She already had Tane's number saved on her phone, had already friended him on Insta and Snapchat.

The PE sub randomly assigned teams—Sadie and Tane on one side and Teddy on the other. Once the game began, Teddy was everywhere, sprinting on the baseline, barking orders. "Move it!" he shouted, and "Block already!"

It's just a game, Sadie felt like telling him, and she might have had a chance if Teddy ever stopped sprinting long enough to make eye contact with her. But instead, it was like Sadie wasn't even there. At junior high orientation in August, Teddy had glommed onto her, nervous and clingy. But in dodgeball Teddy was aggressive and relentless, the same version of himself who'd called Tane a "douchebucket" in front of Sadie's mom.

Unlike Teddy, Tane was laughing during the dodgeball game. He lobbed soft shots at kids who weren't paying attention. Easy outs. "Stay behind me, Sadie!" Tane offered when about half of the kids were sidelined. "I'll block for you." Sadie felt her chest swell beneath the band of

her new seventh-grade bra. She smiled at Mikaela, who'd overheard. Despite Tane's protection, McCoy Blumenfeld whipped a yellow ball at Sadie's calf. The hit stung and would definitely leave a mark. "Jerk," Sadie whispered under her breath as she left the floor.

"You gotta move that ass," McCoy said. Sadie instinctively glanced at her behind. She'd noticed her skating skirt hanging a little shorter than it had the previous year. She'd hoped her mother might just buy a new size without them talking about her "growing body." When she looked back at McCoy, he was laughing with Teddy. The two exchanged a fist bump and scanned their remaining competition.

"You okay?" Tane called after her. His concern had softened her embarrassment. She gave a thumbs-up over her shoulder as she sat down. At least if she was sitting, no one could look at her ass.

The game went on for a few minutes, and Mikaela and Chloe joined Sadie on the sidelines. Eventually, the teams were down to two members each, and then, as if in a teen movie, Teddy and Tane were the final two facing off for the win.

"Team Tane! Team Tane!" Mikaela and Chloe chanted, echoing the Snapchat hashtag. Sadie whipped her head toward Teddy to gauge his reaction. He frowned and stalked his baseline. Sadie glanced at the clock and hoped the bell might ring, ending the game early. Teddy slapped the ball he held against his free hand. Tane stood still, a goofy smile on his face, a green ball balanced between his palms. After several awkward seconds, Tane let it fly, a medium-strength shot at Teddy's waistline.

Teddy probably could have caught it and eliminated Tane if he'd just dropped his own ball, but he didn't. Instead he jumped to his left. "That's all you got, Lagerhead?" he taunted.

"Team Tane! Team Tane!" repeated Chloe and Mikaela and a few others. Sadie's mouth felt dry. She wondered if the substitute teacher would stop things, but he was scrolling on his phone near the entrance to the locker room.

Tane bent to gather three dodgeballs in his long arms. *Get him,* thought Sadie. Any guilt she might have felt about rooting against her oldest friend was overpowered by the shame of McCoy's comment about her butt. Teddy hadn't even reacted.

Ten seconds later, Tane did get him. A couple of balls collided in midair first, and then Tane hurled the other two he held. Teddy almost avoided them both with an agile lunge to the right, but Tane's second shot clipped the heel of his sneaker. It rebounded into the air, and the whole class erupted in cheers. Even McCoy got caught up in Tane fever, raising a fist before he remembered whose side he was on.

By afternoon car pool, there had been a couple of Snapchat and Instagram stories about Tane's so-called cheating. "#TeamTeddy," those said. But they were only from McCoy and Landon. Everyone else had gone back to #TeamTane. He'd won the game, after all.

"Where's your Snapchat story?" Teddy had asked Sadie as they waited for Teddy's mom to pick them up.

"Don't mention Snapchat in the car," Sadie had said. Her mother still didn't know she had it, and she didn't want Alice to know, either. She had buried the app in a folder she'd labeled "Educational" on her iPhone. On the first page in that folder, she had nine icons, programs she'd collected over the last year. They were mom-approved apps that had to do with math facts, or the principles of Euclidian geometry. So far, Sadie's mom hadn't flicked past them to the second screen.

In the car, Teddy hadn't mentioned Snapchat. In fact, they hadn't really talked at all, that afternoon or any time since the game. Sadie imagined him driving home in a similar silence today while she and Tane leaned together over a math problem in Sadler's class.

Evelyn Brown

- - - - -

Evelyn hoped she'd have a few minutes to talk to her daughter when she arrived, but Alice already had her keys in hand. "I have to go," she said as they hugged. Alice kept her arms bent, resisting a full embrace. "I missed an important meeting this morning with the Kerrigans."

"Like the governor?" Evelyn lingered in the hug, even though she could feel Alice's reticence. Evelyn knew Alice's business had been doing well, but Governor Kerrigan would be next level for sure.

"Her daughter. But I had to cancel this morning because . . ." She pointed up the stairs toward Teddy's bedroom and frowned. "Anyway." She disappeared into the mudroom and Evelyn heard the garage door lift. "I'll be back."

Evelyn pulled her Haflingers from her backpack. One of her favorite things about fall was breaking out the wool clogs. As a teenager, Alice had been horrified when Evelyn wore them out of the house.

"Teddy?" She ascended the stairs toward the bedrooms and knocked lightly at his door. When she heard an affirmative-sounding grunt, Evelyn pulled it open. He lay on his back, his sneakers still on, and stared at the ceiling.

"Nana, I just can't talk about it." Teddy dropped his palms over his eyes. Evelyn scanned his long legs, his too-big feet. Alice was right: This kid wasn't the three-year-old Evelyn held in her mind's eye. Still,

teens were her bread and butter. In fact, she consulted regularly with the counselor at Elm Creek Junior High, a capable woman who'd been her graduate student ten or fifteen years before.

"You could try me." Evelyn had reams of files documenting her therapeutic successes. Her open tone and neutral body language were magic, at least with other people's children and grandchildren. Armed with her track record, she'd planned to be the kind of mom that her own teenaged daughter would confide in—one of those best-friend-with-boundaries types—but that was never how things developed with Alice. She wondered if her own secrets precluded Alice's confidences, the space other mothers held for their daughters' confessions already clogged with a lifetime of her own omissions.

"Believe it or not," Evelyn forged on, resolutely hopeful with Teddy, "I still know a ton about junior high." She knew enough, in fact, not to bring up her latest professional research on adjustment disorder in early teens. Not that she thought Teddy's breach warranted that particular diagnosis.

Teddy rolled over and smashed his face into his pillow. "No," he said, and then, as she moved to leave, "Thanks." She smiled at his perfunctory politeness. It was a good sign.

"You know," she said, "there's nothing you could do that would make me stop loving you." She paused, but he didn't respond. She tried again in the car when they picked up Adrian, but Teddy rested his head against the window and said he was tired. Evelyn reminded herself to be patient. It usually took several invitations for kids to finally open up, and she would undoubtedly be back at Alice's to help within the next few days.

When Alice got home, Evelyn had already thrown together a quick dinner of leftovers from the Sullivans' fridge. Teddy shoved rotisserie chicken into his mouth with his fingers, his expression dull. Adrian chattered on obliviously about her collection of Calico Critters. The kids eventually excused themselves, and Alice offered Evelyn a glass of

wine. "Patrick got stuck at work." She sounded apologetic, though this situation was routine. Evelyn nodded yes to the wine. While her marriage to Frank had been toxic in its own way, she often wondered how Patrick's work schedule impacted the kids. And Alice.

"What am I going to do with Teddy at home for a week?" Alice asked.

Evelyn studied her daughter's face, her deep brown eyes so different from her own. She wondered how much of her professional opinion she should offer. "You could use the opportunity to talk," she ventured.

"Right, yeah. But what about my job?" Alice tipped her wineglass up, nearly draining it on her first sip. "It's not as if I can take an unexpected vacation until next Thursday when they let him back into school. I just started working on the Kerrigan project today."

Alice pushed her black hair back from her face, and Evelyn glanced at her wrist, looking for her ubiquitous hair tie. Alice gathered her shoulder-length waves into a high ponytail, a style Evelyn had been sure she'd grow out of. "Can you work from home?" Evelyn asked. "Or is that not the best move for big new clients?" She'd help, obviously, but Teddy probably needed his mother. *And his father.* But Evelyn couldn't remember Patrick ever taking a day off.

"Maybe I could work from home at least half days?" And then Alice blurted, "Do you think I'm too checked out? Like as a mom? I mean, today I found out Adrian can't read and also that Teddy's a sociopath, and I had no idea."

Evelyn couldn't help but smile. "Neither of those things is true." They weren't. Evelyn was one hundred percent certain.

Alice put her head on the table next to her empty wineglass. "I just didn't realize how deficient I've been. I feel like I've been trying really hard."

Evelyn seized on this moment of vulnerability and rubbed her daughter's back, her heart aching. She realized that while she was anxious to share her big update, Alice couldn't process one more thing in

the midst of the current crisis. "You're trying your best." She felt her daughter stiffen beneath her hand, probably reading that assessment as a rebuke. "You're a great mom," she added.

"There are some meetings I can't cancel tomorrow." Alice propped herself up on her elbows.

"I can be here in the morning," Evelyn said. "And after your meetings, maybe you can research a tutor for Adrian? And also"—she hoped her daughter would take this the right way—"a therapist for Teddy?" Evelyn braced herself.

"A therapist?" Alice said. "Really?" She reached for the wine bottle and poured another half glass.

Evelyn shrugged. "Might as well head off whatever is causing this behavioral blip."

"You think it's a blip?" Alice looked hopeful despite the dusky circles beneath her eyes, her concealer worn off.

"Without a doubt." Evelyn patted her back. "You can use this week as an excuse to reset and get some new procedures in order." Evelyn braced herself, hoping the suggestion wouldn't seem like a criticism, but Alice looked suddenly brighter.

"Yeah," she said. "Maybe that's the way to spin it, as an opportunity." She straightened up, and Evelyn dropped her hand back in her lap. She had always admired Alice's gumption, the way she powered through problems and obstacles as if they'd eventually dissipate if she just pushed hard enough. Alice would make it through this rough patch as she had the others, and when it was over, she would be ready to process Evelyn's life-changing news.

Sadie Yoshida

-----

adie had planned her request perfectly. Chloe's party was an
even bigger deal now that Teddy had been suspended. Everyone
else would be there talking about the assembly. It, and the aftermath, would become one of those classic seventh-grade moments. Of
course, no matter when she asked her mother, her chances were hurt
by the failed science test. If only Mr. Robinson had waited to report the
grade until after she'd already gotten permission, then maybe she could
have convinced her mother to let her "follow through on her obligation" to go to the party.

As it was, getting a green light for both the football game and then
Chloe's? With boys? Sadie estimated her chances at about fifty percent. Still, she had to try.

In the car on the way home from skating practice, she started to
build her case. "I talked to Mr. Robinson during study hall," she said.

"Oh great." Meredith swiveled her head at the intersection outside
the ice rink. She told Sadie at least twice per week about the frequency
of accidents here "because people just don't pay attention." Sadie's
mom checked two or three more times before she left the stop sign.

When they'd made the turn, Sadie started again. "Yeah. Mr. Robinson said since it's the first time I've had a bad grade, he'd be happy to
let me do a retake."

"Excellent!" Her mom lifted one hand from her steering wheel and

raised it in a fist. Sadie's skating tights felt hot inside the joggers she'd pulled on after practice. "When are you going to take it? And did he say what the max score could be?"

"What do you mean?" Their Grand Cherokee cruised past Teddy's street and then past Elm Creek Park, where Sadie spotted bright pink paint on the garbage can near the playground, two circles and a thick shaft. *OMG.* She hoped her mom hadn't seen it.

"Like, will Mr. Robinson average what you get with the fifty-six? Or can you just replace the score? Because even if you got a hundred on the retake, if you had to average them, that would still be a C."

"Oh." In sixth grade, they hadn't really talked about grades so much. Sure, Sadie knew ninety percent was better than seventy-five, but it wasn't until she got her first set of junior high midterms that she heard the term "GPA."

"We've got to start thinking about this," her mom had said over dinner that night as her dad had put on his reading glasses so he could see the grades on the portal. "How you do in this one class determines which science you get to take next year. It could impact your whole future. We want to make sure you have the maximum number of college choices."

College was six years away, though, and Chloe's party was tomorrow. "Um," Sadie ventured. "So, there's a football game versus Liston Heights tomorrow?"

"You have synchro, I think." Sadie's mom twirled her hair around her index finger. Her reddish brown waves bounced immediately back when she let the strands go. Sadie had inherited her dad's Japanese hair—straight and black. Although her mother called it easy to manage, Sadie had noticed the depth of the crease between her mom's eyebrows when she lacquered on hair spray to keep it in place for skating competitions. She'd heard her mom muttering to herself about "texture."

Sadie coughed and forced herself to take a breath. She didn't want

to seem too eager. "I checked, and practice ends at five fifteen, so I'd still have time to get there." She looked at her feet, avoiding her mother's eye contact in the rearview.

"What about family game night?" her mom said. "You already missed one for the homecoming game."

"Mom." Sadie rolled her eyes toward the passenger-side window. "I'm almost thirteen. Did you think we'd have Friday family game night all the way through high school?"

Sadie startled as a car behind them honked. "Oh," her mom said, waving into the rearview. "Green light."

Neither of them said anything for the minute it took to get from the intersection to the Yoshidas' driveway. Last weekend before game night, Meredith and Sadie had decorated their "California ranch," as her mom typically described their home, for Halloween, which was also the day after Sadie's birthday. Faux cobwebs stretched over the boxwoods under the living room picture window. It looked cool, Sadie thought, even though she was too old to trick or treat.

Sadie tried once more as they pulled into the garage. "So, the football game? Can I go?"

Meredith turned away from her, her running shoes thudding against the garage floor. "I don't think so," she said. "There's the science test and our family tradition. Both of those things are more important, right?"

Before Sadie could answer, her mom's car door shut, and she disappeared inside.

Evelyn Brown

C "all Julienne," Evelyn commanded her Bluetooth as she pulled out of Alice's driveway.

"Calling Julie-Ann," the speaker said, not quite getting the lovely lilt of the name. Four months ago, tears had streamed down Evelyn's face as she spoke with the baby she'd last seen in the arms of a social worker forty-one years before. The emotion had surprised her. She'd read as many books and articles as she could find in professional journals about adoption and reunion, about the typical arc of these tenuous relationships. She felt prepared to speak to Julienne, and yet the reality of the moment overwhelmed her.

Still, despite her tears, that first conversation had felt easy, effortless even. Later, when she reflected on it, Evelyn felt certain she and Julienne were soul mates of sorts, meant to find each other again. She allowed herself a few moments of outright regret—if only she'd understood at age nineteen what exactly she was sacrificing when she placed her firstborn with other parents—and then she put the feeling aside and made a plan to move forward. "Twice-weekly phone calls?" She suggested. "Lunch on Mondays?" As the months passed, these routines gave way to a more natural connection. She called Julienne when she felt like it.

As Julienne's phone rang in Evelyn's car on the night of Teddy's suspension, Evelyn felt a stab of guilt. She wanted to break down the

pantsing incident with Julienne. She wanted to strategize about Adrian's reading. But it seemed wrong to air Alice's difficulties before she'd even told Alice about the existence of her sister. In fact, to keep things fair, she hadn't even told Julienne Alice's name. "Control the process," Evelyn told herself. "Control what you can control."

This had been among Evelyn's most effective mantras for as long as she could remember. When she'd decided to leave Frank, she'd read umpteen studies on the best way to break the news to Alice. She'd made the decision to get a divorce for Alice's benefit, after all. It wasn't really about her own preference or convenience. While she, the adult, could handle his mood swings and unpredictability, she could see the toll it took on their daughter. She'd rehearsed her announcement over and over again until the words sounded at once calm and sincere when she delivered them to Alice. She still remembered the feel of the microsuede upholstery beneath her Saturday jeans as she delivered her speech, Alice's cool fingers between her palms as Evelyn assured her they'd keep the house. Evelyn had timed the separation for the moment she'd saved enough to buy Frank out of their modest story-and-a-half bungalow in Mills Park, the same house she'd sold last spring in favor of a downtown Minneapolis condo. She'd moved into her new place—new life, really—right before Julienne had contacted her for the first time.

"An older sister," she imagined herself saying to Alice now. She'd have to tell her soon. Evelyn could feel the secret wedged between them. She anticipated Alice's manifested anger. Her daughter had always been stoic, except in the few electric moments she hadn't been. But then Alice would get over it, just as she had the divorce. Evelyn had kept Julienne a secret for Alice's benefit, after all. That was what Frank had always said: Telling Alice would be selfish and pointless. For once, Evelyn had agreed with him. They hadn't known Evelyn would ever meet Julienne. The adoption was closed, just as Alice's had been. She and Frank had only the most basic information about Alice's origins.

Although they had told Alice she was adopted as a toddler, they also repeated as she grew that they didn't have much additional information to share.

When Evelyn had had so much trouble getting pregnant a second time, it felt like karma. She'd called the first pregnancy a "disaster," after all. And then she'd sped through graduate school as if studying other people's grief and regret were a penance for her indelible mistake. When they'd finally brought Alice home, she seemed like an absolute miracle, more than Evelyn thought she deserved after abandoning her first baby.

And then she'd gotten a second miracle: meeting Julienne again.

"Hey!" Julienne answered after the third or fourth ring as Evelyn drove away from Alice's house. "How's your daughter?" She'd texted Julienne that she was helping "A," as Evelyn referred to her.

"She's despondent," Evelyn said. "I don't feel comfortable sharing the details, but her son got in trouble at school."

"I'm sorry to hear that." Evelyn wondered if she detected exasperation in Julienne's tone. Evelyn delighted in the shop talk she and Julienne could employ, as they were both psychologists. When Evelyn had read that detail in Julienne's first email, she felt a shiver up her spine. It turned out that they shared research interests as well, though Julienne had a much larger private practice, and she also facilitated nature therapy groups, a technique about which Evelyn had known virtually nothing.

Evelyn pictured Teddy sprawled on his bed, unwilling to talk to her even though they'd always been close. "I shouldn't tell you exactly," Evelyn said, "but he humiliated a kid in front of his peers. I guess there's been some bullying on his part, though I find that so hard to believe. He's suspended for four days."

"Well," Julienne said, her voice steady, "we know twelve and thirteen are prime years for experimentation with identity permanence." Over the previous months, Evelyn had been studying Julienne's facial expressions. She imagined her now with a slight frown, a wrinkle above

her right eyebrow. "I think therapeutic intervention is indicated, don't you?" Julienne said. "A kid who'd previously been steady and well-adjusted, no behavioral record to speak of, suddenly lands a four-day suspension for bullying? Have you noticed any signs of dysregulation?"

Evelyn felt defensive, suddenly. Julienne didn't know Teddy; she hadn't seen his impish brown eyes, half-hidden beneath his wavy blond hair. This blip, as Evelyn had been thinking of it, was hardly indicative of a personality disorder.

Evelyn's vision flashed a bit, like a lightning strike that made the streetlights flicker. "He isn't dysregulated." Anger clipped her words.

"Hey," Julienne said, her voice softer. "I don't know him. You do."

Evelyn let her shoulders drop. She took a deep breath. "I'm sorry." To her horror, she felt tears well. "I guess maybe I'm not ready to talk." She'd been in so many sessions like this, where the person sitting across the coffee table, ensconced in her aging couch, started to lose control. *Calm down*, she told herself. "I'm overly invested," Evelyn said. "I shouldn't have brought this to you. I'm not ready."

Julienne cleared her throat.

"What?" Evelyn felt wary.

"Maybe it's time," Julienne ventured. "Like I said, I don't know your grandson . . ." She stopped. Evelyn bit her lip. "But I'd really like to."

Evelyn let a silence stretch between them as she kept her eyes on the road in front of her. In a minute, she'd pass the McDonald's she loved to take the kids to after Teddy's soccer games. Everyone ordered caramel sundaes, but Evelyn's was the only one with nuts.

"Not to analyze him, obviously," Julienne said, "but because I want to be part of the family." Her daughter's voice sounded thicker. Was she crying, too? "Isn't that what you want?"

"I do want that. I'm just trying to get the timing right." *Control what you can control.*

Evelyn could hear Julienne's breath before she spoke next, a rag-gedy inhale. "I think we should probably reevaluate," Julienne said. "I

thought we were headed in one direction, but it seems like we might want different things. I want to be like family. But if you can't even tell me your other daughter's name? I'm not sure we can get there."

Evelyn's vision flashed again, the streetlights wavering in the suburban mid-darkness. "I promise you I want to get there." She said it because it was true and also because it was the only thing to say. She slid past the McDonald's, and on the speaker for the drive-thru Evelyn noticed some lewd graffiti in bright pink.

Alice Sullivan

- - - - -

When Patrick finally made it home that night, Alice accosted him in the mudroom. She grabbed his arm and yanked him to sit next to her on the custom storage bench she'd had built for the space. Behind her, the divider between Adrian's and Teddy's cubbies dug into her back. Usually she lingered in here, staring at the Schumacher Birds and Butterflies wallpaper she adored. Now, she felt borderline frantic.

"It's been awful," she said.

Patrick bent over and untied his oxford. "I'm so sorry you had to do it all alone." He lifted a hand to the back of his neck and massaged. "Maybe—" he started, but Alice rushed on, breathless.

"First, Miss Miller tells me that Adrian is a failure, and then I miss the Kerrigan meeting, so I'm a failure. And Teddy? Teddy's more than a failure, he's a . . ." She glanced over her shoulder to check for the children in the kitchen, though she knew very well they were upstairs. "He's a criminal." She accentuated each syllable of the word, and an image of Teddy in an orange jumpsuit flashed in her mind's eye. She covered her mouth.

"No." Patrick put his arm around her and squeezed. She rested her head on his shoulder and breathed in the sandalwood shampoo. She loved its scent a little less now that she knew that Whittaker also used it.

"Teddy pulled Tane Lagerhead's pants all the way down, Patrick,"

Alice said, insistent. "In front of the entire seventh grade. They saw *every*thing." If Patrick had been in the meeting with the assistant principal that morning, he'd understand.

She felt him shudder as he pulled her closer. "Kids are impulsive," he said. "We'll make him apologize."

Alice hoped it would be that easy. "Will you talk to him?" She pulled back, and Patrick leaned over again to untie his other shoe. "My mom didn't even have any luck with him."

"Where is he?" Alice pointed toward the ceiling, indicating his room upstairs. Patrick padded through the kitchen, and Alice set his shoes into the cubby where they belonged.

As she waited for him to return, Alice nervously scrolled her phone. But just as she'd clicked from Pinterest to NextDoor for the latest on the pink graffiti, he was back. The "rocket ships," as Shirley MacIntosh had called them, had been so funny that morning, but now that Teddy had exposed Tane, the paintings felt ominous.

"No luck." Patrick shrugged.

"Nothing?" She balled one fist and gripped her phone tighter in the other.

"Nothing," he repeated. "He's a kid. I did so many stupid things when I was in junior high."

"Like what?" Alice couldn't remember a single story either Patrick or his parents had told her about him misbehaving as a young teen.

"It's a secret." His impish smile materialized, and once again, she could see where Teddy got his charm.

Alice rolled her eyes. "What?" she demanded.

"Okay, look." Patrick pulled her close, but Alice let her arms hang at her sides. He dropped his voice to a whisper. "I had planned to take this to my grave, but if it'll make you feel better, I'll tell you now that I stole a pack of gum from the Tom Thumb on the corner up the street from my parents' house."

Alice snickered. "Okay, fine," she said as Patrick let go.

"And I'm really sorry, hon," he said, "but I have a million documents to review." He pointed at the dining room table, where he set up his de facto office in the evenings. He slid back into the mudroom and grabbed his backpack.

Alice wandered for a few minutes around the kitchen, trying to land on a task, but she couldn't shake her restlessness. Patrick would be leaving that Sunday for a full week in Cincinnati, the first of several such weeks away. She pictured her husband eating a room service cheeseburger on a stiff hotel comforter and realized she wouldn't be free again in the evenings until the Energy Lab case was over.

Alice sent a text to the group chat. She wasn't sure that Nadia and Meredith would take her up on an outing, but she felt desperate to escape the house, to distance herself from her parenting failures. "Quick drink at Cork & Cask? I'm going crazy. Promise we'll be home by 9:30."

Much to her relief, they both took pity on her.

Nadia responded first. "Always here for you," she said. "Just let me change out of my pajama pants." And then Meredith chimed in, affirmative as well. Alice couldn't wait to leave. Teddy's shuffles on the second floor, his intermittent trips to the bathroom and, once, to the kitchen, unnerved her. Thinking about him on the stage with Tane—the poor kid's pants around his shins—it was like the Teddy she'd birthed had disappeared. She didn't know the kid who would have done something like that, plus the textbook in the compost bin and the spaghetti in Tane's lap. None of it seemed real, and yet her misery hung on her like the weighted blanket she draped over Aidy each night at bedtime. Alice hoped her friends knew her well enough not to think she'd failed completely at motherhood despite the day's revelations.

At least in the case of Aidy's reading, there was an easy fix. Alice would start practicing with her immediately. Well, tomorrow. And, she realized with a measure of relief, she didn't have to tell Meredith and Nadia about Adrian's level E. Neither of them had actually been to the

conference. They could think she was I or J with the rest of the second graders. Alice could limit her public failure to her preteen.

As Alice settled at their usual high-top in the back corner of the dim restaurant, she remembered coffee with Nadia just that morning. Thirteen hours ago, her biggest concern had been the Kerrigan meeting. At the office she'd sort of salvaged that disaster with a series of sincere and confidence-inspiring texts to Bea Kerrigan and a grovelly apology to Ramona, her boss. And then, in a miraculous bright spot, she'd gotten word, finally, that the *Elle Decor* feature was a go. A local freelancer would shoot "before" photos of the Kerrigan project as well as one other, and then they'd also feature Alice's own dining room. Photos of her house in one of the nation's leading design magazines? Despite everything, Alice smiled. Ramona would have to make her partner, she thought. The feature would draw a whole new set of clients.

Alice didn't let herself dwell on the fact that she hadn't actually finished her dining room yet. She had all of four weeks still, and the upgrades were just cosmetic—paint, fabrics, tablescapes, maybe a new piece of art with the perfect unexpected frame. Or, if she could work the budget and call in a scheduling favor, a custom paint job by the uber-trendy design duo she had in mind for the Kerrigan rumpus room.

She could get it done. She had to. It was *Elle Decor.*

Meredith arrived just as the server delivered the olives Alice always chose, along with a glass of sparkling rosé. If Cork & Cask had had a full liquor license, she might have ordered a shot of something.

"How's Teddy?" Meredith asked. Alice noticed the twinkle in her eye, a hint of excitement where Alice would have preferred sympathy. But this was Meredith. Even if she enjoyed Alice's misfortune a little bit, she'd still have her back. She had been the one, after all, to get her reinstated at book club after Alice had gotten slightly tipsy and inadvertently insulted Lacy Cushing's selection, *The Scarlet Letter.* Who chose *The Scarlet Letter* for a suburban moms' book club? Alice stood by her

assessment that the novel was "incomprehensible drivel," although she regretted the fervency with which she'd declared it.

Alice bit through the skin of an olive, stopping before she gnashed the pit. She took her time stripping it and deposited the seed as delicately as she could in the empty ramekin, trying to decide how to spin things for her closest friends. She couldn't exactly hide the facts—Sadie and Donovan would have reported them, and besides, she'd invited Meredith and Nadia here to talk.

"Can I tell you what happened when Nadia gets here?" Alice asked. "I'm not sure I can get through it twice." It was true, Alice reasoned, and it bought her some time.

"Good idea." Meredith waved the server over and asked for her usual unoaked Chardonnay. "While we're waiting, let me tell you about this new opportunity at school. I'm so excited."

Alice grabbed another olive and watched the color rise in Meredith's cheeks. Her friend's skin glowed in the low light, her black T-shirt looking somehow a million times more sophisticated than Alice's own camel-colored sweater. Alice wished she'd kept on the necklace she'd worn that afternoon. Statement jewelry could save any outfit.

"Jason Whittaker asked me to start a new discussion group as part of the parent education series." Meredith leaned forward, her hands flat against the dark wood tabletop. "And I'm just so excited, you know? That I'm already being included in Parent Association stuff even though we just got to the junior high? I'd sort of worried that all that time I put in at Elm Creek Elementary wouldn't mean anything now that we've— I mean, the kids—have moved on."

The server slid the wine in front of Meredith, who glanced up with a quick smile. "Any food?" the woman asked.

"No." She shook her head. Meredith never snacked after seven p.m.

"That's great!" Alice raised her glass to clink it with Meredith's. "What's the discussion group?" Somehow, Meredith always had time for these extras, even though she also worked nearly full-time at the

physical therapy clinic. Meanwhile, Alice could barely put dinner on the table, or help with homework, she remembered with a surge of guilt.

"Raising Ethical Teens. Timely, right? In this political climate?" Meredith sipped. "It's so complicated, and there are always missteps. Like this thing with Teddy. I pitched a few ideas to the PA, and this is the one they thought filled a need."

Alice drank again. *Raising ethical teens.* She'd probably have to go to the meeting, both to support her friend and also because, well, Teddy's behavior that day hadn't exactly been ethical. And there had been that text she'd received that morning. *"Can't you do something about this?"* People knew about Teddy's behavior, his recurring failures.

Before Alice had time to respond or to show Meredith the text, Nadia rushed in. Alice felt immediately better. Nadia had changed out of her pajama pants as promised, but Alice could see her University of Minnesota sweatshirt beneath her ancient North Face fleece. Nadia wouldn't talk about ethical teens. She had her hands full at home as it was.

"Honey." Nadia put her arms out as she got to the table, pulling Alice to her in an awkward but fervent side hug. "I've been thinking about you all day. So glad you texted. Tell us everything." She kept her arm on Alice's shoulder as she pulled out a stool. Alice chewed two more olives as Nadia got settled.

"Actually," Alice said, "before I get into it, can you give me the name of Donovan's therapist? You're in with a good one, right?"

Nadia pulled her cell phone from a canvas tote bag emblazoned with the logo for the Minneapolis library system. A few clicks later, Alice's own screen lit up with the contact information for Green Haven Family Services. "Life-changing," Nadia said. "Really. Dr. Martín has been my favorite of them all."

Alice's stomach sank. The Reddys had been in therapy since Donovan was in third grade with very little progress. But then again, Teddy couldn't be that far gone.

"All I know is what Donovan told me," Nadia said, rolling her eyes, "so let's hear the real deal. I'm sure there are a million ways to fix this."

Alice looked alternately at her two friends, so different and yet both equally concerned. She wasn't sure there were a million ways to fix things, but she recounted the harrowing day nonetheless, skipping just Aidy's conference. One spiraling child was more than enough.

Meredith Yoshida

M eredith had read in *Thinking Mother* magazine years ago that responsible parents in the digital age required their children to charge their electronics in the kitchen. Hours alone in their rooms with access to the wilds of the Internet could only lead to folly.

Well, the article didn't say "folly." That sounded like something her grandmother would have said, but she'd taken the advice to heart nonetheless.

And usually she followed the recommendations of another article she'd read in that same magazine about the notion of "privacy." Parents ought to give a little space to their tweens and teens, the writer had argued, and not virtually listen in on every conversation by reading their text messages and scouring their social media feeds for transgressive comments.

Meredith agreed with privacy in theory, but what about safety and supervision? Plenty of "thinking mothers" expressed similar concerns in the comments section of the online article. They'd even provided links to monitoring software, programs that could mirror Sadie's phone and allow Meredith to analyze every incoming message, to comb through each of her daughter's keystrokes. She'd clicked through and marveled at the screenshots explaining such programs. If she bought a subscription, Sadie wouldn't even be able to follow an Amazon ad

without Meredith knowing which product had fascinated her. But that level of snooping, Meredith knew without even asking Alice and Nadia for their opinions, was going too far.

So instead, several times a week after Sadie had adhered to her strict nine thirty bedtime, Meredith stood in the kitchen and scrolled through her daughter's phone. Tonight, after she'd gotten home from Cork & Cask, she looked first at the texts, checking for any fallout from Teddy's nightmare suspension. Though Sadie and Teddy were close, she couldn't find any messages—new or old—from him. Had they had an argument? A message from Mikaela read, "Did you see Sullivan is suspended?" Sadie had simply responded with a thumbs-up.

Meredith switched to Instagram, and Sadie's friends' photos seemed pedestrian enough, though Mikaela Heffernan had photographed the graffiti at Elm Creek Park that Meredith had seen on NextDoor. The same "artwork" had appeared on the McDonald's, she noticed, not that the fast-food restaurant was some kind of community paragon. Mikaela's caption was "Fight the patriarchy," and two laugh-cry emojis. At least Mikaela knew the word "patriarchy," Meredith thought. Still, she was confident in Sadie's relative innocence compared to the other seventh graders at Elm Creek Junior High. Her daughter hadn't even been able to say "penis" aloud when she told Meredith what had happened in assembly. Meredith smiled, remembering the way Sadie had covered her face in the back seat when she'd recounted the incident on the way home from school. Meredith clicked out of the general Instagram feed and onto Sadie's personal profile. She scanned the photos collected there, all the ones going back to the day she had supervised Sadie in creating the account, the day after Christmas in sixth grade. An op-ed in the *Times* about social isolation had convinced her it was time. And the online version of Sadie seemed completely age-appropriate—funny pictures of Stein, their ancient golden retriever mix that Bill had named for Mary Shelley's monster; close-ups of flowers; personalized birthday messages for each of her inner-circle friends.

Meredith didn't quite understand the hashtags, but they seemed benign enough.

Once she felt satisfied, Meredith clicked on a little arrow at the top of the screen she'd never noticed before, right next to Sadie's username, SadieLouWho. It had been an homage, obviously, to their long love affair with Dr. Seuss, never mind that Cindy Lou Who was blond and blue-eyed, and Sadie half Japanese. Meredith had, of course, scoured lists of books by Asian and Asian American authors over the years. The Yoshidas' shelves included volumes by Uchida, Ohi, and Kadohata and other East Asian writers. But still, Sadie had chosen Seuss over and over again as a little girl. Maybe, Meredith worried, she hadn't done enough to help her daughter claim her Japanese identity. She blinked the thought away and tapped the username. A little menu dropped down providing Meredith with an opportunity to select another profile, SadeeLux.

She inhaled sharply through her nose and sank onto a kitchen stool, stretching Sadie's charger toward her. SadeeLux? *What the hell is Lux?* Meredith's eyes bugged as she scanned the pictures in this new feed. She clicked on a close-up of her daughter's lovely face—her deep brown eyes center in the square frame, thick eyeliner drawn above her mascara'd lashes. Meredith frowned. Except for Sadie's skating competitions, they'd stuck to the Burt's Bees tinted lip balms. Sadie hadn't even asked for anything more in terms of makeup.

Another SadeeLux photo featured a selfie of Sadie's pursed lips, bright pink lipstick half applied, the uncapped tube in her daughter's free hand. Meredith scrolled faster. In a third photo, Mikaela sat on the Yoshidas' basement couch, her thighs spread apart, jean shorts barely covering an inch of skin on either side of her crotch. Mikaela's midriff peeked out beneath a green tank top that Meredith couldn't remember ever seeing. The girl's middle finger extended toward the camera, her tongue stuck out. Another photo featured Sadie at her locker door, crammed in a selfie with Tane Lagerhead. "It's #TeamTANE, guys,"

Sadie had written. "It's not that hard to spell." Their cheeks pressed together. Tane looked a little sweaty, probably thrilled to be pulled into a half hug with a beautiful girl. Beautiful and *brilliant*, Meredith reminded herself, despite the shock of discovering this alter ego, a confusing facsimile of the kid asleep upstairs.

She heard Sadie's bedroom door open and rushed to switch the profile back to SadieLouWho, her photos of Stein and flowers. Meredith's heart raced. "SadeeLux," she whispered to herself, overpronouncing the "x," her imagination flashing on a pinup model in a lacy bra. She listened for her daughter's footsteps on the stairs, but they never came. After a minute, Meredith heard the toilet flush and water rush from the tap.

She'd have to confront Sadie in the morning. She knew *Thinking Mother* would have her force Sadie to delete SadeeLux. Or, Meredith reasoned, her heart rate slowing to normal now that the shock had passed, maybe it was smarter to know about the profile and not tell Sadie. She'd get an unfiltered look at this other version of her daughter. And, of course, she could step in if she saw anything truly alarming on the feed.

Did the other kids have secret Instagrams? She grabbed her own phone and googled "secret Instagram." Several articles popped up about so-called Finstas. Now that she saw the term, she thought she remembered reading about them, maybe on a *Thinking Mother* message board. She never would have thought Sadie would be so bold. *At least she doesn't have Snapchat*, Meredith thought.

Or did she? Meredith grabbed at the phone again and swiped through the app icons looking for the little white ghost. No ghost. *Good girl.*

Alice Sullivan

Alice had hoped she'd perk up that night after seeing her friends, but a leaden feeling had settled in her gut. Despite Nadia's assertions that there were "a million ways to fix Teddy," there seemed to be just two: Call a therapist and apologize to Tane.

In a whispered conversation across their pillows with the lights off, Alice told Patrick she'd get both of those items checked off the following day.

"As a start," Alice said.

"The full monty." Patrick whistled again. Alice could see the concern in his brow even in the dark, the heave of his chest as he pictured Tane's pants dropping.

"Did he say anything more before he fell asleep?" Alice asked.

Patrick shook his head, his hair staticky against the pillow.

"The principal—assistant principal"—Alice corrected herself—"acted like Teddy is some kind of sex offender."

Patrick grunted. "Why would he pants a kid?"

Alice shrugged, and Patrick reached across their bed to put an arm around her waist. "Why do twelve-year-olds do anything?"

In between meetings the next morning, Alice retreated to the parking ramp—the only place she could ensure privacy from Ramona—to make the call to Green Haven Family Services, the clinic Nadia had recommended. She felt woozy as a young-sounding male receptionist

took her information and said he'd email paperwork and information on the nature therapy groups that Dr. Martín generally recommended. The receptionist could fit Teddy into one of Dr. Martín's "emergency slots," he said. It would be less than a week until Teddy officially had professional help. Alice thought she might be able to stave off more prison disaster scenarios until then.

Alice steeled herself in the afternoon, when the time came for the apology that she and Patrick had agreed on. Her nausea roared back as she anticipated the call to the Lagerheads. "No issues," Alice's mom said as they passed one another in the mudroom. She'd worked from the Sullivans' in the morning, so Teddy wouldn't be alone. Alice smiled as her mom gave her arm a quick squeeze.

"Thanks," Alice said, but her mom waved her off.

"I've gotta run. Clients." Evelyn skipped down the garage steps. "Call you later."

Alice found Teddy on his bed and told him it was time to call Tane.

"It was an accident," he argued.

"When you hurt someone, you apologize." Alice's patience evaporated as she delivered the line for the umpteenth time.

Teddy lay back theatrically, his head bouncing against his pillow. He kicked a leg up, letting it slam down against his rumpled comforter. So many remnants of toddlerhood stuck with him even as he blustered into junior high. He'd thrashed and protested just like this when she and Patrick had asked him to share toys with Adrian or to stop throwing Cheerios off the tray of his high chair.

"The kid's an asshole anyway," Teddy said. "I mean, do you think he actually likes Sadie?"

"Language. And what? What does this have to do with Sadie?" Alice squinted at him. "Sadie Yoshida?"

"How many Sadies do we know?" Teddy threw his hands up before collapsing them over his face. "Tane just wants to get into her pants."

Get into her pants? Her seventh grader knew this phrase? Alice felt

instantly guilty for watching yet another season of *Bachelor in Paradise* while her children were within earshot.

She blinked a few times, trying to make sense of things. What did Sadie have to do with the assembly? She finally asked, lamely, "What do you mean?"

"He talks about her in band. Says she's hot or whatever, in a Mary kind of way."

"What?"

"Mary. You know. Didn't you say that when you were young? Like from the Bible? Like, the virgin?"

Alice had had "the talk"—many of them, actually—with Teddy. She'd been the one to define the very word "virgin" for him, but she hadn't imagined him using it to describe Sadie Yoshida, the little girl he'd been friends with since he was five.

"Anyway, he's a jerk," Teddy continued. "And I didn't mean to grab his underwear, too. Who wears those loose boxers? I haven't seen those on anyone who isn't eighty."

Alice frowned. "How many eighty-year-olds in underwear have you seen?"

"You've obviously never been in the men's locker room at the gym."

"Clearly." Alice stared at the buffalo-checked sheets she'd chosen for him that summer, a replacement for the boyish striped set that had taken him through the final years of elementary. "But still, you're going to have to call Tane."

"Text," Teddy countered. "No one calls."

Alice had prepared herself for this negotiation tactic, and she held firm. "This is one of those times when we have to call. Believe me, I have no desire to talk to the Lagerheads, either, but it's a must." She had never really connected with Janna Lagerhead, whose leather pants had always looked a little over-the-top at Elm Creek Elementary events. "I'll get us started." Alice grabbed the sticky note from the back of her phone case, on which she'd written the Lagerheads' number. As she

copied it down, she double-checked it against the one attached to the anonymous text she'd received, but it didn't match.

"I'm not talking," Teddy said. Alice ignored him and put the call on speaker.

Janna picked up almost instantly. "Hello?"

"Janna, hi. It's Alice Sullivan." She extended her index finger toward Teddy and employed her sternest expression, eyes narrow and mouth pinched. The kid would deliver his apology. Meanwhile, Janna didn't say anything, and Alice soldiered on. "I'm sitting here with Teddy, and he really wants to apologize to Tane for the incident at school."

I don't, Teddy mouthed, and Alice jerked her palm up in quick signal for him to stop.

"While he intended to pull a prank, he didn't plan to humiliate Tane, and well—" Alice paused. She dropped her hand firmly on Teddy's shoulder, holding him in place. "He's really sorry."

Silence.

Alice nervously continued. "*I'd* also like to apologize." She waited. Would Janna ice her out? She could hear the woman's exhales as she held her own breath.

"Thanks for calling," Janna said finally. "I appreciate that Teddy is sorry. But this goes beyond that, doesn't it? Tane's private parts—the whole seventh grade has seen them." Teddy pressed his lips together, stifling a horribly inappropriate laugh.

Alice hastily pressed the speaker button and held the phone to her ear, lest Janna hear him giggling. "Can you even imagine that kind of trauma for a twelve-year-old?"

Alice nodded. "It must have been very embarrassing."

"Embarrassing?" Janna's voice acquired an edge. "No. This level of humiliation is life-changing."

"Life-changing" seemed a little extreme, but at the same time, Alice couldn't imagine Teddy in Tane's compromised position. He'd

have lost it, she knew. He probably would have refused to go to school for the rest of the week, if not longer.

"So," Janna continued, "I'm afraid Tane is definitely not ready to accept an apology. But I have a question since I have you." Alice's fingers tingled as she held the phone. She felt as nervous as she had at high school track meets, crouched on the starting line, ready to run championship races. "Two, actually." Janna sounded so businesslike, and Alice tried to remember what she did for a living. Something in banking, maybe.

"Of course," Alice said.

"First, have you seen that graffiti on NextDoor?" Alice stiffened. She hadn't even considered that the tags could be related to Teddy's stunt.

"Those don't have anything to do with Tane, do they?" Alice's heartbeat revved. Teddy couldn't have done spaghetti, the compost bin, the pantsing, *and* the pink penises. The last one, for sure, would make her "criminal" pronouncement from the night before uncomfortably true. Alice mentally reviewed the colors of spray paint she kept in her garage workshop. She hadn't done anything pink in ages.

"I hope not." Janna continued. "And what does Sadie Yoshida have to do with this, do you know?"

A second prick of fear lodged near Alice's diaphragm. She remembered Meredith, sympathetic but distant at the wine bar the night before. "Teddy just mentioned her." Alice took a few steps into the hallway.

"Mom!" Teddy whisper-yelled, but Alice turned back and shut his door behind her.

"I was surprised he brought up Sadie."

"This is going to sound a little silly since it's seventh grade," Janna said, "and I definitely don't think this at *all* excuses Teddy." Alice frowned. "But I'm getting the sense that both boys might have a crush on her. And I think, given what Tane has said about the time they've spent together at Quiz Bowl, I think Sadie might like Tane back."

Alice pictured Tane as she'd known him in elementary school, mismatched outfits and those painted nails. *I doubt it*, she thought, and then cringed. She was as bad as her son, judging kids based on appearance rather than character. Alice walked into her bedroom and lowered her voice to just above a whisper. "Teddy did just say something about Tane liking Sadie, but I had no idea that Teddy might feel the same way." Alice thought about Teddy and Sadie swimming together at the Elm Creek pool in the summers, watching movies on either the Sullivans' couch or the Yoshidas'. "I've been friends with Meredith Yoshida since the kids were in kindergarten."

"I know," Janna said. "It's always been you, Meredith, and Nadia, from basically the very beginning." Alice thought back again to Janna's leather pants, her blown-out hair at the Parent Association fund-raisers. Alice had never made an effort to get to know her. "Will you keep me posted?" Janna asked. "Like, if Teddy divulges anything else? Maybe you could ask Meredith? I just want this to end. All of it. The graffiti, too."

"I'll keep you posted," Alice said. *But I'm not asking Meredith*, she thought. The idea of Sadie in any kind of trouble was a complete nonstarter. "Teddy hasn't exactly been forthcoming about his feelings since entering junior high."

"I certainly hope you're considering therapy," Janna said. "I mean, Teddy's behavior is pretty alarming."

Alice sank onto her bed. A sourness stung the back of her throat. "I guess. I made an appointment." What could Alice do but agree? The apology, though, that had been the number one reason for her call. She felt desperate to accomplish it—accomplish *something*.

Alice breathed into silence for a few seconds, and then finally, Janna spoke. "Could he do it via text? I think you're right to make him apologize, but I'm afraid talking would only make things worse."

Teddy Sullivan

The only time Teddy had been allowed to touch his phone after his mom had taken it from his backpack on Thursday was to send the apology text message to Tane. His mom had sat next to him while he did it, watching him type.

"God, could you move?" he said as his thumbs hovered over the screen. He could smell her coffee breath and feel her curly hair brush against his cheek.

"Just type." She sounded angry, but she did move an inch, enough so that it didn't feel like she was sitting in his lap.

He'd written, "I'm sorry. I didn't mean for it to happen like that," and then stalled out. "I don't know what else to say." He dropped the phone in his lap, but she grabbed it and shoved it back into his hands.

"How about what you're going to do differently from now on? Like, how you won't be tripping him in the hallways or dumping lunch on him?"

"I didn't dump my lunch on purpose," Teddy grumbled. That part was totally true. He'd slipped—there'd been spilled milk next to the Quiz Bowl table, and the fall had been just horribly perfect, the pasta arcing off his green plastic cafeteria tray directly onto Tane's premier soccer team shorts. The tripping? That he'd done after Tane had humiliated him in PE, but there was no use trying to explain it to his

mother. She only understood one side of things. And that one side was never Teddy's.

"I hope you can forgive me," Teddy had typed in the text message, imagining what his mother would want him to say, and then tipped the phone toward her and shrugged.

"Fine." She grabbed it and hit send, and then she stared at it for a while waiting for a response. There must not have been one, because she stood to leave.

"Can I have my phone?" Teddy tried to sound normal, not too greedy.

His mother let out a coughlike laugh. "Absolutely not." She spat the last word as if his question were the dumbest thing she'd ever heard.

"When—" Teddy started to ask, but she was already out the door and closing it roughly behind her. He'd try his dad later, he thought.

But the next morning, when he and his father drove to soccer practice at Elm Creek Park, he had just as little luck.

"When we gave you the phone, do you remember what we said?" his dad asked.

Teddy remembered. He'd hoped he'd get a phone for Christmas in sixth grade, but he'd had to wait until his birthday in February. Meanwhile, Sadie had gotten hers on Christmas Eve. For the next two months, he'd stared over her shoulder on their way home from school, looking at other people's Instagrams. When his parents had finally handed over an iPhone—the eight, not the X—they'd given their Spider-Man Speech, as his dad insisted on calling it, even though it wasn't that funny. "With great power . . . ," Teddy repeated, sullenly.

"That's right." Teddy's dad nodded his stubbly chin. "Comes great responsibility."

"But I didn't do anything bad with my phone." Besides the Spider-Man Speech, his parents were also into "logical consequences." Teddy wasn't always sure what that meant, but it had something to do with the punishment being related to the crime. Like, if he didn't eat his

vegetables, he didn't get to have dessert. Or if he didn't put away his laundry, then his room was too messy to have a friend over. But Tane's pants in assembly? That had nothing, as far as Teddy could see, to do with his phone.

Teddy's dad half shrugged and kept his eyes on the road. "Still," he said, "you can't have it." Teddy could see the soccer fields a block or two in front of them. He'd face Tane and the rest of the team in a matter of minutes. He'd asked his mom that morning if Tane had ever responded to his apology text, and she shook her head.

Now, they'd be together in practice. Teddy's legs started to feel twitchy, and he shifted, clicking his right shoe against his left shin guard. He glanced into the back seat, double-checking for the string bag in which he packed his cleats and water bottle.

"Are you nervous?" his dad asked as they pulled into the parking lot. Teddy was, but felt annoyed about it. This was *his* team; he'd been on it for two years before Tane tried out. And the whole thing had been a stupid accident, basically a misunderstanding. "Do you want to talk about anything before you head over there?"

Teddy shrugged and looked over at the clump of kids tying their shoes. He was relieved to see McCoy Blumenfeld among them. He'd always been #TeamTeddy. Landon Severson pulled up in his mom's minivan next to Teddy's window. As Teddy waved at Landon, he noticed his dad looking nervously in the rearview mirror and then craning his neck to see the rest of the cars.

"What are you looking for?" Teddy asked, and then he realized. He was doing the same thing Teddy was: looking for the Lagerheads.

Before his dad could answer, Teddy grabbed his bag and hustled out. It felt weird to have caused his dad's embarrassment. At the last second, he realized he should say good-bye and opened the door again. "Thanks for the ride," he said. "See you after practice." And he re-slammed it.

"Dude," said Landon as they reached the field. "How much trouble are you in?"

Teddy shrugged. McCoy looked up, eyes bulging. But the other kids on the team? Since they didn't all go to Elm Creek, they might not know, and Teddy didn't want to talk about it.

"You don't have your phone, right?" Landon asked, not catching on. "Because I've been texting you. The post on your Finsta was bomb."

Teddy remembered the caption. #pantsdrop, he'd said. Maybe he shouldn't have written that. "Hey," he said as he sat on the sidelines, "I'd kind of like to keep it quiet, okay? My parents don't want me to talk—"

He watched Landon's mouth drop open and turned around to see Tane walking over. The kid had a huge grin on his face. Teddy swallowed hard. "Nothing to see here, fellas," Tane said. Teddy willed himself to look away, but he couldn't. Tane lifted his T-shirt then and showed them the drawstrings of his shorts tied tight. "Double knotted, so I'm safe. Right, Teddy?"

And then Tane held a hand up to Landon for a high five. No, Teddy thought, but Landon did it. They slapped hands. Teddy clenched his jaw. He grabbed his bag and looked over to the spot where his dad had parked and was surprised to see him out of the car. He stood with his hands jammed in his jacket pockets, talking to Teddy's coach near the porta-potty with the pink graffiti. The premier team had hired a new coach that year who'd been a captain at the University of Minnesota when they'd finished second in the Big 10 tournament a year ago. Teddy watched his dad rock back on his heels and then, when he'd finished talking, bob his head. The coach turned to Teddy.

Tane's dad approached the two men then. Jonas Lagerhead towered over them both. Teddy's dad offered a handshake, and while Jonas accepted it, he looked pissed. The coach left the two of them together.

"Sullivan," he said when he got close enough. Teddy's stomach dropped. "Lace up and take three or four extra laps." Looking over Teddy's head, Coach dropped the mesh bag of balls on the ground.

The stack of cones he'd carried under his other arm fell a second later. "Basically," Coach said, "don't stop running until I tell you to. Got it?"

As he got to his feet and started to run toward the goal on the far end of the field, Teddy swiped tears from his eyelids. It had been an accident, he thought. At least he was pretty sure it was an accident. It had happened so quickly, and Tane was so oblivious.

Alice Sullivan

Alice had raced for the shower that Monday morning before her alarm even rang, both anxious and giddy about her upcoming meetings despite the problem with Teddy. The Harrisons, new clients she'd met with once before, would stop in to view the design concepts for their family room, and then Bea and Jeff Kerrigan would arrive after lunch to approve some preliminary sketches. As Alice imagined the Kerrigan design in the *Elle Decor* article, she saw Bea posing for the "before" shoot next to the original pink stove in the retro kitchen.

While they obviously couldn't use the Pepto-Bismol range going forward, Alice had already begun imagining sophisticated nods to the postwar era. Ramona had covered that initial meeting with Bea when Teddy had imploded at school, but Alice was still running point on the project. She'd been back in the office that same afternoon. She'd raced back over to the Kerrigan house and taken measurements. She'd begun work on elevations, sketches to show the couple today.

The only trouble was that she'd have to bring Teddy with her to the office. At twelve, he was perfectly capable of staying home alone, but not now. Not when she had hard evidence that he couldn't be trusted. Alice's mother wasn't available to help until the afternoon and Patrick had flown out to Cincinnati at six a.m. He wouldn't be home until Friday. Teddy had slunk down the stairs that morning in pilled joggers

without combing his hair. *I'll hide him someplace,* Alice thought, thinking of the chair in her office that she could turn inward toward the wall.

WITH FIFTEEN MINUTES before the Harrisons' planned arrival, Alice walked into Ramona Design wearing a slim black turtleneck and an azure statement necklace. Everything was perfect, she thought, except for the sour-looking kid at her side. She rolled her shoulders back and smiled at their assistant, hoping to convey confidence and calm, and then stopped when she saw a tray of fancy-looking pastries on the conference room table between two vases of oakleaf hydrangea. Ramona stood back from the display, considering it. Her high-waisted tweed skirt looked fabulous with her low gray bun.

Alice loved it when Ramona went full luxury in the conference room, but why had she pulled out all the stops for Alice's meeting with the Harrisons?

Ramona glanced at Alice then, tipped her chin up, and grimaced at Teddy. "Isn't there school?" she asked. Ramona was among the most innovative designers in town, but warmth wasn't her strength.

"Unforeseen complications." Alice avoided eye contact. She looked instead at the RD logo that her boss loved so much in a geometric sans serif that contrasted strikingly with the soft hydrangea she preferred for the vases. "He needs to camp in my office during my meeting with the Harrisons." She jerked a thumb toward her space, glass-walled like everything else at Ramona Design.

"What meeting?" Ramona had hired Alice away from a large development firm five years before. They'd both been initially thrilled with the arrangement, though Ramona hadn't seemed to anticipate the number of sick days a mother of two would need. Or the frequent midafternoon departures Alice would make to get to car pool or a soccer game.

Alice made up for it by working in the evenings, but Ramona prized business hours. Last week, when Alice had missed the Kerrigan meeting, she'd let Ramona think Teddy had been sick. She cleared her throat now and glanced alternately at her boss and her son.

"Can I have your phone, at least?" Teddy grumbled.

"Shhh," Alice hissed at him. Ramona had opinions about children. She didn't have kids herself, but, as she often said, she was "an auntie to four." Her youngest nephew had failed to write thank-you notes after the two most recent holidays, and Ramona had told Alice she was considering suspending her gift giving until he improved.

"I have the Harrisons at nine," Alice said, ignoring Teddy. "Their new family room."

Ramona crossed her arms. "It's impossible. I've got the Kerrigans at nine, and I need the conference room."

Alice dropped her bag, a Goyard tote she'd bought when Ramona had hired her, on the jute runner. Her chest started to hurt beneath her necklace. "My meeting's on the calendar. And besides, we're supposed to meet the Kerrigans this afternoon. I have the sketches to show them."

"We almost *lost* the Kerrigan account after your last-minute cancellation." Ramona's face remained placid except for a slight twitch at her temple.

"Can I have that almond croissant?" Teddy walked toward the tray of pastries.

"No!" Ramona shouted, and Teddy startled.

"God." He slunk backward.

"Frankly," Ramona whispered to Alice, though Teddy could certainly hear, "I think it's better if I take point on the Kerrigan project given your distractions." Ramona set her jaw.

Alice turned to her son, seeing him as Ramona must. Had he even brushed his teeth that morning? "Can you go wait in my office?" She pointed at the glass cubicle.

"It's not like that'll give you privacy." Teddy sneered.

Alice felt a twinge in her forehead, the beginnings of a headache. "Go wait in the Starbucks, then." She pointed at the external door.

Teddy held out his hand. "Five dollars?"

Alice took two steps toward him and whispered, though Ramona could surely hear, "Get a table in the back. I'll be right down."

Teddy sauntered out without the cash he'd asked for. The office door swooshed shut behind him.

Alice marched into the sample room, steady on her stacked heels. She pulled a bin labeled HARRISON from the shelf where they kept active projects. "Joanna?" she called to their assistant, who had been paging through receipts while Alice and Ramona negotiated. "Could you apologize to the Harrisons about the change in location, but tell them I'll have hot coffee waiting for them downstairs in the Starbucks?" With the open concept and glass doorless cubes, she and Ramona couldn't very well hold concurrent meetings in their suite. Alice balanced the bin on her hip as she grabbed her bag from the floor. "Check the calendar," she said to Ramona without looking. "It's your system, and I use it religiously."

SWEAT PERCOLATED BENEATH Alice's turtleneck, and she could feel Teddy's eyes on her from the corner of the Starbucks as she finished her opening spiel on colorways for the Harrisons' new family room. Alice hoped Ursula and Jenny hadn't noticed Teddy's glowering, but she imagined they had. They'd both glanced back at him while Alice had reviewed colors and fabrics.

"I'm sorry to stop you." Ursula raised her hand, and she and Jenny shared a look. "It's just that this isn't what we imagined." Alice blinked at the postconsumer recycled textile dangling from her fingers, the one she was sure Ursula and Jenny would choose for their centerpiece sofa. She let it drop on the drawings she'd made of the room.

"Really?" Alice leaned back. "I was sure this was your style." It wouldn't be the first time she'd been wrong about a client's tastes, or the first time a client had completely changed gears between brainstorming and decision time.

Alice would pivot, as she had zillions of times before. "No problem. I've got two other design boards—well, not boards because we're in Starbucks." She thought ruefully of the fabric-upholstered wall upstairs in the conference room. If Ramona hadn't commandeered it, Alice would have tacked up her textiles at the perfect height, under the perfect light. "But I do have other concepts I can show you." She scooped the swatches back into her plastic bin.

"Actually." Jenny's lips quivered beneath her pointed nose. "I think what Ursula means is that this"—she gestured around the café, the worn dark-wood tables, the buzz of overloud conversations, the scowling adolescent in the corner, and just then, the piercing squeal of a baby—"isn't what we had in mind. We saw those other people in the conference room upstairs. Are we, like, not as important as they are? When that couple walked in, your assistant basically pushed Ursula out of the way in order to greet them. I know our budget is on the lower end, but I assure you, this family room is a huge investment for us."

Alice's shoulders rounded. "Not at all." She shook her head. "You're very important to me." And it was true. Projects like the Harrisons' family room were her bread and butter. "It was just a misunderstanding—a scheduling mishap—with my boss, Ramona." She put emphasis on "boss," hoping to signal to the women that she'd been outranked.

"I'm sure that's the case," Ursula broke in, her expression more sympathetic than Jenny's. "But this isn't working for either of us. I don't think you quite got what we were hoping for." She put her hand on her wife's shoulder. Alice wondered how they'd communicated their displeasure to one another during her introductory remarks. She'd missed it completely, just as she'd apparently been blind to Teddy's problem-

atic transformation in seventh grade. "Can we cut this short?" Ursula said. "We'll call you if we'd like to reschedule."

If? Alice deflated. She shook their hands and mumbled her hope to hear from them. As she gathered her things, Teddy slunk back to the table. He slid into the banquette opposite her. "Great meeting, Mom." His sarcasm startled her, and she jerked her head up to study his eyes. She saw a flatness there where she was used to a sparkle. *Who is this kid?* Anger and disappointment melded, intensifying her headache. She threw her bag over her shoulder and turned to walk out. She assumed Teddy would follow her.

ON THE WAY home, Alice felt Teddy's oppressive presence in the front seat of her station wagon like the heat of an oven in summer. She kept her eyes on the traffic, avoiding accidental eye contact. First, her son had traumatized Tane, and now it seemed like he was turning on her.

The anger she'd felt in the coffee shop reignited. Those flat eyes. The bullying. She wondered about Nadia's psychologist. Would Dr. Martín prescribe medication? Would Teddy get worse? As she contemplated these questions, Lakes District Books, a small shop embedded in a strip mall between a Subway and one of those trendy wood-fired pizza places, appeared on her left. Alice veered into the parking lot.

"What are we doing?" Teddy asked, impatient. "It's too early for lunch. I wanted to get home."

"As if I'd buy you lunch," Alice muttered as she roughly undid her seat belt.

"What?"

"You don't need to get home," she said, louder. "You'll just be sitting in your room anyway."

And then, a rage she'd never felt toward either of her children set fire to her limbs. She hurtled herself from the car and slammed the

door shut hard behind her, her breath ragged. She kicked the front tire twice, the rubber satisfyingly firm against her leopard-print flats. After a few seconds of flailing, her embarrassment set in, and she scanned the vicinity for witnesses to her temper tantrum. A woman a few cars down gaped, and Alice attempted a smile. She started toward the bookstore, adrenaline pulsing in her quads and forearms.

Evelyn Brown

E velyn told Alice she couldn't take over for her until one o'clock on Monday, which left her time to have her regular lunch with Julienne. Alice was in crisis, yes, but Evelyn had a life, too. Evelyn had made so many detours around Alice over the years. She'd put her daughter first in nearly every decision, from the fate of her marriage to the trajectory of her career.

Of course, Evelyn was proud of both her relationship with her daughter and her role as an active grandmother. "Put in your time, but maintain boundaries," she'd written in an article about balanced grandparenting for *Psychology Today* when Teddy was younger. She'd also written about the dangers of "competitive grandparenting," the tendency to outdo the kids' other set, but it wasn't even a competition with Patrick's parents. They lived in Indiana and sent twenty-dollar bills for holidays and birthdays. Evelyn, on the other hand, knew the children well enough to choose their most favorite gifts almost every time, no generic gift cards necessary.

And Patrick and Alice readily acknowledged that the Sullivans' life wouldn't even work if Evelyn weren't so involved, if she didn't show up with dinner once a week. Alice was adequately grateful. But Evelyn felt that she herself was ready for a shift. She'd spent countless sessions coaching clients on boundaries. She knew it was past time to enact her own, especially with the addition of Julienne to her daily life.

So, as Evelyn finished her morning class and her office hours, she started thinking about the prosciutto, pine nuts, and charred bread that came with the chopped salad she always ordered at Punch, the wood-fired pizza place she and Julienne had chosen when they'd first started doing these lunches. Both the food and the company were lovely—a highlight of Evelyn's week and a reprieve before she hit the Tuesday grind, when she typically picked Adrian up from the elementary school and supervised both kids for homework.

Evelyn's connection with Julienne had been easy from the start. They had so much in common, including their taste in food. Also, they had the same sturdy body type, the same hazelish eyes. People looking at them would assume they were related. Evelyn sometimes glanced around Punch and imagined other patrons thinking just that, that Evelyn and Julienne were mother and daughter. That familiar feeling *and* eating bread with olive oil and mozzarella? Mondays were Evelyn's dream.

After the tense phone call last week when Julienne had pressed to meet Alice, Evelyn had worried that Julienne would cancel lunch. But when she had texted that morning, Julienne had responded with her usual "Looking forward to it."

Evelyn arrived early. She placed their orders—she knew Julienne's by heart now—and took a seat facing the window. She smiled to herself as she watched Julienne's Acura turn into the shopping complex. Evelyn felt her arms warm with anticipation. She brought her palms together and rubbed them. She'd never take these moments of connection for granted. Evelyn could see Julienne's golden hair swing over one shoulder as she parked in the same row she always chose, regardless of whether there were other, closer spaces available.

Just as Julienne exited her car and positioned her metallic cross-body purse over her shoulder, Evelyn saw Alice's Volvo pull into the lot, too. No, she thought immediately. She looked closer, certain she had to be mistaken about Alice being the driver. What would Alice be doing in the shopping center midday on a Monday? But then she saw Teddy

sitting next to her in the front seat, slumping down, his eyes staring blankly from the passenger window toward Punch. Evelyn's first impulse was to duck, but she controlled herself. *He's not looking at you.* As she parked, Alice turned toward Teddy, her face twisted and angry. Was she yelling?

Meanwhile, Julienne had begun her walk to the restaurant, just two car lengths in front of Alice. Evelyn's heart thudded harder than it did when she forced herself to take the HIIT Over 50 class at the Elm Creek Y. Not twenty feet behind Julienne, Alice had flung herself out of her car and slammed the door. Evelyn rose to her feet. Julienne looked back toward Alice, reacting to the noise. Alice kicked her car like a toddler might, and then, when she realized she had an audience, raised a hand to Julienne to indicate that everything was okay. Everything was not okay, Evelyn could see. Alice shook with rage.

Evelyn held her breath. Punch, she knew, was one of Teddy's favorite takeout places. Was Alice on her way inside? Evelyn considered hiding in the bathroom, but she couldn't, not with her order number on the table. And not when Julienne had just seen her and waved through the window.

Evelyn tried to smile as she sat back down. This wasn't how she'd planned it, the introduction of her daughters. Of course, Alice didn't even know about the existence of Julienne yet. And once she'd told her, Evelyn had hoped the two of them would have coffee on their own, get to know each other without Evelyn micromanaging things. *Sisters,* Evelyn kept saying to herself when she thought of the two of them. She felt at once desperate for them to meet and terrified that it wouldn't go well.

Julienne pulled Punch's door open and Evelyn waved at her while keeping an eye on Alice through the glass front of the restaurant. Just when she was sure Alice was headed inside, she turned to the left.

She's going to the bookstore, Evelyn realized as she collapsed back into her chair.

"Are you okay?" Julienne arrived at the table, blocking Evelyn's view.

"I'm okay." Evelyn felt weak, weak and disappointed in herself. "I ordered the usual," she said, recovering her composure. "I hope that's okay."

Julienne leaned down and hugged Evelyn. Her daughter's scent—a citrusy clean—calmed her.

"Sure you're okay?" Julienne asked. "You look a little shaken." She pulled back to look at Evelyn's face.

Evelyn imagined herself in her office chair, imagined the weight of her session notebook on her lap. What would she advise herself to do in this moment? *Honor your truth*, she thought. "I'm just thinking it's finally time to introduce you to the family," she said. "I'm going to tell A about you tonight."

Alice Sullivan

- - - - -

A lice smoothed her shirt as she opened the door to the book-
shop. She marched to the information desk and cleared her
throat to cue the older clerk. "Where's the parenting section?"
She tried to channel confidence, but her voice wavered. She hadn't
been in Lakes District Books in years, she realized, and guiltily remembered Aidy's reading emergency. She didn't even know what authors were popular with second graders.

The clerk opened his mouth to speak before he looked up at her,
but stopped as he registered her appearance. *I must look awful*, Alice
realized. Her headache had oozed down into her jaw, which throbbed.
She felt a million years old. After the Starbucks disaster, she'd pulled
her hair back into a messy ponytail that didn't match the crispness of
her sweater and necklace.

The clerk pointed toward the back of the store. "It's the last shelf
between adult fiction and children's." Alice moved in the direction
he'd indicated. The parenting books, she found, were arranged by
stage. The baby books in the upper left focused on sleep, establishing
a schedule, and the concept of attachment that had so seduced Alice as
a young mother: the idea that she should strap Teddy to her chest and
never leave him, not even for a millisecond.

Her mother had eventually thrown away that particular tome.

"This isn't helping you," she'd said simply one afternoon when Teddy was no more than six weeks old and Alice had left the bathroom door open while she'd peed. Teddy was still festooned to her front. She had refused to let her mom hold him for even the time it took to relieve herself.

"My book says attachment is the most important thing!" Alice had shouted over the flush. But when she'd made it back to the living room, her mother had already grabbed the parenting book, walked outside, and thrown it in the recycling bin. *Maybe that's the problem*, Alice thought. She'd given up on attachment.

Books about parenting teens were shelved in the lower right of the bookstore section, far away from those about the hopeful beginning.

"Finding everything okay?" Alice realized the clerk had followed her.

"I need a book that explains my seventh grader. He's gone crazy."

The clerk—Dan, his name tag read—looked bemused. "Is this a new thing, like a developmental thing? Or are you worried about mental illness? Because for that, we'd need the psychology section. Or"— he smiled at her—"an actual medical doctor."

"I already called one." Alice felt her voice choke and realized she was on the verge of tears again. "My son started junior high this year. But maybe I've been missing the signs." *Like every parent of a serial killer*, she thought.

Dan squatted in front of the shelf and ran his finger along the books' spines. He pulled out a few, and Alice scanned their titles as he dropped them on the floor in a pile. *The Key to Boys*, one was called. *Reason and Righteousness*, read another, the "Rs" in a formal serif font. *Listen to Me: Transformative Parent-Child Conversations* landed on top. Dan straightened his legs to peruse a higher shelf and pulled one more. "And this one was my personal favorite." He smiled down at the cover where a tween boy nestled in the crook of his mother's arm, grinning up at her. "It's an old one. My kids are in their thirties now,"

he said. "Kind of a classic." *Peace at Home,* Alice read as Dan scooped the volumes from the floor and handed them to her.

Alice pushed them back at him. A tear dropped to her cheek, and she wanted to hug Dan for ignoring it. "I'll take them," she said. "I need all the help I can get."

Meredith Yoshida

- - - - -

Now that Meredith had seen Mikaela Heffernan's short shorts and outstretched middle finger on @SadeeLux, she was less excited that the girls spent a good eight to ten hours a week together at synchronized skating practice. She'd always thought of Mikaela as a solid, salt-of-the-earth type. She got good grades—at least her mother said she did—and she and Sadie wore matching hairstyles on competition days. Once last spring, Meredith and Grace Heffernan, Mikaela's mom, had each French-braided thin purple ribbons into the girls' pigtails to coordinate with the Elkettes' competition dresses. Meredith had watched several YouTube hair tutorials to get the pigtails just right. She and Sadie had each cried a little, getting those braids in, but the photos of the girls had been adorable, nothing like what Meredith had seen on @SadeeLux.

Grace smiled at Meredith as she jogged up the stands at the skating rink on Monday night. Meredith scooted over, clearing a section of her stadium blanket.

"Hey, thanks." Grace sat, and Meredith felt her smile falter. She wondered if she should tell Grace about the crotch shot. Wasn't there some kind of mom code for that? Meredith blinked the images away and decided she *wouldn't* tell Grace. If the photos had shown Mikaela vaping or nude? Then, Meredith thought, she'd have to report. But a flipped bird and a visible belly button? That was a gray area for sure.

"Did you hear about this debacle at school last week?" Grace launched in, her voice low. "Teddy Sullivan and Tane Lagerhead? Mikaela can't shut up about it. And frankly, I'm shocked. Male anatomy onstage in middle school? As if we didn't have enough to worry about."

Meredith cocked her head. *Mikaela can't shut up about it?* Sadie, on the other hand, had barely said anything. Meredith had heard all the details from Alice.

"Yeah," Meredith said, noncommittal. "Seems like a bit of a mess. And have you seen the spray paint on NextDoor? The tags at Elm Creek Park?"

Grace rolled her eyes. "The penises?" she whispered. "Or rocket ships." She giggled. "Do you think that's related? What does Alice say?" Grace bumped against Meredith's shoulder, leaning in. Meredith scanned the stands. She identified a few of the other skating parents by their pom-pom hats and jackets, but the rows were mostly empty. No one sat within earshot of Meredith and Grace. Most people didn't bother to watch practice. Even Meredith tended to multitask during it. But she liked to keep tabs on the Elkettes, too, to see which girls were placed in the center for routines and which ones missed the required sequences.

"About Teddy?" Meredith stalled. She couldn't very well spill all of the details from the wine bar. There was definitely a friend code for that.

"Of course!" Grace bumped her again, prodding. "Come on! You talk to Alice, like, every day, right? Is she freaking out?"

"Right." Was Alice freaking out? She seemed on the verge for sure.

"So? Mikaela says it's something about these hashtags? Some argument that happened in PE? It can't be true that Sadie is involved, can it? I told Mikaela that didn't sound right."

Meredith scooted away from Grace, just a fraction of an inch. "Sadie is definitely not involved," she said. Being friends with Teddy hardly implicated her daughter. Meredith stared at the ice. The girls moved

haltingly into a block formation as their Ed Sheeran competition song blared in the background. They weren't ready, Meredith thought, for a podium finish at next weekend's debut. As if in punctuation to this assessment, Sadie under-rotated her half-loop and fell just then, throwing off the spacing of her entire row.

"Ouch," Grace winced. "She'll get it next time. But Mikaela says Sadie's hashtag-Team-Tane. Have you heard that? I was surprised, since she's been friends with Teddy since they were basically babies. Is Sadie dating Tane? I mean, it's only seventh grade."

Meredith put her hand on the cold metal bleacher beside her and clanked her wedding ring against the edge. *Dating Tane? The kid with the nail polish? There's no way.* Meredith squinted at the ice. Sadie had pushed herself up and quickstepped back into formation. "Sadie's not dating anyone." Meredith hoped her voice sounded light. "And she's certainly not responsible for Teddy Sullivan's bad behavior."

Meredith could see that Sadie had set her jaw. She glued her eyes to her coach's face as she bent her knees for her crossovers. Sadie would fight for every landing, every connection for the rest of the hour's practice. It was a trait Meredith adored in her daughter—her absolute commitment to excellence, especially after a mistake.

"Teddy and Sadie have been growing apart," Meredith said as Sadie planted her toe for a spin.

"Really?" Grace put a light hand on Meredith's wrist, and Meredith repressed a flinch. Grace's curiosity irked her. Maybe she'd go wait in the car as soon as she could break away. She could pretend to have a phone call.

"It's natural as the kids get older," Meredith said. It was true, wasn't it? Friendships changed over time. In fact, her friendship with Alice had changed. They were both busy with work and with their families, and more and more it seemed like they had different parenting philosophies. Alice had told them at the wine bar the other night that she didn't know how to punish Teddy for the assembly stunt. Meredith

thought it was obvious—take away all electronics and institute mandatory counseling. That was what Meredith and Bill would do, anyway. They'd put their heads together and nip it in the bud. Not that Sadie would ever do anything as egregious as pantsing someone onstage at school. "I don't really know what's going on with Alice," Meredith said honestly. "She seems a little lost, right? So you can see that in Teddy's behavior."

Meredith felt a twinge of guilt as she glanced at Grace, whose eyes were trained on the team. Alice would die if she knew Meredith blamed her for Teddy's mistake. The skating coach paused the music and put the girls through several spins. "Count!" Meredith could hear her yell as Sadie's ponytail wheeled straight out from her head with the rotation.

"Hey!" Meredith brightened as she remembered her new endeavor. "I'm facilitating a discussion group at school as part of the parenting education series. It's called Raising Ethical Teens. Can I count on you to attend? I know you care about stuff like that." She thought of Mikaela's bare midriff and her mascara. Grace, Meredith thought, could probably use a little refresher.

"Sounds fabulous," Grace said. "Let me know how I can help."

Evelyn Brown

A duo of open pizza boxes engulfed Alice's counter that night. Evelyn had invited herself for dinner, offering to pick up the pies. She felt only slightly guilty that this would make two pizza meals in a row, two in the very same day. She deserved it, given her commitment to finally telling Alice the truth. She held on to the thought about the pizza, resisting the therapy voice reminding her that edible rewards were rarely productive or motivating. Instead, she imagined the spicy sausage on her tongue and the perfect chewy-crust chaser. The food fantasy kept her mind off Alice's likely reaction to the forthcoming news about Julienne.

And so far, dinner had gone reasonably well. Teddy's scowl, while visible, seemed less severe after the second day of his suspension. Maneuvering around his sullenness in the dinner conversation reminded her of her daughter's own adolescence. She remembered those years in the hazy sort of way that she did Alice's newborn days, the bookend stages both too fraught to recall with absolute clarity. No single incident in either time frame seemed too terrible in her memory, but all together, it made her tired. Poor Alice, she thought, imagining her daughter heading into another tough parenting season. And—she looked at her adorable grandson—poor Teddy.

Adrian sat between Teddy and Alice at the table, trying to engage her brother in her second-grade jokes. Alice poured Evelyn a glass of

red wine, which she promised herself she'd sip slowly despite her nerves. Adrian shrieked with laughter as Teddy and Alice exchanged an eye roll. "What did I miss?" Evelyn asked.

"A joke! The light in the oven, Grandma," Adrian said. "It *burned* out." She squealed. "Get it? *Burned*, since the oven was so hot, but also because that's what lightbulbs do?"

"Aha!" Evelyn chuckled at her granddaughter's earnestness, the little girl a perfect blend of Alice and Patrick with her olive skin and light brown hair. Her waves escaped her ponytail just as Alice's still did.

"How was work?" Evelyn asked her daughter. Alice recounted a horrific client meeting in a Starbucks. She kept saying something about "postconsumer recycled textiles," and Evelyn could only smile. She had no idea which colors coordinated, no clue about the names of fabrics. Her daughter could imagine an entire house, meanwhile, and understand how each tiny element impacted the whole.

"It was embarrassing," Teddy chimed in at the end of Alice's story, though he hadn't appeared to have been listening. "The meeting was a total fail." Evelyn watched Alice's eyebrows furrow and the corner of her mouth twitch.

"You know what?" Alice said. "Why don't you two be excused."

Good call, thought Evelyn. She wiped her mouth with her paper towel napkin and waited for the kids to go, not wanting to get involved if she didn't have to, even though Patrick was out of town.

"Fine," Teddy said, sarcastic. Evelyn had heard that tone in her office from any number of reluctant teen clients. Adrian rested her little head against Evelyn's biceps for a moment as she stood. Evelyn kissed her granddaughter's hair and then reached over and plucked one of the discarded crusts from Adrian's plate. More carbs couldn't hurt.

"No devices!" Alice shouted after the children.

Teddy turned and glared at her; heat rose in the cheeks that still held a childish roundness.

"Obviously, I know that." He stuck his neck out toward his mother,

his hands at his sides. "I'm not an idiot." Saliva spurted between his front teeth, arcing toward the wood floor as he enunciated the "t."

When he'd left, Evelyn snuck a look at Alice. Her daughter's cheeks flushed like Teddy's as she pushed pieces of romaine around the edges of her plate. Evelyn had spied a parenting book on the Sullivans' kitchen countertop when she'd arrived, the classic called *Peace at Home*. She had recommended it in countless therapy sessions over the years. Evelyn had felt another stab of guilt—a frequent sensation these days—as she spotted it. She probably should have recommended it or even picked it up for her daughter over the weekend. She might have thought of it if she hadn't been so distracted by her pending revelation.

"I wish Patrick were home to walk Weasley," Alice said, referring to the cockapoo they'd named for the family in the Harry Potter books. She poured them each another half glass of wine.

Patrick usually walked Weasley. *He's a good guy*, Evelyn thought. *Does tons of chores when he's home*. She'd had to specifically ask Frank to do any routine task when they'd been married. There hadn't been any load sharing in the Brown household. Still, Evelyn had worked hard to prolong the marriage. She'd read hundreds of articles about the impact of divorce before finally filing the paperwork. But there was a much smaller body of research about divorce and adopted kids, the double trauma of losing birth parents and then losing a stable, two-parent home. Evelyn knew that even though Alice *said* she felt relieved when Frank left, there had to have been an impact. She knew as a birth mom herself that no one placed their baby with parents who they expected might break up.

Still, Alice's sanguinity during the divorce had impressed Evelyn. She'd come through. Her daughter was tough. Certainly she could bear the news about Julienne. She'd be able to see how important the relationship was to Evelyn. *Right?* Just as Evelyn steeled herself for her announcement, Adrian's angry scream emanated from the front stairwell.

"Jesus," Alice muttered. She threw her napkin on the table and

marched toward the kids. "Teddy?" she bellowed. Evelyn wondered for the millionth time how such a big voice could come from such a small person. Alice had missed her calling as a teacher, Evelyn thought, or an umpire.

Evelyn couldn't hear the words of the quieter exchange upstairs, but she did note its tenor, Adrian's whiny weeping, and Teddy's incredulous retorts. "Just stop it!" Alice finally shouted, full volume again, and Evelyn heard her feet pound the stairs as she made her way back to the kitchen.

Evelyn pushed the cleaner side of her napkin against her forehead. "Sorry," Alice said.

Evelyn glanced over at *Peace at Home*. There was a whole chapter— Chapter 3, she was pretty sure—on yelling and yelling alternatives. But this wasn't the time to mention it, not right after Alice had used that loud voice. Evelyn trained her eyes on the half-eaten crust she'd taken from Adrian's plate, prepared to let the moment pass. All of a sudden, her breath felt thin. She couldn't put off the Julienne news any longer. It felt like lying, something she'd avoided religiously in her own parenting.

"I have something to tell you," she said.

Alice fell into her chair. "Okay." She drained her wineglass. "What's up?"

Evelyn faltered. "I just want to start by saying I know it's a bad time. You're already stressed, and this is going to stress you out more."

Alice's eyes widened. "Oh my God, Mom. Are you sick?"

Evelyn grabbed her hand. "No, honey. No!" She should have anticipated this assumption and changed her opening. "I'm completely healthy."

Alice took a massive inhale. "Okay, then. It can't be all that terrible. What is it? Are you retiring?"

"Not that, either." Evelyn grabbed her wineglass and took a swallow. As she set it down harder than she'd meant to, a stray drop slid down the side of the goblet and seeped into the tablecloth.

"Then what?" Alice stood to reach the saltshaker and coated the wine stain.

"When I was nineteen," Evelyn began, just as she'd rehearsed, "I got pregnant." She rushed on. "I placed the baby for adoption."

Alice dropped the shaker, holes-side-down. Her mouth hung open. "What?"

Evelyn trained her eyes on the border between the dry tablecloth and the expanding red spot. "It was before you were born, obviously. I was nineteen." She'd said that already.

"Oh my God." Evelyn tried to discern Alice's tone. Hurt? Anger? She took a long swallow of the little wine that was left in her glass. Though she knew, in a therapeutic sense, that eye contact would be most appropriate for this revelation, she found herself staring again at the spill. "I met Julienne in June. That's her name. Your sister."

"But she's not really my sister." Evelyn jerked her head up and studied Alice's face. Alice looked over Evelyn's shoulder toward the darkened windows into the backyard. Evelyn followed her gaze. There was nothing there except their reflections, fuzzy around the edges.

"What do you mean?"

"We're not related. Like, genetically." Alice shook her head. "Or really any other way. Maybe she's your daughter, but that doesn't make her my sister."

Alice Sullivan

-----

lice's head felt fuzzy the next morning, which she attributed to the extra glass of wine she'd gulped after her mother's confession. She already regretted the two times she'd hit snooze on her bedside alarm. Getting out the door was hard enough for the Sullivan family without an eighteen-minute deficit.

Adrian, a habitual early riser, was already lying on the couch in the family room, fully dressed for school and watching two tween girls in a YouTube slime video. Alice squeezed her fingers into fists, suddenly furious at the parents of these slime makers. There were millions of these inane videos, all inspiring Adrian to make a weekly mess of Alice's kitchen.

"Aidy," she said as she flicked on the espresso machine. "Did you have a reading log?" She'd gone to bed without reading to Adrian again, despite the eight-level deficit. She scowled as she imagined the teacher's reaction to another missed assignment.

And then her mind flashed on the headshot of Julienne she'd found, the product of the obsessive googling she'd done instead of practicing with her daughter. Her mother had insisted on telling her Julienne's name, and Alice had started scouring the Internet the second she'd left the evening before. Not five seconds into her search, she'd discovered her unlikely connection to Julienne Martín. Incredulous, she'd taken a picture of the Green Haven Family Services website and texted it to Nadia. "THIS Dr. Martín?!?!?"

"Yes!!!!" Nadia had texted right back. "She's a genius. When are you going?"

Alice had squeezed her eyes shut and pounded the couch cushion in a silent tantrum. She'd have to cancel Teddy's appointment, obviously, but she'd explain that to Nadia later. "Soon," she'd written to end the conversation, and then she'd stared back at the photo of Julienne. With voluminous shoulder-length blond hair, a calm smile, and dusky green eyes the exact same shade as their mother's, Julienne had appeared impeccable on the clinic website. She probably never forgot her kids' reading logs. As Alice had scanned Julienne's bio, every detail inflamed her sense of injustice. Of course Julienne was an adolescent psychologist, just like her mother. They'd have everything in common. Meanwhile, Alice and her mom had always gotten along fine despite their myriad differences. At times, Alice would even have described their relationship as close, though Nadia had once asked Alice at one of Teddy's birthday parties if her mother was always so "guarded and judicious."

Her coffee poured, Alice tried to quell her memories of the details she'd learned the night before, the names of Julienne's children and the identity of Julienne's father. He had been an attractive member of the Notre Dame football team. And talk about guarded: Alice hadn't even known her mother had attended that school before she transferred back to the University of Minnesota. Her mother hadn't even told her when Alice had identified Notre Dame as her own number one college choice. In the midst of her shock, Alice's mom had assured her more than once that she'd protected her privacy by not telling Julienne Alice's name or any identifying details. Her mom seemed insistent that her discretion on that point made everything okay. And for the thousandth time, she'd trumpeted her boycott of social media. "It breaks down protective and healing boundaries," she'd said yet again.

Alice looked back at the slime video and wondered for a split second how Adrian would classify her own mothering skills. She certainly wouldn't say "guarded and judicious," but there wasn't time to dwell on it. "I don't know about the reading log, Mom." Adrian kept her eyes on

the television. "You can check my backpack." Alice grabbed Aidy's kitty-patterned bag from its place in the mudroom even though she knew she should make Adrian find the reading log herself. Alice had a subscription to *Thinking Mother*, after all (a gift from Meredith, which she'd both appreciated and been offended by). But making Adrian check her bag would take too long. They had seventeen minutes to get out the door, and Teddy still hadn't made it to the kitchen. She unzipped the bag to find a crumpled mess of papers held together by bits of blue slime. "Aidy!" she scolded as she pulled the papers out, drawing her daughter's attention momentarily from the screen.

"Oh yeah." Adrian shrugged. "That zip-lock broke." She turned back to her video.

"But where's your homework folder?"

"Check the other pocket." As Alice did it, she imagined Miss Miller wagging a finger at her. What kind of parent took orders from her seven-year-old? Still, she didn't have time to handle the homework situation as *Thinking Mother* prescribed. Alice retrieved Adrian's yellow folder, dingy with stray pencil marks across the front and torn on one corner, despite school having started only six weeks before. She reached inside for the reading log and found a sticky note attached to it, filled with Miss Miller's rounded printing. She'd dated it the previous week, before the break for conferences.

"Please help Adrian remember her responsibilities. If the log isn't complete, I'll hold her at recess to increase her investment."

Meredith and Nadia had both talked about the peril of rescinding recess. Kids needed to get outside. *What a bitch*, Alice thought about Miss Miller, and then felt embarrassed. "Aidy." Alice stomped over to the remote she saw lying in the middle of the floor between the couch and the television. She clicked the video off. "You care about your reading, don't you?"

"What?" Adrian breathed loudly through her nose, annoyed. She twirled her little fingers through her wavy hair. Alice knew *Peace at*

Home would suggest she walk to the couch, sit next to her daughter, and elicit her true feelings about homework. She'd then respond with empathy before insisting she complete the goddamn reading log.

But they only had fourteen minutes now before they had to be buckled into the Volvo and on their way. Alice whisked the log to the kitchen counter and recorded twenty-seven minutes for the night before, though they hadn't done even one. Then she crumpled the sticky note, signed the log, and shoved it back into the folder where she'd found it.

The task fraudulently complete, she tossed Adrian a Nutri-Grain bar from the pantry. "Here's breakfast," she said as the bar sailed toward her daughter. Aidy had reloaded her video.

"I don't like apple cinnamon," she said, but Alice was already racing back upstairs to get Teddy.

She knocked on his bedroom door and pushed it open without waiting. She wrinkled her nose at the stale sleep smell, so different from Adrian's. The room had taken on a musk she assumed was a precursor to full-on puberty. Teddy's curls stuck to his forehead and his mouth gaped.

"Teddy!" She'd set his alarm for seven thirty, a full fifteen minutes ago. "You're supposed to be up!"

Teddy curled into himself. "Go away," he mumbled.

"Go away?" Alice's hair, still damp, swung down, adhering to her cheek as she shook him. "This is not happening." As the seconds elapsed, the chances of dropping Adrian at school on time dwindled. A pain rose along Alice's sternum. "We have to leave," she said.

"I don't have to be anywhere." Teddy pushed her hand from his shoulder and pulled his blanket up.

Alice's rage flared then, and she wished she could tag out, let Patrick do this. But he was in Cincinnati. "Your suspension is not a vacation," Alice growled. "Be downstairs in five or—" She hadn't thought ahead to a consequence and clenched her teeth as she searched for something. "Or I'm emptying your bank account! Adrian!" she yelled. "Turn off the TV and put on your shoes!"

Finally, Alice got Adrian into her booster and honked the horn only once before Teddy stumbled into the garage, his shoelaces untied and his hair matted. They rolled out of the neighborhood, Adrian obliviously humming the theme song to a stupid Disney Channel show, and drove past the house of one of Alice's mudroom clients. The Ramona Design yard sign Alice had stuck in the grass now had a neon penis tagged on it. Alice gasped and slammed on the brakes. Teddy burst into laughter beside her.

Sadie Yoshida

Sadie sat down next to Tane at lunch again on Tuesday. She'd sat with him on Friday and Monday as well, even though her usual friends gaped. She was actually friends with the kids at Tane's table, too, because most of them were on Quiz Bowl. Still, she felt like a girl in a teen makeover movie, crossing the great divide to sit with a "project" kid. Sadie wasn't sure what exactly she was doing, but it felt sort of good. And it wasn't some weird attempt at charity. It had started because she and Tane had both missed Chloe's party on Friday night.

"Your mom thinks you're doing *game* night?" Chloe had said when Sadie broke the news. Chloe looked disgusted, as if she'd just taken an overlarge bite of the cafeteria's tuna salad.

"I know." Sadie had shrugged. "It's like she thinks I'm four. Hey—" She'd pointed at the Quiz Bowl table. "I'm going to sit with the team today, okay? Make sure Tane's focused for next week's match?"

"Don't tell me you have a crush on him now just because you've seen his—" Before Chloe could finish, Sadie whacked her with her lunch bag. It wasn't a crush, and yet Sadie did find herself liking Tane a little more each day. And she knew Tane needed a friend. She'd hated watching Teddy in PE and then onstage, his eyes mean and his teeth clenched. It made her reconsider things. Like, were she and Teddy really even close? Or was it just their moms? "It is our choices, Harry," Dumbledore had said, "that show what we truly are, far more

than our abilities." How many times had she thought about that quote? She was as old now as Harry Potter was when he went into the Chamber of Secrets after Ginny. Sadie was due to step up.

And yes, she admitted to herself but not to Chloe, Tane was kind of cute. He had his height, his floppy hair, and his super white teeth. And neither of them had been at the best party of the year so far.

"Hi!" Tane blushed when Sadie sat down. She grinned. He liked her, she thought. Or at least he was curious about her.

"Hey, so," she said, aiming for casual, "I was thinking about the hashtags."

Tane coughed. "I saw your Insta." His eyes dropped to his sneakers, navy blue with a logo Sadie didn't recognize. "Our selfie with the correct spelling? I actually got a bunch of new followers from that post. They, like, doubled. Not that I had that many . . ." He kept his eyes on the floor.

"That's what I'm thinking," Sadie said. Her confidence expanded as Tane's seemed to deflate. She glanced down the table at the other kids. Yusef, Douglas, and Gretchen, Tane's usual lunch crew, were engrossed in a debate about the prevalence of American president questions in Quiz Bowl finals. It was high, Sadie knew. She'd been bingeing documentaries on the History and National Geographic channels to prep. She'd tried to convince her mom to watch something like that on Friday, but instead it had been *You've Got Mail*, the latest in a series of retro rom-coms.

"You're on the rise," Sadie whispered to Tane. She sounded like a contestant on *The Bachelor*, she thought. "Everyone wants to know more about you."

"Who's everyone?" Tane picked at his thumbnail. Sadie could see that a new coat of purple polish on his index fingers had already chipped. She used to think it was weird that Tane wore the splotches of polish, but now she saw that it was one of the things that made him different. Maybe not cool, exactly, but not your typical seventh-grade boy.

"Chloe. McCoy. Mikaela. Landon." She pointed at their lunch tables. "I think you should put some content out there and capitalize on the hype. You don't have to be just the kid who got, you know . . ." Sadie trailed off. She didn't know how to reference what had happened at assembly. "Pantsing" was what her mother had said, but that word made Sadie feel like puking.

She watched Tane's cheeks for a blush, but it had faded. He looked almost bored as he scanned the lunchroom. "I don't care what people think of me." Tane shook his head and picked up his chicken patty. He took a bite and kept talking, chewing with one side of his mouth. "I can't control what a Neanderthal like Teddy Sullivan is going to do, only how I react to it."

"Is that what Mr. Whittaker told you?" Sadie envisioned the assistant principal clapping Tane on the back during a pep talk.

Tane nodded. "And my mom."

"Well, they're probably right." Sadie opened her lunch bag and pulled out the spring rolls her mother had prepped last night. "And," she said, "I have an idea for your next move." She had decided during game night—when all of her friends were at Chloe's, their Insta stories filled with inside jokes that Sadie only half understood—that she should help Tane strike back.

"Move?" They both watched McCoy Blumenfeld throw a grape in the air and catch it in his open mouth. Landon fist-bumped him.

"Teddy shouldn't get the last word." Sadie snuck a glance at Tane then and smiled at his slack jaw. Tane had already changed so much since sixth grade. He was totally different and completely unique.

Alice Sullivan

Alice disconnected her home Wi-Fi after lunch, checked her purse for Teddy's phone, and then left him alone while she spent the afternoon with Ramona in their office conference room. They caressed tile samples and perused high-res images of slabs of natural stone with intermittent flecks of pink. Despite Ramona's power play with the Harrisons, she was happy to be back on the project that had gotten them into *Elle Decor*. After looking at the calendar, Ramona had quasi-apologized and requested Alice's help.

While they worked, Alice opened her mouth more than once to tell Ramona about the defaced lawn sign in her neighborhood. She pictured the garish fluorescent pink, not at all like the amaranth in the stone they studied, scrawled over Ramona's staid logo, but she held back. She'd stop by the client's house on her way home, she decided, and quietly replace the sign she'd stashed in her trunk with a new one. She should check NextDoor to see whether anyone had posted the compromised logo. *Later*, she thought, her mind already racing, pinging back and forth between thoughts of Julienne and her work.

In terms of the Kerrigan design, the natural stone had been Alice's idea. She'd sketched several versions of a centerpiece table, all with tulip bases. She'd wondered if they couldn't get a little of the pink color back into the kitchen after tearing out the Mamie Eisenhower stove. Pink might satisfy the "whimsical" portion of Ramona's design prom-

ise, and then concrete countertops would adhere to the "industrial chic" idea, which had so pleased Bea Kerrigan.

Alice supposed she should be happy Ramona was still letting her consult. Of course, she was the one with the CAD skills and the LEED certification. All of the big clients these days wanted eco-friendly and sustainable structures. If Ramona didn't have Alice, she'd have to hire someone else. And that would take time. So, for the moment, though things were strained, Alice was back in the fold.

"This." Alice held a ceramic tile next to the on-screen stone. "Imagine this plus the marzipan wall, and the concrete." She kept her voice steady, no question mark in her inflection. After five years at Ramona Design, she knew her boss rewarded confidence. Ramona would undoubtedly need at least an hour to think about whether the pink-marzipan-concrete idea had legs, so Alice quickly excused herself. She had to call Green Haven Family Services and cancel Teddy's appointment.

"I'll be back," she said as Ramona held her chin in her hand and stood next to the screen. "I just need a little privacy for a phone call. Kid stuff." She felt herself blush and raced out of the office before either of her colleagues could react.

Alice's favorite leopard-print flats tapped in the parking ramp as she half jogged to her Volvo. She'd been tempted to tell Patrick that Julienne was the same therapist that Nadia had recommended, but she hadn't. He'd been so supportive, checking in with her multiple times per day even from Ohio, even though Alice knew he was under Sachman's thumb. It had felt good, despite the Julienne setback, to accomplish both the apology to the Lagerheads and the appointment. Canceling would seem like such a backslide, and Alice hadn't had time to seek out any additional recommendations in the eighteen hours since she'd discovered Julienne's true identity. Annoyed, she dialed.

"Green Haven Family Services. This is Griffin. How can I help you?" It was the same guy who'd scheduled her for one of Julienne's emergency early-morning slots.

"Hi." Alice sounded too loud in her station wagon as she spoke over the light hum of the engine. "Um, yes. This is Alice Sullivan. Last week you helped me make an appointment for my son with Dr. Martín?"

"Martín," her mother had said. "Her husband is Spanish." She'd said it with a wistfulness in her voice, as if it had always been her dream to have a European son-in-law. Alice thought of Patrick's parents in Bloomington, Indiana. His dad performed in a jazz quartet, and Patrick himself could play four instruments. That had been interesting enough for Evelyn before, but Alice guessed it couldn't compete with being Spanish.

"Right," Griffin said. "I remember you. Thursday morning." She could hear him clicking, probably verifying the appointment on Julienne's calendar. "Did you have additional questions? Has your schedule changed?"

"Actually . . ." Alice felt hot despite the fall chill and pulled her sweater away from her chest to let in some air. She flicked the heating vent toward the ceiling and stabbed at the climate control fan, switching it to low. "I think I need to cancel."

"Oh no." Griffin held the "o" sympathetically. "Well, we're more than twenty-four hours out, so there won't be a fee. When would you like to come in instead?"

"Um." Alice should have rehearsed her reason. It wasn't as if she could tell Griffin that Teddy couldn't become a patient at Green Haven because Julienne was Alice's secret sister. *Not sister.* Alice shook her head. "I'm just—" Her voice broke.

"Hey," Griffin interrupted. "It's totally normal to have some second thoughts about therapy. I get calls like this all the time. But can I just say? Green Haven is the best." Griffin sounded like he was talking about a new restaurant or the opening of a play. "Dr. Martín is a total pro. You and your son are in great hands."

"Ah," Alice started again. Despite Griffin's earnest pep talk, she needed to cancel. She knew it. But as she pictured Julienne's headshot,

she also felt overcome with a desire to see what she looked like in person. How did her blond hair actually fall on her shoulders? Were the waves as perfect in real life as they were in photos? Alice wanted to study Julienne's mannerisms and facial expressions. She had scoured YouTube in vain for videos. Julienne and their mother—how odd that phrase sounded, *their* mother—had spent so much time together already while Alice had been oblivious. Shouldn't she get a chance to observe, too? To be a secret-keeper instead of the person from whom the truth was kept?

"Maybe I'm overreacting." Alice's mouth went dry. She fell back against the headrest, imagining Patrick's reaction to her keeping this appointment. He'd think she was crazy. Maybe she *was* crazy.

"Keep the appointment," Griffin said, unwittingly egging her on. "I can almost guarantee you won't regret it. One hour is not exactly a lifetime commitment, you know?" He laughed.

"Okay." Alice felt slightly nauseous. "Thank you. You're right."

"Perfect," Griffin said. "Then we'll see you Thursday." He hung up.

Alice imagined Patrick's face for a moment. He'd be shocked at her decision to spy on Julienne this way. "At Teddy's expense," he might say. Except it wasn't at Teddy's expense. Teddy would still get therapy, and if Julienne was as smart as everyone said she was, the therapy would be pretty good. And Alice would be able to tell Jason Whittaker at Teddy's reentry meeting immediately after the seven thirty a.m. appointment that not only had she logged in to the portal, but Teddy'd been to see a psychologist as well. This wasn't all bad. At least, that's what she repeated to herself as she hustled back to her office.

Sadie Yoshida

Sadie had mentioned Tane's Instagram Live video on her story. She'd told Chloe and Mikaela about it. But until she actually logged in at eight thirty, the second she'd gotten to her room after synchro practice and thirty minutes before her phone curfew, she wasn't actually sure that Tane would do it.

But there he was, his adorable hair half-covering his left eye, smiling at her from her phone. Sadie's stomach flipped. She heard McCoy's voice in her head. *"Gotta move that ass."* She saw Teddy's mocking smile in the gym during dodgeball. She remembered the way he'd ignored her at the homecoming game, disappearing instead with Alexandra Hunt, who had now begun wearing a fluorescent pink "This is what a feminist looks like" T-shirt multiple times per week. *Does Teddy actually like feminism?* Sadie thought not. After all, he'd been fine with his friend making fun of her ass.

"Hey," Tane said slowly. "So, this is my first Instagram Live. Shout out to Sadie Yoshida for, like, making me do this." He pointed down at the screen, where he probably saw her username pop up. "Maybe it's the start of my new life? Hashtag-Team-Tane?"

Sadie grinned. How had she not noticed exactly how cute he was before? His skin had a golden color to it, and his eyes were a deep brown. He'd positioned the phone the perfect distance from his face, and Sadie couldn't help but thrill at the revelation that he was doing exactly what she had said, following her directions meticulously. She

leaned forward, hunched over her phone, and glanced up just for a second to be sure her door was closed. Her mother wouldn't understand Instagram Live, and she definitely didn't know about @SadeeLux.

"So," Tane said, and Sadie couldn't help thinking his smile was just for her, though the viewers accumulated. Assuming she'd been first, Tane was up to seventeen. "I'm going to do five reasons you should be Team Tane." He held his hair back with his palm as he looked at a piece of paper, the one Sadie had ripped out of her English composition notebook as they'd brainstormed.

"The first reason is soccer. I've been playing travel soccer for a couple of years, but this year I'm on the premier team for Elm Creek Soccer Association. And also, I'm on the A team at school. That's, like, with mostly eighth graders. So, just in case you're remembering me as a tiny kid from elementary school, things have changed." He laughed a little then. Sadie sucked in her breath.

"Number two." Tane held up his two painted fingernails, the index fingers on each hand. "I'm into color, and I don't care what you think about it."

Sadie blinked. She felt her shoulders creep toward her ears. Tane looked so confident. In seventh grade, it did seem like kids needed a signature something. She had synchro, and recently, @SadeeLux and Quiz Bowl. Teddy had a million friends, and now a bad-boy reputation. And Tane had his total originality. His nerdy chic.

Tane's third and fourth items were cute, but low-stakes. He was the European history and Norse mythology whiz for Quiz Bowl, and he'd reread the whole Harry Potter series five times. "That's not as good as Sadie's six." Tane smiled. Sadie bit her lip and emitted a little squeal. "I'm a Hufflepuff," Tane said, "like Cedric Diggory. So, you know, pretty badass."

Sadie cocked her head to the side. She pictured Tane in PE, telling her to stand behind him; Tane in Quiz Bowl, complimenting her prowess on the geometry and Earth science sections.

"Which brings me to the last reason you should be hashtag-Team-

Tane. It's because Teddy, even though he seems tough and cool, has his own issues. I mean, besides being obsessed with other people's privates. I have it from an inside source that he sleeps with a stuffed otter. So maybe he's not that tough. And he wore Pull-Ups until the fifth grade. So . . ."

Sadie flopped on her back, holding her phone in front of her face. He'd done it. He'd opened the Chamber of Secrets. Or she had. She could see twenty-nine viewers on the video, their emoji responses to the mic drop moment floating up on the screen: laugh-crying; the little face with the tiny round, shocked mouth; the flame.

"So that's it, right?" Tane said. "I hope you're convinced. Hashtag-Team-Tane." And then he was gone, and Sadie started getting texts from Mikaela and Chloe and even stupid McCoy Blumenfeld asking her how she'd known, all before her apps were turned off by her mom at nine o'clock on the nose.

Alice Sullivan

Though Alice had been nervous when she'd left Teddy alone on Wednesday morning, everything had been fine at home. Of course, Ramona had given her a look when she'd packed up just before lunch. "Your kids have really interfered with our business hours lately," she'd said. Alice reiterated her promise to work from home and reminded herself that her LEED certification was paramount to growing the company. Plus, if she left now, she could sneak in a run before dark. With Patrick traveling, it had become nearly impossible to exercise. They'd thought about buying a treadmill when Patrick had been on a different case in Des Moines the year before, but Alice had resisted. She loved running outside away from the children and their ill-timed requests. Plus, there was the expense of the treadmill. She'd been hoarding every penny for that custom paint job in the dining room. She hadn't told Patrick about the plan yet, but it'd be perfect for the *Elle Decor* shoot.

At home, she peeked in on Teddy. He tossed a lacrosse ball from hand to hand and stared at the soccer poster on his ceiling. "I'm going for a run," she said.

"Ugh." Teddy grimaced. "I've been running way too much at practice lately." Patrick had told her the coach had made him do an extra fifteen minutes of laps to punish him for Tane.

As she left, Alice slammed the door harder than she'd meant to and ran quickly down the sidewalk in the crisp October air. Despite her

desire to escape, she pictured her son on his bed. She wondered whether Teddy was depressed. Maybe he was. Her stomach dropped, thinking about it, and she increased her pace. Bullying was a sign of depression, she knew from her extensive Internet research. Of course, she'd balked at the term "bully," but when she'd tested it out at drinks with Meredith and Nadia the other night, neither of them had contradicted her. Even if Teddy wasn't "a bully" in the static sense, clearly the incident at assembly raised flags.

Alice could still taste the olive she'd been chewing when Meredith peered at her over the rim of her wineglass as she summarized the meeting with Whittaker. Alice recognized Meredith's expression as the same one she adopted each time Nadia confessed the latest in her years-long struggle with Donovan's behavior. And since that horrible meeting in Whittaker's office, Alice had barely made eye contact with her son, much less "gotten through" to him. Teddy's suspension was basically over, and she hadn't accomplished anything beyond the apology and the questionable appointment at Green Haven.

Alice shook her arms at her sides as she reached the stoplight at Stable Creek Pass and Appletree Road. Although Teddy hadn't achieved a transformation, Alice *had* done research. She'd paged through her new parenting books and scoured the Internet. It had been a challenge to make herself click on "7 Signs Your Child Might Be a Bully," but she felt she owed it to Janna Lagerhead. As she began it, she wondered about the other mothers who visited the site. Was she like them? Was she like Nadia, who had to go to special meetings at school with all manner of administrative personnel to keep Donovan from getting expelled?

One of the bully indicators in the article was if a kid's friends had "aggressive tendencies." Alice remembered Landon Severson's leering smile at Teddy through the office glass, the admiring way he'd called Teddy a "clown." She pictured the yellow card the ref had held in Teddy's face at a soccer tournament last summer. Did those things count as aggressive? Alice had started to feel ill by the time she got to the

section in the article on bad parenting. If you had "a bad relationship" with your child, that might be a sign he was a bully, she had read. She ran past the playground at the local park, the same place she'd spent hours watching Teddy on the slide and pushing him on the swings. The park board or the porta-potty company, she noticed, had painted over the graffiti. Hopefully whoever was responsible for the tagging would be deterred by the quick cleanup, although she did catch one more "rocket ship" on a trash can at the trailhead.

Before this week, Alice would have said her relationship with Teddy was good, but she couldn't exactly remember the last time they'd spent time together, just the two of them. When Teddy had been little, they'd laughed over board games and silly YouTube videos. Now, Teddy grunted through dinner and spent his free time on the Xbox and buried in his phone. Before last week, she'd assumed that was normal for a twelve-year-old.

Were Meredith's and Nadia's relationships with their kids much better? She thought of the Instagram photos Meredith had posted of Sadie's last synchronized skating competition. The final photo in the series showed Sadie holding up a trophy, her glitter-adorned face peeking out from behind its wide base. Alice had frowned at Sadie's exaggerated makeup. Was that sort of veneer healthy for a tween girl? That much eyeliner? Did Sadie know Meredith loved her just as she was, without any adornment? Alice wouldn't let Adrian wear makeup, she thought, until much later than seventh grade.

A text buzzed in, and Alice looked at her Apple Watch. Nadia had written, "How's it going over there? Need another check-in?"

Alice raced on, heading for the same dirt trail she usually power-walked with her friends on Sunday mornings. Did Nadia, Alice wondered, spend time googling her insufficient parenting? When Donovan had the most minor upswings, Nadia amplified the gains. During one of their September power walks, Nadia had bragged that he'd made it six days without a visit to Jason Whittaker's office.

"That's great," Alice had cooed, while at the same time brainstorming ways to inquire about Donovan's meds and perhaps day-treatment options. Was it really fair, after all, to ask other kids to navigate Donovan's erratic behaviors?

Nadia had peeled off on that walk after an SOS text came in from her husband, Ajay. "Meltdown." Nadia had taken off in a run toward her car.

Teddy and Sadie, by contrast, had pretty much left their meltdowns behind in preschool. Alice had turned her head that day to watch Nadia jog away. "Shouldn't he be more under control by now?" she'd asked Meredith when their friend was out of earshot.

Meredith had shaken her head, the wide brim of her hat almost bonking Alice's forehead. "I know," she'd agreed. "And since Nadia works from home, doesn't she have more time to, like, process with him?" They'd motored past a sluggish-looking set of new parents, a tiny baby strapped in an Ergo to the dad's chest. Alice had flashed a knowing smile. It hadn't been so long ago that she'd pushed Adrian on these walks with her friends, struggling to keep up with Meredith's punishing pace.

"Maybe she's not consistent with her consequences?" Alice had said. "Not following through can really torpedo an entire discipline system."

Meredith had nodded. "That's *Thinking Mother* 101."

Now, a light breeze rustled through the foliage as Alice ran to the lake path, her breath already ragged. Alice decided she'd hit the hills hard. Her legs tensed, anticipating the effort as she charged up the first one. She wondered if Meredith and Nadia ever talked about *her* when she wasn't there. Had they seen Teddy's problems coming and just never told her? Maybe on the days when she'd been the one to peel off early for a soccer game or to take over for Patrick, who'd had to work, Nadia and Meredith had remarked on her laissez-faire failures. Maybe she'd become aware of her obvious deficiencies only when Jason Whit-

taker had thrown them in her face. Alice's heart pounded and, finally, the intensity of her effort distracted her from her thoughts. All she could do was swing her arms and put one foot in front of the other.

When she got home, she grabbed a warm Coke from the secret stash she kept in an unmarked basket in the mudroom and texted Nadia back. "Thanks," she began. "I think things will be okay, but I'm always up for a coffee or a glass of wine." She searched for the right "cheers" GIF, Leo in *Gatsby* raising his champagne, just to be clear that she wasn't overly worried. There was a vast difference between Teddy, who'd just had the one trip to Whittaker's office, and Donovan, who was such a frequent flyer.

Alice toggled to her email. She'd been holding her breath all day for an update from *Elle Decor.* Instead, she had a notification from Next-Door. She'd replaced that yard sign on her way home the other day. The ruined Ramona Design one still lay in the trunk of her car. As far as she knew, she'd hidden the graffiti before it had made the app. She opened the latest digest, which featured a lead story about an owl sighting in Elm Creek Park, where she'd just run. Next came a rant about too-fast driving on Appletree Road. Alice rolled her eyes and glanced at the comments. If you bought a house on the throughway, you had to expect some traffic. She sipped her Coke and felt calmer, grateful for the endorphin rush of the hard workout.

And then she gasped at the last item from NextDoor: a pixilated photo of Teddy and Weasley, the two of them stopped on a walk. Weasley crouched in that comical way of dogs doing their business.

"For some reason, this kid is home on a school day," Shirley MacIntosh had written. "And he left dog poop right on the boulevard. Unacceptable!!! Clean up after your animals!!! It's probably kids like this who are responsible for that vile new graffiti tag, too, don't you think?!!?! And YES, I read your many comments about it not being a rocket ship."

Alice would have laughed if her face hadn't burned with embarrassment. Lots of people used NextDoor. Alice even regularly found

clients on the app after someone queried the neighborhood about freshening a room or choosing a paint color. Many users would recognize Teddy and Weasley. Alice didn't need to be identified as responsible for dog waste. And the graffiti? That couldn't be Teddy. Alice had studied the defaced yard sign. The tag was drawn with some kind of paint marker, and she didn't have any of those in her garage workspace.

Alice scrolled down on NextDoor and her nausea returned. Agnes Godfrey, from whose lawn Patrick had extracted many a sports ball over the years, had left a comment on the dog post. "That kid is Teddy Sullivan on Stable Creek Pass. I'm assuming he's gotten himself in trouble because he's been home from school these last three days, and he doesn't look sick."

Fuck you, Agnes, Alice thought. She felt inclined to leave a counter-comment, but instead she texted Meredith. Meredith would come to her defense. Alice was sure she could defuse the whole thing with some pithy remark about the fleeting nature of youth.

"Can you come to my rescue on NextDoor?" Alice typed. "Our uptight neighbors are threatening to tar and feather Teddy for leaving Weasley's business on the wrong lawn." She hoped that even though Meredith strongly believed in the civic responsibility of picking up dog waste, in this case, she'd do Alice a solid.

Teddy Sullivan

Teddy had been thrilled that morning when his mom decided to leave him alone. He'd even snuck in a little ESPN, grateful that cable didn't rely on the Wi-Fi she had disabled. But by the time his mom had come back and then left again on a run at noon, he was almost bored enough to start reading. He had even eyed his boxed set of illustrated Harry Potter books on the shelf above his desk and was about to grab *Prisoner of Azkaban* when she burst in without knocking.

Teddy sat up. His mom was shouting something about dog poop, her voice high-pitched and harsh. He occasionally heard this tone from the sidelines of a tight soccer game, a shrillness that made his face hurt. Now, she kept repeating "Weasley," which had prompted their cockapoo to appear in Teddy's room, jumping excitedly, his ears level with the side of the bed on each bounce. Teddy tried to turn away from both his mom and the dog, but Alice grabbed his shoulder. "God," he said. "Can you just give me a minute?"

"It's on the app!" she yelled. He had no idea what she was talking about.

"Jesus," he said. "Chill."

She dropped his shoulder and went silent.

Teddy held his breath. He'd told his mother to "chill" once before, and he'd ended up with a two-day Xbox ban.

"Chill?!" Alice yelled, and Teddy moved one hand from his face to his ear, blocking her volume.

Jesus, he thought again.

"Get your ass out of bed," she said, her tone cold, the shrillness replaced with fury. He startled as she slammed the door, leaving him alone again inside.

Teddy rolled onto his back and blinked at the U.S. Soccer Team poster he and his dad had stuck to his ceiling. His mom had insisted they use this putty stuff to hang it. She'd spent, like, an entire weekend scraping off the popcorn ceiling two summers ago. But the poster kept falling, so his dad had added some double-sided tape. "Our secret," he'd said, offering a fist bump.

As he lay there, Teddy tried to figure out what exactly he'd done to get in this new round of trouble. Something about the dog. But he hadn't even done anything related to the dog. He'd walked Weasley each time she'd asked, happy to get out of the house. Although the walks weren't fun, they were something different. It was the same with the yelling, Teddy realized. It was unpleasant to get screamed at, but at least it provided a break from the utter boredom. He wasn't allowed Internet or phone while he was suspended, except to access the school's portal. He finished all of the assignments within an hour each day. Instead of relaxing at home, he knew he was missing everything at school and online with all of his friends.

And besides that, his mom kept trying to "fix" him. She left her stupid parenting books upside down and open, marking her pages. She appeared in his room and repeated lines he knew she must have read in these books, their covers featuring smiling parents and their well-adjusted teens. Teddy and his mom had looked exactly like one of these pairs on last year's holiday card. She still had it stuck to their fridge. And now she'd basically sworn at him and slammed his door. Would they even send out a Christmas card this year?

"Get down here!" his mother yelled from the kitchen. Teddy wished she'd leave again—go back to the office or for another run.

When he got downstairs, his stomach grumbling, she shoved her phone in his face. It was a picture of Weasley taking a dump. "What the hell is that?" Teddy asked.

"Don't say 'hell,'" his mother said.

Teddy turned up his palms. "You just told me to get my ass out of bed, but I'm not allowed to say 'hell'?"

She grabbed a Coke from the countertop and took a long swallow. "I shouldn't have said that."

"We have Coke?" Teddy asked.

His mom slammed the can back on the counter. "Not for you." She looked just like Adrian then, so much that he almost laughed—Adrian refusing to share a Calico Critter. "And why would you leave Weasley's poop in someone else's yard?"

"I ran out of bags," Teddy said. *Chill.* He could feel his mother's anger deflating a bit. He was telling the truth. Sometimes you just didn't have an extra bag. It had happened to his mom, too. He knew it. "Someone took a picture of that and posted it online?" Teddy asked.

"People post all kinds of stuff online." His mom untied the running jacket she had around her waist and put it on. "You can't do stuff like that, especially when you're already in trouble. People are just looking for ways to make you seem like a bad person."

Teddy's arms felt heavy at his sides. "I'm not a bad person," he said. "What are you even talking about?"

"I know you're not a bad person." She said it, but she wouldn't look at him. Instead, she stared into the backyard. Aidy's swing swayed in the breeze out there, and yellow leaves covered the ground all around it. Probably, later, Teddy realized, one of his parents would make him start raking. "Do you know anything about that pink graffiti we saw?"

"The dicks?" Teddy remembered them from the porta-potty and the neighbor's lawn sign. "That's hilarious."

"I'm going to take a walk," his mom said suddenly. "I'll bring Weasley and the extra bags."

"Didn't you just go running?"

"Yeah, but I didn't take the dog." *She just wants to get away from me.* Teddy swallowed. He watched her shuffle back out through the mudroom and saw that she'd left her work bag on the bench. A minute later, she passed Aidy's swing, her shoulders rounded, her shoes kicking up the leaves. As soon as she let the back gate slam behind her, he went to the mudroom himself and shoved his hands into her bag, feeling for his phone. Finally, he found it in a pouch with a bunch of random gift cards.

He felt a tiny bit guilty for going behind his mom's back, but he had to know what was happening at school before he returned the next day. He grabbed a charger from the junk drawer in the kitchen island and headed for the upstairs bathroom. He planned to stash the phone under the sink behind the extra rolls of toilet paper if she came back too quickly. His fingers shook a little as he plugged it in and waited for it to power up.

And then suddenly his screen filled with notifications. He dismissed a bunch from Instagram and Clash of Clans, and then he opened Snapchat. The first message was from McCoy. In his pic, McCoy's eyes bugged out. "DUDE," he'd written as the caption. "A stuffed OTTER?" And that was when Teddy started to panic.

His stomach lurched. He pictured the soft toy he kept under his pillow, shoved in his pillowcase whenever he had a friend over. It was cute, with tiny plastic eyes that Teddy liked to run his thumb over as he went to sleep. On the tail, the fur was almost totally worn, the fabric like a web where the fuzziness used to be.

But how did McCoy know about the otter?

"What otter?" Teddy messaged back, one eyebrow raised in his selfie.

McCoy's next photo was just his forehead, but the message said it all: "Tane made an Instagram live. #TeamTane is blowin UP."

Teddy gazed at the closed bathroom door. He listened for his

mother. Nothing. He opened Instagram and relogged in to his Finsta, @TedBaller420, and clicked on @SadeeLux's story. "Wasn't that epic?" she said into the camera, her eyes shining and her lips a weird orange. "I mean, if you weren't already hashtag-Team-Tane, you probably are now, right? I mean, right?"

Teddy collapsed onto the closed toilet lid, his arms and legs weak. "What the fuck," he whispered as her video picked up in the next story. "I mean, regardless of what you thought of him before, you've got to respect him now, rebounding like that from the assembly."

Teddy didn't follow Tane on Instagram, but he found @Tanger easily enough. He clicked on his story, and a video came up, the one McCoy had mentioned.

Holy shit, Teddy thought as Tane delivered reasons one through four that people should like him. As he watched, Teddy recalled last weekend's soccer practice, Tane's long legs wheeling past kids who'd been on premier for years while Teddy ran punishment laps around the field. He remembered the high fives Tane had exchanged with Coach and McCoy. He saw Sadie in PE, smiling at Tane even when he was in the final moments against Teddy in dodgeball.

Tane's video moved to reason number five, and Teddy's back molars ground together as he heard Tane casually, meanly expose his biggest secrets. He could still feel the Pull-Up against his skin, feel the warmth of its fullness in the mornings when he had to throw it away. An eleven-year-old in diapers. He'd hated himself. And now everyone knew.

In spite of his age, he found himself beginning to cry. He rubbed furiously at his eyes with one hand and gripped the iPhone hard between the fingers of the other.

"Fuck," he said again. He heard the downstairs door slam and Weasley's nails clicking against the kitchen floor. He was out of time. He flushed the toilet to cover for himself and clicked the DM button. He was so mad at Sadie he almost didn't care about getting caught with his phone. She knew him better than almost anyone. They'd been at car

pool and day camps and their parents' dinner parties together. And now Sadie had told everyone what a loser he was, what a baby.

"SLUT," he wrote in his message to her, the word appearing at his fingertips without his having to think about it, the worst thing he could imagine writing. "YOU STUPID FUCKING SLUT."

Meredith Yoshida

Meredith frowned at Shirley MacIntosh's photo of Teddy on NextDoor as Nadia sat down next to her in the conference room at Elm Creek Junior High.

"What are you doing here?" Meredith asked. She hadn't expected Nadia at the Parent Association meeting.

"Hello to you, too." Nadia smiled. "I'm the chair of the learning differences subcommittee, remember?"

"Oh right." Meredith should have been glad to see one of her oldest and best friends, but something about Nadia sitting so close threw her off. She wanted to make her own impression on this new group of parents—without her posse from elementary school. *Oh well.* "Have you seen this?" Meredith tipped her phone toward Nadia and tapped the picture of Teddy.

"Yikes," Nadia whispered as Assistant Principal Whittaker greeted everyone. While he spoke, Meredith put her phone facedown on the table and mentally reviewed her ideas for the ethical parenting seminars. Her lips moved as she ticked through her talking points. Her first topic, she thought, would be "Is ethical parenting possible?" It seemed the primary question at the intersection of ethics and family life was whether parents were truly capable of prioritizing the common good over individual achievement. Many of the psychologists quoted in the articles Meredith had read seemed to think that living an ethical life in

the privileged suburbs was an impossibility, but Meredith thought *she* could do the right thing. Even Sadie's choice of sport, synchronized skating, proved her daughter's commitment to the common good. A different kid, one more concerned with her individual success, would have chosen to compete in singles, rather than trying to blend in with eleven other girls, none more sparkly than the others.

"Let's start with reports," Whittaker said. "How about the learning differences support subcommittee?" He smiled at Nadia, and Meredith wondered why she got to go first.

Nadia beamed. "I just want to say that I'm so pleased that the PA has made space for the learning differences group. It means so much to be included." Meredith felt a twinge of guilt for forgetting she'd even be there. She eyed the plate of store-bought chocolate chip cookies in the center of the table and stood to grab one. Her arm obscured Nadia's face from half of those seated. "Sorry," she said.

Nadia ignored her. "In our group, we invite a guest speaker to the first half of each meeting, and then we proceed in conversation."

"How are numbers?" asked Julie, the eighth-grade PA president.

"Well, given that a full quarter of the student body has either a 504 plan or an IEP, our numbers are relatively low." Nadia frowned. "We get ten to fifteen parents at each meeting. But they're engaged parents."

"Any ideas to beef up attendance?" Whittaker asked. "I'd love for parents experiencing challenges to feel less alone. I see a lot of kids in my office who aren't actually discipline problems, but rather struggling with learning."

Nadia nodded emphatically. Meredith knew Donovan himself had been one of those kids in the assistant principal's office. "I think adding an evening or weekend meeting would really help," Nadia said. "Lots of people work."

Work was always Alice's excuse, anyway, thought Meredith. Among Meredith's own talking points was a proposed lunch-hour gathering.

She hoped the timing would accommodate enough working parents. Even Alice could technically make lunch, but she had never been the PA type. She always had other priorities. That magazine photo shoot had been the latest distraction. And of course Teddy's suspension, and now NextDoor. Meredith wondered why Alice couldn't see that things like the PA should actually be her priority, given her problems at home.

Meredith started to jiggle her leg under the table, anxious for her turn to talk. While Nadia's group was important, only a quarter of the families in the school—by her own admission—could possibly benefit from her efforts, while ethics impacted everyone.

"Great," Whittaker said as Nadia finally finished. "Next?" Meredith swallowed the last bite of cookie and reached for the tiny cup of coffee she'd poured at the reception desk.

She swallowed the dregs, then began. "I'm thrilled to bring the concept of ethical parenting to Elm Creek Junior High for the winter session." She smiled and scanned the group of eight. "Ethical parenting is the idea that parents consider the common good—the community and the world at large—when they make decisions about their children, rather than only thinking about individual success."

"How fascinating!" Nadia interrupted. "That really dovetails nicely with—"

Meredith put a hand on Nadia's biceps. "Could I just explain my vision for the four-part series?" She tried to keep her voice light, but she'd rehearsed this. And frankly, not everything had to overlap with the agenda for the learning differences support group.

Nadia raised her eyebrows, and Meredith detected a touch of mocking in her smile. "Of course," she said.

"Thanks." Meredith looked at Julie. "I was thinking four lunch-hour meetings, each time reacting to a stimulus, like an article or a video about how we can be more community-minded in our parenting decisions." She pulled a printed list from her handbag. "I previewed a bunch of resources if anyone's interested." She laid the paper in front

of her. "And then, at our last meeting, the group could produce a document with strategies, like ten tips for making ethical decisions." Meredith thought about delivering the decision-making document to Alice. She'd seemed so confused about how to get Teddy to understand the severity of his actions.

"Great," Julie said. Meredith relaxed as she glanced around the table. They were loving it—even Whittaker, who smiled broadly. "Now that I have a kid in high school," Julie said, "and the college pressure is ramping up, it's really easy to lose perspective on what's actually important."

Nadia straightened up again and glanced at Meredith as if for permission. "I think kindness and empathy are a huge part of it, which is what I was going to say before. If we focus on empathy, behaviors across the board will improve. We've all seen that pink graffiti, right? That's just a symptom of the same problem."

Whittaker's eyes widened. "Does anyone have a tip on that?" he blurted. "I've been worried that the culprit is an Elm Creek Junior High kid."

Meredith flashed to the wine bar gathering two nights before. She remembered Alice's description of Teddy's horrifying stunt at assembly. Wouldn't a kid who'd pantsed someone in public think rather lightly of a little spray paint? And Alice had seemed less remorseful than mortified. It was all about how people would see *her*, and not about how Teddy's behaviors impacted others. The ethical parenting group would be tailor-made for parents like Alice, who seemed not to understand the interconnectedness of it all. The women around the table shook their heads and murmmered. No one had a lead on the graffiti.

"Well anyway," Whittaker said, "I agree one hundred percent, Nadia." He knocked the table for emphasis, as if Nadia had invented the whole concept of empathy. "I think this is a great idea."

"Would you like to see the list of resources?" Meredith picked up her handout and held it across to Whittaker.

"Thanks, Marilyn." He didn't even look at her as he took it.

"Mere*dith*." She enunciated the final syllable.

"Sorry," he mumbled.

"How will we advertise this?" Nadia asked. "How can we get the right parents in the room?"

Meredith felt her irritation rising. Nadia had barged in on her presentation, and Whittaker hadn't even learned her name. Of course, he knew Nadia because of Donovan's issues. It wasn't fair that he ignored her just because Sadie had never landed in his office for discipline. "Well, it's for everyone," Meredith said crisply.

She thought of Alice again then, who excused her own deficits by asserting that other people had it easier. Alice never made time for the PA, but apparently had time to scroll NextDoor in the middle of the workday and ask for bailouts. Meredith raised her voice. "But it's especially for parents of kids who are acting out. Mr. Whittaker, perhaps you could issue personalized invitations to kids who are at code red in the portal? Or kids who've been suspended." Meredith looked at Nadia, whose eyes had gotten rounder as Meredith continued.

"We wouldn't want to single anyone out . . ." Nadia gave her a look.

"Or we would," Meredith said. "We want to make sure the families who are making things difficult for the community—and let's be honest, obviously I'm talking about recent events that have veritably flooded my daughter's Instagram account. Nudity in the seventh-grade assembly? That kind of public humiliation? Certainly the Sullivans would be good candidates for a little training in ethical parenting." Meredith felt a swift kick to her shin under the table.

"That's right! I heard all about that nightmare." Julie turned to Whittaker. "You must have had some serious consequences for that one." Her forehead wrinkled, although it scrunched less than Meredith remembered it doing at back-to-school night. Maybe she'd touched up her Botox.

Whittaker put his own forehead in his hand. "I'd rather not get into it, Maril—Meredith."

Meredith rolled her eyes. "Well, it's a little late for that, right? Five hundred seventh graders already saw the whole banana?"

Nadia kicked her again.

Nadia Reddy

-----

can't save Alice from herself." Meredith looked at her phone as she and Nadia walked to the parking lot after the Parent Association meeting.

"Yeah, but you don't have to tell the entire PA leadership about her problems," Nadia said.

Meredith picked up her pace, and Nadia lagged a step or two behind. "I'm talking about the NextDoor thing." Meredith summarized the post she'd shown Nadia inside. Nadia tried to take it all seriously, but really, the dog poop incident was totally peripheral to the actual problem with Teddy and Alice. Teddy wasn't even the one who owned the dog. The real issue was Alice's obsession with how Teddy's mistakes would make her look. In fact, all of the parents at the PA meeting had the same issue: They all tried to excel vicariously, and Nadia was sick of it.

It wasn't like she didn't understand the impulse to own the kids' behaviors, to answer and apologize for them, but she'd been forced eons ago to release it. Donovan insisted on being his own person. She hoped to tell Alice about this revelation, to speed her along to acceptance after Teddy's suspension.

"People really should be picking up after their pets," Meredith said.

"Really?" Nadia caught up to her as she stopped next to her Jeep. She swatted Meredith lightly on the arm, much more gently than she

had kicked her in the meeting. "She's your friend! And should Shirley MacIntosh really be shaming minors on social media? What are you so mad about?"

Meredith shrugged. "I have to get back to work. Call you later?" She opened her door, and Nadia sighed. She crossed the parking lot to her Leaf (she'd downsized and gone electric after Donovan had gotten so involved in nature therapy) and reset her own forgotten NextDoor password.

"I'm on it." She texted Alice along with a screenshot of her response to Shirley MacIntosh. "We've all been caught without supplies," she'd written. "Playing gotcha with the kids in the neighborhood and identifying their names and addresses in a public forum is hardly the purpose of this app. It's mean and also dangerous. Let's remember to act like adults!"

"You're the best," Alice typed back. "I was trying not to bother you when I sent it to Meredith, but I'm super grateful you responded." She added the kiss emoji.

Nadia drove the two miles home and stood for a moment in front of the landscaping. She and Donovan had added a blue aster to their pollinator garden last year, and the cheery daisylike flowers, fresh even into October, contrasted with her apprehensive mood. Clearly neither of her friends had seen the Instagram Live video, the one during which Tane had revealed Teddy's secret. Nadia remembered Alice fretting about sending Teddy to sleepovers and overnight soccer camp with Pull-Ups. She'd worried about what would happen if kids found out he wet the bed. Nothing Alice tried—not the fancy alarm or strategically timed wake-ups—had solved Teddy's bedwetting. In the end, it had just been time.

"Hey," Nadia typed to Alice. "Now that we've taken care of Next-Door . . . How's Teddy taking the Instagram fallout? I suppose you've confiscated his phone? Maybe you haven't seen it?"

Alice wrote back, "I'm keeping his phone for-fucking-ever."

"But have you looked at his Instagram? Donovan showed me a video from Tuesday night that might involve him."

Alice's reply ellipsis popped up and then disappeared again. Nadia sighed and stared at the aster. She knew Alice and Meredith didn't understand what it was like to have a kid constantly in trouble. Though she didn't want Alice to feel her pain, exactly, she was sort of relieved to have some company in Jason Whittaker's office.

Nadia's phone pinged. "I know you're trying to help," the text read, "but Teddy's blip—it's not the same thing as what's going on with Donovan."

A shot of anger seized Nadia's arm, and she almost dropped her phone, wanting to erase Alice's message. She tried to help, and her best friends pushed her aside. If she were less of a person, she'd log back in to NextDoor and delete her supportive comment. Of course Teddy didn't pick up dog shit. Teddy, with his blond curls and boundless entitlement, didn't do anything for anyone. Sure, Donovan was a total handful and yes, at times he drove Nadia and Ajay bonkers, but at least she wasn't lying to herself about who he actually was.

Meredith Yoshida

M eredith wrapped the bricks of tofu in paper towels and squeezed them between two plates. If she fried the tofu, maybe Sadie would eat it. Her daughter needed a good healthy dinner. The ride home from synchro that night had been oddly silent. Meredith knew something was wrong, but Sadie wasn't talking. The moment they'd gotten inside, Sadie had torn up the stairs and closed her door. This was happening more often now that she was in junior high. It was normal, Meredith knew. The social and academic pressures ramped up in seventh grade, even if Meredith didn't factor in distractions like Teddy's behavior in assembly. Teddy, come to think of it, had been at the center of a couple of Sadie's recent upsets.

There had been the evening that Sadie had come home crying from the Elm Creek homecoming football game. She'd seemed totally fine when Meredith had picked the kids up at school, and then the second they'd dropped Teddy at his house, Sadie had lost it, sobbing in the car. She'd never provided the details but implored Meredith not to say anything to Alice.

Meredith frowned as she leveraged all her weight against the top plate, soaking her tofu paper towels. Maybe the union she and Alice had formed when the kids were at kindergarten round-up all those years ago was set to dissolve. Maybe their friendship had run its course. Teddy had proven himself a bad influence. She'd had the thought on

the way home as she passed the McDonald's with the obscene graffiti on the drive-thru console.

She hadn't discussed her hypothesis with Alice, but the timing of the tagging was highly suspect. It had appeared the same week as Teddy's stunt at assembly, and both things involved male anatomy. It couldn't be a coincidence. Meredith thought Alice should search her house for pink spray paint. If Teddy was the culprit, she'd find some evidence.

Meredith heard the garage door open. Bill was home. Maybe Sadie would talk to him. It was rare that he was the one in whom their daughter confided, but everything seemed different now that Sadie would be thirteen in a week.

"Smells great!" Bill kissed Meredith's cheek as the back door slammed shut behind him.

"I've barely started." Meredith pointed at the onions and peppers in the pan and then cut her newly pressed tofu into bite-sized chunks.

"How are things?" Bill walked back to the doormat and slid off his shoes, replacing them with slippers that looked a little worn. She would put a new pair in his stocking at Christmas.

"Meh," Meredith said. Before Bill could follow up, she asked, "Actually, could you fry this?" She handed her spatula to him and dumped in the tofu with a squirt of prepared ginger and a couple of cloves of minced garlic. "I want to check on Sadie."

"She okay?"

"I think so. Just press the tofu hard with the back of the spatula for a couple of minutes and then flip it." Meredith clicked cancel on the beeping rice cooker and jogged up the stairs. She tapped on her daughter's door and waited a second before cracking it open. Sadie's bedside lamp cast a golden glow over the pink-and-yellow quilt, the same one Meredith had purchased when Sadie first graduated to a big-girl twin bed at age three. Sadie lay on top of it, facing away, but Meredith could feel her energy. She wasn't asleep.

"Sadie?" Meredith said lightly. "Dinner's almost ready."

Sadie sniffled, and Meredith rode a wave of panic. "Honey?" She walked around to the far side and sat on the bed.

"It's nothing," Sadie said, her voice choked. She lifted a hand to cover her blotchy face. Meredith thought back to a *Thinking Mother* article that had described helping a teen regain calm.

"Breathe," she said. She put her hand on Sadie's back, where she could feel her rapid inhalations. "Slower," she commanded, exaggerating the sound of her own respiration as a model.

"Mom," said Sadie after a few slow cycles. "Really, it's fine. Didn't you read something about how crying is normal for tween girls? I remember we talked about it." She sniffed again. Meredith stood to grab a tissue from the box on Sadie's bookshelf. She passed it to her and sat back down. Meredith stroked Sadie's back, her daughter's Elkettes sweatshirt soft beneath her hand.

"Sure," Meredith said, "crying is great, but it's also good to talk about it. What happened?"

Sadie rolled her face into the quilt. "I don't want to talk about it." She paused. "Really."

"Can I guess what's bothering you? And then you can tell me if I'm close?" The *Thinking Mother* article had suggested this tactic.

Sadie lifted her head, but trained her gaze on the pink rag rug, another holdover from toddlerhood, that matched her quilt. Meredith had thought about asking Alice to redesign Sadie's room as a gift for her thirteenth birthday. "But even if you guess," Sadie said, "I don't want to talk about it."

"Humor me," Meredith charged on. "Let me see." She took a breath and squinted, making a show of thinking. "The Spanish test was really hard. Am I close?"

Sadie shook her head. "That test was ridiculously easy. I think I got a hundred."

Meredith smiled. She'd expected as much. "Okay." She raised a finger to her lips and pressed. "You lost to Dad in Parcheesi again last night?"

Meredith could see the beginnings of a smile. "Yeah, right," Sadie said.

Meredith's next guess would have to be closer to the truth, and then she'd have a chance at getting Sadie to spill. She remembered @SadeeLux and the exaggerated close-ups her daughter had posted, her deliberate rule breaking. She took another slow breath in, akin to the ones she'd just demonstrated. "Something happened on Instagram?" She tried to keep her voice low-key. Sadie's eyes clouded; her Parcheesi smile faded.

"That's closer," she admitted. "But I still don't want to talk about it."

Thinking Mother advised "following your tween's lead." Meredith forced herself to lean over her daughter's prone body and offer a cuddle. As much as she hated to do it, she'd leave the conversation here, to show Sadie she trusted her judgment.

Plus, she could smell the ginger from downstairs. The stir-fry would be done.

"Dinner!" called Bill just then.

"Come eat," Meredith said.

NEITHER MEREDITH NOR Bill had any luck with Sadie over the tofu. Sadie diplomatically relegated the protein to the sides of her plate. She then politely refused Bill's offer for a Parcheesi rematch, and when her apps went off at nine p.m., Sadie glumly plugged her phone into the kitchen outlet.

"Sure you're okay?" Meredith asked for the umpteenth time.

"Mom." Sadie rolled her eyes as she shuffled back to the stairs. "It's normal."

Maybe so, thought Meredith, but she should still check Sadie's phone. Once her daughter had been in bed for fifteen minutes, Meredith began looking at texts and then @SadeeLux. At first, everything

seemed fine. The same. In today's post on Sadie's profile, Sadie and Mikaela stood next to one of their lockers, duck faces and arched eyebrows. Sadie had thrust her hip out in the affected way of influencers and red-carpet celebrities. At least Sadie's and Mikaela's torsos were covered.

Meredith clicked on the little paper airplane in the upper right corner of Sadie's feed, the one that took her to direct messages. Her shoulders immediately tensed as she read the first thread. There was a message from @TedBaller420 in all caps. "SLUT."

Meredith blinked rapidly, her body frozen. "Bill?" she called, her voice not loud enough to reach him in his study, where he'd retreated after Sadie went to bed. She'd tell him in a minute, when he was out. Hands shaking, she screenshotted the message and then clicked into @TedBaller420's profile.

It had to be Teddy Sullivan. As the page loaded, Meredith swallowed against a flash of nausea. Meredith had known Teddy since preschool. She'd laughed at his bright, Kennedy-esque smile and his slapstick sense of humor. This little kid, Sadie's lifelong friend, had called her a slut? No wonder Sadie was sobbing.

The photos on @TedBaller420 were all Teddy's. He'd posted a soccer selfie and a sunny group photo from the homecoming game, that same night Sadie had also burst into tears.

"Bill?" Meredith said louder.

"One minute," he called. "Just hitting send."

Meredith felt faint. She walked to the dining room and collapsed into a chair. She stared at the surface of the burlwood table, the grain irregular and undulating. That was how Alice had described it when Meredith had asked her advice on what to get. She had sent her to a Room and Board outlet and insisted Meredith use Alice's industry professional pricing. "Elevated," Alice called the table when she'd come over for a glass of wine the night it was delivered, and then she'd forwarded Meredith three choices of fabric for the chairs.

Meredith thought about texting Alice now, sending her the screen-shot of Teddy's message. But what the hell would Alice do about it? She couldn't very well send three options for making it right. Teddy could never take back what he'd written. And it wasn't as if Alice had any control of him. Ever since the end of sixth grade, and maybe even longer, the kid had been in a slide. He'd been free-falling toward delinquency without any of the usual parental checks. Alice had more in common with Nadia, Meredith realized, than with her.

While she waited for Bill—one minute was always closer to ten—she opened her email and began composing a message to Jason Whittaker.

Alice Sullivan

- - - - -

W hy are you being so weird?" Teddy asked on Thursday morning. They'd gotten up early, and Alice had promised him a donut and Starbucks, her most reliable bribe, if he went to the therapist—to Julienne's office—without complaining.

"I'm not being weird." Alice whipped her head to the left to check for oncoming traffic. She thought back over the morning and wondered how she'd tipped Teddy off. She'd tried so hard to keep it together, despite the tumultuous week that had left her feeling constantly dizzy.

Yes, she'd cried a couple of times. She'd have told any of her friends they were justified in their tears if they'd had the week she did. She'd lost it after the NextDoor post and then again after the text exchange with Nadia on Wednesday afternoon, but she'd been careful to sob only in the bathroom with the shower running. The kids couldn't have heard.

And of course she'd feverishly scoured Facebook for more pictures of Julienne, but only after her kids were asleep. They didn't know about their nana's secret. And, perhaps most importantly, Alice had deleted the browser history that showed her searches related to sociopathy in adolescents, the ones that had left her breathless and sweaty.

When Patrick showed up on FaceTime in the evenings for quick chats with them all, Alice applied undereye concealer, but still her

husband could tell she wasn't quite okay. "I know this is hard," he'd said to her after he had talked to each of the kids. She had tried to downplay her misery, but last night, she'd wiped a few tears before they'd said good-bye.

"I am so sorry about this stupid trial." He'd reached toward the screen, as if he could touch her face via Internet.

Alice had shrugged. "We always knew it would be like this."

They hadn't known, though, that the Energy Lab trial would coincide with Teddy's meltdown and Alice's mother's revelation. And in the dark alone, with Patrick in Cincinnati, Alice imagined Teddy falling in line with each and every bullet point she'd read in the articles about adolescent sociopaths. Google said, actually, that it wasn't "sociopathy" but rather "conduct disorder" in kids, but that didn't make the reality less alarming. "Withdrawn," she recited to herself before she fell asleep at night, thinking of the first criteria. "Unremorseful." It was true that Teddy never seemed to feel completely sorry for the embarrassment he'd caused Tane.

"You're being super weird," he muttered now in the car on the way to Green Haven. "Is it because you're making me go to therapy?"

Alice passed the McDonald's where she and her mother took the kids too often. Even in the winter, she went at least once a week for a sundae. This time, she did a double take when she saw the familiar pink graffiti on the drive-thru order box.

"I know, right?" Teddy said. "That shit is everywhere."

"Language," Alice said. "And therapy is a good idea for everyone." Alice had already used this line three or four times with Teddy.

"Then why don't you go?" Teddy asked.

They'd been down this road, too. "I have gone at times in my life. Your grandmother is a therapist." She resisted a sideways glance at her son. *He'll put me back in therapy*, she realized, this child whom she used to understand so well. Plus the Energy Lab case that was turning her into a single parent. Plus insulting and alienating her closest friend

via text. Plus Julienne. Plus spying on Julienne. Alice shoved that last thought out of her mind. She deserved a little head start after being lied to for her whole life. She'd worry about how to explain herself after she decided whether Julienne was, at the basic level, a good person.

"You know you can't make me talk, right? The counselor—Dr. Martín? She can't make me talk."

"No one can make you do anything." Alice accelerated onto the highway. "But I can buy you a donut if you play along."

"ALICE SULLIVAN," SHE said, smiling at the young man at the reception desk. She looked over her shoulder at the empty lobby, glad there weren't any witnesses. This early appointment—the emergency slot—had its benefits.

Alice had called her mother the night before, just to be sure that Julienne didn't have any identifying information about Alice's family. "I told her I had to wait until you were ready," Alice's mom had repeated. "I've been calling you A." She'd sounded imperious about it, righteous, as if she hadn't kept Alice in the dark for a full thirty-seven years before this week.

Alice's mother had a way of explaining highly emotional situations in an utterly detached manner. "I've decided to divorce your father," she'd said, for example. Alice could still hear the coolness in her mom's tone, could still see her pushing her hair matter-of-factly behind her ears on that long-ago Saturday morning. Then her mom had launched into a summary of the finances that made it possible for them to stay in the house even though Alice's dad had already left on a "business trip" from which he'd never return. Alice had been twelve herself then, she realized. Though she'd agreed to monthly calls with her father after the split, it had been nicer with him living in Nashville, hours and hours from daily contact.

Alice glanced at Teddy beside her. She couldn't imagine leaving him at this point in his life, speaking to him only for a few hours each year. "Right!" said the receptionist in Julienne's office. "I remember talking with you on the phone. I'm Griffin. Thanks for coming in after all. And this is Edward?"

He looked at Teddy, who blinked at him, silent.

"Teddy," Alice said to Griffin, when her son didn't speak up. "That's what he goes by." She opened her palm and gestured toward him, as if presenting him in a pageant. She instantly regretted it and shoved her hand into her jacket pocket.

"Great." Griffin pulled a piece of paper from a tray next to his computer and attached it to a plastic clipboard. "Intake." He handed the form to Teddy. "Dr. Martín will be right with you." Alice eyed a Keurig in the corner. "Help yourself to beverages," Griffin said.

Teddy dropped the clipboard on a chair in the waiting area and headed straight to the machine.

"Your form," Alice whispered.

"Hot chocolate," Teddy said, full volume.

Alice wondered how many parents found themselves in public arguments with their kids here.

As Teddy shoved a pod into the machine, Alice looked at the questions on his form. Teddy would have to write about his interests, times he'd felt successful. Alice sucked in her breath when she got to the section about family history. "Are your parents married or divorced?" the questionnaire asked. And then, "Do you think their relationship is good?"

What would Teddy say about her marriage? What would she have said about her mother's?

"Mom?" Griffin called to her from the desk, and Alice jerked her head up. "That form is just for Teddy, okay?" She flipped the clipboard over, embarrassed. She hated being called "Mom" by other adults in front of her kids. "I've got another form for you, actually, that you can

fill out while Teddy's in session." Alice's heart fluttered. She hadn't imagined the part of the morning that would include Teddy being alone with Julienne while she waited outside.

The phone on Griffin's desk rang then, and Teddy plopped down in the chair next to her. She could smell the sweetness of his hot chocolate. Meredith, she knew, would be thinking about the drink's corn syrup and hydrogenated oil ingredients, but Alice felt resigned. It was smart of Julienne to give the kids sweet drinks in the lobby, ply them for their openness.

"Teddy?" Alice jerked her head at the familiar voice and gaped at the woman who'd appeared. Julienne Martín sounded exactly like her mother. Her hair, that familiar blond, was pulled back in a low ponytail. She wore glasses with dark plastic frames, but the glasses were really the only difference between her mother and Julienne. Julienne's eyes, her smile, her stature and posture—all of it was uncanny. Alice blinked four or five times, shocked.

Teddy was on his feet. "I didn't do this yet." He grabbed the clipboard.

"It's okay." Julienne smiled at Teddy and then peered at Alice. "We'll go over it together. Mrs. Sullivan?" Alice resisted a flinch.

She'll know, Alice thought, but she willed herself to her feet. She twisted her mouth into a smile. "Hello." To her horror, her voice broke, and she realized she might cry.

"This way." Julienne turned, ignoring the emotion. *She's probably seen it all.* A therapist wouldn't be surprised by her tears, though Alice hoped to hide them from Teddy. She looked down at Julienne's shoes as they moved into a hallway behind the lobby. She wore those flats Alice had seen advertised on Instagram, the ones made from recycled water bottles. Alice had considered buying a pair for her mother's birthday the previous spring. They were exactly her style.

Julienne's office smelled of lavender and oranges, and Alice fairly collapsed into the love seat that Julienne indicated. Despite their unnerving physical resemblance, Julienne's office was nothing like Alice's

mother's old one. That had been a small room at the back of their house with an entrance off the porch. Alice had grown up hearing muffled voices through the walls.

"Okay," Julienne said. She sat in a wingback chair upholstered in an understated neutral houndstooth. *Stylish*, Alice thought. She glanced at the floor lamp over Julienne's shoulder, a brass parabola with a linen drum. Alice had used a similar one in a client's guest bedroom a year ago. Teddy slurped his hot chocolate beside her. "I usually do a few minutes now with us all together," Julienne said, "and then Teddy and I will talk for about forty minutes more. At the end, I'll bring you back in and we'll plan next steps." She made a mark on her notepad. "Sound good?"

Alice glanced at Teddy, who'd raised his eyebrows at her over the top of his drink. "Yes," Alice said for both of them. "Sounds good." She'd started sweating, and she shrugged out of her coat.

Julienne's eyes twinkled as she smiled at Teddy. "I'd love to hear from you. What brings you in today? Are you willing to share?"

"It's not my choice." Teddy put his cup on the coffee table in front of the love seat. Alice looked for a coaster, but there weren't any. There were, she noted, rings from other beverages marring the table's surface. "But I got in trouble at school, and I'm suspended, and my mom said we had to come here. If I behave, I get a donut." He smirked at her, and Alice ducked her chin to her chest.

"Okay," Julienne said, unfazed. "And Teddy, have you ever seen a counselor before? Ever done any therapy?"

Teddy shook his head. Julienne made another mark on the clipboard, and Alice wondered when they'd get to the marriage items she'd seen on the questionnaire. "But my grandmother is a therapist," Teddy offered.

Alice coughed and looked up. She hadn't considered that Teddy could give identifying details about his nana while they were here.

"Would you like some water, Mrs. Sullivan?" Julienne asked. "There's some in the lobby. I could just . . ."

"No." Alice shook her head. "I'm fine. So sorry. Call me Alice." She

glanced at Teddy, who curled his lip at her. His expression reiterated his query from that morning: *Why are you being so weird?*

Julienne looked at her notes. "Alice, why don't you talk a little about your goals for Teddy, and then he and I can get started."

Alice had been so focused on her own goal of getting here—getting a head start on Julienne—that she hadn't thought about her hopes for her son. She wanted him to get back into school, obviously. She wanted him to be the kind of person who cared about others, who didn't take pleasure in humiliating his peers. She wanted him to appreciate her, to be honest with her. "I just want him to be okay," Alice said finally, her voice wavering again. "I want him to be a good person."

She felt tears gather at the corners of her eyes and swiped them away. Teddy picked up his hot chocolate and lowered his nose to the rim of the cup. She realized her comment made it seem like he wasn't a good person already, but she couldn't think of a way to backtrack.

"Thank you." Julienne smiled at her, and as she did, her eyes crinkled in exactly the same way Alice's mother's always had. The right side of her mouth smiled more than her left, a quirk so familiar that Alice felt faint.

"Why don't you wait in the lobby," Julienne said, standing. "And Teddy and I will get to know each other."

Alice thought again of the marriage questions on the form. Julienne would have a complete picture of her through Teddy's eyes, before they'd even met in a normal way. And when they did meet in a normal way, Alice would have to admit that she'd put Teddy's treatment at risk in order to spy on Julienne. It was no wonder Teddy struggled. Alice was basically delusional. *She* was the one who needed a therapist.

Still, what could she do in the moment? Alice tried to smile at each of them as she walked out, though her whole face felt bruised.

Teddy Sullivan

Look," Dr. Martín said after his mom had left, "I know you don't want to be here. No one wants emergency therapy." He looked up from his hot chocolate. "But together, we can work to help you get what you *do* want. What is that, do you think?" Her glasses slipped a little on her nose, and she pushed them up.

"What?"

"What do you want?" Dr. Martín repeated. She didn't sound impatient, exactly, but rather sort of insistent. He scanned the room. Dr. Martín had several shelves' worth of trucks, trains, and dolls on the wall to his right.

"What are those?" he asked.

"For the littler kids." She held her pen over her notepad, ready to write. "I've got some things for my older clients, too. Drawing supplies and Model Magic, but not for you yet." She smiled, but just barely. "You seem like the kind of person that can just tell me your goals first. Then, once that's done, I'm guessing you'll want to know the fastest, easiest way to get there." He bit his lip. "Nobody wants to do therapy forever, even though the nature groups I run are pretty fun." She smiled then for real and nodded at him. "So? What do you want?"

Teddy blinked a few times, and he exhaled through his nose, fast enough that he could hear it. He put his hot chocolate down again and gripped the armrest of the love seat. He wondered what to say that would make his answer right.

"Just say it." Dr. Martín squinted at him. "Don't think too hard."

"I want to start junior high over." Teddy felt his shoulders relax once he'd confessed it.

"Great." Dr. Martín made a note. "Of course, I haven't yet figured out time travel. But it's a place to start." She smiled again, and Teddy felt like she really did approve of him. "Now tell me more."

"Nothing has gone the way it should go." Teddy felt his voice catch. For a horrified second, he wondered if he might cry. He had noticed the three separate Kleenex boxes in Dr. Martín's office, but he forced his tears back. He'd cried just yesterday about that goddamned Instagram video. Before that, it had been in the back seat of his mom's Volvo after he missed his penalty kick in the semifinal shootout last summer.

"Like what?" Dr. Martín's voice was softer, but still demanding.

"I don't like my teachers as much as I liked Ms. Tierney." He hadn't thought of it until he said it. His sixth-grade teacher had clearly enjoyed him. They'd joked around, whereas his junior high teachers seemed suspicious of him. "My grades aren't all As." He'd expected to have all As. His mom had told him when he was in fourth or fifth grade that "all As" was how she'd gotten into Notre Dame.

Dr. Martín stared at him.

"The school soccer team is a joke. And," Teddy added, "I was busier because I had to do ECSC and school soccer both."

"Elm Creek Soccer Club?"

"How do you know?"

"My son plays for Liston Heights." Teddy winced. His team had lost to Liston Heights Premier twice that summer. He didn't remember seeing her on the sidelines. "He's older than you are," she explained without him asking.

"Liston Heights is really good." He wanted to ask how old Dr. Martín's son was, but he wasn't sure that was allowed.

"And what about girls?" she asked after a moment. "Or boys. Any romantic interest?"

Teddy blushed. "At the end of sixth grade, we all got phones," he said, though he realized it didn't make sense.

Dr. Martín wrote something else, and he half stood to see. He expected her to pull the paper back toward herself, hiding it from him, but she did the opposite.

"Kids are usually curious about what I'm writing down," she said. "It's about them, after all." She flipped the notebook toward him and he saw that she'd written his name at the top, and then without him noticing, she'd written "middle school do-over," and below that, she'd added "phones at the end of 6th."

Dr. Martín stared at him, and Teddy looked down at his lap. It seemed like he was supposed to say something. "Okay?" he tried.

"So now you know," she said. "It's just a list of things that I want to remember." He nodded. "So, tell me about why the phones changed things."

Teddy thought back to the sixth-grade graduation party. The text Sadie sent him on the bus on the way there before the chaperones, including Meredith, made them put their phones in this giant plastic tub, not unlike the one in which Dr. Martín kept the Duplos he could see on her shelves.

"Do you think Tane likes me?" Sadie's text had appeared on Teddy's home screen.

As he read it, it became harder to breathe. Tane had gotten to be the third tallest kid in their class that spring. Teddy had noticed he'd passed him right after spring break. And not only that, Tane had abandoned his short pants. He wore joggers all of a sudden, like all of Teddy's friends, including one pair from Adidas. And he had a new pair of shoes, too: Brooks with laces instead of his usual Velcro.

Tane had asked if he could join the football game Teddy played at recess. He didn't ask Teddy, but rather Ryan. Ryan always followed the school's Welcome Rule, even though everyone knew they were too old for the babyish directive about inviting everyone to play.

And then Sadie had wanted to know whether Tane liked her.

"Don't know," Teddy had texted back.

"Find out?" He could see Sadie's black ponytail a few seats in front of him on the bus. He had found it between Mikaela Heffernan's blond waves and Sylvie Acheson's short brown pigtails. He wondered if the other girls were reading Sadie's texts.

As he looked, Sadie turned around and smiled at him, her eyes flashing. She held her phone up over the back of the seat, so he could see it. *Text me back,* she mouthed.

Tane Lagerhead? The kid's parents said he couldn't get a phone until the beginning of junior high. He's in the board game club. "Okay," typed Teddy. What else could he say to Sadie? No? He'd text her later that he couldn't find out. No way Sadie and Tane could be, like, a thing.

"Teddy?" It was Dr. Martín, pulling him back. He looked at her glasses and at her notepad. He swiveled toward the Duplos on her shelf.

"I never really thought much about talking to Sadie until I had to type it in a text."

Sadie Yoshida

Sadie's dad was never home on school mornings, which was why she was so suspicious when she found him, his top button undone, pacing around the kitchen so close to the time her mom usually drove her to the junior high.

"What's going on?" She glanced at the table where someone had laid a place mat and a paper towel. "Why aren't you at work?"

Her dad smiled. "Aren't I allowed to take a slow morning? Spend a little time with my girl?"

Sadie frowned. She opened the fridge and grabbed the orange juice. "Where's Mom?" She'd smelled pancakes from the second-floor landing, and she watched her dad flip the three he had on the griddle. Pancakes were usually a Sunday morning thing. Her dad whipped them up after he'd finished whatever long run was in his training plan. They'd eat them together while her mom power-walked with Alice and Nadia.

Her dad didn't look up from the stove. "She had to stop by the junior high for a meeting."

"What meeting?" Sadie grabbed one of the tiny glasses her mom insisted on for juice. "Too much sugar," she'd say if Sadie tried for a bigger cup.

Her dad waved his spatula in the air. "Some wellness thing."

Good guess, Dad, Sadie thought. Meredith's favorite committee

was student wellness. She used to teach the yoga classes at Elm Creek Elementary until it had gotten too embarrassing for Sadie to be the teacher's kid.

Sadie stood next to her dad, who still wasn't looking at her. Something felt off. She scanned the kitchen counter, where she usually kept her phone. The charger was there, but the phone was missing. "Have you seen my phone?" she asked.

Her dad pointed at the table near the back door. "Over there."

"What's it doing there?"

"Ah . . ." Her dad put the first of the pancakes on a cobalt plate and handed them to Sadie. He scooped three new blobs of batter onto the griddle. *Stalling*, Sadie thought, suddenly nervous. She stood still, waiting for an answer. "Well, your mom took a look at your phone last night, sweetheart. It's one of those things that parents do."

She walked to the table, mentally scanning through the messages she'd received recently. Nothing major on her texts, and Meredith didn't know about Snapchat or Finsta.

"Grab a fork," her dad said, pointing at the silverware drawer. "Eat up."

"Does Mom's meeting have something to do with my phone?" *It couldn't, right?* But why was her dad being so weird? She backtracked to the refrigerator for the syrup.

Her dad held his spatula aloft. "Do you have two Instagram accounts?"

"No," she said automatically, though she could feel her face heating.

"Sadie?" His voice wasn't angry, exactly. It was the same tone he used if she forgot to empty the recycling or left her dinner plate on the counter instead of putting it in the dishwasher.

If he's asking, they probably already know. Sadie sat down, poured her syrup, shoved a hunk of pancake in her mouth. She stared at a brownish stain on the blue place mat. Should she deny the Finsta? It might get her in worse trouble. Warm pancake stuck to the roof of her mouth, and she grabbed her juice glass.

By the time she wiped her mouth with the back of her hand, her dad had taken the next three pancakes off the griddle. He stared at her over the counter. "Well?" he said. "Did you want to revise that answer?"

Sadie stuck out her lower lip and blew her breath out, defeated. She rubbed a tense spot on her shoulder. "Fine," she said. "Yes, I have a Finsta. Everyone has them."

Though she wasn't looking, Sadie could hear three more pancakes sizzling. Ordinarily, she'd love the cozy, starchy smell, but with the backdrop of her parents discovering her secret, the sweetness of the syrup made her stomach turn. She pushed her plate away after just the one bite.

"Can I have my phone?" she asked.

"Yes." Her dad glanced at her. "But Mom and I want you to know we'll be having a serious talk tonight."

"Fine," Sadie said. She stood and grabbed the device. "I'm not hungry. I'll be ready in ten. Are you driving me?" She looked at the clock and bounded upstairs to her room before her dad could answer.

She clicked on @SadeeLux as soon as she'd closed her bedroom door. If they knew about this account, they'd seen all the photos. Her mother now knew she wore her skating makeup at school. She'd probably figured out that Mikaela had come over to the house when no adults were home. And she might have read her DMs.

Sadie held her breath and pain radiated down each of her arms. She thought back to the evening before, the horrible moment when she'd seen that message from Teddy. She'd known he'd be furious about the video, but he'd been acting like such a jerk with the dodgeball thing and the homecoming game. And hadn't he done something so much worse to Tane than she'd done in that video? Showing everyone Tane's actual naked body?

A stuffed otter wasn't really a big deal. Probably half the kids in their class had their own stuffies or blankies. Sadie looked at her bookshelf where she herself kept Ansel, the floppy-eared rabbit she'd begged

for on a family trip to South Dakota when she'd been in the third grade.

But as she thought about Teddy's otter, Gigi, she knew it was the Pull-Ups that made Teddy write that horrible thing to her. She'd found out about them on a camping trip their families had taken the summer after fifth grade. She remembered the smell and Teddy's sleepy embarrassed eyes as he whispered about it with Alice outside the kids' tent. When Teddy had gone to the bathroom, Sadie had peeked in his duffel bag and seen the extra ones, like diapers but bigger, with gray and blue stripes that were meant to make them look like real underwear.

She dropped her phone and pulled her jeans on, trading her night shirt for her favorite pink V-neck.

"We'll talk about it tonight, right?" Sadie asked her dad when she slid into the car next to him. "Because I don't want to talk about it right now."

He seemed relieved to agree, and he didn't insist she get in the back seat, where she usually sat when her mom drove.

WHEN SADIE GOT to school, Meredith was waiting for her outside the office, her hands in a ball.

Great, Sadie thought, instantly horrified. She stalled just inside the doorway searching vainly for an escape. Everyone else's mothers seemed to understand that parents didn't come into the junior high, at least not during passing time when everyone was in the halls. But Sadie's mother had already seen her. She beckoned her with frantic waving. Sadie scanned the rest of the foyer. Kids streamed in through all four glass doors. She didn't see any of her friends, thank God. She usually met Chloe and Mikaela near the library after they'd grabbed their stuff for first period. This morning, though, with the pancakes and the Instagram, she was running late.

Sadie slumped as she walked toward her mother. She looked back over her shoulder, calculating the number of witnesses. When she stood in front of her, she tensed, ready for a whisper-shouted scolding about the Finsta and the secrets, but instead, her mom pulled her into a hard hug, her breath a little shuddery. "I'm so sorry," she whispered into the top of Sadie's head.

What? Sadie hugged back with bent arms. She patted her mom's back, hoping to shorten the embrace. She imagined the eighth graders laughing at her as they walked by.

"Mom?" she tried. "This is a little much for school." She dropped her arms to her sides, hoping the movement would prompt her mom to let go. It sort of worked, but then her mom seized her arms and pulled her closer. Sadie looked at the floor and tried ineffectively to shake free.

"Are you okay?" her mom demanded.

"Mom, yes." Sadie took a step back, but her mom followed. Sadie was sure she could hear snickers behind her. "Let go," she whispered. "This is really embarrassing."

"Oh, Sadie, stop." Her mom sounded annoyed, but to Sadie's immense relief, she did let go. "I'm just so worried about you, honey," she continued, her words tumbling out fast. "I had no idea you'd gotten into this Instagram mess, and now those horrible messages from Teddy. I just had to tell Mr. Whittaker right away. Don't worry, though. We'll get it taken care of."

"Wait," said Sadie. "You read the DMs and told Mr. Whittaker?" *And this was her mother's idea of helping?* If Mr. Whittaker knew about the DMs, he'd probably also learn about the video. People knew that she was the one who gave Tane the intel.

Her mom's voice got louder still. "Of course I told Mr. Whittaker! Teddy was completely out of line. And cruel! I just wish you'd told me last night when you were so upset. I'm here to support you." Sadie closed her eyes and started to shake her head, but her mother's voice rose in crescendo. "We'll deal with the fake Instagram later, Sadie,

because that's a clear violation of the trust we've established, but cyber-bullying?"

Sadie held up a hand to stop her. "Mom," she tried again.

"Dad and I just won't abide that, Sadie. We won't!"

A kid bumped into Sadie's mom's shoulder. "Sorry," he mumbled as he looked back at them and laughed.

"I have to go to class." Sadie took some quick steps in the direction of her locker.

"Okay, sweetie!" her mom shouted after her. "Dad and I are here for you." Sadie scrambled away as if escaping a monster in a horror film.

Alice Sullivan

When they got in the car, Alice handed Teddy a bakery bag with a chocolate long john inside. The end of the session had been fine. Julienne had been complimentary about Teddy—"extraordinarily open and self-aware," she'd said—and Alice had faked her way through plans for more appointments, which they obviously couldn't have. Alice had collected herself during a quick run to the gas station for the donut. Teddy had cooperated and even seemed happy about the idea of continuing therapy. And now, Alice braced herself all over again for the reentry meeting they'd have with Assistant Principal Whittaker in fifteen minutes.

"Thanks." Teddy admired the chocolate icing. If only it were always so easy to please her children, Alice thought. He bit off about a third of the donut, and Alice backed out of her parking spot and tried not to get her hopes up that he'd confide too much in her. One session, after all, could hardly change their whole lives; plus, she hadn't stopped sweating, worrying at every moment that Julienne would realize her ruse.

"It wasn't as bad as I thought it would be," Teddy said, mouth full. "Are we going to school?" He seemed almost excited to get there. Alice felt surprised by this and realized with a start that she couldn't remember the last time he'd anticipated school. She flashed on a pajama day the elementary had had a couple of years ago. She remembered his

toothy grin that morning as he'd danced in his slippers. But since then? She realized he hadn't seemed happy at school in a long time.

The optimism she felt about his attitude faded as soon as they walked into the junior high and saw Jason Whittaker, who stood with his hands in his pockets outside the glass-walled office. "I've been waiting for you," Whittaker said. Teddy tossed the empty donut bag into the wide-mouthed garbage can as if he were hefting a free throw. Alice wished he hadn't done that. *Wrong tone*, she thought, and she put her hand on his arm.

"What?" He shook her off.

Alice smiled. "Is everything all right?"

"I'm afraid not." Whittaker turned and gestured for them to follow. Alice asked Teddy a silent question with her eyebrow. *What did you do?*

Teddy shrugged. "Nothing," he whispered, but he kept his eyes on the floor, the tile morphing to carpet once they'd made it into Whittaker's office. Alice doubled back to close the door behind Teddy and stared at the row of succulents on Mr. Whittaker's filing cabinet. She was tempted to reach a finger out to touch the smooth leaves of the echeveria. *Is it artificial?*

Alice started speaking, nervous. "We had a great meeting with a therapist this morning. We've spent some time reflecting on the incident, and Teddy has texted Tane to apologize—"

Whittaker interrupted. "Usually, these meetings go one way." He ran a hand down his cheek, pulling his lower eyelid so Alice could see the pink flesh on the inside. "But I got a disturbing email this morning about something Teddy posted on social media."

Alice shook her head slightly, as if shooing away a fly. "Impossible," she said. "I've had Teddy's phone the whole time he's been suspended. He's had no access to social media."

"Mr. Sullivan?" Whittaker looked at him, his mouth slightly open. Alice swiveled toward her son and was stunned to register an admission in Teddy's features. She almost reached over to wipe a speck of choco-

late from the corner of his mouth but stopped herself. Teddy said nothing.

"What?" Alice could hear her panic and wished for what seemed like the thousandth time that week that Patrick were next to her.

Whittaker clicked his mouse and his eyes ran over his screen. Alice craned her neck to see what he was looking at. Email, she thought.

"Mr. Whittaker?" she prompted after several more seconds.

He folded his hands. Alice could hear her heartbeat in her ears.

"Can you tell me anything about some Instagram messages you sent to Sadie Yoshida this week?"

Teddy's chin fell. His breath heaved out in a giant sigh.

"Instagram?" Alice nervously swiped the chocolate on Teddy's lip. As she did it, Teddy lifted his hand and batted hers away. The first of his tears fell then, and Whittaker reached across the philodendron on his desk—definitely artificial, Alice decided—and offered him a tissue.

"I DID IT because of the video," Teddy said after Mr. Whittaker showed them the DMs on his monitor. Alice reached into her purse to retrieve his phone from the zippered pouch where she'd kept it, but Teddy stopped her.

"I haven't had time to sneak it back in." He bent over his backpack and pulled out the iPhone. Alice's jaw dropped. She had clearly failed his suspension. That was definitely what Whittaker was thinking.

That and also that Teddy was the kind of boy who tried to keep women in line with insults like "slut."

Alice shuddered. "How did you even know that word?"

"I'm in seventh grade." Teddy said it as if that explained everything.

Whittaker pointed at the phone in Teddy's hand. "Can I see what made you so angry that you decided to send that message?"

In a few clicks, Teddy had it. He held the phone out to the side so

both Alice and Whittaker could see the Instagram Live video from opposite sides of the assistant principal's desk. Alice closed her eyes when Tane mentioned Gigi. *Not by name at least,* Alice thought, as she pictured the raggedy stuffed otter. She put a hand on Teddy's shoulder when Tane talked about the Pull-Ups. Teddy had cried so many times about them, humiliated each morning for years. Alice and Patrick had held their breath the first week Teddy had gone without them, just days after the start of sixth grade. And then, when nearly a month had gone by without an accident, Alice had slipped into his room while Teddy had been at soccer practice and taken the leftover briefs in their plastic package. They'd never talked about the transition.

"What does this have to do with Sadie?" Whittaker asked when the video ended.

Teddy sniffed, and Alice handed him another tissue. "She's the one who told him. She's the only one who knew."

Alice's heart broke a little then. "How did she know about the Pull-Ups?"

Teddy shrugged. "Camping, probably. Anyway, she told him, and he told everyone."

"We can't be sure about that," Whittaker said. He looked stern, but also sad. "You know, Teddy, when I first saw Mrs. Yoshida's email about your DMs, I'd planned to send you back home with your mom to continue your suspension. But now? I think it might be better to keep you here on campus while I investigate. I'm going to send you to the Quiet Room until lunch."

Teddy rolled his eyes. "The Quiet Room?" Alice had never heard of it.

"It'll be better than having to answer people's questions," Whittaker said. "You'll have a little privacy as this blows over."

Alice thought about arguing. Tane was certainly equally at fault. He should also see the inside of the so-called Quiet Room. But before she could speak up, she noticed the relief in her son's face.

"Why don't I plan on calling you by the end of the day?" Whittaker suggested to Alice.

She nodded and held her hand out to Teddy. "Give me your phone."

ALICE HELD IT together in the school office, focused on Teddy's emotion instead of her own, but in the parking lot after she'd said good-bye, she bent over her steering wheel and sobbed. Tears dripped onto the black leather interior as the engine idled. She called Patrick on speaker but got his voice mail, which was probably for the best since she wasn't sure she could form words, or even explain the train of events that had gotten her to this level of despondency. And, she remembered, she hadn't even divulged the appointment with Julienne. Obviously he'd disapprove. It was the stupidest of her ideas since her own adolescence.

But Patrick wasn't available anyway. He was never available. Alice cried harder. She usually pictured their healthy savings account statements when she missed him this intensely, but this time it didn't help. At the rate she was going on her own, it didn't matter if they had money saved for college—she wouldn't be able to get the children there. They'd be in jail before their eighteenth birthdays. Alice bent in half, letting her hair cover the sides of her face as she bumped her forehead against the heated steering wheel.

Eventually, she sat up and took several shaky breaths. She flipped open the sun visor and checked her face in the mirror. She was a mess, as she'd predicted—all blotchy with raccoon eyes. She grabbed a McDonald's napkin from the center console, a remnant from one of their ice cream runs, and stemmed the carnage with spit. If she weren't already hours late for work, she'd go home and touch up. But she had to get into the studio. She pulled out of the lot, scanning quickly for witnesses to her breakdown. None, thank God.

When she got to Ramona Design, against all odds, she managed

the most fruitful session she and her boss had had in months. They lost themselves in the newest fabric memos from Schumacher. They'd chosen an "unparalleled"—Ramona's favorite word—russet performance velvet upholstery for the Kerrigans' living room settee, both having the same inspiration at the same moment. They'd then pored over Osborne and Little floral linens and also mahogany antiques. The space would be spectacular, Alice knew. Given the ample budget, it would be their most striking work to date.

By the time Alice excused herself to head back to the car pool line just after three, she felt hungover, whiplashed back into Teddy's drama. It wasn't actually her day to do the driving, but Alice had gotten just one spare text from Meredith that morning, a terse proclamation that, given the circumstances, she didn't think they should share pickups. "For the time being," Meredith had added.

Alice wondered if there was any way back to their friendship from an all-caps "SLUT." She thought of Adrian and worried there wasn't. As the mother of a daughter, she knew that no matter the provocation, Teddy had crossed a line. She started crying again thinking about it. She couldn't call either Meredith or Nadia, she realized, after telling the latter that Donovan was worse than Teddy. Maybe she could at least apologize for that.

As she settled, sniffling, into the car pool line, Alice scanned the assembled cars for Meredith. She didn't see the Jeep and turned her engine off as the school preferred. No need to contribute to greenhouse gases on school property, at least not while the weather was still temperate. Just as she'd closed her eyes beneath her sunglasses, her phone rang. Elm Creek Junior High appeared in the caller ID, and even though Alice expected to hear an update from Jason Whittaker, her stomach lurched. The sour remnants of the squash soup she'd had for lunch stung the back of her throat.

Alice imagined Whittaker on the other end of the call, his unlined face pale under the LEDs. "Alice Sullivan," she said, anticipating his voice.

"Mrs. Sullivan, it's Jason Whittaker. I have some updates." Alice appreciated at least one thing about Whittaker: He didn't beat around the bush. Before she could even acknowledge him, he rushed on. "I've finished an investigation, and I've determined that though Teddy was completely out of line with those DMs, he was definitely provoked. In addition to the video we saw this morning, there's been some conflict around hashtags."

"Hashtags?"

"A power struggle between Teddy and Tane. Other kids took sides online."

Alice flashed to Nadia's warning about the hashtags at coffee before Aidy's conference and then to the mysterious text she'd received about Teddy laying off. She hadn't heeded the warnings because her son wasn't "that" kind of kid. She'd never once talked to a school administrator about anything but fund-raising. And now here she was just a week later, on close personal terms with the assistant principal. Alice's whole body felt heavy. The RAV4 in front of her began its trek around the circle. Alice started the car and inched up as well. She caught sight of Teddy's blond mop just outside the school's main entrance and felt a slow sadness radiate from her belly. "Okay," Alice said. "Where do we go from here? I'm in the car pool line. Teddy's about to get in." She watched him spot the car and lift his chin in a grown-up acknowledgment.

"He can come back to school tomorrow, but I'm going to have all three of them—Teddy, Tane, and Sadie—meet with the social worker individually."

Alice watched Teddy wave over his shoulder to McCoy Blumenfeld. Maybe, she thought, he hadn't lost all of his friends in the bedwetting scandal. "Sounds reasonable," she said. "And you'll keep me posted?"

Teddy opened the passenger door and sat beside her, not making eye contact as he shoved his backpack down by his feet.

As she hung up with Whittaker, another call came in. Ramona, she read on the Volvo's display unit. Though she knew she should take it,

she pressed the button next to her steering wheel that sent her boss to voice mail. She'd already broken the car pool rules by being on the phone at all. The last thing they needed was another infraction. Plus, Teddy's hangdog expression compelled her to try to talk to him.

"Are you okay?"

He shrugged. "I spent the day in the Quiet Room. They made me go to the cafeteria early before the lunch bell rang, so I didn't see anyone."

Alice wasn't sure what to say. It seemed the wrong tack to remind him about the Pull-Ups, the potential need for privacy.

"Do I have practice?" Teddy asked.

Alice envisioned the calendar. She kept a whiteboard in their mud-room, a marker color for each of their responsibilities. She pictured Teddy's green. She'd printed the name of the field where the premier team would meet on today's date. "At seven, I'm pretty sure." And then she imagined going through the car pool line all over again at the elementary school to retrieve Aidy. She imagined dragging her daughter to Teddy's soccer practice. Maybe her mom would come over with takeout, Alice thought, even though she'd just been there on Tuesday. She'd text her. She hated to ask for extra help, especially now with Julienne, and yet facing her exhaustion on her own seemed impossible.

Evelyn Brown

Evelyn eased her Camry into park in front of Julienne's house. Her heart thudded against her seat belt, and she tried a cognitive behavioral approach to calming down. *What's the worst that could happen?* she asked herself. *The kids don't like me?* She knew, rationally, that her track record with teens was pretty strong. She'd routinely cracked hard cases in her clinic. *You genuinely like kids,* Evelyn told herself. *And you'll especially like these kids. They're your grandchildren.* She felt her spine straighten and a smile overtake her face. More grandchildren! She'd hardly allowed herself to contemplate the possibility when she first learned Julienne's identity.

Evelyn's secondary infertility had been a terrible shock when she and Frank had started trying for a baby. She had been rigid about birth control after her premature pregnancy with Julienne. Never once had she considered that she'd have difficulty conceiving again, and by then, four years after relinquishing her newborn, her desire for another child nearly doubled her over. After Alice, her grandchildren had been the great miracles of her life. She'd loved feeling their little hands in her hair as she had rocked them to sleep, and delighted again in their morning faces when they stayed over at her place.

She'd missed so many childhood moments with Julienne's kids, of course. It was hard for her to accept that they were teenagers already. Though she'd thought of Julienne incessantly, she hadn't allowed her-

self to picture her firstborn as an actual grown-up. Evelyn unlatched her seat belt and checked her hair, a no-nonsense bob, in the rearview mirror. She felt inside her bag for the gifts she'd brought, a gift card to a movie theater for Laura, and an equally valued one to the sporting goods store for Miguel. Julienne opened the front door then and stepped onto the porch. Her blond hair hung to her shoulders, and she raised a hand to her brow, blocking the late-afternoon sunlight.

"Hi!" Evelyn called. Her hand shook as she pressed the lock button on the key fob and dropped it into her canvas tote.

"We're so excited!" Julienne said. Just then a man appeared at her shoulder. Rafael, Evelyn presumed, as he put an arm around her daughter. They were nearly the same height with similar builds. Evelyn wondered for a moment what it was like not to be dwarfed, physically or emotionally, by a partner. She shook the memory of Frank away as she navigated the Martíns' front steps. Her breath came shallow as she stuck a hand out to Rafael. Her heart had begun its pounding again, and she imagined this man in a tux, her daughter in a white gown. She pictured Julienne's adoptive mother watching them marry from the front row of a church. If there had been a chair to sit in just then, amid the pain of this phantom memory, Evelyn would have fallen back into it.

"It's so nice to meet you," Rafael said.

Evelyn smiled and willed herself steady.

"Are you okay?" Julienne asked.

"Just overwhelmed," Evelyn managed. "This is such a joy."

She hugged Julienne and breathed in her citrus perfume. She should ask for its name and buy a bottle for herself. It made sense that she'd like it, as she shared so much of her daughter's chemistry.

"Come in." Rafael gestured toward the door. "The kids are in the kitchen."

In fact, the kids were not in the kitchen, but rather crowded inside the door frame.

"Hi." The boy, Miguel, stepped backward, taking a seat on the stairs just beyond the entryway.

Evelyn's therapy instincts kicked right in. This was her grandchild, yes, but also just another teenager. "I'm Evelyn," she said. "I'm so excited to meet you." She walked forward, her legs suddenly sure, with her hand outstretched. As he smiled at her, she could see glimpses of her own smile, the left side slightly off-kilter. "And you're Laura." The girl stood close to her shoulder, and Evelyn thought she might want to hug. She opened her arms just slightly, offering, and Laura latched on, gripping Evelyn's rib cage with a surprising ferocity.

"She's a hugger." Julienne laughed. "Let's head into the kitchen. Rafael made some treats."

Julienne's kitchen couldn't have been more different from Alice's. Alice had just replaced her dark wood cabinets with sleek gray ones. Alice's sharp-edge countertop sat free from clutter except for a stainless-steel soap dispenser next to the tall faucet. At Julienne's, Evelyn noticed a pile of papers at one end of the counter, opened envelopes sticking out at odd angles. In the center sat a hand-painted serving dish piled with thick chocolate brownies. Evelyn tried to imagine Patrick arranging brownies on a decorative platter and almost laughed aloud. Neither Alice nor Patrick had time (*took time?*) to bake.

"Tea, Evelyn?" Julienne grabbed a mug.

Evelyn nodded and opened her bag. "I brought something for each of you," she said to the kids.

She pulled out the cards she'd chosen, blank in bright colors that she'd found at the Walgreens near her condo. She'd written short, nearly identical notes in each of them, versions of "I can't wait to get to know you."

"Should I open it now?" Miguel asked. His eyes were dark like his father's.

"Sure." Evelyn grabbed a brownie from the tray. "Your mom says you're a big soccer player."

Miguel smiled. "He scored three goals in two games last week," Rafael said.

"Dad," Miguel chided. "We don't need to brag." He held the gift card and grinned. "Thanks. This is my favorite store."

Evelyn winked at him. "I may have heard that from someone."

"Is this so weird?" Laura asked suddenly, grabbing her arm again. "Like, to meet us after all this time? Can you even believe we're related?"

Evelyn put her hand against Laura's as she slid onto a kitchen stool. "What do you think?" she asked, employing a therapy technique. "Does it feel weird to you?"

"Totally." Laura's eyes bugged.

Julienne laughed. "You can see I've prioritized openness with our feelings," she said. "Therapist's kids and all."

Evelyn grinned. "Did you know I'm a therapist, too?"

"That's another thing that's weird," Miguel said. He grabbed a brownie and took a too-big bite. It reminded Evelyn of Teddy.

"What's your position in soccer?" Evelyn asked, knowing already that he was a left wing. She'd memorized every detail of Julienne's descriptions—soccer, student council, the theater productions Laura had worked on as part of the props and set crews.

"Left wing." Miguel spoke around his full mouth. Evelyn could see Rafael's instinct to correct him for talking while chewing, a slight lean forward and an intake of breath, but he resisted. *Good work, Dad,* she thought to herself. Parents had to limit their corrections to appropriate moments. Telling Miguel to keep his mouth shut in front of Evelyn would have only embarrassed and alienated him. *Patrick,* Evelyn thought, *could take note.*

"My other grandson is a striker." As she said it, she felt her heart rate accelerate again. She hadn't shared nearly as many details about her existing family, after all, with Julienne. She hadn't even told the names of Alice's children. But now, with these kids in front of her, open and

accepting despite the awkwardness, Evelyn could see that more omissions would only impede her relationships.

She anticipated Miguel's next question, and decided before he could speak that she'd answer it: "He plays on the premier team for Elm Creek Soccer Association." She glanced at Julienne. Her daughter's eyebrows shot up. "He's twelve. Seventh grade." She grabbed her mug.

"The Elks!" Miguel said. "That team is pretty good."

"Oh yeah? I usually go to a bunch of the games. Maybe I could go to some of yours, too?"

"I'm fourteen," Miguel said, "so I follow a lot of those U13 guys on Instagram, even the kids from Elm Creek. What's your grandson's name?" He laughed. "I mean, your other grandson."

Evelyn held her breath, fighting tears. She wanted to scoop up these kids and erase the years of separation. She glanced at Julienne to check whether she, too, felt the joy and wistfulness that had overcome Evelyn, but she couldn't quite read her expression. She smiled at Julienne reassuringly. She patted Laura's knee. Her granddaughter had pulled her stool up as close to Evelyn's as she could get it.

"Teddy," Evelyn said, her voice clear. "Teddy Sullivan."

"IS ADRIAN AT school?" Evelyn asked Alice the next morning. She could hear the echo of speakerphone and imagined her daughter sitting at the helm of her Volvo. "Are there other people in the car?"

Evelyn had been nervous to dial, worried that today's ask would be the stressor that tipped Alice over the edge. "I'm alone, Mom." Alice sounded exhausted, just as Evelyn had feared she would.

"Are you okay?" It seemed an inadequate query, and yet the most salient she could think of.

"I don't know."

Evelyn had felt guilty telling Alice she couldn't help the night be-

fore. She hadn't even gotten Alice's SOS text until she'd grabbed her phone to find a photo of Teddy and Adrian to show the Martíns. As she waited for Alice to say more, Evelyn picked at her fingernail where the mauve polish she'd gotten after a lunch date with Julienne had started to peel. A half-moon shape of the lacquer came away between the tips of her fingers, leaving a naked spot near her cuticle.

"It's just, Teddy's reputation." Alice sounded hopeless. "He did this other thing now. Made a stupid comment on social media and—"

"Who cares what other people think of Teddy?"

But of course, Alice had always cared about public opinion. Evelyn knew this. Appearances, after all, had become her daughter's life's work as an architect and interior designer. Alice's desire to impress had seemed inborn. She'd collected only accolades all through middle and high school, cultivating her teachers' and peers' impressions of her. Alice herself had affixed the "Notre Dame Mom" sticker on the back window of Evelyn's old Subaru the same day the acceptance came in. The Notre Dame architecture dream had been pure irony, Evelyn marveled, as Alice didn't even know her mother had started at the very same school, transferring away only when her pregnancy mandated it.

"It's hard to be a pariah," Alice said. "Even you'd agree with that, right? It's hard to be a delinquent?"

"He's not a delinquent." Evelyn pictured her grandson. Even during this blip, she could see his inherent sweetness.

"We started therapy," Alice blurted. Evelyn wondered if she'd meant to tell her, or whether she'd just happened to call her in a weak moment. She felt pleasantly surprised by the news. She'd expected Alice to drag her feet on making the appointment, if not on purpose then because she was so overloaded with Patrick out of town.

"That's great. How did it go?"

"He talked. He—" Evelyn could hear Alice breathing, almost a wheeze on the inhale. "*We*. We liked her."

"That's a huge step. Whom did you see? Do I know her?"

"My friend Nadia recommended her."

Evelyn felt a wave of hurt that Alice hadn't asked her for a referral. "Good." Evelyn kept her tone neutral. *This is about Teddy's health*, she told herself. *Not about your ego.*

A pause extended between them. "Mom?" Alice said finally. "It seemed like there was some reason you called?"

Evelyn doubted her purpose. Maybe this wasn't the right day after all.

"Are you there?" Alice queried, her voice louder. "Can you hear me?"

Evelyn knew that if she didn't say it, it would mean more secrets, more distance. She'd always felt just a sliver of separation between herself and Alice, and now that she knew Julienne, that their connection felt so immediate, she couldn't bear to keep herself insulated.

Evelyn went for it: "I met Julienne's kids last night. That's why I wasn't free to help you."

"Wow." Evelyn couldn't read her daughter's tone. When Alice didn't say anything else, she charged forward. "And I—well, I know I told you I would protect your privacy—but it was so awkward trying to tell them about my life." Evelyn stood from the couch where she'd been sitting and walked to the window. Her new condo looked over downtown Minneapolis, the buildings a pleasing blend of heights and styles, the names of which Alice knew but Evelyn had never internalized. She squinted at the skyline, biting her bottom lip and hoping Alice would understand.

"What are you saying?" Alice's voice got louder.

"I'm saying I'd planned not to reveal your names, but I did share them after all. It just felt right, and I didn't want to manufacture more secrets. Alice, I feel so terrible for keeping this big thing from you for so long. I didn't want to repeat my mistake." Evelyn heard her voice shake. "I had to be authentic. Miguel—that's Julienne's son—he asked about Teddy's soccer, and he asked Teddy's name, and well . . . it just seemed wrong not to tell him. I know this isn't what we talked about."

"Oh my God."

Alice was on the edge, if not over it. Evelyn thought about hanging up and giving her more time to process. She'd expected the transition to be hard for Alice, but she also wondered if, since Alice had been adopted herself, she'd be more attuned to what Evelyn was feeling in the aftermath of her reunion with Julienne. She tried to shift focus. "If at some point you want to engage in a search for your own birth parents—"

"This isn't about me," Alice said, her tone cold. "It's about you and your choices and how they're impacting my life."

Evelyn studied her finger, the little space where the nail polish had chipped. "Well." A heaviness overtook her and she sat back down on her couch. "I did make a choice. It seemed like the best choice in the moment, and I'm sorry it seems you can't understand. You both mean the world to me." She waited. Certainly, Alice had noticed the sacrifices Evelyn had made to be a good mother to her. She'd turned down that professorship at Cal Berkeley so Alice wouldn't be uprooted during high school. She'd passed on a Fulbright so Alice wouldn't have to spend unsupervised time with Frank. Although now that she thought about it, she wasn't sure Alice even knew about these concessions. Evelyn's version of "good motherhood" had included making secret sacrifices for her daughter.

"I'm glad to hear we mean so much to you." Alice's sarcasm felt like a lead vest.

Evelyn dropped her gaze to Alice's senior picture, which sat framed on her antique end table. Her daughter had worn her letter jacket for the photo, the sleeve filled with bars and stars, another reminder of her accomplishments. If only Alice cared as much about Evelyn's opinion of her as she did about everyone else's.

"Julienne has a sense about these things." Evelyn plowed forward. "She introduced me to her adoptive mother, and Alice, you can't believe how natural it was, even though it was also so weird."

"Wait, you met her *mother*?" Alice's anger had flared again.

"It was important to Julienne." Evelyn softened her tone, an attempt to be gentle. "It's also important for you two to meet. I'd like for you to plan a coffee with her." This had been Julienne's suggestion, actually. A neutral ground, she said, where she and Alice could meet in "a spirit of curiosity." It had sounded lovely to Evelyn when Julienne had used the phrase, but she knew if she repeated it to Alice, she'd spoil it.

"You want me to meet her, like, without you there?"

"Are you driving right now?" Evelyn asked. "Should we talk later?"

"I'm pulling in to my office."

If Evelyn could go back five minutes, she might have skipped this call, but now, she figured she should just finish it. "Well anyway, Julienne thought it might be best to meet you one-on-one, to really get to know you."

Evelyn could hear that Alice had taken the phone off speaker. She imagined her sitting in her parking spot, her features pinched. "I can't really do this on your timeline, Mom."

Evelyn pulled the phone away from her ear and fought her own anger. She felt betrayed by Alice's reaction. Meeting Julienne had been so healing for Evelyn. It felt like filling a deep and craggy hole that she'd sidestepped for her entire adult life. Months after her first conversation with Julienne, she felt restored and safe. She realized she'd thought that the miracle of becoming a mother to Alice would have fixed her thirty-seven years ago, but it hadn't. One child simply couldn't replace another.

"It's your choice about getting together with her," Evelyn said.

"It's clearly *not* my choice." Alice opened her car door and slammed it again.

"I'll send you her number in case you decide to do it. She already has yours."

"Oh my God."

"You'll be nice, right?"

"Jesus, Mom." Evelyn winced at Alice's sharpness, but then she said, "You know I'm always nice."

Sadie Yoshida

On Saturday, Sadie caught sight of her mother in the third row of the auditorium for the Quiz Bowl match versus Liston Heights. Her mom gave her a thumbs-up as the team got settled onstage. Sadie hadn't been sure that her mom would even watch the tournament after how angry she'd been about Mr. Whittaker's call on Friday.

"You told kids about Teddy's bedwetting?" Sadie's mom had seemed shocked.

"But he called me a slut," Sadie tried.

"And that's *not* okay, but Sadie"—the wrinkle between her mom's eyebrows grew cavernous—"you told about the Pull-Ups first. That was a huge secret."

There hadn't really been any consequences for Sadie at home after Mr. Whittaker had called, but she still didn't think her mom was quite over it. From the stage, Sadie returned her thumbs-up and pulled her purple uniform shirt flat against the white thermal she'd worn beneath it. She had a matching white ribbon in her hair.

The team would face Liston Heights for the championship. Sadie could see the trophy, a two-tiered thing with red accents, just offstage.

First place would be good, Sadie thought. She imagined her Instagram post, and her mother's Instagram post, celebrating the accomplishment. It might erase some of the disappointment Sadie had seen

in her mother's face after Whittaker's call. Plus, the team expected a win.

Tane and Gretchen and Yusef had made it clear that only a defense of Elm Creek's title from the previous school year would do. And Sadie had barely eked out a seat on the A team, narrowly defeating Douglas Lim in a paper-and-pencil test on key dates in American history to make the squad. Douglas, for his part, had parked himself in the front row of the auditorium. He'd been a good sport about losing, but Sadie felt him looking at her. He'd be happy if she made a mistake and Mr. O'Connor, the faculty advisor, put him back on the A team for the next tournament.

If Sadie didn't make it next time, she wouldn't be able to sit on-stage next to Tane. Their arms wouldn't bump. She wouldn't high-five him after the victories, as they had this morning, twice. Plus, she wasn't sure there was any point in being B squad. If she didn't make A, she should probably quit Quiz Bowl.

Still, despite her desire for success, as soon as the match began, Sadie could feel that things weren't going her way. First, she'd mistaken the composers Telemann and Handel. Next, she'd buzzed in with Shintoism when the correct religion was Sikhism. Worse, she knew the team expected her to know about Asian religions because her dad was Japanese, even though their family wasn't at all religious. Finally, and while making eye contact with her mother in the third row, Sadie failed to feed "the Emancipation Proclamation" to Gretchen as the policy mentioned in the first paragraph of MLK's "I Have a Dream" speech, despite her presumed prowess in American history. She glanced at Douglas and caught his self-satisfied smile.

When Liston Heights celebrated at the end of the match, the trophy shone in the lights of the theater as the opposing kids hoisted it. Sadie offered a sad handshake to Douglas on her way to meet her mom. She'd looked for her in the audience as the match wound down, but her mother had already left her seat.

Sometimes, Sadie knew, her mom got too nervous to watch her compete, either in synchro or now in Quiz Bowl. Rather than sit for the whole thing, she lapped the building or removed herself to the lobby. But this time, she wondered if her mother wasn't just nervous, but also embarrassed, wishing Sadie had known more answers. Wishing she'd won.

"You'll probably get to play next time," Sadie said to Douglas, who nodded. She thought she saw him make eye contact with Yusef behind her. Yusef, she knew, had been #TeamDouglas the whole time, although Quiz Bowl hadn't yet made it to Instagram in the same way Teddy and Tane's feud had.

Sadie walked out of the auditorium without even looking at Tane, who, as their captain, had accepted the second-place trophy. Her whole idea about the next steps of their relationship—the Snapchat messages she'd imagined sending him that night, the plans she'd suggest for off-season training—had depended on them winning the tournament. Now they'd failed to keep the Elm Creek streak alive, and even though Quiz Bowl was a team activity, Sadie's three mistakes seemed to cement her as the weak link. Even though she'd answered correctly about square roots, Georgia O'Keeffe, and William Faulkner earlier in the day, when it had mattered in the championship match, she'd failed.

"Sadie!" Tane caught up to her just as she'd made eye contact with her mom in the lobby. He put his hand on her arm to stop her walking and she felt herself blush. He was touching her, and her mom was watching.

She looked up at him and remembered his cute face in the Instagram video. His hair fell in his eyes, and she thought that if she were a high schooler in a Disney movie, she'd reach up and brush it aside. Instead, he did it for himself, taking his hand from her shoulder and leaving a hot spot in the place he'd touched. "You did great today," he said.

Sadie glanced at her mom. That wrinkle in her forehead deepened.

Was she mad because Sadie had failed at Quiz Bowl or because Tane had touched her in the lobby?

"I didn't. I sucked." She looked at her shoes, red lace-up Keds that she knew her mom wouldn't let her wear after the first snowfall in a couple of weeks.

"I'm glad you were here," Tane said, and Sadie felt a spark of something in her chest, something in addition to the hollowed-out disappointment of losing for the team. Gretchen and her mom approached and offered high fives.

"We were good until that last one," Gretchen said sadly.

"What are you talking about?" Gretchen's mom said, slapping Sadie's hand. "You all did great. I didn't know half of those answers."

"Sadie?" Sadie's mom called across the lobby. "Sadie? We have to go." She pointed at the parking lot and walked out ahead of her, not waiting to see that she'd follow.

Meredith Yoshida

Meredith could feel Sadie's disappointment radiating from her. Her daughter collapsed against the back seat and leaned her head against the window. The white ribbon Meredith had tied around Sadie's ponytail hung limply over her neck, where Sadie's downy hairs fell from her elastic.

Meredith had encouraged Sadie when she had first mentioned Quiz Bowl (who wouldn't want their child engaged in an academic competition, after all?), but she found herself disliking it more and more with each rapid-fire question. The kids didn't even wait for the whole question to be read; they buzzed in recklessly, guessing answers. What amazed Meredith was how often they were right. She herself had never heard of the Haber-Bosch process and couldn't come up with the term "heliocentric," even from the audience. The only questions she'd been sure of were the ones about nineties rock music and anatomy. She'd been most impressed that Tane and Yusef seemed to be experts on Smashing Pumpkins and Blink-182.

"That was so embarrassing," Sadie mumbled.

Meredith glanced back at her as they drove past the hardware store. Alice had recommended that Meredith buy adhesive squares there for the hooks she wanted to hang inside Sadie's closet door for synchro medals. Meredith had just complimented the way Alice had displayed Teddy's soccer trophies on floating shelves in his room. *It's a little*

much, Meredith remembered thinking, but then she'd asked Alice's advice on how to create something similar, if a little more low-key.

"Second place isn't really embarrassing." Meredith remembered the squirming discomfort she'd felt in the audience when Sadie couldn't name the Emancipation Proclamation. Even Meredith had known that one. Meredith guessed it had been brave of Sadie to put herself out there, but as the synchronized skating coach always said, "Don't compete if you're not ready." Maybe she hadn't been ready.

"Elm Creek hasn't lost in, like, five years." Sadie's voice sounded far away.

"Tane didn't seem that disappointed in you." Meredith blinked into the rearview but glanced quickly away when she saw that Sadie had startled, her neck suddenly as straight as if she were standing center ice, waiting for her music to start.

"We're just friends." Sadie sounded defensive.

Meredith pictured Tane's nail polish, the way it reflected the light as his arm stretched forward in Warrior 2 when she'd taught the yoga unit in elementary PE. She'd of course imagined Sadie dating someday, but she hadn't thought about Sadie dating *now*. Or dating someone who'd just had his junk revealed to the entire seventh grade.

"Friends is good," Meredith said mildly. "Friends is all you should be in junior high."

Sadie leaned her head once again against the glass. "But he'll probably be embarrassed for asking me to be on the Quiz Bowl team. It's going to suck to have to tell people we lost the streak."

"Do people really know about Quiz Bowl?" Meredith couldn't imagine anyone caring that the kids had lost. It wasn't like there'd been spectators from school.

"I wanted to be better."

Meredith smiled as she turned into their neighborhood. She and Bill encouraged Sadie's tendency to continually strive for perfection.

Her coaches had commented on it since she was a little girl wearing the crash pants Meredith had purchased on Etsy to protect her hips from continual bruising. Maybe because of the extra padding, but mostly because of what Meredith came to think of as Sadie's superior single-mindedness, she refused to give up on a skill until she'd nailed it.

"Maybe you should refocus your energies on synchro? Or something else? Not everything we try is the thing for us." *And it would be fine to create a little more distance from Tane.*

Meredith pulled up next to the Yoshidas' mailbox, grabbed the envelopes and catalogs out, and handed the stack into the back seat for Sadie to flip through. It was an old tradition of theirs, dating back to Sadie's preschool days when she was just learning to distinguish their names. "M" for "Meredith," "W" for "William," and then very occasionally, she'd squeal as she came across an "S" for "Sadie" or her given name, "Sarah," which Meredith imagined she might want to use when she became a professional.

"I got something from the Service Division of the United Nations?" Sadie asked, and Meredith's adrenaline blasted through her forearms.

"What does it say?" The previous spring, Meredith had asked Ms. Tierney, Sadie's sixth-grade teacher, to nominate Sadie for a service award after Meredith had finished her two-year stint as director of the lower school service club. Meredith heard the envelope rip. Her heart pounded as she idled in the driveway and watched the garage door go up.

"It says, 'Congratulations.' Mom, I won some kind of award?"

"See?" Meredith said. "This is the kind of recognition that comes from investing in the activities that really match your talent." Meredith remembered the rapid-fire Quiz Bowl questions, the emphasis on speed over thoughtfulness. "Doesn't it feel great to be noticed for something that really matters?" Meredith peeked at Sadie as she pulled

into her parking spot. Sadie ran a finger over the embossed certificate. Meredith thought of the adhesive hooks on the back of Sadie's closet. Maybe a certificate from the UN should be framed and visible. Surely Sadie's commitment to the betterment of others deserved as much wall space as Teddy's soccer trophies.

Alice Sullivan

When she got to the studio on Saturday, Alice found she couldn't sit still. Patrick had been bleary-eyed from his late-night flight home from Cincinnati when she'd told him she needed to catch up after a week of single parenting. Even though she was swamped, she'd hesitated to leave the house. Patrick's warmth in the bed calmed her, and his heavy arm around her middle was enough to make her weep. But still, she was barely keeping Ramona at bay. Patrick could help by taking Teddy to soccer, she reasoned. He could review Aidy's homework folder.

Even though Alice was alone in the bright office—sun zigzagging through the glass partitions—she found she couldn't think about tile choices or the Mamie Eisenhower pink or the new mudroom she'd contracted with a book club mom, even though she herself hadn't attended book club since July. All she could think about was Julienne in her office, her golden hair resting over her shoulders, Teddy's tentative smile on his way out of the appointment. He'd liked her. And now, before she'd even had time to plan her next move, her ruse was already discovered. She'd have to confess it to her mother.

Just as she was imagining her mom's potential shock, a text message buzzed in from her. "Here's Julienne's number again," she wrote. "Please call her." And then, "Or text." Finally, in a separate message, "XO, Mom." Alice rolled her eyes. Her mother always signed her text

messages. She wondered how she signed the ones to Julienne. Surely, there was no need to go by "Mom" when Julienne had been an adult when they'd met. And Julienne had her own mom, in addition to Alice's.

Alice tried to imagine Julienne's face when their mother had revealed Alice's identity. She must have maintained perfect placidity. *Of course she did.*

Alice shook her head. She'd figure out how to fix the Julienne mess after she'd actually accomplished something at the office. Alice started on her easiest project. She began to sketch another new mudroom. Each one was a version of her own entryway, and half the book club had hired her already. She chose a different, whimsical wallpaper for each client, never duplicating the birds and butterflies she'd done for herself. As she penciled in hashmarks indicating the seagrass baskets she always recommended, she thought again about how Julienne hadn't told Evelyn about the appointment. If Julienne had ratted her out, their mother would have scolded her. There wouldn't have been the "XO, Mom" text. Instead, that message might have read, "WTF?"

But why hadn't Julienne told her? Was she adhering to a kind of patient-client privilege? HIPAA? Regardless, now Alice would really have to reach out to Julienne. She'd have to admit she'd brought Teddy to Green Haven under false pretenses. And she'd have to tell Teddy that he'd need to see a different therapist. Even worse, she'd probably have to tell him why. She'd counted on him hating Dr. Martín, she realized. She'd assumed he'd resist further appointments. She'd underestimated both him and Julienne.

Alice abandoned her sketch and googled "changing therapists." Twenty minutes later, she was still mired in articles about the "therapeutic relationship" and "getting a second opinion on your child's diagnosis." She shifted uncomfortably in her seat periodically, usually when she came across the word "diagnosis." She hadn't considered asking for one from Dr. Martín, though perhaps Julienne had had one in mind. Not "conduct disorder," she hoped, remembering the adoles-

cent precursor to sociopathy. She searched "ADHD," which was milder than conduct disorder and treatable with medication. And wouldn't ADHD explain Teddy's impulsivity? She felt self-satisfied when she read "impulsivity" as the first symptom of ADHD on the website she clicked. She had moved on to a paragraph about "low frustration toler-ance" when she heard the office door open. Ramona appeared.

Alice instinctively smoothed her hair and regretted not putting on makeup. Even on a Saturday, Ramona looked impeccable in a cash-mere boucle tunic over thick leggings and slouchy ankle boots.

"What are you doing here?" Ramona's eyes were wider than usual, rimmed in eyeliner, and she didn't return Alice's smile. Alice quickly scanned her memories of the last few days, wondering what she'd done wrong. She'd been checked out, sure, but she hadn't missed any addi-tional meetings. She'd logged a new project on their Slack workspace. The mudrooms were boring, but steady.

"Just getting organized," Alice said. "Patrick's been traveling, and I needed a little time . . ." She trailed off. Ramona had pulled her phone from her handbag and wasn't listening. Suspicion replaced Alice's ini-tial sheepishness. "What are *you* doing here?"

Ramona scowled at her phone. "I scheduled a meeting."

Alice glanced down at her hoodie and frowned. She wasn't exactly client-ready. "A client meeting? On Saturday?" As far as Alice knew, Ramona had never done that.

"Not exactly."

Alice cocked her head. She stared past Ramona into the confer-ence room, where the tile and countertop samples they'd assembled for Bea Kerrigan lay in neat piles across the table. She noticed for the first time an enlarged set of her original drawings tacked up on the fabric wall next to the television screen. "Then what is it?" she pressed.

Ramona walked into her glass cube without answering. Alice fol-lowed her, not bothering to put on the running shoes she'd kicked off under her desk. "What aren't you telling me?"

Ramona's eyes hardened. Alice recognized the same look she'd given her when she'd been forced to take the Harrison meeting to the Starbucks. "It's a journalist, okay?" Ramona said. "I'm doing a casual natural-light shoot and answering a few questions."

"But that's great!" Alice peered at her, trying to discern the catch. Ramona could have made the appointment for Friday, when they'd both been there. Alice felt slow; the fog that had descended on her beginning at Adrian's parent-teacher conference and continuing through the meetings with Jason Whittaker overtook her. She'd been failing to connect even the most prominent of dots in the last ten days.

"Maybe you could go?" Ramona gestured around the office. "I hate to ask that, but it's not as if we can really achieve privacy here." Alice followed her gaze. Their assistant's desk, now that she thought of it, was remarkably clear. The sample room looked freshly tidied.

A glimmer poked through Alice's fog, the beginnings of a realization. "I'll stay," Alice said, testing it. "I can help with background and make sure your hair and makeup stay fresh. What's the publication?"

Ramona sighed. Her shoulders tensed. She dropped her phone on her desk, and the thud made Alice jump. "Okay, look." Ramona's anger blazed. "I didn't want to tell you this, but *Elle Decor*—"

"Oh, Ramona." Alice spun on her heel. She marched back to her desk and began packing her files for the Kerrigan rumpus room and the new mudroom into her bag.

"Alice, you have a lot going on." Alice shoved her feet into her running shoes as Ramona stood in her doorway. "It seemed like you weren't in the right headspace to really represent the firm. Your kids are having a moment, right? I told *Elle* they'd still want to photograph your dining room. They've asked for an Easter tablescape. Are you doing the custom painting?"

"I can't talk to you," Alice said. She'd joined the firm with Ramona's assurances that they'd become equal partners, that Alice could buy in eventually. And now, when she'd secured their first national

media coverage—the feature that would break Alice out as a first-class practitioner—Ramona had stolen it. "And good luck with the Kerrigan project on your own."

She wasn't sure if she meant it—she had the rumpus room file in her tote—but she raced to leave, nonetheless. As Alice yanked open the door to the hallway, her phone buzzed. She glanced at it. "Alice, it's Julienne," the text read.

"Shit!" Alice shouted. Before she could throw the phone into her Goyard, her eyes skimmed Julienne's next message. "We should probably talk, yes?"

She clenched her fists as she strode toward the exit, but not fast enough to avoid the woman who smiled hopefully at the top of the stairs. With her expensive haircut and bulky camera bag, this was definitely the photographer from *Elle Decor.* "Excuse me?" she said, and Alice had no choice but to stop. "Can you direct me to Ramona Design?"

Sadie Yoshida

That night, after the Quiz Bowl defeat and just four days shy of her thirteenth birthday, Sadie sat on the floor of her room with a clear sight line to the door. If her mother cracked it open, Sadie would be able to toggle out of Snapchat without her seeing the screen. Her mother still didn't know she had the app, even though she had discovered the Finsta. Given everything—the Finsta, the video, the call Mr. Whittaker had made to her mom on Thursday—Sadie was sure she should have been in much bigger trouble. But her parents just seemed confused.

Luckily, they'd both been distracted by the UN Service Award. Her mom had written yet another email to Mr. Whittaker after dinner describing what Sadie had done to get it. There'd been all those hours at the food packing place and all the winter clothing drives at the elementary school.

Sadie thought about Tane's hand on her shoulder that afternoon, the warm feeling that had lingered even after he'd pulled it away. She'd felt that warmth with Teddy once, too. They'd been on the way to the homecoming game, their arms brushing each other's in the back seat as Sadie sat in the middle between Teddy and Donovan.

Sadie had been so excited to go to that football game. It was the first time she'd been allowed to go to an event like that without a parent. But as soon as her mom dropped them at the high school, Teddy had

beelined toward Alexandra Hunt at the concession stand. Sadie had been stunned, but Alexandra did have the biggest bra cup size of anyone in the seventh grade. By halftime, Teddy and Alexandra had been sitting together in the stands near the eighth graders. Sadie had seen their arms touching just as hers and Teddy's had an hour before in the back seat of her mom's Jeep.

On the ride home she'd watched Teddy and Alexandra Snapchat. He hadn't even noticed she was looking. Now, Sadie pushed away the residual embarrassment she felt about crying in front of her mom that night. Nothing had really happened, and yet she'd been so sad. Nobody—not Teddy and not her mom—really understood her.

When the stuff with Tane started happening last week, she had felt better. She and Tane were both Quiz Bowl nerds. Tane had been happy to see her at his lunch table. Sadie had helped him after the assembly. People mostly felt bad for him instead of making fun of him. The improvement was a lot because of her. Maybe this was her chance to take things to the next level.

"Football game?" Sadie asked Tane in a Snapchat caption. The last home game was that weekend. The pic she sent was of her raised eyebrow, her right one. She had darkened it with pencil that day, just like she did for her skating competitions.

Tane's reply photo showed the underside of his chin. Not the most attractive angle, but it made Sadie laugh. "Sounds good," he said.

"It's a date?" Sadie used a filter to make her eyes look extra wide. She held her breath as she waited for his reply. She was ninety-nine percent sure he'd say yes, but the one percent made her tense.

"I guess." Tane cheesed with a hyperextended thumbs-up. *Adorable*, Sadie thought. She flopped back on the floor, contemplating her next message. She flattened her shoulders against her rag rug, the gradations between the fabric twists pleasantly firm against her back.

She had about six minutes until her nine o'clock phone cutoff. Sadie puffed her cheeks for her next Snap, aiming to make Tane laugh.

She held the phone above her face, and her hair looked extra shiny in the low light against her pink rug. She sent the photo without a caption.

Tane snapped back in an instant, a silly grin on his face. He, too, seemed to be lying on the floor, a crumpled sweatshirt in the frame above his head.

"Are you lying down?" she typed back. "Me, too." It felt risky, this message. Sadie remembered Teddy and Alexandra near the concession stand, and then later, their arms pressed together in the bleachers.

She had to read Tane's reply three times before she was sure she understood it. He'd written, "Show me your Ts?" The picture was of his gray T-shirt. She could see his arms reaching up to take the selfie of his chest.

Sadie gasped and dropped her phone on her stomach. She could hear the low murmur of her parents still talking at the kitchen table downstairs. She watched her cell phone rise and fall on her belly with her breath. Had he really just asked? Of course, they'd talked about this kind of thing in health and wellness class, and her mother awkwardly brought up sexting when they were alone in the car together. But all of that had been hypothetical. Now, she had Tane, who was a real boy. He was a nerd, like her. Did this mean they trusted each other?

Sadie wished she had a little more time to think. If she did, she might text Mikaela for advice. But of course, she knew what Mikaela would say. Mikaela was the one who wore her cutoffs so short that her butt cheeks showed. She flaunted her bra straps. She'd been sent to Whittaker's office for a midriff violation at least three times that fall.

And Sadie only had four minutes until her apps would go off, the phone yielding to her mom's parental controls.

"Show me your Ts?" *He for sure meant tits, right?* Sadie blushed just thinking of the word.

But this was Tane. Tane from Quiz Bowl with purple nail polish. He'd never dated anyone, as far as Sadie knew. He'd probably never seen a girl's anything. Being his first seemed appropriate, given what

they'd been through. Plus, she rationalized, Snapchats disappeared. It wasn't Instagram Live.

Sadie glanced at her closed door and pulled her white shirt up over her bra. She pulled just one of the cups down and felt goose bumps form all the way up her stomach. She held the phone over her head and squealed, the thrill of taking this snap matched by the fear of getting caught.

Hurry, she thought as she set up the pic, her nipple—she *hated* that word—in the center. Her hair swirled over the rug and just a sliver of her chin showed in the upper corner of the frame. She captioned the message, "I've never done this before," and sent it to Tane.

Alice Sullivan

- - - - -

O
n Sunday, after Patrick had Ubered back to the airport for the second week of the Energy Lab trial, Alice locked her bedroom door and made herself call Julienne at their pre-arranged time.

"I'm so sorry," she began as soon as Julienne answered. Alice flashed back to the call with Janna Lagerhead she'd made just nine days before. *Let this be the end of big dramatic apologies for a while*, Alice thought. And then she remembered she still had to grovel to Nadia.

"Let's start fresh." Julienne sounded just like she had in the session with Teddy: calm, friendly, and commanding.

"Good idea." Alice breathed deeply and channeled Oprah.

"First, I'd love to talk about Teddy for just a minute, since you already brought me in on that."

Alice shivered. "Of course." She slid down on her bed, resting her head against her leaf-print sham.

Julienne launched into a thorough description of the nature therapy groups Nadia had told her about. "Perfect for Teddy," Julienne said. She spoke for several minutes about walking barefoot outside, which seemed to be a key component of her program. "Earthing," Julienne called it, and Alice was grateful she wasn't having this conversation live. Her eye rolls became more and more exaggerated as Julienne spoke about dirt and electrons. *Oprah*, she thought.

"I know it sounds crazy," Julienne said, "but I could forward you the research that shows that earthing increases antioxidants and decreases inflammation." Alice blinked as she registered again the similarities in Julienne's voice and her mother's, their cadence and tenor remarkably alike. "And, anecdotally, in my practice I've seen an almost one hundred percent success rate in the improvement of sleep."

Alice imagined Teddy's protests against "earthing" with Donovan on the weekends. "Teddy doesn't have a problem with sleep," she said.

"That's good news." Julienne sounded dispassionate. "But usually in these cases of emotional dysregulation, we're seeing sleep disruptions on some level. You might just not be aware of them."

Alice gritted her teeth and swallowed a retort about how she thought she knew her child well enough. She clearly didn't. Otherwise, she wouldn't have been blindsided by his behavior, and they'd never have ended up in Julienne's office in the first place. And, Alice realized, if she were a better decision maker, she wouldn't have snuck into Green Haven to do reconnaissance at her son's potential expense. Alice threw an arm over her face, the flannel of her shirt soft against her cheek.

"Look," Julienne said, "I'll be honest with you. You've made things awkward here, right? But based on what Evelyn has told me, and based on my conversation with Teddy, I feel strongly that he could benefit from our program. He's a great kid." Alice's heart swelled just a little. Julienne could see Teddy's goodness from just one session. "Your family," Julienne continued, "you don't really get outside much, do you? And even thinking of your job, you're singularly focused on interiors?"

Alice frowned and sank deeper into the duvet. What was wrong with being focused on interiors? And Teddy played soccer outside all the time. She was about to say so when Julienne continued. "Teddy mentioned he plays soccer?"

Alice felt vindicated. That was an outdoor activity. Adrian even "earthed" during the games, barefoot on the sidelines. "He does. We spend a lot of time outside," she added, "watching him."

"That's one of the great paradoxes of organized sports. It seems like you're doing the right thing—your kids are outside and learning life lessons about winning and losing, right? But parents don't consider the impact of the fungicides and pesticides that those fields are doused in."

Alice increased the pressure of her arm against the bridge of her nose.

"We're talking neurotoxicity that can cause long-term health effects that in many cases outweigh the benefits of the exercise in the first place."

Alice tried to keep her voice level. "I feel like with all the research we've seen on childhood obesity and addiction to social media . . . Being outside at all is probably worth the risk? And," she added, "doesn't your kid play soccer?"

"Yes, and I pad my stats with forest bathing." Julienne laughed, the same chortle Alice had been hearing her whole life from her mother.

"Forest bathing?" Alice felt her quads tense.

"It's the Japanese practice of being in nature."

"Okay."

"So I'm going to recommend my colleague Milo Underhill's group," Julienne said. "He's great, and seeing as I'm related to Teddy, it wouldn't be appropriate for me to continue his treatment. That's obvious, right?"

Alice flopped her free arm on the bed and stared at the ceiling. "I'll have him do the group." It seemed the only option, both to appease Julienne and also because it wasn't as if she had a backup therapist waiting in the wings. "But—" She couldn't hang up without making a last request, even though she could feel her cheeks heating. "Could we please not tell my—our—um, Evelyn?" *God damn it!* "About this? I'd really rather she not know that I . . ." Alice tipped her head back.

"You'd rather she not know that you risked your child's mental health in order to spy on me?" Julienne said it lightly, but Alice deflated further.

"I said I was sorry," Alice offered.

"I really don't want secrets getting in the way of my relationship with Evelyn. There have already been too many of those, don't you think?"

"Mmm-hmm." Alice cringed.

"But," Julienne said confidently, betraying none of the awkwardness that Alice was drowning in, "I'm not actually allowed to tell Evelyn. HIPAA and all. You know"—she paused—"ethics."

"Right." Alice turned her face into the covers.

"I recommend that you tell her, though," Julienne continued. "Like I said, there are too many secrets. And what are the chances, anyway, that she never finds out?" None, Alice realized, chastised. She imagined introducing Teddy to Julienne's family someday, as her mother would undoubtedly desire.

As soon as Alice hung up, she felt itchy with tension, like she needed to go for a long, hard run. As she changed into her workout clothes, she realized the miles wouldn't make her feel better unless she also cleared her conscience. Calling her mother seemed too hard, but she could start with Nadia. She opened her text app and clicked on the thread in which she'd said that Donovan was worse than Teddy. She shook her head at her hubris. "I'm an idiot," she wrote. "And I'm so, so sorry."

Tane Lagerhead

– – – – –

Everything felt different when Tane walked through the front door of Elm Creek Junior High on Monday. He couldn't stop thinking about it. He saw Sadie's shiny skin and the brown of the nipple— even the word made him shiver. He could almost feel little ridges like goose bumps around its eraser-tip center.

Over and over again on Sunday, and again that morning during breakfast and on the bus, he'd checked his phone to verify that the whole thing had indeed happened. If he hadn't taken a video of Sadie's snap with his mom's old iPad, the one he'd used all the time before he'd finally gotten a phone, he might not have even trusted his memory.

If he'd screenshotted Sadie's pic, she would have gotten a Snapchat alert, but since he took a video on another device, it would be his to keep. She'd never know. His one chance to see actual boob. He had planned to tell Sadie that he was kidding about the pic when she refused. "LOL," he'd planned to type.

But he was ready when she responded just in case. And then she'd done it. Once he had the video on the iPad, he'd messaged it to himself and deleted it from the tablet.

Tane looked down at his favorite striped T-shirt that morning, his joggers, his navy Brooks. He had given up on coolness in elementary. He was the weird kid, the mythology whiz and Quiz Bowl captain with

purple nail polish. But somehow, none of those nerd flags had mattered that weekend when he'd asked Sadie for the picture.

He looked up from his phone as the bus rolled past Elm Creek Park. "There it is!" shrieked Mikaela Heffernan from the back. He swiveled his head in time to see another hot pink dick, this one painted on the garbage can near the soccer field. The spray painter had added a hashtag near the right ball, but nothing followed it. The girls were still laughing about it when Tane pressed play one more time on his phone. There again was the proof of his changing life: Sadie Yoshida with her bra off.

At school, he could hardly wait for math class, the first time he'd see her during the day. He wondered if he was supposed to treat her differently now or maybe put his arm around her. She found him in the hallway after choir, in the passing time before math. She'd detoured, he realized, to meet him. He smiled and tried hard not to stare directly at her chest.

"Hey," she said. Sadie yanked her ponytail in the same way he'd seen her do in Quiz Bowl, usually when she was stumped about an answer.

"Hey." He froze. Would they pretend that nothing had happened?

She leaned in and whispered, "I can't believe I, like, did that." Tane looked over her head at Mikaela, who was staring at the two of them from down the hall. Did Mikaela know about the Snapchat? So far, Tane hadn't told anyone.

"I can't believe it either," Tane said.

They walked away from Mikaela, each carrying an algebra textbook. Tane tried to think of something to say, but all of his ideas—*What did you do last weekend?* or *Have you thought of a Halloween costume?*—seemed stupid. Finally, he landed on "Did you do your math homework? Number five was impossible." And then he blushed. It was true that number five had been impossible. He tried to imagine Sadie lying on that pink rug, the one he'd seen in the picture, with her

book open. He glanced down at her chest at the same time she looked up at him.

"The homework was really hard," she agreed.

Don't be weird, he told himself, and then asked another question about rational numbers.

"You can text me about that stuff," Sadie said as they took their seats. "I usually get the homework."

"Cool." Tane dropped his book on his desktop and flipped through his notebook to the most recent problems. Sadie turned away from him to talk to Chloe Cushing. *Has Chloe ever seen Sadie with her bra off?*

Stop it, he commanded. Now that he'd gotten his first conversation with Sadie over with, things could be normal, right? Normal by lunchtime? Normal, except that he could look at that pic whenever he wanted. He could see it a million times a day if he felt like it. And he was pretty sure that most of the seventh grade, not McCoy Blumenfeld and definitely not Teddy Sullivan, had ever gotten something like that from an actual person, and definitely not from someone as hot as Sadie Yoshida.

Alice Sullivan

- - - -

Teddy appeared in Alice's door frame after she'd read with Aidy and tucked her in. Alice felt victorious after twenty-seven minutes of actual level E reading and held a tepid cup of chamomile in both hands.

"Can I have my phone?" Teddy blurted.

Alice smiled. She'd been waiting for this request but also "taking his lead" as her parenting manuals suggested.

Before she could answer him, Teddy piped up again. "Don't you, like, need me to have it in order to pick me up from soccer?" He paused. "Or whatever?"

Solid effort, she thought. "Yes," she said, and then steeled herself. "But I've made some adjustments to our family rules." She took a breath. Alice had been skeptical when Meredith had told her about the monitoring software she'd installed on Sadie's phone last winter. Alice remembered thinking that parents should demonstrate trust in their kids. Now, Teddy had proven totally unworthy. Meredith, once again, had been right. Not that Alice could give her any credit, seeing as they weren't speaking. The sense of accomplishment she'd enjoyed after finishing the reading dissipated.

As Alice prepared to launch into her phone plan with Teddy, she felt nerves flutter beneath her breastbone. Before last week, it had never occurred to her to be wary of her child. He'd been an open book—not al-

ways perfectly behaved, but always easy to figure out. Now, she couldn't help thinking of the Phil Donahue show, those episodes her mother had watched when Alice was little, parents crying about their teens' reckless behavior. Her mother used to talk back to the television screen. "Open your eyes!" she'd say, as if raising teens were just common sense.

"What adjustments?" Teddy asked.

Alice glanced at herself in the asymmetrical mirror she'd hung over her dresser. Her eyeliner had migrated past her lower lid, and she wiped the smudge away with her index finger. "Why don't you sit down." Alice pointed at her duvet, the large printed leaf pattern rumpled in the places she'd already sat. She walked to her closet to retrieve Teddy's phone from a summer handbag, a new hiding place where he'd never look.

"I'm going to give this back to you, but you'll have to sign a contract." She'd done online research for this part and edited one she'd found on some parenting expert's website. She plucked a printed copy out of the drawer in her bedside table and handed it to Teddy. "Take a look." She sat beside him. "Dad and I have agreed on these conditions, and if you're in agreement as well, you sign. And then you can have your phone back."

She sipped her tea while he read the rules.

"You're going to look at my texts?" Teddy asked.

Alice had gone back and forth on this point. "I'm not going to read every one, and I didn't purchase the cloning software." Teddy looked blank, so she added, "That's the type of program that lets me see all of your keystrokes—everything you type and everything you click." Teddy's nostrils flared, an expression she remembered from his toddlerhood. "I *didn't* get that," Alice reiterated. "But Dad and I will periodically scan your text messages. And you'll have to let us do it at will."

"At will?" Alice couldn't quite read his tone, but so far, he wasn't yelling or screaming. He hadn't stormed back to his room and slammed the door.

"It means whenever we ask, you have to let us. Why don't you keep going?" She pointed at the contract. "You see you'll have to delete your Finsta." She felt embarrassed just thinking about his alter ego, @Ted-Baller420. As if he even knew what 420 meant. She'd searched his room from top to bottom when he'd been on a mandated walk with Weasley and found absolutely no evidence of drug paraphernalia, thank God. "And Dad and I can look at your Instagram anytime."

"No Snapchat?" Teddy asked.

"That's right." Alice felt her confidence building.

"But everyone has it. People use that now instead of texting."

"It's non-negotiable," Alice said. She tried to sound like Julienne, calm but definite. "You'll have to decide whether it's worth having a phone without it."

"What's this about parental controls?" Teddy arrived at the bottom of the page.

"Your phone will turn off at nine p.m." She'd stolen this rule directly from Meredith. "I've installed an app on my phone that controls it. It'll turn off all of your apps except calling."

"That's completely unfair."

Alice glanced at herself again in the mirror, hoping her face reflected her determination. *Not bad*, she thought. "You can choose," she told Teddy. "You can either sign this contract, or not have a phone." Teddy held the paper taut between his hands and Alice wondered if he might tear it up. "After all," Alice said, aiming for lightness, "Dad and I didn't have cell phones until we were in college."

"College?" Teddy's eyes bulged, and Alice nodded. "Okay," Teddy finally said. "It's not like you're giving me a freaking choice."

Alice winced at "freaking," though it could have been worse.

She grabbed a pen from her nightstand and held it out to Teddy. "Sign at the bottom."

"Really? We're actually signing?" Teddy sounded pissed but stared greedily at his phone. Alice glanced at the time on her alarm clock. It was already 8:14. Teddy's apps would automatically turn off at nine.

"I want things to be official," Alice said. "No Finsta, no Snapchat, no angry DMs or texts. Talk to Dad and me if you're upset about something online." She held the phone out to him. "You've got forty-six minutes until the apps turn off."

Teddy left her room without saying anything, his thumbs already scrolling.

Teddy Sullivan

— — — —

Whittaker said Teddy's new class schedule, which he started on Tuesday, would give him a fresh start. The assistant principal had separated him in classes from all of his friends, and it wasn't until Teddy made it to the lunchroom that he even saw McCoy or Landon or Sadie. Her birthday was the next day, he knew—October 30, just a day before Halloween. She'd had about eight ghost-themed birthday parties over the years. He wondered if she was having one this year, if he just wasn't invited.

"Do *not* approach her," Whittaker had said that morning, as if she were a nuclear bomb. Teddy had been required to check in with the assistant principal in his office before he went to first hour. Things had been better when he'd never even spoken to Whittaker. Now, Teddy knew how the guy's shampoo smelled—the same, he thought, as his dad's. Teddy had sometimes used the brown bottle himself, though now he wouldn't do that again.

Teddy promised Whittaker he wouldn't speak to Sadie either, even though she was the one who'd started it. He didn't even *want* to talk to her. But then, on that very first day of his new schedule, she walked into the cafeteria just ahead of him. He thought about turning around and moving to the back of the line, but they made eye contact when Sadie looked over her shoulder. She didn't mean to look at him. Teddy knew that. She was probably checking for one of her friends. Or for Tane.

Teddy looked quickly away, a sourness rising in his throat. He let a few kids push in front of him, stalling near the stack of cafeteria trays, and he felt better when McCoy pulled up next to him. "Hey." Teddy flashed a peace sign.

McCoy slapped his shoulder, which seemed normal. He'd never said anything about the video, thank God. McCoy hadn't even mentioned Gigi or the diapers.

Just as Teddy was planning what to say next—should he bring up that evening's soccer practice? Tomorrow's math test?—he felt the tray of the person behind him dig into his back, just above the waistband of his pants. He turned, irritated, and then gasped when he made eye contact with Tane. "*Avoid*," Whittaker had said about him, too.

"God, Lagerhead," Teddy said. Whittaker hadn't covered what to do if Tane approached *him*. He couldn't very well ignore him when he'd run into his back. "Watch it." He glanced at Tane's hands, looking for his nail polish, but Tane's index fingers were tucked beneath his tray.

Tane didn't say anything, so Teddy turned toward the lunch lady, who deposited a fistful of mini corn dogs on his tray. "Shut up," Tane said, quiet enough so only Teddy could hear. His response was so delayed that Teddy couldn't even remember what he'd said to prompt it.

He grabbed a serving of limp-looking fries from under the heat lamp next to the corn dog station. "I can't believe you did that to me, man," Teddy whispered. "Those things you said in that video."

"Are you kidding?" They'd reached the end of the serving line and Teddy could see that across the lunchroom Sadie was getting settled with the other Quiz Bowl kids. Talk about betrayals. Had Sadie totally rejected Chloe and Mikaela? Why did she like the Quiz Bowl team so much better? Teddy had seen Douglas Lim's Finsta post the previous night about taking Sadie's spot in the next competition.

Teddy felt his forearms tense, and he thought again about Sadie and Tane planning the Instagram Live. They'd probably done it right there at their lunch table. She knew exactly what to say to humiliate him the most.

"It doesn't change anything, you know. You're not suddenly Mr. Popular," Teddy said, his whisper fervent. "It takes a lot more than that. One video and you're the best? And Sadie is, like, your girlfriend? Is that what you think?" Teddy was sure that if Whittaker were here, he'd separate the two of them. The corn dogs rolled precariously on Tane's tray, and Teddy fought the urge to hit the bottom of it and send his food flying. *Not worth it*, he told himself, remembering the hard plastic chairs in the office, the smell of Whittaker's shampoo. He and Tane walked toward the condiment station.

"You think what I did was worse than what you did?" Tane's voice sounded choked.

Teddy gritted his teeth. "It was so much fucking worse. You told everyone everything. And at assembly I thought you had gym shorts on under your joggers like usual. That was an accident."

"In some ways I should be thanking you," Tane said. "Before that assembly, I had no shot at winning that hashtag thing, but now everyone's on my side." Teddy saw McCoy waiting for him near the cashier, his deli sandwich and chips in hand. Teddy pointed toward their usual table, and McCoy walked away.

"Do you think this stupid hashtag thing means anything?" Teddy tried to sound firm, but even he had to acknowledge his uncertainty. "Remember just last year when you had to get Ms. Tierney to make us let you play football? Nobody actually likes you. You're still you."

"Me, but with a girlfriend." Tane smiled down at him as he pumped ketchup from the industrial-sized dispenser.

"Sadie Yoshida?" Teddy shook his head.

Tane shrugged. He licked ketchup from the tip of his thumb.

"You can't just say that if it's not true. You have to prove something like that."

"I don't owe you anything."

"Like you said, I put you on the map with that assembly." Teddy took a step away toward his friends. "If you have a girlfriend now, it's actually all because of me."

"Oh my God," Tane said to his back. "Do you have, like, the world's tiniest dick or something? Is that why you're such an asshole?" Teddy turned around in time to see Tane swivel his head, checking for adults that might have overheard him.

Coward, Teddy thought. "You're lying. I knew it. Nail polish never gets girlfriends. It just makes you totally fucking weird. Who would go out with you?" Teddy walked toward McCoy. At least four of their soccer teammates were at their usual table, a spot saved for Teddy. Things, he thought, might just be okay.

And then suddenly Tane was next to him again. "Check your DMs," Tane said, spit gathering at the corners of his mouth. He whipped his phone from his pocket and clicked a few times before storming away.

Teddy felt his cell phone buzz as he sat down. They weren't allowed to have phones in school, but the lunchroom monitors didn't seem to care, and in any case, Teddy's back was to them. He checked his messages.

"Whoa," he said aloud. "Jesus Christ." He blinked several times at the video Tane had sent, a video of someone opening a Snapchat on an iPhone. The photo showed a girl with her top partway off. Teddy's eyes bugged.

"What?" asked McCoy.

"Dude, I can't even believe this." Teddy beckoned him closer and held his phone under the table. Once McCoy was watching, he showed him the DM.

"What the fuck?" McCoy breathed. "Who even is that? Where'd you get it?"

Teddy looked over at Tane's table. Tane stared at them, his mouth slightly open.

"I think it's Sadie Yoshida," Teddy said. Actually, he knew it was her. He'd seen that rug a million times. They'd built Duplos on it as little kids.

"Send me a screenshot," said McCoy. "That's freaking legendary."

Alice Sullivan

— — — — —

Alice stared at her oily store-bought tortellini and sad-looking microwaved peas. "A starch, not a vegetable," she knew Meredith would say about the peas. But Nadia would remind her that at least dinner wasn't something truly terrible like Coke with a side of Doritos. Alice felt grateful for both the Nadia in her head and the one in her text messages who had responded to her apology with a heart emoji. "Thanks," she'd written. "Onward."

Still, Alice had thought about throwing some baby spinach on everyone's plates. She had a plastic tub of it in reasonably good shape in the refrigerator, but the kids wouldn't have eaten it anyway. She put a piece of pasta in her mouth and felt the cheese ooze around the al dente noodle as she bit. "What was for hot lunch?" Alice hoped they'd had something healthy, so she could absolve herself of this five-minute meal.

Her chin dropped when Adrian said, "Mini corn dogs." Her daughter smiled around a mouthful of pasta. "And guess what, Mom?" Alice caught a glimpse of mashed peas mixed into the white sauce as her daughter chewed. "Guess what Nana told me when she picked me up?"

Alice felt her shoulders tense. She hadn't followed through on Julienne's suggestion that she tell her mother about the session at Green Haven. In fact, they hadn't really spoken since Alice had promised to contact Julienne. Her mom had agreed via text to the usual Tuesday

pickup. Alice could probably have escaped work early given the state of her collaborations with Ramona, but she wanted to get some of her simpler projects finished and invoiced in case she decided to leave for good. She and her mother had passed in the mudroom when Alice had arrived at home. Alice hadn't invited her to stay for dinner. "What did Nana tell you?"

Adrian's smile went comically wide, her eyes bright. "I have a new aunt and cousins!"

Alice coughed, a tortellini catching in the back of her throat.

"What?" Teddy asked.

Alice stood from the table, still coughing, and filled a glass with water. She faced away from the children longer than she needed to. She finally managed to choke out a question: "Nana told you that?"

"Yeah! Is it a secret?" Adrian got up on her knees, her face alight. "When she picked me up today, she said I would be meeting my new aunt and cousins soon. Mom, can you believe it?"

"What are you even talking about?" Teddy scowled at his sister. "And is she allowed to sit like that?"

"Worry about yourself," Alice said automatically. She wished Patrick were here. How could she explain the complexities of Julienne alone and on the fly? She couldn't believe her mother hadn't at least given her a heads-up. "Yes," said Alice. She couldn't very well deny it. "Well." She glanced up at the swatches she'd painted on the dining room wall, research for the custom job she still hoped to procure. "I was waiting for the right moment to talk to you both about this, but yes, Nana has recently met a family member we never knew about."

Alice channeled Oprah again and simultaneously imagined shouting at Siri after dinner to dial her mother on speakerphone. "When Nana was very young—" Alice began. "Did she tell you this, Aidy?"

"She said she had a baby when she was too young to take care of it. She said it was just like your birth mother, Mom. That's why Nana took care of you, remember?"

Alice felt her eyes narrow. She resisted this connection to Julienne, and she definitely didn't want to consider their similarities in discussion with her seven-year-old daughter.

But even as Alice imagined unloading on her mother about the inappropriateness of her revelation, she knew she'd lose the argument. After she confessed the trip to Green Haven, her mom would say that Alice had started it. Alice had been the one to leverage her own child's well-being against her curiosity.

"I do remember," she said to Aidy. "And now, Nana has met her baby. She's all grown up. She's older than Daddy and me." Alice watched as Teddy shoved three tortellini in his mouth at once. She'd have to tell him, eventually, that Dr. Martín was Nana's mystery baby. She hoped by then he'd be fully invested in Milo Underhill's nature therapy. "Do you have any questions?" Alice asked, though she hadn't really explained anything. *Listen to Me* had suggested that parents only answer the questions kids actually ask, rather than to go on about things they weren't ready for.

"I have a question," Teddy said. Alice swallowed a sticky bite of pasta and grabbed her water glass for a chaser. She braced herself: Teddy had a glint in his eye, a ferocity she'd seen in his bedtime negotiations and on the soccer field.

"Go for it," she said.

"Why is this family always so fucked up?"

Alice wilted. *Was it true that the family was fucked up?* Maybe they were—Teddy's suspension, Aidy's delayed reading, Nana's secret daughter.

"I don't know." She looked at Patrick's empty seat. If he were here, he'd have dealt with the swearing.

"Mom!" Aidy shrieked, pointing at Teddy. "He said 'fuck'!"

"And also"—Teddy transferred a clump of peas onto his fork with his fingers, ignoring his sister—"who's taking me to soccer practice?"

Evelyn Brown

Evelyn had thought about playing off her confession to Aidy as an accident. It could have been. She was helping Alice even though she was behind on her own writing and had emails from at least four advisees in the hopper. She was distracted, and she could say she'd accidentally mentioned Julienne.

But Alice knew Evelyn better than anyone, had watched her spin and process her life events in real time for thirty-seven years. Evelyn never divulged without premeditation.

In reality, when Evelyn blurted the truth about Julienne to Adrian, she felt a sort of catharsis. As she claimed her firstborn daughter more and more times, as she told a few friends, a colleague, and Alice, the solidity of Julienne's place in her life felt heavier and more. And better.

And their upcoming Thanksgiving dinner would normalize things further. Evelyn had already imagined the family photos she'd take, how Adrian and Laura would look standing side by side. She imagined Teddy and Miguel exchanging stories from the soccer field. To think, her grandchildren had played on neighboring teams, and the boys were just eighteen months apart in age. They could have played together! The image both thrilled her and made her deeply sad. She could never get back the time she'd missed with the Martíns, a fact that made it all the more important that she integrate them as completely and immediately as possible.

So as Adrian had sat in the back seat and sweetly asked, "How was your day, Nana?" the first and only thing Evelyn had wanted to say was, "It was a great day because I got to talk to my new daughter."

And that was true. Every day was great because she got to talk to her new daughter. And so she'd said it, out loud into the Camry, her declaration seeming to reverberate against the rear window.

Evelyn had held her breath, waiting to see if Adrian would react. A couple of beats of silence went by, and Evelyn started to feel relieved. But then, Aidy asked, "Mom is your daughter?" Her face arranged itself just exactly like Alice's always did when she felt confused, her left eyebrow cocked and her little mouth scrunched in a slight frown.

Evelyn had weighed her options for a moment. She could have backtracked at this point, but she'd always believed in telling children the truth. "I know." Evelyn had smiled—a real, relieved smile. "But I have another daughter, too."

She expected Alice's call right when she got it, had even predicted that she'd be on speakerphone in the kitchen, listening to the sounds of Alice rinsing dishes in the background. Although she wasn't Alice's biological mother, she knew her on a cellular level. She'd lived her childhood, she'd been there when she'd become a mother herself. Evelyn knew her admission would set off ripples, and that was why she was already in her car. She had been driving to Alice's neighborhood when her daughter's call came in. She had the file she wanted to share with her ready on the front seat.

"I hadn't planned on telling Adrian," Evelyn said. "But in the moment, Alice, it just seemed right."

"I was blindsided!" Alice yelled.

"Where are the kids?"

"Are you suggesting I'd have this conversation in front of them?" Evelyn turned the volume down. "You're the one who told Adrian—my *seven*-year-old—a secret you kept from me for thirty-seven years and then didn't even give me a heads-up about it."

Evelyn parked her car in front of Alice's house and peered through the front window into the living room. She knew Alice was standing in the adjoining kitchen, just out of view. "It seemed like we were making progress. Julienne said the two of you talked. She said you had some updates for me?"

Evelyn had broken into an outright grin over lunch the day before when Julienne had said that she and Alice had spoken live. She'd even clapped her hands over her pine nut and prosciutto salad, imagining the two of them together in conversation. She pictured them for a moment as little kids, building something out of Legos in the house in which she'd raised Alice. That image, too, like the one of Teddy and Miguel on the soccer field, had taken her breath away. Now, Alice was suddenly silent on the other end of the line.

"Alice?" Evelyn turned up the volume again, now that her daughter had stopped yelling.

"Okay," Alice said. "So, you know how my friend Nadia recommended a therapist for Teddy?"

"Yes. You were so smart to get right on that. I'm really proud of—"

Alice rushed on, "Well, the therapist was Julienne at Green Haven. I took Teddy there." The words came so fast it took Evelyn a moment to make sense of them. "Like, we saw her," Alice said.

Evelyn squinted at the line of houses on Alice's block. "You what?"

"You know," Alice said, her voice sounding strident again over the Bluetooth, "you're the one who kept a secret for decades. For my whole life. You could have told me at any time that Julienne existed, but you didn't. I just needed to see her for myself, and it was a coincidence! Nadia really *did* suggest her, and I'd already made the appointment when you told me who she was."

Evelyn gripped the gear shift and squinted. "Okay, but are you telling me you risked Teddy's mental health to, what? Like, spy?" Evelyn didn't wait for Alice to answer. "That's kind of crazy, Alice."

"You said we're not supposed to say 'crazy' anymore." Evelyn

breathed in. She had told Alice to eliminate the word "crazy" from her vocabulary. She'd read new research that it reinforced mental health stigma. "You have to know, I wanted to tell you about your sister," she said. "I wanted to tell you from the time you were a little girl." Evelyn remembered almost spilling the news on Julienne's birthdays in multiple years. "Your dad was the one who was always against it."

"That's a cop-out." Alice still sounded angry. "You're always telling me each person is responsible for her own decisions. Right? So this was your choice. And now you've taken away my choices." Evelyn could hear a cabinet door slam. "I wanted to decide how to break this news to my kids."

"It's not really your news to break." Evelyn flinched. Alice wouldn't like that, the implication that something regarding her children was out of her control. But she was learning this lesson anyway, right? With Adrian's reading and Teddy's discipline problems? The Julienne news was just one more example of something she'd have to roll with. Before Alice could answer, Evelyn continued. "Look, can I come in? I'm outside. I figured this would be an issue, and I wanted to discuss it in person."

"God, Mom." Evelyn watched Alice walk into the family room and peer out the window, verifying that indeed, Evelyn's car was there. Evelyn raised her hand in a wave, though Alice probably couldn't see her in the dark. Alice hung up.

Evelyn killed the ignition and pulled the collar of her fleece jacket up. Alice had never been one of those adopted children who seemed consumed by curiosity about her biological origins. Even as a teenager, Alice had been content with just the most basic health information. She'd never even asked for her birth parents' names. Evelyn thought that maybe when she divorced Frank, Alice might feel a sense of loss that guided her back in history, but it was only after the intake appointment at her OB-GYN when she was newly pregnant with Teddy that she'd posed any specific questions. "Do you know how long my birth mother's labor was with me?" she wanted to know. "Did she need a c-section?"

Evelyn hadn't known those answers. She still didn't, though she knew quite a bit more now than she had then. For most of Alice's life, Evelyn felt relieved by her daughter's ambivalence. She'd seen patients who fixated on their "bio parents," as she called them. The kids and adoptive parents in these cases seemed decidedly different from one another. Although Evelyn would never say "ill-suited," she did think it sometimes—a highly athletic mom and a kid with no hand-eye coordination, for example, or a dad with a PhD and a son who couldn't for the life of him maintain a 3.0.

Of course, a biological bond never guaranteed an easy affinity. And despite their disparate DNA, Evelyn had always felt completely connected to Alice. And, Evelyn realized with a touch of pleasure, Alice now needed her more than ever. There was the sudden storm in her own nuclear family, and the arrival of Julienne in her family of origin. Evelyn would support her as she always had.

She grabbed her file and traversed the front walkway, making a more formal entrance than she usually did through the garage.

"You should call first before you just show up here," Alice said as she opened the door.

"I know." Evelyn encouraged her clients to set boundaries all the time, and in almost all areas of her life, she adhered to them perfectly. "It's just that this is an emotional situation, and I wanted to follow up in person." Evelyn raised her eyebrows. "And now I know you've met Julienne."

"I don't need to be scolded." Alice walked away from her toward the kitchen. Evelyn looked down at her own pilled yoga pants and compared them to Alice's brand-new-looking ones. The wool socks Alice wore over them—gray with turquoise contour lines—made the casual outfit somehow chic.

Evelyn glanced up the stairs, where she assumed the kids were. Neither of them seemed to have heard her come in. "But it was wrong, right? To go to Green Haven? How did you think it would play out? Obviously we'd all realize eventually."

When they'd reached the kitchen, Alice collapsed onto the stool where she usually sat. She pulled out her ponytail and then refastened it, an old habit. "I told you, okay? I made the appointment before I knew. And yes"—she raised a hand and lowered it again in concession—"I guess I couldn't resist."

"Okay." Evelyn laid her file folder on the counter, thinking of the several pieces of legal paper she'd shoved inside. It was Frank who'd always loved the yellow lined paper, but Evelyn had gotten accustomed to using it, too. She'd kept pads around even after they'd split. "I get that, and so I hope you'll also understand what I'm going to tell you next."

Alice put her head down, her forehead touching the counter. "No more surprises," she said, and for a moment, Evelyn doubted her purpose.

"Just one more." Better to get it out, she realized, than to keep another omission between them. "I just want to clear all of the air." Alice raised her head and blinked slowly.

Evelyn craned her neck around Alice's shoulder to be sure the kids were still upstairs. "I'm not sure where you are on this these days, and I definitely didn't want to overstep." Alice rolled her eyes at "overstep," but Evelyn pressed on. "I've been doing some research," she said.

Alice sipped ice water from a narrow-lipped mason jar. At least, Evelyn thought, she wasn't having a second or third glass of wine.

"I think it's going to work out with Milo Underhill," Alice said. "Julienne recommended her partner for Teddy. It was insanely awkward after what I did, but I think we're set on the therapist front."

"Not that." Evelyn went for it: "I'm talking about you. About your birth parents."

"What?" Alice stood and opened the pantry. She extracted a handful of fun-sized Snickers bars and dropped them on the counter. She opened one and shoved it whole into her mouth.

Evelyn wondered if she'd have to repeat herself.

"I didn't see that coming," Alice said, her mouth full.

"Really?" Evelyn had figured with all of the adoption talk, Alice would have at least considered her own origins. "You really haven't been feeling any enhanced curiosity about your birth parents?"

"Mom." Alice's long eyelashes fluttered. "I don't know if this is the best time."

"You're saying it hasn't come up for you at all, even with my news?"

Alice unwrapped a second Snickers. "Is this therapy?" Evelyn could still see the remnants of the first candy bar in Alice's mouth as she shoved in the second one.

"Okay," Evelyn said. "But now that I've brought it up, I feel like I should be totally honest. I did a little Internet research using the birthdays I have. Julienne told me how she'd done it to locate me. And now I've done it for you."

"Mom!" Chocolate spewed from Alice's mouth. She grabbed a cloth from the rim of her sink and hastily wiped the steely gray counter. Evelyn studied her daughter's face. The dark hair at her temples had just the slightest hint of gray. Her collarbones, always visible, seemed to jut a bit more than usual under her formfitting athletic shirt.

"I have their names and birthdays." Now that Evelyn had started, she couldn't resist. She opened the folder she'd prepared, the information transcribed neatly on the legal paper. "They don't live in Minnesota anymore, as far as I can tell," Evelyn said. "If you feel anything like I felt after meeting Julienne, if you recognize something in yourself that you didn't even see before—" Evelyn reached for her daughter as she felt tears coming, but Alice slid her stool back just a few inches, putting herself out of reach. "I just want this for you," Evelyn said, her voice quieter now. "I want you to feel whole, too."

"Really?" Alice grabbed a third Snickers, and Evelyn knew she'd be sick. "Because it feels like you're trying to eject me from the family."

Meredith Yoshida

Meredith glanced again at Alice's text as she sat down to lunch in the clinic's break room on Wednesday. "Happy birthday to Sadie. Can we talk?" Meredith pried open her glass bento. She and Sadie were both having smashed chickpeas with pita. Meredith had included a stick of Trident in each of their lunch bags to counteract the red onions. She'd snuck a Kit Kat, the first of the newly opened Halloween candy, into Sadie's as a birthday treat.

Meredith could still feel the warmth of Sadie's body pressed against her in the school hallway last Thursday. It had been hard to leave her there after Teddy's messages, even though Sadie insisted she was okay. Clearly, regardless of what she said, she wasn't herself. Goading Tane into making that Instagram video was completely out of character, though Meredith could see why she'd done it. She was just trying to help him recover some of his social standing after Teddy's cruel prank. Sadie always had rooted for the underdog. Meredith loved that about her. And now she was officially a teenager. It was normal, Meredith knew, for teenagers to have lapses in judgment and to make mistakes.

Meredith could have ignored Alice's text, but she decided to be the bigger person. She'd embody the behaviors she hoped to instill in her daughter.

"I'm not ready," she'd typed. With each letter, she felt her anger

balloon. "I'm not sure I'll ever be ready." Her thumb had throbbed as she'd hit send, Teddy's all-caps "SLUT" flashing in her mind's eye.

"Okay," Alice had written back, "but it seems like they've both done thoughtless things, right? Maybe we can move past this. Onward? I'm working with Teddy on his sense of significance, and we started therapy."

Bullshit, Meredith thought. *Excuses, rather than real contrition.* She wouldn't respond. Teddy had called her daughter a slut, and even though Sadie had played a role, "slut" was a line in the sand.

Meredith opened the clinic's charting software on her laptop. She might as well multitask, to prepare for the onslaught of afternoon patients. She didn't want to spend her evening catching up when they'd be celebrating Sadie's birthday as a family. Meredith had two dozen cupcakes on their kitchen counter ready to send along to synchro practice. Mikaela and Chloe were set to come over for a sleepover on Friday.

Her phone pinged just as she was about to pack up. She sighed, half expecting another plea from Alice, but instead the message was from her daughter. Before she slid it open, she looked at the time: 11:24. Sadie should be in class. A shot of fear froze Meredith's arm.

"Don't panic," read the first text. Too late. Meredith felt a swell of terror beneath her rib cage and quickly skimmed the next message. "But something's happening again with Teddy. And Tane."

Meredith's first thought was that Teddy had a gun. *Of course he doesn't have a gun*, she chastised herself, though it was easy to catastrophize about school shootings when they seemed to happen every other week.

"And Mom," another text read, "don't freak out, but there's something about me."

Meredith blew a long breath out, an attempt to expel her anxiety. Sadie's was certainly a junior high girl thing, the kind of problem she'd been dreaming about solving since the ultrasound tech had shouted "Pink!" in the exam room.

"Whatever it is," Meredith wrote, "we'll tackle it together tonight. I'm sure we can solve it." Meredith had been a whiz at navigating the social scene as a teenager.

"But Mom, it's out there."

"What's out there?" She shoved the remaining half of her lunch into her thermal bag. "Just tell me. What's going on?" Meredith kept her eyes on the response bubbles, waiting.

"There's a picture," Sadie finally wrote. "I don't know why I did it, but Tane asked for a snap, and I sent it."

Meredith gaped at the message, and then she jerked her head up as the door to the break room opened.

"Are you okay?" Meredith's colleague Adriana crossed from the door to where she stood. Meredith jerked her phone toward her chest, hiding it.

"Whoa!" Adriana took a step back and put her palms up.

Meredith kept her head down, embarrassed. "I'm so sorry," she said. "I think this might be an emergency." She forced herself to type the next question, "What kind of picture?" She closed her eyes as she waited for confirmation, praying she was wrong. A few seconds later, she felt her phone pulse.

"My chest," Sadie had written. "With half my bra off."

Meredith's legs shook with adrenaline. "I have a family emergency," she blurted. "Adriana, can you get Jill to cover for me?" She didn't wait for an answer or clear her lunch or grab her computer. She just ran.

Alice Sullivan

We have to talk." Ramona stood at the entry to Alice's office. Alice filled a seagrass basket with files from her desk drawer. Fabric and wallpaper samples stuck out of her folders, options she'd planned to show Ramona or clients in upcoming meetings.

That morning, Alice had backed up all of her electronic files and all of her drawings to her personal Google account. She wasn't sure she could sustain a studio on her own, but she planned to ask Patrick that weekend to review her noncompete clause just in case.

"You're distracted," Ramona continued. "It's obvious." Alice looked up in time to see Ramona gesture at her whole person, sweeping her hand down the length of Alice's torso as if criticizing her outfit. Alice looked down at her green V-neck. There was nothing wrong with it. There was nothing wrong with that or her black jeans, and certainly nothing wrong with her leopard-print flats. Nothing about Alice conveyed distraction.

And while Alice definitely had a lot going on—an understatement, she thought, before pushing the admission out of her mind—this was Ramona grasping at straws. She needed excuses for stealing *Elle Decor* and excuses for not treating Alice as the partner she deserved to be.

"I made a new Slack channel for a powder room remodel," Alice said. "I sent you the wallpapers for the Kerrigan rumpus room. I booked three estimates for the O'Brien kitchen. I'm getting my work done."

Alice collapsed a framed photo of Teddy holding newborn Adrian in a hospital bed and put it in her basket. In the picture, Alice had the kids encircled in her arm, her plastic ID bracelet wrinkled against Teddy's five-year-old elbow. "But for the rest of the week," Alice said, "I'm going to get my work done at home. We need space."

Alice had always felt under the microscope in this glass office, but it was worse since Ramona's backstabbing, the way she'd undermined Alice's growth.

"Working from home isn't really part of our agreement." Alice fell into her desk chair and woke up her computer. If she looked at Ramona, she'd lose it. So instead, she thought of Oprah and scanned her desktop for files she'd missed. Alice felt her teeth grit. She felt the same anger from the night before when her mother had given her that folder. Everyone seemed to want to expel her.

"I can think of a lot of things that weren't part of our agreement." Alice racked her brain for a list. "For instance," she continued, triumphant, "I'm pretty sure it's not part of our agreement for you to schedule client meetings in the conference room when I've already—"

Alice's phone rang then. She startled at the caller ID: Elm Creek Junior High. "Shit," she said aloud, and then she regretted it. If she was trying to appear put together, swearing wouldn't help. Without looking up she said, "I have to take this." Ramona crossed her arms and stayed put. "Do you mind?" Alice asked as the phone buzzed against her palm. Of course, even if Ramona moved, Alice still wouldn't have any privacy in this goddamned office. She pushed her chair back and rushed past her immobile boss, jostling her slightly. She hit the answer button on the phone once she'd reached the reception desk. By the time she'd said, "This is Alice Sullivan," she was safely in the hallway.

"Jason Whittaker." His tone was flat, almost regretful.

Alice froze. "What is it?"

"We'll need you here right away. Hold on—" She could hear muffled talking then, something about "getting Officer Larson" and "isolation." Alice wrapped an arm around herself, feeling chilled.

"Can you give me any information?" Alice raised her voice to speak over whatever else Whittaker was doing.

"Sorry," he said, "it'll be easier to talk when you get here. How soon can you come?"

Alice looked back at the office door. She could see Ramona flipping through the basket she'd packed. Ramona had already plucked out a couple of fabric memos. Alice seethed. The samples weren't the property of Ramona Design. Alice herself had called the companies and requested them.

"I'll be there in ten." Although Alice feared whatever Whittaker needed to tell her, she was more than happy to escape her boss.

Meredith Yoshida

Meredith called Bill from the car, but she could barely speak the words to explain the emergency. *Poor Bill*, Meredith thought. He had pretty much ignored Sadie's foray into puberty. Meredith had bought the next sizes up in clothes and skating costumes. But they hadn't approved any makeup or dating. Meredith had insisted that she and Sadie shop for bras together, and Sadie had shrieked when Meredith had asked to come into the fitting room. Meredith hadn't mentioned it to Bill when she'd slipped some organic cotton menstrual pads under Sadie's sink.

"Do you want me to meet you at school?" Bill asked.

"You won't make it," she said. Her husband was three suburbs away as Meredith pulled into a parking spot in the junior high's back lot. After she turned off the car, she closed her eyes, steadying herself. Sadie was the kind of kid who did Service Club and Quiz Bowl. How could she also be the kid who sent naked photos?

Meredith shivered just thinking about it, and then she forced herself out of the Jeep and into the school. *Was there any way they could deny the photo was of Sadie?* Though Meredith dreaded seeing the picture, she knew she'd have to study it, to memorize every pixel. As she speed-walked past the choir room, strains of "Let the River Run" escaped into the hallway, and Meredith realized Sadie might need a lawyer. The thought stopped her for a split second, and then she propelled herself forward again.

She rounded the corner to the front office and saw Alice standing at the reception desk. Her trench coat brushed the back of her black jeans. She noticed Alice's favorite leopard-print flats and felt a surge of rage. She should have let Sadie's friendship with Teddy run its course in elementary school. Instead, Meredith had continued to throw them together. Sadie had witnessed Teddy's downward spiral, and now she was participating in it.

Of course, Alice looked impeccable, as if appearances could fix everything. Meredith assessed her own work uniform: Nike running pants and an Elm Creek Ortho polo shirt layered over a black tee. She wished she'd had time to change.

The receptionist looked past Alice. "Mrs. Yoshida? Just a moment. I'll be right with you."

Alice spun, her face pale and eyes wide. "Meredith," she said. "What are you doing here?"

Meredith stiffened. Alice didn't know? Her fury intensified as she imagined her finding out about the photo. Alice would try to blame Sadie, no doubt. Meredith flashed back to her comment about due process when they'd all discussed #MeToo on one of their power walks last summer.

"Did you give Teddy his phone back?" Meredith demanded, her voice a gravelly whisper. "Why would you do that?"

Alice looked baffled. "I installed that software you recommended. The one with the app control."

Meredith moved up to the desk and signed in on the clipboard. She avoided eye contact with the receptionist. *How will I ever make eye contact with anyone in Elm Creek ever again?*

"To be honest, Meredith," Alice whispered as she followed her to the chairs outside Whittaker's office, "I don't even know why I'm here. It must have been too awful to tell me on the phone." She tried for a laugh then, but it came out as a croak. "Do you know?"

Just then, Whittaker's office door clicked open and Jonas Lagerhead, his white-blond hair slicked back, walked out.

"As I said—" Whittaker kept talking as he trailed Jonas. "Tane's waiting in the Quiet Room at the back of the library. You can go pick him up there and then come back to sign out."

Jonas glowered at the assistant principal. "I'll sign him out now," he said. "Save time." *That's against the rules*, Meredith thought, and then shook her head. Who cared about sign-out rules at a time like this?

Meredith jumped up. "Am I next?" She followed Whittaker into the office without looking back. The overhead lights reflected off the waxy leaves of a lush-looking plant on Whittaker's desk. Meredith reached out and rubbed a leaf between her thumb and forefinger and realized with a shot of embarrassment that the plant was artificial. She dropped both hands into her lap.

"Well," said Whittaker awkwardly.

This man has seen my child's breast, Meredith realized. She blinked hard. "Do you know how this happened? Sadie would never just *do* this kind of thing."

"I'm still piecing things together," Whittaker said.

"Where is Sadie?" Meredith's mouth felt dry, the lights too bright.

"I've got her in the nurse's office," Whittaker said. "I've been keeping the three of them separate."

Meredith clasped her hands and leaned toward the assistant principal. "I just feel like I have to tell you that Sadie hasn't done anything like this before. She's been the opposite of a wild child for her entire school career." *Wild child?* Meredith squeezed her knuckles. *What was she talking about?*

Mr. Whittaker's face remained neutral, his eyes flat. "Mrs. Yoshida, the fact that I hadn't met Sadie before last week tells me that she usually runs the straight and narrow. But the Instagram video was troubling. And now this photo. As I said, I'm working with incomplete information. What do you already know?"

No, thought Meredith. *Don't give him anything*. She'd call Bill about a lawyer. "All I have is a couple of text messages from my daugh-

ter." Meredith imagined the assistant principal looking at the picture again then and her stomach lurched. "Have you seen it?" she blurted.

"Look," he said, palms up, "I know how shocking something like this has to be."

"You don't," Meredith said. The man couldn't be more than thirty years old. He had the remnants of a zit on the left side of his chin.

"Do you have children?" Meredith asked. "Any girls?"

"No. Actually, I just got engaged." He smiled faintly, and Meredith felt like slapping him.

"Congratulations," she managed. "Well, this will be hard, but just try to imagine you have a daughter." Meredith felt her words coming more quickly. "And then imagine she's thirteen years old and some little pervert pressures her to take a topless photo." Whittaker pulled at his collar and coughed. "Now imagine him showing it to all his skeezy friends."

"Um . . ." Whittaker looked over Meredith's shoulder as if he hoped to be interrupted.

"I'm sorry," she said. She reached out to the plant again and felt its thick plastic leaf. "There's no way Sadie would have done something like this unless she was massively coerced." Meredith shifted her gaze to a row of potted succulents on the filing cabinet. *Also fake*, she thought.

Whittaker leaned back in his chair, his hands curled around the armrests. "I asked her a couple of times why she did it, and she says she doesn't know."

Alice Sullivan

Ten minutes after Meredith's meeting with Whittaker started, Sadie appeared with a police officer, a stout woman with her hair in a neat chignon and a gun in her holster. Alice held her breath as they walked to Whittaker's office. The officer knocked lightly and held the door open for Sadie. The two disappeared inside, and Alice made stunned eye contact with the receptionist.

"Police liaison officer. They don't have those in the elementary schools." The receptionist looked quickly back to her computer screen.

A gun? Alice thought. *For junior high?*

This had to be Sadie's first time in any discipline situation. Meredith said Sadie had straight As. And now she was in a meeting with the police.

Alice grabbed her phone from her bag and texted Patrick. "Emergency meeting in Whittaker's office." On the one hand, she felt guilty for alarming him when she didn't know all the facts. But on the other hand, she couldn't face the police alone. "I'll let you know what happens."

Alice leaned her head back against the glass wall of the office and closed her eyes, blocking out the kids passing in the hallways. A few minutes later, she opened them again when Meredith and Sadie exited Whittaker's office ahead of him. Meredith refused eye contact, and Sadie's slumped posture conveyed dejection. This was not the Sadie she knew—none of her usual confidence or precociousness. In fact,

Sadie's whole body seemed to sag, her shoulders rounded around her chest. After they'd passed, Alice stood.

"Come on in," Whittaker said. "I've asked Officer Larson to join us."

Alice forced herself forward, unable to speak. She judged the police officer to be about forty-five, given the wrinkles around her eyes. She didn't smile or stand as she offered her hand to shake. "I'm Cindy Larson of the Elm Creek Police Department, currently assigned to the school."

Once she'd taken the seat next to Officer Larson, Alice tried again and felt relieved that she could indeed utter words. "What's going on?" she asked. She scanned the room, remembering the blank walls and the dusky sandalwood smell. Alice fixed her eyes on the artificial plant on the edge of the desk.

"I hate to do this today just as we've gotten back to normal," Whittaker began, "but we've uncovered a troubling situation this morning, and given Teddy's recent history . . ." He coughed. Alice closed her eyes as she had outside, as if waiting for a jury to read its verdict. "Well," Whittaker continued. "It's especially troubling for him."

Officer Larson scooted her chair closer to Alice's. "This might sound shocking," she said. Alice glanced again at her gun. "But we've determined from interviews this morning that Teddy has distributed a photo of Sadie Yoshida's breast to several members of his soccer team."

Officer Larson's round face blurred in front of Alice. The sandal-wood smell—one she usually associated with warm feelings—became oppressive. Alice fanned her face with her hand. The silence in the room stretched.

There had to be a mistake. Sadie Yoshida would never, ever photograph her naked breast. Alice would have laughed at just the idea of Meredith's daughter doing something so illicit.

"But I turned off Teddy's phone apps after nine p.m.," Alice said stupidly. Nothing, she realized, would have prevented him from sending the photo earlier in the day. Officer Larson gave her a pitying smile, and neither she nor Whittaker spoke. "Why would Sadie take such a

photo?" Alice's voice sounded like a whine, which she hated. "We've known her since she was a little girl."

Whittaker nodded. "I agree it seems totally out of character for Sadie, but junior high is prime time for impulsive behavior, and in this case, it seems like we might be dealing with a bit of a love triangle?"

"What?" Alice was having a hard time following. She wished she could tag out, that Patrick could just give her a report of the meeting later, after the fact.

"I'm thinking this might have something to do with Teddy's actions at assembly two weeks ago." Whittaker coughed again. "With Tane." As if Alice needed a reminder.

"To be fair," Alice said, "I'm not sure that was so much of a decision related to Tane as a terrible impulse. You just mentioned impulsivity? I read an article about ADHD last week." She'd make an appointment, she thought, with Teddy's pediatrician for a formal evaluation.

Officer Larson's cocked head conveyed judgment, and Alice looked away, her eyes drawn to her leopard-print shoes. "In any case," Whittaker said, "Tane seems to have bragged about his relationship." He rolled his hand in the air. "With Sadie, I mean, by sending Teddy the picture I mentioned."

Alice blinked at him.

"Uh, the picture of Sadie's breast," he clarified.

Whittaker's face faded in and out of focus. "Wait," Alice managed. "What exactly did Teddy do?"

Whittaker gave an exaggerated nod and seemed relieved to be back on track. "We learned about the photo when another parent, the mother of someone on Teddy's Elm Creek Soccer Club team, reported that she'd seen it on her child's phone last night." Whittaker dropped his chin and looked up at Alice, as if she were being scolded. "We do recommend, Mrs. Sullivan, that parents periodically check their children's text messages and emails."

"I do check!" Alice blurted. "I just told you I'd started that!" She

jumped then as a text notification dinged. "Sorry." She grabbed her phone and flicked it to silent. "And this soccer mother knows for sure her son got the picture from Teddy?" His phone was supposed to be a practical purchase, helpful for rides and trips to the mall. Alice had read alarmist pieces about the catastrophic mistakes teens made with their phones in every publication from *People* to the *New York Times*, but she couldn't believe this meeting was actually happening to her. "I'm assuming you've talked to Teddy about this?" Alice asked. "What's he saying about it?"

Alice caught a look between Officer Larson and Mr. Whittaker. "He denies it," Whittaker said, "but we've got it now from more than one source."

Alice remembered the Spider-Man speech Patrick had given to Teddy when he'd unwrapped the iPhone. Her husband would be so disappointed to learn it hadn't done any good. Officer Larson jumped in. "I'm afraid we need to talk about the seriousness of what Teddy has done."

"I understand the seriousness," Alice said, "but we do want to verify that he actually—"

Officer Larson held up a finger. "You'll find he actually did." The compassion Alice had first detected in her gaze fizzled. "And I need to tell you that sharing pictures of girls' breasts via text message qualifies as distributing child pornography. It's Minnesota statute."

"Well, then Tane's guilty, too?" Alice remembered Jonas Lagerhead striding angrily from the office, no police officer at his side.

Officer Larson frowned. "We obviously can't discuss the disciplinary actions we may or may not have taken against other students."

Alice felt the backs of her thighs slide forward on the straight-backed chair. Dry air spread across her tongue. Officer Larson peered at her. "I'll have to file a police report," she said. Alice wondered what would happen if she slid all the way off her chair and lay on the ground. "But," Officer Larson continued as Alice imagined the feel of the carpet against the back of her neck. "Our county DA hasn't been pressing

charges for minors under the age of fifteen, at least not for first-time offenders."

"You're filing a report?" Alice's voice echoed in her head. "Teddy's only twelve."

"I know it sounds extreme." Whittaker swallowed hard, his Adam's apple shiny under the LED lights. "But what Teddy's done is actually a crime."

Nothing in any of Alice's parenting books had included instructions on what to do if your tween got arrested. She ran a hand over her jeans and wished she were home in her sweat pants. This outfit, including her favorite shoes, had turned against her. "Where is Teddy?" Alice asked.

Whittaker nodded toward the wall on his left. "He's on his way from the social worker's office." Alice felt hot.

"We should look at other schools," she blurted. "Or move. My husband's been working in Cincinnati. Maybe it's nice there?" Whittaker squinted at her, and Alice heard the office door open. She expected to feel enraged when she saw Teddy, but instead she wanted to throw both arms around him. All of his blustery defiance had gone. His eyes looked tired and his head bowed. Alice remembered the couple of times he'd dropped his McDonald's ice creams on the sidewalk after soccer practices. This was like that, only sadder.

Teddy Sullivan

As soon as they left Whittaker's office, Teddy's mom took his phone. "Where's your locker?" she asked. Her face looked gray. He pointed down the hall, and she walked next to him in that direction, silent. After Teddy had opened it, his mom dumped everything from his locker shelves into his backpack.

"We don't need it all," Teddy tried to say, but she emptied it anyway. The stuff that didn't fit in the backpack, she put in her work bag. She took down the pictures of soccer players he'd hung on the door, crumpling them as she pushed them behind her laptop sleeve. Teddy looked up and down the hallway, checking for witnesses. Only the English teacher with a classroom across the hall seemed to notice them. He gave Teddy a wondering look.

Teddy tried to swallow his fear, to push the police officer out of his mind, but his limbs shook with it. For a second, he thought he'd have to sit down right there in the hallway. "We don't need the pictures," he whispered to his mother. She didn't say anything.

In the car, she never turned toward him. She revved her engine out of the school's driveway and took her turns faster than normal. Teddy gripped the armrest and spread his fingers for stability.

When they pulled into the garage, Teddy's mom got out before he'd even unbuckled his seat belt. His whole body felt heavy as he shuffled inside. His mom's shoes—the animal print ones she liked so

much—lay on their sides in the mudroom. He could hear her stomping up the stairs and guessed he should probably go to his room, but he didn't want to follow her to the second floor. He didn't want to see her eyes flash while she avoided looking at him.

Once her door slammed, he figured he could tiptoe up there. As he did, he could hear her opening and closing her dresser drawers. He briefly wondered whether she'd hide his phone in the same place she'd stashed the Xbox she'd bought them for Christmas last year, in the drawer beneath her bed with the bulkiest of her sweaters. Teddy still remembered the date on which he'd found that Xbox. It had been December 16, when Alice had taken Weasley for a walk before dinner. He'd worried for the next nine days that his pretend "surprised" reaction to the gift wouldn't be convincing enough, but neither of his parents suspected anything. Adrian had asked him later, "Did you know?" Teddy surprised himself then with a seemingly heartfelt shake of his head.

Teddy had almost crossed the threshold of his room when he heard his mother's voice, muffled but sharp. He couldn't hear all of her words, but a particularly loud "No!" reached him. He backed out into the hallway. His arms felt leaden, his fingers tingly. He'd never, even before a penalty kick in soccer, felt so seized by fear. Who was she talking to?

"I don't know," she said. "The police officer said they haven't been charging kids under fifteen lately—too few resources for too common a problem, which I guess is supposed to make me feel better? To know that other kids do this kind of stupid shit?"

Teddy recoiled at "shit" but forced himself forward again, closer to his parents' door. He'd crept out here once in the previous summer, woken in the night by a bad dream. He'd stood outside their door, feeling his heart exploding in his chest, and realized he was too old to open it.

"I'm not sending him back," his mom said, louder now on the

phone. "I texted Ramona to tell her I needed time. I'll have to home-school him."

Teddy's eyes widened. *Homeschool?* There was a kid on the Elm Creek Soccer Club premier team who was homeschooled. He wore the kind of ugly sports goggles that fastened behind his head. Nobody passed to that kid unless the coach screamed at them to do it. Teddy had heard him mention the periodic table and Jesus in equal frequency on the sidelines.

"I can't calm down, Patrick," Alice said, quieter. Teddy leaned his head closer to the door. He thought he heard her flop down on her bed. "The police are involved." She paused, and Teddy held his breath. "Okay." His mom's voice cracked, and he heard a hiccup. "Thank you. I know."

When Teddy realized she was crying, he took two quick steps back-ward and nearly tripped over Weasley, who'd arrived at his feet. Teddy's hand shot out to brace himself against the wall, his fingers hitting just beneath the painting of a horse he'd done in third grade. Teddy re-membered the day they'd gone to the frame shop to pick it up. The clerk had gently unstuck the masking tape on the brown paper wrap-ping, and Teddy had been thrilled to see his art looking so official. He'd run his hand over the wooden frame and onto the glass. No one had been irritated with him for leaving a fingerprint. The frame shop guy just wiped it away with a cloth.

Had Teddy ever made his mother cry before today? Probably, he thought. Alice was a relatively easy crier, tearing up during commercials and at the end of Pixar movies. But she'd never cried over something like this. Not that he knew. His mom should be out here in the hallway, Teddy thought, yelling about his punishment, not locked in her room crying. His "logical consequence" should be something to do with elec-tronics, right? Of course, she'd already taken his phone, but the photo? The police officer? Even Teddy knew he deserved something worse than anything he'd gotten before. His mother's tears proved it.

He suddenly felt his legs gain sturdiness beneath him, and he had

his own idea of what it would take to make things right. He walked straight down two flights of stairs into the Sullivans' finished basement. He roughly unplugged the Xbox from the TV in the half-finished den and marched back upstairs with it in his arms.

In the garage, he grabbed a hammer from the box of tools his mom kept on a worktable in the corner and slammed it down on the top of the console. He'd pictured pieces scattering over the table, but he found he couldn't break the Xbox outright. He used two hands on the hammer and whacked as hard as he could. When he picked it up to check he heard pieces rattling inside it. Then he put it down and hit it over and over until he was sure it would never work again. Maybe if it was really broken, if he gave up gaming forever, that would be enough to make things okay again.

Alice Sullivan

Patrick walked into the kitchen with a beautiful bouquet from Arts & Flowers on Thursday night, and Alice burst into tears for the second time in as many days. "It's orange," she said, nonsensically, her chest heaving. "And thanks for coming home early."

"The woman at the shop said you liked king protea." Patrick put the vase down on the counter and wrapped his arms around her. "Is that a flower?"

"Yes." Alice sobbed. "I love them, especially with those orange roses." She'd been a frequent customer at Arts & Flowers. She typically left an arrangement in each of the homes she finished working on. The staff had put in extra effort on this one, finishing it with dried sprigs of Italian ruscus.

Patrick put his nose in the top of her hair, and she squeezed him harder. "They look like sea anemone," he said, referring to the king protea. Alice nodded. Her face slid against his dress shirt. She breathed in his Old Spice.

"Where's Aidy?" Patrick asked. Ordinarily, she'd be there in the middle of their hug, wedged between them and angling to be picked up. But tonight it was only Weasley at their feet. Alice had looped his leash around her wrist, a preemptive measure to keep him under control during trick-or-treating.

"She's at a friend's house." Alice could hear her heart beating slower now that her husband was here. She felt sleepier and heavier, and she

scowled into one of Patrick's buttons when the doorbell rang. It was the second trick-or-treater of the night. "She's an angel." Alice laughed then, through her tears. "I mean, that's Aidy's costume."

Patrick released Alice and walked to the door with the painted bowl they always used for Halloween candy. When he returned, Alice sent him to Teddy's room, hopeful that a male influence could make a difference. Meanwhile, Alice opened the door for five or six more trick-or-treaters, all while restraining their overexcited cockapoo.

In between visitors, Alice grabbed one of the rocks glasses Patrick liked from a kitchen cabinet. She'd chosen Farrow & Ball's Purbeck Stone color last year when she'd had the cabinetry painted. The doors' glass insets revealed her wedding crystal and the brightly colored chip-and-dip set Evelyn had gifted Alice on her thirtieth birthday. The effect most often gave her a jolt of satisfaction, but not tonight.

Alice had just dropped ice into the glass when Patrick slumped into the kitchen, his return trek from Teddy's room less enthusiastic than his departure. His eyes drooped at the corners as they did when he sacrificed sleep for more than a night or two. He'd put in endless hours on the Energy Lab case.

"I figured you'd want bourbon," she said.

"You read my mind." Patrick grabbed the bottle from the cabinet where they kept his Maker's Mark, as well as some random liqueurs they'd purchased for stray cocktails over the years. The doorbell rang.

"We should probably start locking the booze up," Alice said as she grabbed the candy bowl and walked to the door. "Now that Teddy is getting older." When she got back, Patrick had poured a double and held the bottle out to her. She waved it away. "Did your parents keep the liquor cabinet locked when you were a kid?"

"I wasn't interested in my dad's scotch." Patrick raised the glass to his nose. They'd both tried alcohol in high school, Alice knew, but everything seemed riskier now for Teddy. If anyone in the room had a cell phone, you could wreck your whole life with a couple of beers.

Patrick took a long swallow.

"What did Teddy say?" Alice's stomach twisted.

"Not much," Patrick admitted. "He said he wasn't thinking when he sent the screenshots. Same thing he said to you." Alice had hoped that having Patrick home would have softened Teddy. She at least wanted him to explain the broken Xbox, which they'd discovered when Aidy had tried to play Just Dance after school the day before.

There'd been more crying after that, first Aidy's wails and then Alice alone, her face smashed into her sham.

"Did he say anything about Sadie?" Alice asked.

Patrick bit his lip, and then the doorbell rang again. Patrick went this time. While he usually exclaimed over the neighborhood kids' costumes, tonight he barely spoke. Alice could hear the Snickers thudding into the kids' plastic pumpkins.

As soon as he was back, Alice reentered their conversation. "Tell me what he said." She flattened her hands against the natural stone countertop. The delicate gray grain would have looked great—neutral yet sleek in the background of the *Elle Decor* shoot, maybe with her cerulean Dutch oven on top. That brilliant orange trivet she'd picked up at an estate sale could have peeked out beneath. She glanced then at the orange flowers, and she felt the anxiety that she'd battled all week creep again into her arms. Her husband was here now, but he'd be gone again in seventy-two hours.

Patrick scratched his ear and looked over her shoulder. "Teddy said that if Sadie was dumb enough to take that photo, of course she knew people would see it." He slid his drink back and forth on the counter, clanking the ice against the sides of the cut-glass tumbler.

Alice wilted. They'd gotten no further with Teddy than passing the buck? She'd thought there'd been some real remorse mixed in with the shortsighted Xbox smashing. He'd done it, he said, to show he was sorry. "We can start nature therapy," Alice said. "He actually wants to do that." She still hadn't told him about Julienne—the fact that it was her clinic Alice had visited. It had been easy to omit details with Patrick traveling and chaos at home.

229

"That's good for now." Patrick gulped his bourbon. "Can he do individual sessions, too? I feel like the more steps we take, the faster he'll be able to get back to normal. Go to school. Deal with soccer."

Alice turned away from him, her relief about him coming home suddenly replaced by irritation. "Honestly," she said, "at this point who cares about soccer?" She opened the pantry door for something to do with her hands and then slammed it again. "We just had a meeting with the police!"

"I care about soccer." Patrick seemed oblivious to her rising alarm. The doorbell rang again.

"You haven't even been here!" She gripped the sides of her head with rigid fingers, startled herself by how quickly her mood had changed. But how could Patrick question any of her choices when he had disappeared for weeks while she tried to hold their crumbling children upright all on her own? "And you've always cared more about sports than school!" She fought an impulse to storm to their bedroom, to throw herself down again on her duvet.

Patrick disappeared to appease the trick-or-treaters, and when he returned, he put a warm hand on her shoulder. "Hey," he said, still calm. "I'm taking it seriously. I know it's been harder for you." She turned back to him, though she could feel her pulse throbbing in her temples.

Patrick took another gulp of bourbon, his expression a mix of plaintive and placid. "But," he said, "I don't think you can actually home-school him. He needs a school, and you have a job."

Alice collapsed onto her kitchen stool, her stomach churning. "But Elm Creek clearly isn't working. It's toxic!" As she said it, she knew the truth of it. "The social dynamics, the soccer team, the teachers he hasn't connected with . . ." She trailed off, and her anger ebbed as quickly as it had boiled. *What's wrong with me?* Alice's eyes found a familiar spot above the back window where a dot of white paint from the trim marred the matte, silvery color of the wall. "Also, Teddy seems

incapable of making the right choices at that school." If she had to keep him home, isolate him from his peers to make sure he wasn't arrested, that's what she would do.

Patrick took her hand and brought her focus back from the paint mistake. She'd fix it this week, she decided, rather than spending any more time looking at it. It would take about ten minutes and the right-sized brush. "Do you really think you'll be able to get him to do school at home? Like, if you're his only teacher?" The bell rang again.

Alice pulled her hand back, not entirely ready for a full reconciliation, and headed to the door. After she'd tossed about six pieces of candy in each of the kids' pillowcases, she roughly turned off the porch light. *Enough.*

Back in the kitchen, she thought for a minute. "Maybe there's some kind of online school he could do. I've heard ads for those on the radio." She reached for Patrick's bourbon and took a sip. Patrick stifled a laugh as she winced. She slid the glass back toward him and kept talking. "The Elm Creek counselor probably knows." Alice imagined Teddy on a laptop on the stool next to hers, their respective work spread over the countertop.

But Alice doubted how many projects she could do at home, especially if she continued to alienate Ramona. "Do you remember what kind of noncompete I signed?" Alice asked.

Patrick shrugged. "Standard, I think." *Just like the phone contract we put in front of Teddy,* Alice thought. *What a joke.*

"I'm going to get my laptop." Patrick looked up the stairs toward the kids' rooms. Alice noticed his hair was getting long, the shaggy blond waves at the back of his neck matching their son's. "We can research the online schools."

At least he was trying. *But he'll be gone again before I know it.* Alice grabbed the bourbon and sucked a melty ice cube into her mouth, rolling the remnants of alcohol around her tongue.

Sadie Yoshida

Things at home could have been worse, Sadie realized. Again, she hadn't really even gotten in trouble. Rather, her mother had gone hypervigilant on her phone. Snapchat was discovered and gone. Instagram disabled. All that was left was texting and calling and a couple of educational games, but given the fact that the police had been involved? Sadie knew it could have been much, much worse.

The police. If someone had told Sadie even a week ago that she'd be in trouble with the school police officer—that boxy woman with the broad shoulders and the chest that strained the buttons on her thick, navy uniform top—she would have laughed. She'd only seen Officer Larson before with the kids who vaped in the bathrooms. She hadn't even known the woman's name. But now, Officer Larson had explained to her, slowly and using the words "breast" and "nipple" repeatedly, that taking a photo of her own body was illegal.

Even more horrifying than that was the idea that her dad had seen her boob. *He saw it, right?* It didn't seem possible that her mother could have kept it from him. Sadie was pretty sure her parents had discussed the Elm Creek soccer players, too, and how many of them had also seen the picture. She'd walked into the kitchen a couple of times to that awkward feeling that everyone had stopped talking the moment you showed up. It was junior high lunch table 101.

Obviously, Sadie wished she could go back to that moment in her

room and simply not take the picture. She'd message Tane an eye roll emoji instead. They'd still be sitting together at lunch instead of each suspended. Mikaela had texted her about sixteen shocked GIFs when Sadie had told her what she'd done. "Even I've never sent a nude," Mikaela had written.

Really? Sadie thought. *After the crotch shots and the lipstick? Could I really be the first one?* After Mikaela's reaction, Sadie decided not to tell Chloe.

"Don't tell Chloe," Sadie had texted back to Mikaela. "Or anyone else." *Fat chance*, she said to herself, sounding like her mother in her own head. If she'd just sent that emoji to Tane instead of the picture, everything would be fine. She'd still be able to look her dad in the eye.

Despite the photo, her dad had made his famous pancakes that weekend, but when he put the plate down in front of her, he looked at her forehead instead of at her face. He didn't sit down with her for even five minutes before leaving for his run, an "extra-long one," he said, without turning to say good-bye.

Meanwhile, her mom spent a good chunk of the morning on the phone. Sadie could hear some of what she said, even with the study door closed. "That hardly seems relevant," Sadie heard her say once. "This is about the safety and well-being of a thirteen-year-old girl!" After she nearly shouted those words, her volume decreased. Sadie stood outside the door. She wouldn't lean her ear against it, she decided, but she'd stand closer, with a better chance to hear at least bits and pieces. After all, the conversation was about her.

"Walt," Meredith said, "I hardly think the record of a junior high soccer team is more important than the club's adherence to its values." *Walt is Chloe's dad*, Sadie realized. But she had no idea what he had to do with the picture.

Meredith paused then, and Sadie inched closer to the door. "Of course I value my daughter's privacy, Walt, but I also want these kids punished, and frankly, I'm surprised that you don't agree. What if, and

I hate to do this to you because I'm currently living this nightmare, but what if this photo were of Chloe? Then would you want Tane Lagerhead and Teddy Sullivan wearing the Elm Creek jersey? Be honest with yourself."

Sadie shivered, though she wore a heavy Elkettes Synchro sweatshirt. She slid her stockinged foot back and forth across the smooth wood floor outside the office and caught a glimpse of herself in the gold-framed circular mirror. Alice had hung it for them over a little table in the hallway. She frowned at the Elkettes logo on her shirt, a skate blade attached to the bottom of the big block "E." Suddenly, she couldn't imagine putting on her eye shadow and slicking her hair into a high bun. The person she'd been in the selfie she'd sent to Tane wasn't the same girl who'd so recently cared about spins and crossovers.

There was silence for a few seconds, and Sadie wondered if Chloe's dad had hung up, but then her mother piped in again, as loud as she had been before. "Well," she said, "I can't imagine the larger community will agree with you. That seems like blaming the victim. Not a good look, Walt, in 2019."

Sadie heard the desk chair roll back. Her mother's footsteps thudded toward the door. There was no time for Sadie to move before it opened, so she decided to pretend to be on her way to the powder room.

Her mother's eyes narrowed when she saw her, and Sadie felt herself hold her breath, but she exhaled again when her mom breezed past into the kitchen. "Everything's going to be okay," her mom said over her shoulder. "Don't you even worry."

She'd said that a few times already. Officer Larson had, too, when she'd explained about the charges. Mikaela had even said not to worry, after she'd expressed her surprise. Everyone assumed Sadie would be worried. But she wasn't, exactly.

Things would change, right? They had already changed in junior high. She'd already lost Teddy. She already sat at a different lunch table than she had before. And there would be more changes the older she

got. People might see her differently. Mikaela and Chloe might make comments about her no longer being a "Mary." Or they might start sending their own secret photos. Although it would be complicated, Sadie thought it would be okay. The only thing she wasn't fine with— the thing that made her feel like crying—was her dad looking at her forehead and going for that extra-long run. He hadn't peeked in on her before bed in the last few days, either.

Him seeing that photo—that was one thing she really wished she could undo.

Nadia Reddy

- - - - -

When Alice slumped toward her in the trailhead parking lot on Sunday morning, Nadia could immediately see her exhaustion. Alice's shoulders drooped, and her curls seemed relaxed, as if she hadn't washed her hair in several days. This was how Alice had looked after Aidy was born. She'd been thrust back into sleepless nights for the first time in five years. Nadia and Meredith had exchanged smug glances behind her back, both happy that their kids were sleeping through the night and out of diapers. Not that Nadia hadn't wanted a second child. She had, desperately, but seeing Alice with a baby—disheveled and with milk stains on her stretched-out T-shirts? It looked hard. And now Alice looked rough again, even though her kid could walk and talk. She looked rough probably *because* her kid could walk and talk.

"I'm considering homeschool," Alice said as she and Nadia started down the path. Alice had suggested a park across town from their usual spot. Nadia knew she was trying to avoid running into Meredith.

"Homeschool?" Nadia tried to imagine Alice teaching Teddy algebra at her gorgeous kitchen counter, a Martha Stewart–esque centerpiece between them. In her imagination, neither Alice nor Teddy was smiling. "Doesn't that seem extreme?"

"Teddy can't do school." Alice's voice sounded flat.

Nadia rubbed Alice's back. "Oh, honey," she said. "I've thought that so many times about Donovan, but it's not true. Not only *can* he do it,

but he has a *right* to do it." She dropped her hand and pumped her elbows, energized by the opportunity to share some of what she'd learned in these last few hard years. "Having a behavior problem doesn't mean a kid is unworthy of education." She glanced over at her friend. Alice's eyes were focused a few feet down the trail in front of them.

Alice picked up the pace. She did that sometimes. Usually it was Meredith who tapped her shoulder or tugged her jacket sleeve. "Whoa there, NASCAR," Meredith had said once, which had made them all laugh. This time, Nadia just tried to match her.

"What do you do?" Alice asked. "How do you handle it?"

Nadia felt at once irritated and relieved that one of her friends seemed finally interested. "You mean being the mom of the bad kid?" Nadia hop-skipped to keep up. Alice shuddered, and Nadia wondered if she might cry. Nadia nudged her. "You're supposed to say, 'But Donovan is *not* a bad kid.'"

"I know that." Alice finally looked over at her, her eyes teary and color rising in her cheeks. "Donovan's not bad. But other people think that. Right?"

"You know what really mattered to me?" Nadia remembered Donovan's suspension in fifth grade, the chair-throwing incident that she knew all of the kids and parents had still discussed weeks after it happened.

"What?"

"What my friends thought of me." Honesty, Nadia knew, was the best way to help Alice. "The days when I imagined—when I knew—that you and Meredith thought I was failing? Those were the days that I felt the most lost." Leaves skittered behind them on the path. Nadia sniffed the chilly November air. "The most alone," she added.

"I'm—" Alice started to give the apology that Nadia had craved for years, a continuation of the text she'd sent the previous week. But just then Lacy Cushing and Meredith came toward them around a bend. Nadia saw them first and slowed her pace. A few seconds later, when Alice realized Nadia had fallen behind, she stopped entirely.

"Shit," Alice said, just loud enough for Nadia to hear.

"It's okay." Nadia wasn't sure if she was speaking to Alice, to Meredith, or to herself.

For a split second, it seemed like Meredith and Lacy were stopping as well, which would have created a made-for-Hollywood showdown in the county park, but then Meredith revved her pace again, swerving to the right side of the path to give Alice a wide berth. "Let's go," she said to Lacy.

Lacy raised her eyebrows and made eye contact with Nadia. They hadn't been friends since Donovan had bitten Chloe in kindergarten, the seven-year-old incident still the reason Lacy had never accepted an invitation to one of the threesome's wine bar evenings, the reason Nadia had quietly dropped out of book club and never returned.

Suddenly, Alice shouted, "You're not even going to say anything?" Nadia swiveled her head between her friends.

Meredith kept her back to Alice but raised her right hand, middle finger extended. Nadia gasped. "The whole point of this park was to avoid you!" Meredith yelled.

"I warned you!" Lacy yelled inexplicably. "I told you Teddy was out of control." The two of them walked on.

Alice's arms fell limply at her sides. She pressed the heel of her palm against her forehead. "Christ," she said.

"Let's go." Nadia squeezed Alice's shoulder.

They walked in silence for a few minutes, except for the deep breaths Nadia could hear Alice take every thirty seconds or so. Cleansing breaths, she thought, imagining herself in the sauna after yoga, eyes closed against the heat. "What did Lacy mean when she said she warned you?" Nadia asked.

"I think she texted me the morning of Aidy's conference, before the assembly," Alice said. "I got a text asking me to do something about Teddy. It just hit me when she said that. Isn't she friends with Janna Lagerhead?"

"I think? But you know, she hates me, too. So." Nadia trailed off.

"The nature groups?" Alice said finally. "You think that's what's been making a difference for Donovan?"

Nadia felt a swell in her chest, a moment of pride. So her friend had noticed Donovan's progress after all. "Yes. You've met her, right? Dr. Martín?"

"That's a long story." Alice picked up the pace again. "But yes."

Nadia waited, wondering if Alice would continue, but instead she pivoted. "I can't believe my kid is a criminal."

"Your kid isn't a criminal." Nadia took another hop-step.

"He is." Alice sounded determined. "I'm not even exaggerating. It's just a fact. And now that I know what this feels like? This total agony of having outside proof that I'm a terrible parent? Even though I've tried to do everything possible to not be one? I'm just . . ." She slowed down. Nadia felt her quad seize up as she put the brakes on. She felt both sad for Alice and also just a tiny bit vindicated. She'd been the one feeling so lost all along, and now Alice had a taste of the lack of control Nadia had always experienced. "It just changes the way I look at things," Alice said.

Nadia wondered if she was thinking back on some of the times she had avoided asking about Donovan. She and Meredith had never said that they thought Donovan's behaviors had something to do with her parenting, but it was clear in what they didn't say. Nadia had stayed in the friendships because she knew they just didn't *know*. But now Alice *did* know.

"Nature therapy," Nadia said. "But don't do homeschool."

"But—" Alice stopped again and grabbed Nadia's arm. "It's better than being embarrassed. Everyone hates me. We can't go back to Elm Creek."

"Keep walking," Nadia said. She physically pulled her friend for a while, and then finally Alice found her rhythm again. Nadia patted her back intermittently. She'd feel better, Nadia knew from experience, if she got good exercise. Eventually, as Alice's breathing slowed, they

talked about Nadia's clients and Ajay's mother's upcoming visit from India. Alice mentioned linens on sale for the basement bedroom Nadia kept for her mother-in-law. Apparently, everything was twenty percent off at CB2.

Nadia felt accomplished as they reached the end of the trail. She'd talked Alice down, gotten her through her first encounter with Meredith, and even distracted her. Just as she'd begun a self-satisfied sigh, the sign marking the trailhead came into view. Nadia stopped short again, her quad seizing the same way it had when they'd encountered Meredith and Lacy.

"Oh my God." Alice ran forward to the sign, her arms stiff at her sides. She reached out to touch the bright pink graffiti, the same tag Nadia had seen on NextDoor and at the McDonald's.

She tilted her head. "How could Shirley MacIntosh think that was a rocket ship?" Despite Alice's distress, she laughed. The fluorescent drawing was clearly a penis.

"Have you seen this mark before?" Alice spun toward her. She kept her finger on the sign where the painter had added a hashtag followed by two "Ts."

Nadia squinted. She hadn't seen the hashtag before. But it was certainly hard not to think the initials stood for #TeamTane or, maybe worse, for #TeamTeddy.

Alice Sullivan

A lice crossed her arms as she and Patrick stood in the doorway to Teddy's room. "Mom," he said. "I told you, it's not me. I wouldn't do that."

A month ago, it never would have occurred to her to ask him whether he'd graffitied the park. But now, he'd basically been arrested. "Teddy?" Patrick prodded. Alice looked at her husband's clenched fists and felt grateful that someone else was playing the heavy.

"God!" Teddy flopped facedown on his bed. "What kind of person do you think I am?"

Alice thought to remind him that he was the type of person who pantsed Tane and distributed child pornography. Compared to those offenses, what was a little graffiti?

"We're glad to know you don't have anything to do with it," Patrick said diplomatically. He stretched his fingers.

Still, when Teddy got in the shower later that afternoon, Alice and Patrick searched his room again, as she had after discovering his 420 Finsta.

"No pink paint," she texted Nadia.

The reply came immediately: "None here, either." She added eight or nine pink hearts to the message.

On Monday morning, with Patrick gone again in Ohio, Alice made a tense call to Ramona to let her know she was officially off the Kerri-

gan project. There just wasn't time between Cincinnati and Teddy and the pink graffiti and Adrian and, for Christ's sake, the names of her birth parents (which she hadn't even had a moment to think about) to navigate a tense collaboration with her boss on a potentially career-defining, to-the-studs remodel.

She did regret reneging on Bea Kerrigan, though. She truly liked her. But if these last weeks had taught her anything, it was that she just couldn't do it all. If she invested in the Kerrigans, something else would drop. She pictured Teddy in front of a judge and shivered.

Later that morning, she went into Teddy's room again without knocking. He shrank back toward his headboard, startled.

"You've lost the privilege of privacy," she said before he could complain. She wasn't actually mad at him anymore, and they both knew it. He'd been colossally stupid, yes, but in her heart, Alice didn't think Teddy was an inherently bad kid. It felt like a relief to Alice, like she was dealing with a lost child rather than a deranged one. Teddy seemed relieved, too, she thought. He recovered from the surprise of her entrance, and his right arm and leg each hung limply off the side of the bed.

Alice sat down next to him. She expected Teddy to turn away, but he didn't. She paused, gathering herself. Her heart fluttered uncomfortably in her chest and she pulled at the sleeve of her running top with the opposite hand. "I've got to tell you something," she began, and then she stopped.

The call from Walt Cushing had come last night. She'd whispered about it with Patrick as they fell asleep. He was the one who'd always handled soccer—tryouts and tournament berths. She'd been spared the responsibility of delivering bad sports news, but now that Patrick had left for the airport at five thirty that morning, she was stuck with the worst news of all. "I'll do it over FaceTime," he had offered, but Alice had said no. She'd handle it in person.

"What?" Teddy's mouth drooped at the corners; his eyes looked sleepy.

"The Elm Creek Soccer board has a zero-tolerance policy for bullying. Do you remember signing that player agreement?"

Teddy blinked at her. "We never read those." She realized with a pang of regret that it was true. She and Patrick had just had him sign the codes of conduct without reading them. They were always in a hurry, and the paperwork was always due.

"Well, anyway," she said. "You signed it. Now, the soccer club knows about the picture of Sadie, and well—" She paused here, but then spat it out. "You're off the team."

"I'm off the team?" He still sounded groggy. "But I didn't even have anything to do with that picture. Tane sent it to me. Is *he* off the team?" Teddy sat up and faced the wall away from her. He swung both legs to the ground.

"Dad asked that." Alice squeezed her hands into fists. "They said they couldn't tell us what's happening with other players, but I assume Tane is also out. I know this is harsh." Alice felt like crying herself as Teddy's shoulders began to shake. "We asked them to reconsider, but they said they have to stand by their policy."

Teddy grabbed his gray comforter and balled the corner in his lap. Alice had purchased it that summer, as part of a mini room makeover to celebrate the beginning of junior high. She'd painted the wall over his bed a dark red and framed a Tottenham Hotspur jersey, which she'd centered above his headboard. On the opposite wall, Alice had installed the shelves for his trophies and hooks for his medals.

"So," Teddy said finally. "I'll just go back to the C1 team?"

Alice's heart sank. "No," she said. She ran her hand over the buffalo-checked sheets she'd found on clearance, masculine enough for a teenaged boy.

"No?" Teddy repeated.

"The Elm Creek Soccer Association has a zero-tolerance policy for the entire organization. You can't play for them at all on any team."

"Wait." Teddy finally turned to face her. "Soccer is over, like, for the year?"

Alice held her breath and squinted. She watched his tears well. His chin fell, and he raised his palms to his eyes as if to force them back in.

"It's over for the year," she confirmed. "I'm so sorry." He sniffled, and she remembered his heaving sobs in the back seat of the Volvo last summer when he'd missed that penalty shot. Even though he'd started to look so old, he was still so young. Alice reached a hand out to rub his shoulder, but he shrugged it away.

"And also, while I'm here . . ." She knew she was pushing her luck, and yet waiting felt like it would be like lowering the hammer twice.

"What?" Teddy said. He stood and approached the trophy shelves. He ran his finger over the engraved plaque from last year's state championship. That was the game the Elks had lost in a shootout.

"We're going to try online school," Alice said. "I found one. You're not going back to Elm Creek."

"You're kidding." Teddy's voice was thick. He wiped his nose on his sleeve and then took the second-place plaque and walked to his closet. Once he had the door open, he grabbed one of the couple dozen string bags they'd collected at events over the years from a storage bin. He shoved the plaque roughly inside. Teddy carried the bag back to the shelves, grabbed another trophy, and dropped it in. Alice flinched as the figurine on top disappeared below the nylon. "I'm not doing online school. This whole thing is stupid."

Validate his feelings, Alice reminded herself, channeling advice from *Listen to Me*. "I can see how it feels stupid," she said. "But in-person school isn't really working for you right now." She swallowed. "Obviously."

Teddy added two more trophies to his bag and then handed it to her. "What about your job?"

Teddy stared at his white ankle socks. "You're more important," she said. She felt tears coming and shook her head, hoping to circumvent them.

"God, Mom," Teddy said. He turned away and loaded another string bag half-full with trophies.

State your expectations firmly, but kindly, Alice told herself. *And then follow through.* "I'm going to give you a little time to process this, and then we can log on and I'll show you the school Dad and I chose." Teddy walked toward her, and as he dropped the string bag at her feet, the awards inside thunked together. He turned back to his closet and procured another bag. "I thought—" Her voice was quieter than she'd planned for the "firm but kind stage." She pressed on. "I thought we could do some joint work sessions at Starbucks."

Teddy scooped six or seven medals off the hooks underneath the shelves and punched the whole handful into the bag, the metal clanking. "You think a Frappuccino is going to get me to agree to never see my friends again?"

Alice imagined herself replacing the trophies later, when Teddy was feeling better. "I thought the Starbucks might sweeten the pot." She forced herself not to react as he grabbed the participation awards from the three- and four-year-old house leagues.

"I'd throw in a chocolate croissant on each visit," she said, flailing.

Teddy didn't answer. Alice walked to him. She took the Most Improved plaque and held it out to him. She had one more carrot. "You don't need to do this forever," she said. He took the plaque, put it in the bag, and then held the whole thing out to her. "Let's try it for a month, and if it's not for you, you can go back. Or maybe we'll try a new school."

Teddy stepped around her toward his closet. He grabbed one last string bag—a souvenir from a Colorado tournament he and Patrick had attended the previous summer. Alice's mother had been shocked that they'd planned their whole vacation around a twelve-year-old's sports team. "A month?" Teddy said. Alice couldn't read his tone. Teddy plunked the last two trophies into the string bag and moved over to his desk, where Alice had set up a wire rack for certificates. He folded

the pile of cardstock roughly in half and shoved it into the bag. "Can you adios this stuff?" He held the last bag out to her. "I don't want it anymore."

Alice wasn't sure what to say. Maybe she should argue or make him take it to the garage himself. "Okay," she said finally, deciding to avoid the fight.

Meredith Yoshida

-----

don't have any reason to hide." Meredith texted Nadia on the morning of the first ethical parenting discussion group. Nadia had offered to lead it for her, "given the circumstances," but Meredith had no desire to cede her position, especially not to Nadia. Nadia had sided with Alice, walking with her in the park together the day before, and now she was trying to take over the group. But Meredith knew she shouldn't be chagrined. The photo was only Sadie's first offense. Donovan was the one with the track record. And the more Meredith thought about it, the less she could even really call Sadie's misstep an offense, regardless of what the law said. Sadie had clearly been pressured by Tane. Her daughter couldn't even articulate why she'd taken the photo; she just kept repeating that Tane had asked for it. Surely that was the bigger crime—eliciting the photo. And then Sadie had been taken advantage of by Teddy, a boy that Meredith herself had encouraged her to trust. This was classic #MeToo. Sadie, while careless and shortsighted, was a victim.

Meredith had told Sadie that every woman she knew had fallen under the spell of a bad boy at some point in her life. Perhaps they were actually lucky Sadie was having this near-ubiquitous experience when she was still so young, before college transcripts or permanent records. Officer Larson had assured Bill and her that nothing from this blip would show up on background checks. The DA had decided against

pressing charges. Sadie wouldn't face consequences beyond Whittaker's suspension, and that would end by the following afternoon.

"I'm going," Meredith told Nadia about the ethical parenting group.

"Well, I'll be there to support you," Nadia had said. She'd added a pink heart emoji to the message.

That sentiment annoyed Meredith, especially after she'd seen her at the park with Alice. *Who does Nadia think she is?* Meredith wondered. *Switzerland?*

On her way to the junior high, Meredith stopped at home and slipped on a new top from Anthropologie and her favorite green pants. She curled her hair, too, going for loose waves that seemed like she hadn't tried too hard. If she looked unperturbed, others would assume she was.

"Where are you going?" Sadie had asked. She was snuggled up on the couch with a book while Bill worked from home in his study, loosely supervising her. They'd confiscated her phone for the duration of the school days, forcing her to fill her suspension with wholesome activities. Meredith had noticed that she and Bill had each used the word "wholesome" more in those few days than ever before in their lives.

Meredith didn't think the news of the photos had spread much beyond her immediate friend group. She'd told Lacy Cushing, but Lacy was a vault when it came to secrets. Plus, Lacy was married to Walt, whom she'd encouraged to adhere to the Elm Creek Soccer board's no-tolerance policy. Later, she'd gotten a sympathetic text from Grace Heffernan that she answered with a quick "We're handling it." It turned out Sadie had told Mikaela about the photo during an evening when they'd let her have her phone. After that, Meredith made her promise not to tell anyone else. She kept Sadie's phone on the kitchen counter or in her own pocket. "Reputations," Meredith had said, not quite looking at her daughter, "are incredibly hard to repair. Better to just keep them intact."

"Why should I say I'm suspended, then?" Sadie had asked.

"Tell them you're sick." This was the first time that she'd asked Sadie to lie. Of course she and Bill valued honesty, but this situation called for discretion.

Meredith knocked on Jason Whittaker's doorjamb when she arrived at school. "Are you joining us for the ethical parenting group?" Her smile felt tight at the edges.

"I've got your copies." Whittaker pulled a stack of taupe-colored papers from a bin on his filing cabinet and handed them over. "I'm impressed you're still willing to facilitate given Sadie's circumstances." Meredith eyed the fake plant on his desk. Now that she knew it was artificial, she wondered how she'd ever been fooled.

"It's possible to practice ethical parenting in times of adversity." She'd rehearsed this response. "In fact, it's arguably the most important time."

Whittaker put his palms up. "You're right. I hadn't thought of it that way."

"Will you be sitting in?" Meredith hoped he'd make an appearance at the beginning to give the group some legitimacy. But then she preferred that he leave. Parents might not be as open about their challenges with a school administrator in the room.

"I thought I'd stop by to greet folks." Meredith felt her eye twitch. She hated the word "folks." It sounded so affected.

"Perfect," she said.

"And then I'll see you tomorrow, right? For Sadie's reinstatement meeting?"

Meredith nodded and retreated from the office. She repositioned her nylon grocery bag on her shoulder, feeling the weight of the pumpkin chocolate chip muffins she and Sadie had baked the night before, along with her favorite rectangular porcelain serving dish and some thick paper napkins. She glanced at her Garmin and found there were eight minutes before the meeting convened, enough time to arrange the chairs and lay out the snacks.

When she arrived in the conference room, a mom she knew from elementary, Lynne Graham, had already commandeered the head of the table. Meredith visualized the RSVP list from the week before and didn't remember Lynne's name. She hoped she'd have enough copies.

"How are you doing?" Lynne asked, her eyebrow cocked.

Meredith startled at her conspiratorial tone. Lynne wouldn't know about Sadie. "I'm fine." Meredith smiled. "Great." She set the copies down on the table and began counting chairs.

"I'm so glad to hear it," Lynne said. "It's basically everyone's worst nightmare, right? I'm so surprised it was Sadie who did it first, though. She's been such the straight-and-narrow type. I mean, what a shock."

Meredith dropped her bag on the floor, forgetting about the breakable serving dish.

"Are you okay?" Lynne's smile looked snide.

"What are you talking about?"

"Oh." Lynne's forehead wrinkled. "Did you forget that Larry is on the Elm Creek Soccer board?"

Meredith wilted. She had, in fact, forgotten that Lynne's husband was on the Elm Creek Soccer board. She'd called Walt Cushing about Tane and Teddy, but she hadn't thought about the other board members who'd find out about the photo. She hadn't thought about their spouses and children.

Meredith bent down and pulled the serving dish—unscathed from the fall, thank goodness—from her bag and placed it in the center of the table. "Of course Larry is on the board." Meredith kept her eyes on her treats. "I had forgotten. But, Lynne, can you help me out? I'd really like to keep this as quiet as possible. It's not that I'm embarrassed, but just for Sadie's sake."

"Well, sure . . ." Lynne trailed off as Meredith pulled the muffins out and arranged them on the tray. "But I think it might already be sort of widespread? And now with that graffiti at Elm Creek Park? I've seen it in a few neighborhoods, too. That's related, right?"

"Ethical parenting?" A seventh-grade mom that Meredith recognized as Jess walked in.

"Welcome!" she said, grateful for the distraction from Lynne's insinuations. "I'm so glad you could be here. Jess, right?"

Jess slung her handbag onto the corner of a chair and grabbed a muffin from the tray. "These look amazing," she said. "I'm really excited we're doing this. There's so much to talk about, especially in the new junior high frontier."

Meredith nodded as a couple of other moms walked in. She could see Jason Whittaker in the hallway just outside the room, chatting with Nadia.

"I mean," Jess continued, "talk about the ethics of all this social media stuff." She took a bite and then pointed at the muffin with her free hand. "Delicious!" she mumbled, mouth full. Other parents got settled. Meredith tried to make eye contact with each one, to welcome them. Jess swallowed and kept talking. "I know all about the Finstas, right?" she said. "But now it's really Snapchat you have to worry about."

Meredith held her breath. A surge of nausea overtook her as she sat among the women.

"Right," interjected another mom. "I read that that's where they post their"—she paused, leaned forward, and whispered—"nudes." Meredith gripped her copies. "How scary, right?" the woman continued. "Of course, our kids are still far too young for that sort of thing. Can you imagine?"

"Not too young, unfortunately," said Elizabeth Hunt, whom Meredith knew from book club. "In fact, Alexandra told me she heard rumors this week about kids sending nudes. Meredith, have you heard anything about this?" There was something accusatory about Elizabeth's inquiry.

Meredith shoved the top of a muffin in her mouth and motioned to her chomping jaw, stalling. Lynne jumped in. "I think it's just a couple of boys spreading things around."

Elizabeth nodded. "Alexandra said something about the Elm Creek soccer team. Of course, I'm all for girls reclaiming their sexuality. Don't you think part of ethical parenting is educating our kids about feminism? Both the boys and girls could be part of the fourth wave."

A chocolate chip caught in Meredith's throat. "Maybe we could table the discussion about sexuality." She coughed. The last thing she needed was people forming opinions about her and Sadie before they got to know them. The real Sadie was the UN Service Award. Meredith felt desperate to bury her Snapchat.

"But sexuality has everything to do with ethics!" Elizabeth unzipped her jacket to reveal a "This is what a feminist looks like" T-shirt in bright pink. "In fact, Grace and I and the girls have started a radical feminism club." She pointed at Mikaela's mom, who lifted her sweater to show the same T-shirt. "We're meeting with the girls again this afternoon. It might be perfect for Sadie given—"

"It's two kids from the soccer team," Meredith blurted. She kept an eye on Whittaker and Nadia outside and willed the women to shut up. She had an agenda, and it didn't include Sadie's foray into exhibitionism.

"How do you know?" Jess asked. She seemed guileless, but Meredith wondered if she'd heard the rumors, too. "Sadie isn't involved, is she?"

Shit, Meredith thought. "Absolutely not." She shot a look at Lynne, whose eyebrows nearly reached her hairline. And then she added, "I heard about the photos from a friend."

Meredith pictured Alice's face and felt furious. Alice had never really owned up to Teddy's faults. All that mattered to the Sullivans was soccer. "I'm pretty sure Teddy Sullivan is involved." It felt right to Meredith, saying Teddy's name aloud. He should be the subject of the rumors, not Sadie. It wasn't Meredith's or Sadie's fault that Teddy had sent the picture to kids on the soccer team. That had been inexcusable. "It's serious," Meredith continued, her words coming fast. "I guess the police are involved." She stood then after delivering this last line. She

didn't want to see how Lynne Graham reacted or hear what any of the mothers said next. "I'm going to the restroom," she said over her shoulder, "before the meeting starts." She excused herself past Whittaker and Nadia, who appeared deep in conversation.

She tried to keep her pace reasonably slow as she left, and she heard Jess say, "My Ian did say Teddy's been absent a lot. And I know Alice and Patrick have been stretched pretty thin with work. I guess they missed the signs?" Meredith had put enough distance between herself and the other mothers by then that she didn't hear any of their replies.

Evelyn Brown

The tension between her and Alice was the thickest Evelyn could remember, but she insisted again that week on doing Aidy's Tuesday pickup. Alice had given her the sparest of details about Teddy's continued suspension. Evelyn had opinions, grandmotherly and professional, about the situation, but she had decided not to ask any follow-up questions just yet about online school. It didn't seem right to completely isolate him socially. The better course—what she would have recommended to Alice if she had asked—was integration with supervision.

Evelyn had said to Alice on the phone that she'd pick up Aidy as usual, and then she'd announced that she'd make risotto for dinner. She'd stay and eat with the family whether she was invited or not, because she had to talk to Alice about Thanksgiving. It wouldn't be easy, but the holiday was just three weeks away. If Evelyn was really going through with her plan—and frankly, she was determined to—she had to break the news now. "I know you're busy," Evelyn said before Alice had time to refuse her offer. "Let me help."

And by the time Alice had returned home that evening, dressed more casually than usual in wide-leg jeans and a turquoise blouse, the nutty smell of the Italian dish permeated the kitchen. Evelyn stood at the stove stirring as Alice collapsed on the sectional in the adjoining family room. She pulled the white chenille blanket, rumpled already from Aidy's reading session, over her lap.

Now, Evelyn turned off the stove, the risotto all done but for the Parmesan, and perched on the edge of the sofa near her daughter. A multicolor rug spread beneath her feet, its hues uneven like watercolor.

"So," Alice said. "Everything okay here? Where are the kids?"

Alice peered through the archway into the dining room, checking for them. Evelyn followed her gaze and took in the gorgeous arrangement of orange flowers at the center of the Shaker-style oak table. Evelyn also surveyed the large square color swatches Alice had painted on the adjacent dining room wall, one a darker gray than her kitchen cabinets and one a lighter blue. Alice was always updating something or other, never satisfied though most of her house already looked like the "after" shots on a makeover show.

"They're upstairs. They've been fine. The dining room looks gorgeous. What are you doing with the paint?"

Alice flashed a tired smile. "I'm experimenting for Thanksgiving," she said. "And I've been taking photos for my professional Instagram."

Evelyn put her hands in her lap and stared at Alice's profile, her slight physique. And then, though she couldn't quite decipher Alice's melancholy mood, Evelyn launched into her agenda. "I want to talk about Thanksgiving, actually."

"I ordered the turkey," Alice said. "The heritage organic kind from that butcher in Liston Heights? Didn't you like the darker meat?"

In fact, Evelyn had found the fancy bird to be tougher than their usual Jennie-O, but there was no point in admitting it. "Actually, I'm hoping I can help you. You've been so busy, and there's a bit of a crisis, right? I'm hoping to take something off your plate." Evelyn looked back at the flower arrangement. The whole spotless house belied the turmoil that Evelyn knew her daughter was feeling. She pictured her own living room, the stacks of stray books on the end and coffee tables, teacups that Evelyn had forgotten to put in the dishwasher at the end of various workdays.

"I'd like to have Thanksgiving at my house this year," Evelyn said, definitive.

"What?" Alice jutted her chin.

"Yes." Evelyn forged ahead. "I know you've hosted for years—"

"At least ten years!" Alice interrupted.

Evelyn had known she'd be upset. She lapsed into her therapy voice, an attempt to quell Alice's anxiety. "I want to invite Julienne and her family. Did I mention she has two teenagers? Plus her husband? I think they'd be more comfortable at my place. And I definitely don't want to impose on you by adding to the number." Evelyn pointed at the dining table. Although it was striking in its simplicity, the matching benches definitely wouldn't accommodate four more.

"But I was already experimenting with centerpieces. I have a whole-sale rug on order. I reserved the turkey." She threw an arm out toward the dining room.

"I'll use the turkey." Evelyn could concede to the dark meat if it made Alice feel better. "And I'm actually taking two things off your plate—you won't have to finish the dining room. That would have been a challenge, right? And you won't have to worry about the Thanksgiving dinner. You always kill yourself with that. Maybe instead you could just bring the cornbread rolls the kids like so much?"

Evelyn looked at the watercolor rug, the places where the pink diffused into orange. She pushed away her guilt over Alice's obvious distress, the tightness of her jaw and her simultaneously wild and hollow eyes. Evelyn felt bad about taking Thanksgiving, of course, but this was a onetime thing. And Alice was nearing forty years old. Evelyn had structured her entire life around her daughter. Now that she was middle-aged, there could surely be some balance in their relationship, rather than Evelyn always taking on the supporting role.

"It might help," Evelyn pressed on, "if you'd call Julienne again before then. I'd appreciate it if you'd put in a bit more effort. Especially after . . ." Evelyn paused, not sure how to describe Alice's therapy transgression. "What happened," she said.

Alice closed her eyes as she pulled the blanket up to her chin. "Okay,

Mom." She didn't move. "Let's have dinner. I know you'll want to get home."

Evelyn's anger sparked. Alice had waltzed in, her dinner made and her kids cared for. After everything Evelyn had done for her, all the sacrifices she'd made and continued to make, Thanksgiving at her house just one time didn't seem like that big of an ask. Evelyn marched to the kitchen, lit the burner under the Dutch oven, and poured her premeasured Parmesan into the risotto. She stirred aggressively, then dropped the spoon next to the pan and grabbed her coat. "I'll go now," she said, hustling toward the impeccable mudroom. "Your dinner's ready."

Alice Sullivan

— — — —

When Patrick called that night, Alice, too, had an agenda. With Thanksgiving on the horizon, she couldn't wait any longer to confess her big mistake to her husband. But she decided to start with the other news: "My mom wants to host Thanksgiving this year."

"What?" Patrick asked. "Why? She didn't like that organic dark meat?" Alice could hear the laughter in his voice, and she held on to that warmth. His reaction would be less affable when she told him what she'd done.

"Was the turkey really that bad?" Alice stared at the ceiling. Their bedroom ceiling was the first she'd scraped of that dreaded popcorn. It had taken a full weekend, and by Sunday dinner Patrick had been ragged from entertaining four-year-old Teddy.

"How often do we even look at the ceiling?" he'd said, exasperated. But Alice knew that was the secret of a well-designed space. She thought out every detail, even elements people didn't realize they were seeing.

"The turkey was fine," he said now. "Great. You know I love dark meat. I was kidding. Why is your mom hosting Thanksgiving?"

Alice put her left hand on her forehead. She could feel the cool platinum of her wedding band against her skin. "Okay," Alice said. "I did something really stupid."

"What?" Patrick sounded distracted. "Does this have to do with the holiday?"

"Sort of, or at least I think it does." She'd just have to spit it out. "You know how Julienne is a therapist?"

"Yeah."

"Well, she's Donovan Reddy's therapist, so Nadia had already recommended her to me when I found out who she was."

"That's a funny coincidence," Patrick said.

"So that's where I took Teddy," Alice blurted.

"What?" Alice felt impatient now for him to understand what she'd done and to forgive her for it.

"I'd already made an appointment with Dr. Martín when Mom told me who she was. I thought about canceling it, but I didn't. We went." Alice moaned. "Without telling her who we were."

Patrick laughed.

Alice blinked. "Why are you laughing?"

"Because that's so stupid, Al." He kept laughing. "I mean, what did you think would happen?"

Alice chuckled herself, so relieved by his response that it didn't even occur to her to be offended that he'd called her stupid. "I just wanted to see her." Alice laughed harder, imagining the scenario from Patrick's point of view.

"Did you, like, consider going in disguise? Like a spy? So when you met her later in real life, she wouldn't know it was you?" His guffaws came faster, and Alice heard him snort, which elicited a squeal on her part. She rolled onto her side and curled into a ball, her whole body shaking with giggles.

"I'm so dumb," she said finally, when they'd each caught their breath.

Patrick sighed. "So, because you did this ridiculous spying, your mom feels like she can move Thanksgiving to her house?"

Alice pushed her hair off her face. "I guess," she said. And then,

when Patrick didn't say anything right away, she added, "I guess that's fair?"

"Yep." Patrick started laughing again. "I'm just imagining you with one of those glasses-and-nose disguises, like with the big fuzzy eyebrows."

Alice's stomach hurt. "Stop!"

"Okay," Patrick said, "but now what? Is there a new therapist, or what?"

"Yeah. Miss Perfect recommended her partner. A guy. And a nature therapy group." Alice imagined Patrick barefoot in the forest, his blond hair ruffling in the breeze. She snorted again, on the verge of losing it.

"Fine." Patrick chuckled one last time. "So," he said, mischievous, "what are you wearing?"

"Are you for real right now?" Alice sat up and rolled her eyes. Her teeth felt fuzzy, and she still had garlic on her breath from the risotto. "I'm wearing dirty flannel pants and your Twins T-shirt with the holes in the armpits."

"Mmm," Patrick said. "Sexy."

Alice laughed. "I'll talk to you tomorrow."

Sadie Yoshida

Normally, Sadie's mom didn't pick her outfits for school. "Comb your hair," she'd sometimes yell toward the bathroom while Sadie brushed her teeth and washed her face.

Before this whole thing had started, Sadie used to hide her eye shadow and mascara in her backpack. There'd be no point in doing that today, she knew. Her mom planned to get to school seconds before the bell, so Sadie wouldn't have time to touch up in the bathroom. The late arrival was just one way in which Sadie was supposed to become a totally different person. They'd covered the others in the awkward meeting with Whittaker and Officer Larson the day before. The meeting passed in ten minutes, thank goodness. The adults said stuff about appropriate boundaries and self-respect, a phrase that made Sadie squirm.

Officer Larson had been especially aggressive and cringey. "Listen," she'd said, leaning uncomfortably close to Sadie, so close that Sadie could smell her mint gum, "besides the fact that underaged nudes are illegal, you've got to own your power. Don't let boys' stupidity bring you down. You got it?" Sadie wondered whether Officer Larson knew about the new radical feminism group. Maybe she had one of those pink T-shirts like Alexandra Hunt's.

Sadie's mother had contributed comments in the reinstatement meeting about remembering where Sadie came from, about "auditing

her decisions," about being "purposeful as she got older regarding the people with whom she associated." That was what Sadie's mom had said—"with whom." She'd rehearsed that line for sure, Sadie thought. She'd probably written it out after reading tons of articles about how to coach your daughter through "a difficult time." Sadie had found multiple back issues of *Thinking Mother* around the house during her suspension.

Her mother had read other articles in the past about how it was bad to focus on appearances. She regularly corrected her grandmothers when they complimented Sadie's looks. ("June," she'd say to her dad's mom, "we're putting our emphasis on Sadie's intrinsic qualities.") Nevertheless, the night before Sadie went back to school after the suspension, her mom had flicked through the shirts in Sadie's closet.

"Don't you think it'll be weird if I don't look normal?" Sadie had asked as she sat on her bed. She'd pulled her knees up to her chest and rested her chin on them. Her boobs squished against her thighs. They felt bigger than they had before. They *were* bigger, she knew. She pictured the way the skin poked out of the bras she and her mom had bought that summer, little soft pouches escaping next to her armpits. At some point, Sadie thought, Meredith would notice that she'd grown out of them and a new set would appear in her underwear drawer. That was always the way she moved up sizes. New skating tights or a bigger leotard just magically appeared in her bag.

And with the bras, her mom had seen that stupid photo anyway, Sadie thought. She should know Sadie had gotten bigger. It was obvious.

"I think you should aim for a good impression," Meredith said, her back to Sadie as she pawed through the closet. "Make a clean break from the person who would take that picture. Show that you're moving on."

Sadie lowered her nose into the crack between her knees, feeling her leggings against her cheeks.

"And real pants," her mother was saying, "Jeans. Not leggings." She pulled jeans from Sadie's drawer and threw them on the bed. "Just for tomorrow."

In the morning, Sadie put on the skinny jeans and pink cotton sweater. She'd layered a T-shirt underneath to smooth out the lines of her bra and tried to act normal when her mom pulled into the car pool circle.

"Something else will have already happened," Sadie said, mostly to herself. "People will be over it."

Meredith nodded. It wasn't true, Sadie knew. None of them had ever sent a nude before. And with all three of them—her, Teddy, and Tane—suspended and, like, breaking laws? People would definitely still be talking about it.

"Can I have my phone?" Sadie's mom sighed as she reached for her purse. She lifted the flap on the front pocket and took out Sadie's iPhone with the floral *Moana* case.

"Texting and calling only," her mom said.

Sadie got out of the car without answering. She shoved the phone into her back pocket, rolled her shoulders, and headed straight to English without even stopping at her locker. None of her friends were in Mr. O'Connor's class, so it'd be an easy start. She slid into her seat just as the bell rang.

Mr. O'Connor looked up with narrowed eyes when he got to her name on the attendance list. "Welcome back." He didn't sound friendly.

Do all the teachers know about the photo, too? Mr. O'Connor didn't call on her once during their discussion about strength and perseverance in *The Old Man and the Sea*. When Sadie stopped at her locker before science, she was relieved to see Chloe waiting for her there.

"Hi," Sadie said. "Thanks for waiting." Chloe had never once not waited for her, but Sadie wasn't sure where they stood. Maybe Lacy

and Walt, Chloe's parents whom Sadie had known forever, had told her not to talk to Sadie. Maybe they thought she was a bad influence.

"Duh." Chloe smiled mildly. The two turned simultaneously toward the science labs, and Sadie felt her heart pound as they caught a glimpse of Tane in front of them. His head floated above most of the crowd. She wondered if he felt as weird about being back as she did. "Things are different for boys," Sadie's mom had said about two hundred times.

"Are you nervous?" Chloe asked. She pointed at Tane.

"Sort of." Sadie caught McCoy Blumenfeld staring at her as they walked past his locker. He waggled his eyebrows, and Sadie realized he'd probably seen the picture, too. She winced, imagining him staring at her boob. "Do your parents want you to stop hanging out with me?" Sadie hadn't planned to ask Chloe this, but the question bubbled out of her.

"What?" Chloe bumped against her shoulder. "No!" Her voice sounded warm, but she seemed jumpy.

"But?" Sadie remembered her mom on the phone with Walt, asking him what he would have done if the photo had been of Chloe. *It would never be of Chloe*, Sadie thought. Chloe had convinced her to spend recesses in fifth grade picking up sticks on the soccer field next to the playground. "To make sure kids don't trip in PE," she'd said. Chloe wasn't about to take her top off. Her idea of risk taking was a slice of pepperoni pizza instead of plain cheese in the school cafeteria.

"But nothing." Sadie recognized a stubbornness in Chloe's voice, the same tone she used to get her way about sleepover activities or hairstyles for synchro.

Sadie felt woozy as they approached Mr. Robinson's door. Inside, Tane was already in his assigned seat near the front window. Sadie couldn't follow Mr. Robinson's lesson during science. It was something about the food chain. Energy transfer, she thought he said. Chloe, whose seat was kitty-corner from Sadie's, had two full pages of notes by

the end of the period. Meanwhile, Sadie had spent the entire time staring at a red patch of skin on the back of Tane's neck. It expanded a little bit as he scratched it, and Sadie wondered if maybe it was a bug bite.

When it came time for lunch, the biggest land mine in her day, Sadie grabbed her insulated bag from her locker. Her mother had packed one of her favorite bentos, turkey roll-ups and apple slices with cinnamon sprinkled on them. There'd be some celery sticks, Sadie knew, in one of the other compartments. And maybe, if she was lucky, some chocolate chips. Chloe was getting hot lunch, so Sadie stood alone.

She stared at the Quiz Bowl table. Gretchen and Yusef were there already. Gretchen animatedly talked with her hands. Probably, Sadie thought, they were discussing how Douglas Lim would come off the bench and help them to victory. Tane wasn't there yet.

"Stay away from him," Sadie's mother had said. "Just act like he's not there."

She headed toward her old table once Chloe got out of the hot lunch line, a piece of cheese pizza and a bag of chips on her tray. Tane strode in front of them, passing so close to Sadie that she could feel the air move around her as he went by. He didn't look back at her, though she knew he must have seen her. And, in a majorly shocking move, he veered away from Gretchen and Yusef's table and went straight to McCoy and Landon's. They high-fived him when he got there. Sadie watched as he pushed his hair out of his face and sat down. She thought for a millisecond that he might have glanced at her, but if he did, it was so quick it hardly counted.

Chloe elbowed her. "Come on," she said. And Sadie followed her to their old table. Mikaela and a few other girls raised their eyebrows at her, but Chloe kept talking.

"I was watching a YouTube tutorial," Chloe said, "about French braids that start from the bottom and go up." She pointed at her hairline just below her right ear and then touched the back of her head.

"And then, that's where your ponytail goes. That would be cool for synchro, right?"

Sadie nodded, but she realized she didn't care. She took a deep breath and felt her bra tighten uncomfortably around her rib cage. She glanced over her shoulder at Tane, McCoy, and Landon. *No Teddy.* Her mother had told her he'd be homeschooled. She'd thought that was so unlucky, but now that the seventh grade seemed sort of ruined, she wasn't so sure.

Teddy Sullivan

Teddy had known better than to ask his mom for his phone in the days after Officer Larson had made that speech about pornography and the district attorney. He waited a full week after that horrible meeting in Whittaker's office, and then carefully planned his request.

He'd been taking online homeschool lessons on persuasive speeches, and he was ready for real-life practice. "It's Landon's thirteenth birthday," he said when his mom looked up from her computer.

She'd stopped wearing makeup, mostly. When she had meetings, she at least combed her hair. A couple of times per day, he heard her on the phone with the office.

"Oh?" she said now about Landon. She blinked at him, as if she were confused.

"And I have just one special request." Teddy planted his feet shoulder-width apart and puffed his chest. "I want to text him 'happy birthday.'"

His mom shook her head. "Teddy, we've discussed this." They hadn't, really, but that argument wasn't part of his plan.

"But, Mom, I have some reasons. Just listen." She opened her mouth to speak, but he kept going. "Please!" he said, louder than he'd meant to.

His mom pushed her computer away and frowned at him. "Okay," she said, though she didn't look enthusiastic. "I'm listening."

"I have three reasons." Three, he'd learned in those online lessons, was a good number. He'd start with the weakest reason and end with the best. "First, I know I need supervision, so I'm asking you to turn the texting app on just for a few minutes, but you can sit next to me while I look at it. You can watch what I text to Landon. Nothing bad will happen."

Teddy's mom nodded. Her eyes looked a little less flat. "Second, I totally get my punishments, right? But I don't think you meant to make it so I could never have friends again. I'm not in school, I'm not in soccer, and I'm not allowed to have a phone. Is that kind of isolation really good for a kid? Do any of your books recommend that?"

He knew he was right about this one. A day or two of lockdown seemed reasonable, but a lifetime ban from social interaction? That couldn't be healthy. And it had been smart of him to mention her parenting books, to "cite the research," as his online teacher had said.

"One more," he said before his mother had time to break in. "I'm going to reenter the world eventually, right? So if you sit by me—if you watch me—you can help me make good decisions." Teddy sighed then; his arms relaxed. He hadn't realized he'd been flexing.

He locked eyes with his mom, and she looked at him for what seemed like a long time. Finally, he smiled at her. A big grin, the kind he remembered flashing from the back seat when he'd beg for a caramel sundae after soccer. It almost always worked.

She laughed, and he kept smiling. "Come here," she said. She stood from her computer and reached for him. A hug? Teddy didn't particularly want one, but it seemed a small price to pay for some text messages with his friends.

He laid his head against her shoulder and let her squeeze. She smelled like Tide and coffee. "Okay," she said before she let go. "Okay. We'll do it this evening when Landon's likely to be home, so you can see his replies."

Alice Sullivan

Alice left Teddy alone when she went to grab Aidy from the car pool line. Things had mostly been going better in the last week. Aidy had books labeled "G" in her bag these days. And though Teddy's online school—his omnipresence in the house—served as a daily reminder of the trouble they'd all been through, Alice felt the tiniest bit relieved, panic quelled for several days. If Teddy couldn't go to Elm Creek, he couldn't make terrible choices there. If he didn't have access to his phone, he couldn't engage in toxic social media. He still had the Internet because he had to do his online school on the family laptop, but Alice supervised him. She *really* supervised him.

Things were going reasonably well with the kids. And so, of course, work was a disaster. The line her mother always used was, "You can have it all; you just can't have it all at the same time." The truth of the adage had never stopped Alice from trying.

Now, Ramona had told Alice she wouldn't have access to the conference room going forward, as she wasn't actually partnering with her on any projects. And there'd been another defaced Ramona Design lawn sign that appeared on NextDoor. "What's this #TT?" Shirley MacIntosh had asked in her post. Ramona had started a conversation with Alice about it on Slack. "Could it be possible that your son is doing this?" she asked, without even a hint of sympathy. "That's what my sister heard from her neighbors who go to Elm Creek Junior High."

Patrick hadn't had time to review Alice's noncompete, not with the Energy Lab case in its final push, but he'd be home soon. *Until the next time we get Sachman'd.*

Teddy was waiting for Alice when she and Aidy tramped through the mudroom after pickup. "Aidy, take off your shoes!" Alice called. Her daughter stopped, braced herself against the door frame, and slid each of her light-up sneakers off, leaving them in the middle of the runner, the same one Alice purchased for at least eighty-five percent of her mudroom clients. "Nope!" Alice corrected as Aidy ran out, her tights sliding on the wood floor.

Aidy sighed and slumped back in. She grabbed her shoes, roughly pulled out her assigned seagrass basket, and dumped them inside with an imperious look at Alice.

"Thank you!" Alice went overboard cheerful and then shared an eye roll with Teddy. Her irritation morphed into a genuine smile. Teddy had been a fun kid before junior high, she remembered. Maybe he could be fun again.

He held out his locked phone to her. "Let's text Landon," he said.

She hung her jacket on a hook and traded her shoes for slippers. "Okay." She took the phone and pointed at the dining room table. They sat together on one of the sturdy benches. Alice loved the family feel of the thick half-trunk seat. She navigated to the app on her phone that let her control his device and pressed the requisite buttons.

She set his phone on the table between them, and they both watched it come to life. She and Patrick had flat-out deleted Instagram and Snapchat, but a long string of texts popped up, including a zillion messages on a group chat with Landon and McCoy and a couple of other kids from soccer.

"Let's just start by texting Landon," Alice said. She glanced at Teddy, whose eyes sparkled at the prospect of connecting.

Teddy typed and then tipped the phone, so Alice could see. "Dude," Teddy had written. "HBD. Maybe we can hang soon." He'd added a cartoon avatar of himself with a party hat on.

She nodded, and he pressed send.

"Now, can I read the group chat?" Teddy's hands shook as he asked her, and she almost laughed at his anticipation.

"Sure, but I have to see." Teddy didn't argue. He clicked the thread and scrolled back. There seemed to be hundreds of messages. "Whoa," Alice said.

"Yeah, and just remember most of it's on Snapchat." She tried to read some of the comments, but Teddy paged back too quickly. Finally, he stopped. "Okay," he said. "Soccer . . ." He flipped ahead more slowly.

"Great win?" Alice read aloud. "They won against Liston Heights last weekend?" A message from Landon read, "I didn't think we could do it without T & T, but we did. Way to show up, boys." Alice put a hand on Teddy's shoulder, not sure if he'd prefer that the team won or lost without him, but he shrugged her off. He'd stopped smiling and scrolled down a little further.

A day or two later, McCoy had written, "Tane at striker? What do u think?" Alice frowned.

Teddy dropped the phone. "Tane's playing?" He flipped through a couple more messages with the screen flat on the table, his friends' assessments of Tane in Teddy's old position.

"Maybe this is—" Alice reached for the phone, but Teddy yanked it away. "Hey," she said, a warning in her tone.

"Sorry," Teddy spat, though he sounded sincere. "I just have to . . ." His breath caught. Alice leaned farther over Teddy's shoulder.

"Why does Tane get to play, but not Teddy?" Landon had asked.

Derrick had written, "My parents say it's because Tane has a better lawyer."

"He has a lawyer? Do we have a lawyer?" Teddy sounded desperate.

Alice had no idea whether the Lagerheads actually had a lawyer, but Derrick's mom was an assistant coach. She might know. "Honey, we don't have a lawyer," she said.

"But Dad's a lawyer!" Teddy stared at her. "Can he get me back on the team?"

"I don't think this is a good idea." Alice picked the phone up and moved to delete the group chat. She also felt angry about Tane but tried to hide it. Consequences should be consequences for everyone. She'd call Patrick as soon as she could distract the kids. Just then, a reply text came in from Landon, the notification louder than either of them expected.

Teddy grabbed the phone back. "Let me see." Alice let him hold it away from her and watched his face. As he read, his eyes went flat. She saw nothing of the mischievous sparkle she'd enjoyed during his persuasive speech the night before. Eventually, he put the phone back on the table, stood, and stared over her head at the swing in the backyard.

"Take it," he said. "I don't need it." He walked toward the stairs without looking back.

Alice's chest ached as she picked up the phone and read Landon's reply: "Oh man! You're alive. Hey, thanks. I'm having a party this weekend, but I know you can't come. And actually, since you're not on ECSC anymore, my parents say it'll be good to have some distance. And, like, I know I need to think about my reputation. L8R, man."

Alice's fury made her vision blur as she held the power button on the side of the phone until the whole screen went black. As if none of those kids had ever made—or would ever make—a mistake.

LATER, PATRICK GROANED when Alice told him about the texts, about Tane at Teddy's old position.

"Walt Cushing is the head of commercial lending for Twin Cities Federal," Patrick said. "I know they've done a bunch of work with Prince Development. Doesn't Janna Lagerhead work there?"

Alice googled. She found Janna's gorgeous headshot on the Prince Development webpage. Alice pictured her leather pants. "She's the CFO," Alice said, breathless. She'd known Janna had a high-powered career, but she hadn't realized she was an executive.

"Ugh." Patrick sounded dejected.

"What?"

"She'd be involved in every transaction, and she probably does millions of dollars' worth of business with Twin Cities Federal. With Walt Cushing."

Alice felt sick. So Meredith's connection with the Cushings was enough to get Teddy barred from the club, but not enough to overpower Walt and Janna's financial relationship. Plus, there'd been whatever lawyer Derrick referenced.

She'd try to explain all this to Teddy, but he wouldn't understand how these kinds of adult negotiations sidestepped fairness. She was glad, at least, that Teddy didn't have to go to school, to see the kids in their uniforms on game days and experience the isolation firsthand.

Before she walked upstairs to Teddy's room, she poured a Maker's Mark on ice. It was Patrick's favorite, but it would steel her nerves. When she got to Teddy's room he hid his face in his pillow. "Mom," he said, "I'm fine, but I just don't want to talk."

"But I have some answers." Alice pressed on. "I could try to explain—"

"Tomorrow," Teddy said. He stuck in his earbuds to make sure she got the message.

Evelyn Brown

A week had gone by since Evelyn had told Alice about Thanksgiving. It had been a week without phone calls and without her usual Tuesday with Aidy. Still, Evelyn sent periodic text messages and hoped that in a few days, they could move on from the risotto incident. Evelyn had been angry, obviously, when Alice responded so negatively to the Thanksgiving change, but in the days that followed, she reminded herself that Alice was under a great deal of stress.

"Just remember," Evelyn wrote to her midweek, "you can do this!" She'd included a GIF of Arnold Schwarzenegger from the "Hans & Franz" days of *SNL*. Aidy had shown her how to text those. She hoped the humor would break Alice's silence, but Evelyn didn't get a response.

"Did you try nature therapy?" she wrote a few days later. Julienne couldn't confirm whether Alice had agreed to go ahead with care at Green Haven, but she hoped so. She smiled as she imagined Julienne's earthing protocol. It was hard to picture Teddy doing it, wiggling his toes in the mud and again in the drying grass. Most often when Evelyn had seen Teddy outside, he wore soccer cleats. Evelyn pictured him sitting quietly during forest bathing.

"Yes." Alice wrote back the one word, and that was enough. The fact that he was doing the program delighted her.

"Good for you, honey." Evelyn wanted to prop Alice up, to tell her that despite every setback, she was doing okay. It wasn't easy to get an

almost-teenager into therapy, and Alice had gotten him not only to the office, but to the nature group. Teddy, Evelyn knew, was in the best possible hands, in the care of each of her brilliant daughters.

And so, a few days after Teddy's first nature therapy group, Evelyn thought the timing might be right to send her first family email—one to both Julienne and Alice at the same time—about her desires for Thanksgiving. She'd write in the spirit of admiration she truly felt for each of them. They were in a good place with each other, she reasoned. Teddy was safe at Green Haven, and Thanksgiving was only two weeks away.

Evelyn wrote "THANKSGIVING PLANS" as the subject line of her email, and couldn't help but start with "Girls!" as a salutation. She grinned to herself and clapped her hands, the sound echoing in the exposed ceiling of her condo. What a thrill to address them collectively. She kept typing: "There's been a slight change in the plans I shared with you, Alice, in that Julienne has agreed to host us. Rafael is going to offer a Spanish take on the traditional Thanksgiving feast, and I think it'll be really something."

Please accept this, Evelyn pleaded with Alice from afar as she continued.

"This will be a special Thanksgiving for many reasons," Evelyn went on. "For one, I'm hoping to get my first full family photo. I know I might be overdoing it, but I'm thinking it would be great if everyone wore blues and greens to unify the look. I'd love to frame this shot! I know blue and green aren't typical for Thanksgiving, but I figure not everyone has red, orange, and yellow."

Alice, Evelyn knew, looked great in red, but it really wasn't flattering on her or Julienne. Evelyn smiled again thinking about Julienne's coloring. It still amazed her she and Julienne shared so many physical features.

"Now for assignments," Evelyn typed. "Rafael is going to provide us with some Spanish flavors, but that doesn't mean we have to forgo the

Brown family favorites." Evelyn wanted the Sullivans to feel comfortable, too. "Alice, I already asked you to bring some cornbread rolls. Julienne said it would also help if you'd do the mashed potatoes. I'm sure that will work, right? I remember Aidy liked helping with those last year."

Evelyn realized she didn't know what Laura and Miguel liked to help with. She'd pay close attention this year, file every detail away.

"Love you, girls." Then she cut and pasted the time and address. Evelyn felt so overjoyed that she cried a little as she clicked send. Never in a million years would she have imagined a Thanksgiving with both of her daughters and all four of her grandchildren. Although Alice had been angry about the change in plans at first, Evelyn knew she'd pull it together for the big day. She had always made Evelyn proud, and she certainly would in this case, when the holiday had always meant so much to both of them.

Sadie Yoshida

On the Wednesday before Thanksgiving, Mr. Robinson frowned at Sadie's forehead when he put her ecology test upside down on her desk. Sadie knew right then that she hadn't pulled it off. She'd thought that maybe the last-minute cram session—the emergency texts with Chloe about population sampling and food supply—would carry her through. She grabbed the stapled test packet and closed her eyes. She could hear other people's high fives and sighs as she crossed her ankles and rubbed the tops of her boots together.

When she opened her eyes, she looked directly at Tane. He smiled down at his paper, flipping the pages. Of course he'd done well. He did as well as anyone in Quiz Bowl on the science questions. He'd probably read dozens of articles already about the food chain, about biological diversity and consumptive use, and about whatever other terms Sadie had forgotten when it came time to take the stupid test. Tane, she noticed, didn't think to look back at *her*. That was one of the worst parts of this. His reaction to the photo and the aftermath had been the ultimate cliché. He hadn't messaged her since they'd been back at school. Officer Larson had been right when she'd said Sadie had ceded her power to a boy.

Sadie peeled the top of her test off the desktop just high enough to see Mr. Robinson's purple felt-tip writing. She dropped it again before she could make sense of it, not wanting to internalize the truth that she

already knew. The bell rang then, and everyone stood. Sadie did, too, placing the facedown test on top of her notebook and folder. "What'd you get?" Chloe asked.

"I haven't looked yet," Sadie said. "I know it's bad."

While she was afraid to see the results, she felt oddly detached from them, as if caring about how she'd done on a science test was something the old Sadie would have done.

"Sadie?" It was Mr. Robinson.

Chloe's mouth formed an O. "See you at lunch," she whispered.

Sadie nodded and turned toward Mr. Robinson's desk. "What do you think?" The teacher leaned back in his chair and folded his arms across his belly.

"Um," Sadie said. She looked down at the upside-down test. "I haven't looked yet. I know it's not, uh—" She looked over Mr. Robinson's shoulder at the set of three test tubes he kept in his bookshelf, each with a single daisy sticking up over the lip. "I know it's not good."

Mr. Robinson raised an eyebrow. "It's a D." Sadie swallowed.

"And, since you've already used your retake this quarter, that grade sticks, Ms. Yoshida." Sadie hated when teachers called kids by their last names with Ms. or Mr. Maybe it was supposed to make her feel older, but it actually just made her feel embarrassed and weird.

"Okay." She backed toward the door, hoping that was all.

"Hold on." Mr. Robinson sat up straight. "I want to make sure you know that means your midterm grade is a C."

A C. On my report card. Sadie tried to imagine her mother's face, her mother who said that grades weren't important—that hard work was what really mattered—but who had never gotten anything lower than an A– in her life.

"So what's your plan?"

"What?"

"What's your idea," Mr. Robinson said slowly, "about how to change course? You don't seem like the kind of person who gets Cs. Am I right?"

She felt herself blink a couple of times. She wondered if he was saying this because she was Asian, if that was why he thought she wasn't the type to get a C.

"Aren't you on Quiz Bowl?"

"Was," Sadie said. "I got bumped." And then an idea came to her. "I know what I'm going to do."

Mr. Robinson turned his palm up and pursed his lips, signaling for her to continue. He looked like such a weirdo. Did he know that?

"I'm going to quit synchro."

"Synchro?" Mr. Robinson asked. "Like swimming?"

"Skating," Sadie said. "It takes a ton of time, and it's sometimes late at night. If I quit synchro, I'll have more time to study."

The idea seemed perfect to Sadie just then. Her mom had told her, after all, that she'd have to become a completely different person in order to leave the photo behind. She'd also leave the glitter and the hair bows and the leotards. They didn't look right anyway with her bigger boobs.

Mr. Robinson seemed pleased. "We all have to make tough decisions sometimes when things are spiraling. Talk to your parents about it."

Sadie walked out of the science lab thinking about her mom. She usually had a tea in hand as she sat in the stands during practice watching the team move in and out of their formations. She had her own Elkettes sweatshirt that she wore for competitions. She'd tell her mom that night, Sadie decided, about both the team and the C. Both at the same time.

Meredith Yoshida

Meredith dropped her cell phone into the center console and closed the lid as soon as Sadie was buckled into the back seat after school. The most important factor in whether teen drivers adhered to distracted driving laws was parental role modeling. Meredith never touched her phone when Sadie was in the car. On days like today, that was especially difficult. There were a million things to check on before they drove the three hours south to her mother's house for Thanksgiving.

"Everything go okay today? Ready for vacation?" Meredith asked as they passed the school's empty baseball diamond. The grass in the outfield had turned a rusty brown. Meredith hated Minnesota winters, and the damp air smelled like snow. The weather matched Sadie's gloomy energy.

"Yeah."

"Classes fine?" Sadie used to give unlimited details about her school days without prompting. Not that long ago, Meredith and Bill used to roll their eyes behind Sadie's back, wishing she'd skip some of the play-by-play. But now, in seventh grade, it seemed like Sadie told only the bare minimum, especially after all of this trouble.

"It was all good, Mom, but I have to tell you something."

Meredith gripped the steering wheel hard. "What?" She glanced at the rearview, checking to see whether Sadie was crying or looked scared. "Did something happen with the boys?"

Sadie shook her head. "No, it's not like that."

"Then what?" Meredith's voice had gone high. *Calm*, she reminded herself, though the mantra sounded like a shriek in her head.

Sadie tipped her chin up, her throat exposed. Meredith forced herself to watch the road. "It's just science."

Meredith felt her grip relax a bit. Academics, she could deal with. "What about it?"

"Well, don't freak out."

Calm, Meredith told herself again.

"It's just, Mr. Robinson told me today I'm getting a C. Like, for the midterm. It'll be on my report card."

C, Meredith repeated to herself. *Calm*. She tightened her grip again on the wheel. What was it with this teacher? Sadie had never scored poorly on anything in her life, at any point in her schooling. And then, this one guy in this one class—

"And," Sadie said. Meredith gritted her teeth. "I've been thinking." Meredith sped through a yellow light, anxious to get home. "It's time for me to quit the Elkettes."

Meredith pressed harder on the gas. She imagined Sadie with her tight French braids, the silky purple ribbons. She pictured the shelves in the basement where they'd lined up the old pairs of skates. "We can trade these in," Bill had said. "Get a discount on the next pair." But Meredith couldn't do it. She wanted to remember their only daughter wearing skates at all of her different ages. When she looked at them on her way to the laundry room, she remembered the first spins, the first jumps, the first podium finish for the Elkettes, Sadie holding a trophy bigger than herself.

"It's just, my priorities are changing," Sadie said. Her voice sounded distant, as if she were speaking to Meredith through a tin-can phone. "And I obviously need more time for my studies." The stoplight in front of Meredith flipped from green to yellow. Her distance from the intersection was too far to make it, even if she floored it, and instead she

slammed on the brakes. Sadie's head thudded against the headrest as the car ground to a squeaky halt. "Mom!" she shouted.

"Sorry," Meredith muttered. She couldn't think of anything else to say, not about the C, not about the Elkettes. She still flashed on the photo multiple times per day, the image of her half-naked daughter sneaking into her consciousness while she performed neck and hip mobilizations in the clinic. Her first thought about Sadie's new revelation was to call Alice to vent. Together, they'd talked about parenting teenagers in a detached sense, laughing nervously about other people's problems. Sadie's teen years were going to be solid, Meredith had been sure of it. But now Sadie seemed worst-case-scenario, and Meredith couldn't call Alice.

She watched the cars stream in front of her through the intersection, their headlights bright in the murky fall afternoon. She could hear Sadie breathing hard behind her. Meredith wondered what Alice was doing this afternoon. Did she supervise Teddy for online school? She remembered the pink "rocket ship" she and Lacy Cushing had seen on the trailhead sign at the park after they'd passed Alice and Nadia that day. Lacy had pointed backward, her thumb indicating the path where Alice walked behind them. "If you ask me," she'd said, "that disgusting graffiti is his fault, too."

"Do you know anything about that pink graffiti?" Meredith asked now.

"Hmm?" Sadie blinked.

"Those penises," Meredith said. She watched her daughter flinch at the word but carried on. If Sadie was sophisticated enough to send a nude photo, certainly she could handle hearing the medical terminology for male anatomy.

"Oh." Sadie kicked at the floor. "Not really."

"Not *really*?" Meredith's "calm" mantra dissolved, and she found herself shouting. "Sarah June Yoshida, if you know a *single* shred of information about—"

"Chill!" Sadie yelled, and after she'd succeeded in interrupting, she was quieter. "Mom, chill."

"Don't you dare tell me to chill—"

"Look!" Sadie interrupted again. "The only thing I've heard about those tags was when Grace and Alexandra talked about their feminist club."

Meredith remembered the T-shirts she'd seen at the ethical parenting discussion. "What about the club?"

"They said at lunch that it was such a relief that after decades of people's obsessions with, um . . ." She paused.

"What?" The light turned green and Meredith broke the eye contact she'd been maintaining through the rearview mirror.

"It's just, they said, after like everyone being obsessed with women's bodies, it was nice to see some male parts." Sadie coughed. "Like getting attention, or something."

THE ROUTE TO Meredith's mother's house in southern Minnesota, a small town thirty miles from the nearest Target, took them out of Elm Creek past the Sullivans' neighborhood. She imagined Alice's spotless kitchen. Alice's turkey would come out perfectly in an All-Clad roasting pan. She'd post the proof on her professional Instagram.

Bill had turned on an investment podcast in the car, and they'd all been quiet for several minutes. Meredith stared at the brown Minnesota landscape, trees void of leaves but not yet covered in snow as Bill drove the Jeep out of the metro. Finally, Sadie spoke softly from the back seat. "Does Grandma know?"

Meredith leaned back against the headrest and blinked at the withered cornstalks in the field outside. She thought about asking, *Know what?* But it was obvious.

"No," Meredith said. She knew she should try to sound upbeat, but she felt so tired, her eyelids heavy. She had whispered to Bill about synchro and the C as they'd loaded their luggage. He had hugged her and said they'd talk later. But when? They'd be in her mother's four-room house all weekend.

"You didn't tell her?" Sadie sounded small. Usually Sadie approached challenges with bravado, shoulders back. Meredith pictured her right arm out, chin lifted as the Elkettes glided onto the ice to take their positions before their music began. Sadie never showed a hint of reservation. Where would she hone her confidence now that she'd apparently left skating behind?

"I didn't tell her." Meredith kept her eyes on the fields.

A few seconds later, her daughter broke in again. "Because you're embarrassed?"

Meredith looked at Bill. He paused the podcast. They'd both been mortified, of course. Bill hadn't so much as made eye contact with Sadie since Meredith had shown him the photo. What dad wants to see that? What *mom* does? Beneath her intense anger at Alice and at the boys who'd shared the picture, she knew that yes, she was embarrassed. She was shocked and appalled and humiliated that her daughter was the one who'd made such a public and stupid mistake.

Bill shrugged, deferring as usual. "I guess, yes," Meredith said. She turned and caught Sadie's eye. Her daughter's skin looked peaked, her eyes tired, too. "It's not the kind of thing I like to tell my mother."

Sadie's lips pressed together. "I know," she said. "I know I'm such a disappointment." And then she turned toward the driver's-side window. Meredith followed her gaze to the opposite-direction traffic, to the families headed to the city for the holiday.

Alice Sullivan

The first thing Alice noticed were the planters on Julienne's porch—big, matte metal vats filled with fall foliage and artfully placed sticks. *No way she did those herself,* thought Alice as Patrick pulled up to the curb in front of the house. She scanned the neighbors' steps for similar displays and thought she could see another stick-and-greenery arrangement three doors down. Cardinal Gardening, she suspected, a company she regularly recommended to clients. Alice and Patrick had discussed skipping the "family reunion from hell," as Alice had taken to calling it, but in the end, she'd decided on the path of least resistance. She could suck it up, she told herself. She'd perma-smile for a couple of hours in the hopes of preserving her relationship with her mother. Plus, if she refused to go to Julienne's, she'd have to explain to the children why they were carving a turkey alone, and after everything else, she just didn't have the reserves.

Julienne's house was decidedly bigger than the Sullivans', and Alice could see the netting for a trampoline beyond a wide-slatted fence.

"They have a tramp!" Aidy shrieked, spotting it simultaneously. She threw open her door the second Patrick had put the car in park and ran straight across the grass. Her navy dress bounced over white tights and black dress shoes. Adrian had chosen that dress herself, alleviating any guilt Alice might have felt about either adhering to the dress code or breaking it. Patrick, too, had donned one of his usual blue quarter-zip

pullover sweaters and gray pants. Teddy had khakis and a blue-check oxford that more or less matched Patrick's outfit. Alice looked down at her own wine-colored dress. She didn't own a similar blue or green one, she reminded herself as a twinge of regret seeped in. Blue was her mother's color. And besides, the dress code email had been ridiculously insensitive. Still, Alice had grabbed a navy pashmina on her way to the car, a concession she could throw over herself for the photo. She peered after Adrian, who had opened the gate and begun scrambling up to the deck of Julienne's trampoline. Her unbuckled shoes lay on their sides in the grass.

Alice thought about calling Aidy back but decided against it. Instead, she grabbed a cast-iron pot filled with mashed potatoes from the floor near her feet and turned back toward Teddy, who'd carried the cornbread rolls in his lap.

"Got 'em," he said, before she'd even asked him to help. She smiled. They hadn't fought in days. Donovan had come over on Monday night, and the two boys had watched a movie and played cards. Nadia had sipped wine with her in the kitchen, and they'd barely mentioned Elm Creek, except to discuss new pink graffiti that had popped up on a RE/MAX realty SOLD sign. Alice had been relieved to note that the vandals hadn't limited themselves to Ramona Design.

"Has Donovan heard anything new about the tagging?" Alice had remembered his prescient warning to Nadia about the hashtags and their recent tandem searches of the kids' rooms for paint.

Nadia had shaken her head. "He still doesn't know."

At Julienne's, Alice sighed as she walked past her mother's car, parked right up next to the Martíns' garage door. As Alice approached the porch, the front door opened. Julienne looked statuesque in a navy sheath dress with long sleeves. Alice's breath caught as she took in the similarities again between this woman and her—their—mother. Julienne's blond hair, blown out and with some kind of product in it for shine, fell perfectly to her shoulders, one side swinging forward as she opened her arms to take Alice's potatoes. Or maybe to hug her. Alice

wasn't sure, and she reflexively drew the Le Creuset pot (red, she realized, like her own dress) back toward her body.

"Julienne!" Patrick said then. He stepped in front of Alice, breaking up the stilted moment. "It's so lovely to meet you." Patrick reached around her in an easy hug. "Thank you so much for having us."

"It's my pleasure." Julienne winked at Teddy. "Hello again. Weird connection, huh?" Alice had explained it before his first appointment with Milo, and to her great relief, he hadn't asked too many questions about the "amazing coincidence."

"Now that I know who you are," Teddy said, "I can see you look exactly like Nana." Julienne's smile broadened, and her eyes seemed to sparkle with the pleasure of the compliment. Alice fought to maintain a neutral expression, but she could feel her left eyelid twitch.

"I'm afraid our daughter has gotten ahead of us." Patrick smiled. "She caught a glimpse of your trampoline and made a run for it."

Julienne laughed. "My Laura saw her through the window and was more than happy to abandon her job of napkin folding to go out and do a little jumping." Julienne turned around. "Come in," she said over her shoulder. "Your mom's in the kitchen, chopping romaine."

Your mom.

Patrick put his hand on Alice's shoulder and massaged. They followed Julienne through the dining room, past a 1980s oak table and chairs. The chairs, Alice noticed, had charming spindle-style legs. A cheap yet adorable cornucopia lay on the table in the middle of a burnt-orange runner. There were simple, hand-lettered name cards next to each brown place mat.

"Beautiful table," Alice said. And it was, in its own way.

"Thanks." Julienne flopped her wrist toward the candlesticks and the cornucopia. "Laura and I love to add to our kitsch collection. We shop the T.J. Maxx HomeGoods. You know the one on Main and Excelsior? That"—she pointed at a ceramic turkey on the sideboard next to two small vases of mums—"was one of our favorite finds."

"Love it." Alice faked enthusiasm. In her dining room, the sideboard would have been adorned at either end with tight bouquets in tin buckets. She'd have chosen bells of Ireland, orange roses, dahlias, and spider mums. Sometimes Adrian picked out a few miniature pumpkins and gourds at the farmer's market while she shopped, and those, too, might be placed in groups of three. Not this year.

"Maybe T.J. Maxx is below your standards, since you're a designer?" Julienne laughed as they entered the kitchen. There was a smokiness to the aroma, something richer than the normal herb blend that Alice usually stuffed into the cavity of their bird.

"It smells wonderful," Alice said, ignoring the comment about T.J. Maxx. "Hi, Mom." Her mom kept chopping. Alice could see her smile from the side, her cheeks flushed and a dish towel slung over her shoulder. She looked completely comfortable with Julienne's knife in her hand, Julienne's cutting board beneath a pile of lettuce. Her mother put the knife down and wiped her hands on her borrowed apron.

"I caught a glimpse of Adrian through the back window—" She stopped as she registered Alice's red dress, the slightly flared skirt swirling as Alice stepped forward, her arms still encumbered with potatoes.

"Blue or green," her mom said quietly. Her smile evaporated. "That's what I asked for."

Alice felt light-headed. Patrick shook hands with Julienne's husband, who'd set down his wooden spoon. "I'm Patrick." His voice filled the room, louder than usual, and Rafael responded with a hearty hello.

"Let's put your potatoes here." Julienne steered Alice toward an empty burner. "And Teddy? Those can go right here." She gestured at her Corian counter, and he deposited the rolls.

Alice's mouth went dry as she looked out the back window at Adrian and Laura. Julienne's daughter was perfectly dressed in a light green top and navy pants. On the trampoline, Laura held Aidy's hands, and even through the glass, Alice could hear her daughter's laughter.

"This is Miguel," Alice's mom said to Teddy.

"Dude," Miguel said to Teddy, "do you play COD?" The two disappeared immediately upstairs. Alice's head started to hurt, a needle prick right in the middle of her forehead. She opened the sliding glass door to the backyard and waved hello to Laura.

"Mommy!" Adrian shrieked. "Laura double-bounces me. Watch!"

The two held hands, and Laura buckled her legs at the close of one of her jumps, sending Adrian's way up, so that both her and Laura's arms were fully extended.

The girls looked like they'd been cousins forever. "Hi, I'm Laura." She giggled. "Obviously."

"Did you know she's my cousin?" Adrian ran to the mesh side of the trampoline in front of Alice, pressing her hands against it. "My *actual* cousin? And living in the same exact town?" Alice would have laughed at her earnestness if it weren't for her blackening mood.

Laura walked over, too, her feet sinking into the webbing of the trampoline as she approached. Her eyes matched her mother's and grandmother's. "I'd be happy to babysit sometime," Laura said. "And my mom said Aidy's working on her reading? I could help."

Aidy. A nickname for family and close friends, and yet Laura commandeered it. "That's nice. Adrian, why don't you come inside now?"

Laura smoothed Adrian's hair. "Oh, I'm sure we're fine for a few more minutes," she said. "It takes forever to actually get the dinner on the table. We'll come in five?"

Adrian ran back to the center of the trampoline, her arms out for Laura's. "Let's keep jumping!"

Neither looked back at Alice to gauge her reaction. She thought about insisting that Adrian leave the tramp, and then imagined the scene: herself standing on tiptoes, reaching into the enclosure, trying to capture Adrian, who was rapidly becoming too big to physically commandeer. She pulled closed the sliding glass door and looked back at the adults.

"Those just need a warm oven," Alice said, pointing at the rolls

Rafael had unwrapped. The ceilings felt low, the bronze pendant lamps closing in over her head.

"Alice, could I chat with you for a moment?" Her mom appeared at her side. She'd removed the apron to reveal a lapis sweater Alice had never seen before.

"Let's get a glass of wine first?"

"Of course!" Julienne piped in. "Sorry for not offering sooner. Red or white?"

"White," said Alice, just as her mother said, "Red."

Rafael, busy with a gigantic pile of cilantro, laughed. "Not totally in sync today, eh?"

"Good thing we've got both." Julienne seemed overboard cheerful.

After Julienne poured their wine, her mom gestured toward the dining room. "Let's take the photo soon, okay?" Julienne suggested as they left. "Before everyone is overstuffed from dinner?" She laughed and rubbed her stomach. "Or maybe I'm just thinking of myself." She walked to the sliding glass door and signaled for Laura and Adrian to come in, which they did immediately without negotiation.

Rafael picked up his phone from the countertop. "I'll text the boys to come down."

Alice's mom grabbed her by the wrist and pulled her toward the ceramic turkey in the dining room. "Why would you wear red?"

Alice shook her arm free. "God," she said. She was immediately transported back to high school, to one of the few times she'd missed curfew. Alice had found her mother sitting rigidly on their brown tweed sofa, waiting with her arms folded. "I don't look good in blue," she said now. Even when she'd been in high school, Alice had been allowed to choose her own clothing. "I'm here, aren't I?" Alice gestured toward the cornucopia. "We're doing your Thanksgiving."

Patrick appeared in the door frame then, his smile watery. "Photo time," he said, just before Julienne followed him into the room, the kids and Rafael behind her.

"Mom!" Teddy's face looked flushed as he trotted up to her. "Miguel and Rafael do soccer drills every Wednesday afternoon at the park with some Liston Heights Premier kids, and Miguel said I could come. Can I come? That would be off the hook."

Alice blinked at him. "Um," she murmured.

"They're a year older!" Teddy jumped a little, his whole body filled with excitement. "It would be such a good opportunity, especially since I don't have a team right now. Can you even believe my luck?"

Rafael ruffled Teddy's hair and said, "We're having a special session tomorrow morning since we don't have school." He raised an eyebrow at Alice, who took two steps backward and ran into one of the dining room chairs.

"Oh my God, Teddy!" Miguel said. "You should sleep over! We can play COD and then go to soccer. I'll let you borrow one of my practice jerseys."

"Yes!" Teddy high-fived him. He didn't even look at Alice for permission.

"I don't think—" Alice glanced at Patrick, who shook his head subtly.

"Should we stand on the front porch?" Patrick forged ahead with the photo.

"Fine." Alice gulped her wine.

In the foyer Julienne put her arm around Alice's mom. "Where would you like everyone to stand?" Her voice was expansive and generous. The two of them touched their temples together in a side hug. Alice frowned.

Her mother shook the navy pashmina, which Alice had draped over the bannister, to unfold it. On the front steps, Laura had begun arranging people. "Why don't you stand in the middle, Evie, since this is really your photo."

Evie? Alice fought an eye roll.

"Who's Evie?" Adrian asked.

"That's what we call our grandma!" Laura pulled Adrian to a spot at Alice's mother's left. "You can call her that, too."

"Do you like that better than Nana?" Adrian looked at her grandmother, who seemed not to hear.

"Should we put the other kids around her?" Laura asked.

"I think so," "Evie" said. "What do you think, Julienne?"

Alice clenched her teeth. "Do you have a lot of experience in photography, Julienne?"

"Alice, come here," her mother said. *Come here?* Her mother held out the pashmina as Alice stepped toward her. She bent down and wrapped the scarf around her like a hair salon cape, covering her entire torso and also her arms, including the hand in which she held her wine. "There," she said. She took a step back and scanned her. "Now, I wonder if you could perhaps stand behind Teddy and Adrian." She put a finger to her lip and squinted. "We'll hide the red."

"I think—" Julienne broke in, her smile magnanimous.

"Fuck it," Alice said before she could finish.

She felt Patrick's hand clamp down on the back of her neck, but she evaded him. The pashmina fell to the ground in front of her, and Alice stepped on it, not caring that it was cashmere. "I'm not going to hide in the back of this picture because you don't like my fucking dress."

"Mom!" Adrian yelled, her little voice high with alarm.

"Alice," Patrick said, trying again.

"It's fine." Alice turned toward the backyard. Even as she left the group, she wasn't sure where she was going. To the trampoline? "Why don't you arrange everything," she shouted over her shoulder, "and then when you've got it, maybe I'll come back to be the goddamn photographer." She pictured herself standing in front of the blue-green family, the women with their perfect blond hair, matching heights, and pink cheeks. She pictured Julienne's perfect teenagers. She heard her mother's disappointed voice in her head: *Blue or green. That's what I asked for.*

This was really it, Alice thought. The final failure. She already had kids who couldn't cut it in school. Her work was limited to brainless mudroom remodels. And now she'd alienated her mother and her mother's new family. Without thinking, Alice raised the hand in which she held the wineglass and hurled it, its liquid sloshing from the rim as the goblet smashed against Julienne's siding, sprinkles of crystal showering the dogwood shrub below. She stood frozen for a moment, agog at the mess she'd created, and wished fervently for the last few seconds back.

Instead, she heard shouting behind her—Patrick's voice above them all—but she didn't look. Instead she veered into the backyard and jogged toward the sliding glass door. Her cornbread rolls still lay on the counter. She grabbed both them and her purse, which she'd hung on one of the kitchen stools, and turned back outside. The family was coming in the front now; she could hear some uneasy laughter. Patrick was saying something about pictures of the grandchildren, and Alice fumed thinking about Laura and Miguel flanking her mother, on equal footing with Adrian and Teddy. She waited for a moment for Patrick to reappear, and when he did, she waved him into the backyard.

"What is wrong with you?" he asked her. "You need to fix this." He seemed in equal measure concerned and bewildered.

"But I hate it here." Alice's face burned. She put the rolls down on the grass and palmed away hot tears.

Patrick put his hands on his hips. Alice could tell he was trying not to lose it himself. He hardly ever did. He'd never throw a wineglass against someone's house. She wouldn't have, either, before today. "Okay, fine," Patrick said, "but could you, like, get it together? Set a decent example for the children? You're basically having a temper tantrum."

"I have to go." Her crying had intensified, and she heard herself emit a little wail.

"You have to *go*?" Patrick put a hand on his brow. "You can't go. That's going to make everything worse."

"I have to," Alice said. She took a few steps toward the car. "I'm really sorry. I can come and pick you up when it's over." And then she stalked past the trampoline and back to the Volvo, realizing only when she'd gotten there that she'd left the cornbread rolls on the Martíns' lawn.

Sadie Yoshida

Thanksgiving felt like both a relief and a giant bummer. Usually, Sadie and her dad ran the Winona Turkey Trot when they were at her grandmother's house, but he hadn't mentioned registering this year. In fact, she and her dad hadn't really talked much at all since she'd sent that Snapchat, except when her mom made her tell him at the dinner table about an article she'd read for social studies or a math problem she'd finished.

"Your dad will help you with your current events project," Meredith had said one night last week as Sadie cleared her plate.

"You need help?" Her dad had already put on his reading glasses, had already grabbed his laptop from the counter and loaded Twitter. Sadie caught a glimpse of his usual political news.

"I've got it," she'd said.

When Sadie had stood in the kitchen on Tuesday night, the night before they left for her grandmother's, she pictured last year's Turkey Trot T-shirt and almost started to cry.

"Can I help you with something?" Her dad sounded like he did when he was on a call for work.

The question was on the tip of her tongue—"Are we going to run the Turkey Trot on Thursday?"—but instead of asking it, she just filled a mug with water and took a long sip. "No," she said. "Just thirsty."

- - - - - - - -

AFTER THANKSGIVING DINNER, Sadie stood at the sink, an orange dish towel in hand. Sadie's grandma playfully hip-checked her. "Did you like the yams?" she asked. Sadie had loved marshmallow yams since she was tiny. Her mom always said it was because they were candy, not vegetables.

"I loved the yams, Grandma." Her grandmother had already put on her dish gloves. She wore her famous Thanksgiving sweater-vest over a plaid flannel. The vest featured an appliquéd cartoon turkey, its feathers a mix of fall colors. Grandma's earrings were mini cornucopias. "Kids *and* my patients appreciate my enthusiasm," she always said when Sadie's mom teased her about her holiday-themed attire. Sadie herself loved her grandmother's holiday spirit. A card arrived in the mailbox for each of the minor holidays, usually with a five-dollar bill tucked inside.

"So . . ." Grandma's voice trailed off, and Sadie watched as she peered over her shoulder into the adjacent family room. Grandma had folded her crocheted afghans over the back of the couch. Sadie's mom fiddled with the remote, and her dad scrolled on his phone. "What's up?"

The question sounded both casual and loaded. "Nothing," Sadie said automatically.

"Skating? Junior high? Everything's going well?"

Sadie's stomach dropped. She thought about her decision to quit the team. "Well," she said, softly, "actually, I've been thinking of spending some time working on something else. I told my mom I'm quitting skating. Maybe she told you?"

"Quitting?" Her grandmother dunked a wineglass into the cloudy dishwater and rubbed the rim with a blue sponge. "But don't you love skating?"

She handed Sadie the glass to rinse and grabbed another. "I—"

Sadie thought about the cool air on her cheeks as she jumped, the times she and Mikaela did dryland practice, moving through their routines in their sneakers. "I used to love it," Sadie said.

Grandma shrugged. "We all change as we get older. Interests change." She bumped her hip against Sadie's again. Sadie was almost as tall as Grandma was now. By summer, she thought, when her mother measured them standing back to back as she had a few times a year since fifth grade, Sadie would have passed her. "I recently took up beading," Grandma said as she handed her another glass. "Did I tell you that?"

"I still like skating." Sadie felt her face heat. She opened the cabinet for the glasses.

Grandma stopped washing. Sadie stared at the pumpkin socks she always wore on Thanksgiving, afraid that she'd say too much if she made eye contact.

"If you still like skating, then why are you quitting the team?"

Sadie felt her eyes fill, and no matter how hard she blinked, she couldn't exile the tears. "The uniforms are too tight." As she breathed in, she felt her bra strap digging into her back. "That's stupid." She wiped her eyes with the dishcloth and then worried immediately that it was gross.

"Get over here," Grandma said. Sadie returned to the sink, and Grandma threw an arm around her, her glove dripping on Sadie's sweater. Sadie put her head against Grandma's shoulder and sniffed. "Now," Grandma said, "I'm going to attack the yam pan, and you're going to tell me what exactly you're talking about. Because, to be honest, I don't really get it."

Sadie laughed and grabbed a Kleenex from the counter. Grandma had put her favorite holiday Beanie Baby right next to the box, a turkey wearing a pilgrim's hat. "You can have my Beanie Baby collection when I move to Arizona," she'd told Sadie last year. Sadie's mom had rolled her eyes, but Sadie had touched the turkey's wattle. She could imagine it in the Yoshidas' kitchen next to the refrigerator.

"I'll tell you," Sadie said. "But it's a little bit of a long story, and you might not—" She paused and looked over her shoulder again. Her parents were on the couch, an afghan over their legs, both watching what Sadie assumed was football. "You might not think of me the same way afterward."

"Honey, nothing you could say would change the basic facts. Grandparents are professional lovers. That's what we do. If you think there are any grown-ups alive who haven't made big mistakes, you're wrong. So, let's hear it."

Without looking at her—while staring mostly at her pumpkin socks—Sadie told the whole thing. She told about the homecoming game when she thought she'd be with Teddy, but Teddy chose Alexandra. She told about how she'd wanted to go to Chloe's party, and her mom had said no. She told about making the Quiz Bowl team and then her massive choke at the final match. She told about Douglas Lim's smug smile from the front row, knowing he'd take back his spot. And she told about the picture. About Tane's message, "Show me your Ts," and her wild, reckless response.

When it was all over and the yam pan was rinsed and in Sadie's hands, ready to put away, Sadie finally looked up. Grandma's gaze was on the archway between the kitchen and the family room, her eyes wide and her head cocked. Sadie followed it and saw her mother standing there, tears in her eyes and her body sort of hunched.

Alice Sullivan

When she got home, Alice slammed the front door, kicked off her shoes, and ran upstairs to her bedroom. She yanked the zipper of the red dress down, wriggled out of it, and balled it up. She threw it in the back of her closet next to her summer sandals and grabbed a pair of black leggings. Her Elm Creek Soccer sweatshirt lay in front of her nightstand, where she'd thrown it off the night before. Once she'd turned the sleeves right-side-out and forced it over her head, she collapsed onto her bed and pushed back the hairs that had fallen into her face. She took a few breaths, felt her heart rate slow, and involuntarily replayed the scene at Julienne's. She saw the glass smash against the siding. She watched the crystal leave her hand and heard the explosion as it shattered. There had been a big leftover piece of glass in front of the dogwood. Alice remembered a thick unbroken section from the bottom of the goblet, a razor-sharp parabola rising out of the woodchips. Had Adrian cried?

Alice would have cried if her mother had thrown a glass. She had cried when her mother had locked herself in her room that one time after the divorce and repeatedly slammed something—her fists?—against the wall. Alice had been five minutes from calling her grandmother for help when her mother had finally emerged from her room, her eyes red but her face calm. "Let's order Vietnamese," she'd said then. The next morning she'd muttered about the importance of emotional release.

Alice had left Julienne's with the car. She pictured the Volvo in the garage and then imagined Patrick standing outside Julienne's house with his Uber app open. All this chaos, and Thanksgiving was usually her favorite holiday. Guilty, Alice padded down to the mudroom, where she'd thrown her handbag on the bench next to a pair of pink stretchy gloves that hadn't made it into their assigned basket. She grabbed her phone.

"I'll come and get you," she typed to Patrick. She stared at the labeled bins on the shelves.

Her phone buzzed. "We're having pie," Patrick wrote back. "Rafael said he'll drive us home later. I'll drive Teddy back tomorrow morning for soccer. No need to sleep over."

Alice collapsed onto the built-in bench and tucked her stockinged feet into the extra storage shelves beneath her. They were all there— her whole family and her mom—eating pie at Julienne's. While her first inclination was to pour an overflowing glass of wine, she decided instead on action.

She'd left pandemonium at Julienne's, but she could stem it at home. She'd start her organizing in Adrian's room. She'd clean out her bookshelves, find the lost reading logs, make some kind of spreadsheet. She couldn't take back that glass. She couldn't even pick up the shards herself, as she'd run out of the house like a teenager, but she could be ready for when the family got home.

And sure enough, when she heard them pile into the mudroom an hour and a half later, she had rearranged all of Adrian's drawers and reorganized her bookshelf by genre. She ran down the stairs to greet the family, though a little knot of anxiety gripped her as she intercepted them in the kitchen.

"I'm so full," Teddy was saying.

"Yeah," Patrick added. "Can't believe Mom missed the pecan pie."

"There was pecan pie?" she asked, her voice softer than she'd meant for it to be.

Adrian stopped short when she saw her. She put her little hands on her hips. "You left!" she said. "And you broke that glass. I can't believe you did that."

Teddy raised an eyebrow at her and walked by. "Beast mode, Mom."

Patrick shook his head, though she could tell he'd already halfway forgiven her. "That's going to be hard to repair," he said. "You'll have to send something from Arts & Flowers. Maybe a new glass." He reached for her. "Or a set of them."

Evelyn Brown

~ ~ ~ ~

Evelyn let Alice's first call that night go to voice mail. She had been drying the last of Julienne's wedding china when it came in. Evelyn ignored Alice's second call, too. Instead, she hugged the Martín family at the door. She apologized for what seemed like the fiftieth time to Julienne and Rafael for Alice's behavior.

"Hey," said Rafael finally, with conviction. "First, you're not responsible for Alice's choices; and second, these things—all these relationships—are going to take time." This from the one adult in the room who didn't have a degree in psychology. Evelyn knew he was probably right, and yet still, when she got to her car, she drove down the block, pulled over, and pummeled the steering wheel with her fists until the pads of her hands hurt. Tears dripped off her jaw onto her new blue sweater. Alice had been selfish and immature. She had wrecked Evelyn's whole reunion. And she'd abandoned her family at a virtual stranger's house for Thanksgiving dinner.

A *virtual stranger's house.*

It was that phrase that compelled Evelyn to pull over again on the next block when Alice called for the third time.

"Yes?" she said. Her voice sounded cold, which matched how she felt.

"Mom." Alice was breathless. "Thank God you picked up. Mom, I'm so sorry."

Evelyn waited. She felt her shoulders drop a bit, hearing Alice's frantic tone, reminiscent of the times she'd missed curfew as a teenager, desperate for Evelyn to understand the one random and insignificant thing that had kept her from meeting her obligation.

"I can't believe I did that. It's true I was angry that you canceled my Thanksgiving and that Julienne's seemed to be the only place you were willing to go, but my behavior. The glass. I acted like a toddler."

Evelyn sat silent. She looked at the streetlight across from her car. Its brightness illuminated the lawns of the houses in which she could still see gatherings taking place.

"Mom?" Alice asked. "Are you there?"

"I'm here."

Alice sighed. "I wish you would say something."

Evelyn raised her hand and dropped it again. "You threw Julienne's Waterford against the side of her house and tore off. You behaved ridiculously. Laura cried at the table because it was so awkward."

"I know—" Alice began, but Evelyn cut her off.

"Alice, how is Teddy supposed to have a reasonable handle on how to behave, on what's in bounds and what's out-of-bounds, when his mother is throwing a first-class temper tantrum at a perfectly nice family holiday?"

She could hear Alice suck in her breath. She saw her toddler face, indignant in the toy aisle about Evelyn's refusal to buy her a He-Man action figure. She'd chucked that, too, in her toddler fury. Evelyn remembered having to jump out of the way, lest it hit her thigh. "A perfectly nice family holiday?" Alice's voice rose.

"Yes!" She remembered Alice's screams then, the way Evelyn had had to carry her like a potato sack out of the Target, abandoning her cart. She'd had to send Frank for toilet paper and 2% milk when they'd gotten home.

"Mom." Evelyn could hear a door slam, and she imagined Alice leaving the mudroom to stand in the garage. Even that space was clean,

bikes hanging from industrial hooks mounted on the walls. "You can-celed my traditional holiday and forced me to have dinner at the home of some woman I don't even know, claiming that she's my sister. She's not, in any way, my sister. You're genetically related to her, and I get that that's incredibly important to *you*. But honestly? I'm just not ready to join in."

Heat coursed through Evelyn, a fire that originated in her belly and raged through her limbs. Before she could form any words, her arm shot out toward the Bluetooth controls on the console and she hit the button to hang up. "No!" she shouted, not caring whether Alice heard it. After she'd ended the call, she leaned back in her seat and let the fire smolder. Once she could breathe again, she put on her turn signal and eased back into traffic.

ON SATURDAY, EVELYN felt the fire ignite again when Julienne sug-gested an uncharacteristic coffee. They'd been getting together on Mondays for lunch, but this was just two days after Thanksgiving. They'd meet for a quick latte in between Miguel's indoor soccer games. Julienne had emphasized "quick."

"I'll just meet you at the games," Evelyn had suggested. She was an experienced soccer fan, after all, perfectly capable of chatting on the sidelines. Besides, then there'd be more time with Miguel and Laura. She was finding it hard to get enough of them. She'd made an Insta-gram account just to follow them, and she pressed the heart button on each of their photos, checking for updates between clients.

But Julienne had insisted on coffee. "I think we should check in," she'd said. And then she'd been quiet.

Evelyn thought about the advice she sometimes gave clients who were prepping for difficult conversations. "Ask for a meeting," she'd encourage. "Speak your truth." And so her heart pounded as she

waited for Julienne in the Caribou Coffee adjacent to the soccer dome. It wasn't terrifically cold yet, but the indoor season had started. Kids and parents filed in and out of the pressure-controlled, inflatable structure. Julienne and Alice had probably passed one another there before, unknowingly. The thought of them brushing shoulders, not realizing their connection, gave Evelyn the chills. Evelyn herself might have been inside the dome at the same time as Julienne, watching on an adjoining field. She thought she might have known it if it had happened. An electricity crackled between them, Evelyn thought. They'd talked about it. Julienne herself described it as a force field.

The proximity of her daughter through all these years—just one suburb between them, a divide Evelyn crossed at least weekly—still took her breath away. She chewed a nail as she waited for Julienne to walk into the coffee shop. Fear prickled in her fingertips. She remembered snippets of Thanksgiving—the smashing glass against the side of the house, Laura's wide brown eyes wet with tears. That gathering, Evelyn knew, had changed things.

Just as she'd taken the top off her decaf latte and blown into it, her daughter walked in. Her thick hair swirled around her fleece jacket. Evelyn's heart ached seeing her. Julienne's smile was warm, but there was a hint of tension in her forehead, a wrinkle above her right eyebrow.

"I'll just order." Julienne pointed at the counter. "And then I'll be right there."

Evelyn took a tentative sip of her coffee and flinched against the heat. She blew on it again.

"Hi," Julienne said after she'd ordered. She unzipped her jacket and sat in the chair opposite Evelyn, one eye on the barista. "I'll pick mine up in a minute." They'd laughed at their first meeting about their identical orders. The decaf lattes with single pumps of almond syrup were one of many little things they had in common. They also shared a penchant for Uni-ball Rollerball pens, along with an extreme distaste for bacon.

"I'm sorry again about Thanksgiving," Evelyn blurted. This wasn't how she'd planned to start.

Julienne leaned forward and put her chin in her palms. She let her hands slide up, running her fingers through her hair. Evelyn could see gray roots at her temples, the same place she'd first gone gray, and the same spot where she'd noticed silver in Alice's hair a few weeks before. "It was a little much, I think." Julienne glanced at the counter. The barista poured milk from the silver pitcher, swirling it over the top of the coffee. "Hang on." She stood to pick up her drink. Evelyn watched as she grabbed a sleeve and a top for the cup.

"It's too hot," Evelyn warned her as she sat back down.

Julienne shook her head. "I like it almost scalding." She took a sip and closed her eyes as she swallowed. Evelyn forced herself to wait. She spread her palm on her jeans and pressed each finger into her thigh in succession, a silence strategy she'd developed in her clinic over the years.

"So," Julienne said finally, "I haven't been able to sleep the last couple of nights."

Evelyn studied Julienne's face. Now that she'd said something, Evelyn could see that the corners of her eyes drooped slightly. "I just think there are clear signs that we're taking things a little too fast."

There it was. Evelyn wilted.

"I mean, you could see it, right? The crystal shattered against the side of my house?" Julienne raised a palm toward Evelyn. If they were having a conversation about their clinical work, they'd be in agreement: The patient wasn't ready. The patient needed more time.

Evelyn felt her face flush. She undid the top button of her cardigan. "But this isn't about what Alice wants."

"Not entirely, no." Evelyn recognized the tone, the therapy voice. Julienne operated from a rational stance, and Evelyn had only a marginal command of her emotions. "But, Evelyn—" Evelyn winced. They hadn't really come to an agreement on what Julienne would call

her. Of course, it was unreasonable to expect that after all these years, "Mom" would feel appropriate, but her first name? It felt just somehow too distant, too impersonal. *"I'm* not comfortable with Alice's discomfort. It's too much. Let's just take a step back."

Evelyn bit her lip and took another sip of the too-hot latte. The sweetness of the almond syrup burned her throat on its way down.

Meredith Yoshida

— — — —

Meredith drove Sadie to school on the Tuesday morning after Thanksgiving break. "Just so you know," she said, "I'm not embarrassed by you." She thought back to her stunned sadness in the kitchen of her mother's house, the ache of listening to Sadie lay out her missteps to her grandmother.

"It's okay, Mom." Meredith glanced at her but couldn't read her expression. "Did you see the portal this morning? I'm rebounding in science already. Even Mr. Robinson held me after class yesterday to say my lab notes were good."

Meredith smiled and her chest started to hurt a little bit, the spot right beneath the necklace Bill had gotten her for Mother's Day when Sadie was two, a silver charm engraved with an "S" hanging from a delicate chain.

"You don't need to have a good grade in science," she said. She was surprised to find that at least on some level, she meant it.

"What do you mean? I'll totally have a good grade in science." Sadie hugged her backpack to her chest in the back seat.

Meredith flashed to her own report cards, the straight As she'd gotten in the sciences all the way through college, the scores in the 98th and 97th percentiles respectively on the quantitative and analytical sections of the GRE. And she did love her career in physical therapy. She loved working at the clinic, a position she'd gotten in part because of her

long history of hard work and obsessive studying. But had those grades made her parents love her any more than they already did? She thought of her mother in the kitchen with her dishwashing gloves. She visualized that ridiculous turkey sweater-vest. Meredith's mother didn't care that she'd aced her GREs. She only cared that she came to visit and brought Sadie with her.

Meredith was surprised to find herself choking up. "It's not that you can't have a good grade in science," she said to Sadie. "It's just—" She swallowed. "I've been thinking since your conversation with Grandma."

"Mom," Sadie said again, as she had twice already when Meredith had tried to talk with her about it, "I'm sorry for bringing up everything to Grandma. I know I should be careful about who I tell. I get all of that. I just—"

"Hey." Meredith kept her eyes on the road. "You're in charge of your story." For the first time in Sadie's life, Meredith wished she sat in the front seat. She wished she could touch her just then and squeeze her forearm to let her know she meant what she said.

She glanced at Sadie in the rearview mirror, and the two made eye contact as Meredith pulled into the turn lane near the school. She was grateful for the red light. Maybe Sadie would say something before they got to the car pool circle. Meredith held her breath. "Mom?" Sadie's voice was small.

"Hmm?" Meredith tempered her anticipation, not wanting to force the moment. *Let your child lead*, all the articles said.

"I'm sorry about the picture." It was a whisper, almost, and Meredith felt a tear crest the lower lid of her eye. "I'm sorry I disappointed you."

"It's not about me," Meredith said. She grabbed a tissue from the travel pack she kept in the cup holder. "It's about who you are and who you want to be." She dabbed her nose and tried to take a cleansing breath without letting on to Sadie that she'd started to cry. The light turned green, and Meredith turned into the school drive. Why couldn't they have a few more minutes?

"I won't do it again." Sadie's voice was steady. "And I know I can get a good grade in science." Meredith peeked at her. Sadie squared her shoulders. Her chin bobbed as she nodded to herself.

"Honey?" Meredith pulled up next to the curb and waved at the school security guard, a corpulent guy in a blazing orange security vest. Bob, Meredith thought his name was. Sadie moved to open the door, but Meredith reached back for her, not quite touching her arm. Sadie stopped, surprised. "Nobody gives a shit about your science grade," Meredith said.

Sadie's eyes widened and she blinked twice. Meredith could see the corners of her mouth turning up. She had never once sworn in front of Sadie. Meredith and Bill had decided when she was a toddler that they wouldn't ever swear, actually, within earshot of their daughter. Sadie had spent most of elementary school thinking the s-word wasn't "shit," but "stupid." "Mom." She laughed. "I don't know what this is. I mean, I appreciate it? But let's be real. You've always, *always* cared about my grade in science."

She moved again to open the door, but Meredith said, "Stop." The security guard motioned her forward. She pulled the car up, but then braked again, twisting her body so she faced the back seat. "I've changed my mind." Meredith opened the center console and pulled her cell phone out. "Your grades are your grades." She held the icon for the portal app. She turned the phone, so Sadie could see it wiggling, primed for deletion.

Sadie's mouth dropped open. She looked in that moment just exactly like Meredith's mother used to when she came home with a funny story from work. Meredith laughed, and then she clicked the "X" on the portal app decisively with her index finger. "Done," she said. She showed Sadie the screen. The icon had disappeared.

"I don't know what to say." The security guard motioned for a car behind Meredith to go around. She was holding up the line, obviously, but she didn't care. "Maybe I should say, 'Who are you and what have

you done with my mother?'" Sadie opened the door, and Meredith let her. She dropped her phone back into the console.

"Have a good day," Meredith said. And then, because she couldn't help it, "Make good choices."

She felt liberated as she drove to the clinic that morning, and not even a fresh penis painted on the dugout of the school's baseball diamond could ruin her mood.

Teddy Sullivan

On Tuesday morning, Teddy's mom interrupted the easiest, most boring online lesson on quotation marks. The English class was taught by a white lady with a pixie cut who preferred that the kids call her "Tawna," and Teddy barely had to pay attention to get ninety percent or better on the assessments.

"We're leaving in fifteen minutes for a tour at a charter school," his mom said.

"Are you going to wear that?" Teddy asked. She hadn't been putting on real clothes since Thanksgiving. She was wearing black leggings and the same Elm Creek Soccer Association sweatshirt he'd seen on her every day since she'd smashed that glass at Julienne's house, but at least she turned his texting app on for a couple of supervised hours each evening, a success of his argument about isolation, he'd guessed. Miguel had texted him after the dinner. "Dude," he'd written, "see you tomorrow on the field."

"Sorry about my mom's anger management problems," Teddy had texted back.

"Epic," Miguel had answered immediately. "I'll remember that Thanksgiving for a long time." He'd added soccer ball and martini glass emojis. The drink made Teddy feel a little uneasy.

"I'll change," Teddy's mom said. She brushed at what Teddy assumed was a tea stain on her stomach, but he realized it could also

have been a food item from any of the dinners or lunches they'd had in the last four days. If she would change, Teddy thought, he'd be happy to visit whatever school she wanted. Also, he'd get a legitimate break from Tawna. The kids in the radio ads for Twin Cities Online Academy seemed happy, but who were they kidding? This shit was bleak.

By the time Teddy buckled his seat belt fifteen minutes later, his mom had not only changed her clothes but also showered. She hadn't washed her hair, but she smelled like his dad's soap. His dad, for his part, had headed back to Cincinnati on Sunday night as usual. That was bleak, too.

"What is this school, and do they have sports?" Even though online school had made him a little desperate, Teddy still had standards.

"It's called Echo. It's an environmental charter," Alice said. "It looked cool, and Milo recommended it."

"An environmental charter?" Teddy thought about the gardening beds at Eastwood Nature Center, the winter wheat stalks that had sprouted so quickly after he, Donovan, and Eddie had planted them at their last nature therapy group. "Like science?"

"That, and going outside every day and experiential learning," Alice said. "For wellness. And other stuff." She rolled her wrist around to indicate the other stuff.

"I've never heard of it." No kids in the Elm Creek Soccer Association and no kids at any summer soccer clinic or any camp he'd ever gone to had mentioned "Echo" as the name of their school.

Maybe, thought Teddy when they arrived, that was because the school was tiny. It was one of four schools inside a building that used to be a high school when his mom was a kid. His mom pulled the door open for the Echo office. Through the glass, Teddy watched a guy at the desk who looked like he'd barely graduated from high school. He wore a rumpled flannel and looked like a younger version of Milo. As they approached, Teddy could see sweat beaded on his forehead.

"Welcome!" He looked up, and Teddy read "Jasper" on his name badge. "I see we've got a tour this morning. Are you the Sullivans?"

Jasper stuck a hand out toward Alice, but then pulled it back. "Sorry," he said. He flipped his palm over, looked at it, and then offered it again. "Dirt check. I just came in from the garden. I was helping the fourth graders harvest the last of their spinach. They'll have salad for lunch."

Jasper offered his hand to Teddy, too. "It's clean," he said when Teddy hesitated. "You're good." Jasper's hand felt damp. He'd definitely washed after doing whatever he was talking about with the spinach.

"Is it only salads here for lunch?" Teddy asked.

Jasper laughed much harder than Teddy expected.

"No, dude," Jasper said. "There's a regular cafeteria, too." He grabbed a clipboard from a tray and scanned a calendar. "Today it's meatless lasagna and California medley. We do try to limit animal protein." Jasper nodded at them, as if obviously they would limit animal protein. "But I guess we're still having the cheese."

"Okay," Alice said. "That sounds good. So"—she leaned in and read his name tag—"are you our tour guide, Jasper?"

"Affirmative!" Jasper said. He took a tissue from the box on the reception desk and wiped his forehead. "Should we get this party started?"

Teddy snuck a sideways glance at his mom. Was she liking this guy? He was pretty much the opposite of Mr. Whittaker. Whittaker had his necktie knotted so tightly Teddy thought he'd have trouble turning his face. His mom's eyebrows had lifted, and she looked like she was about to laugh. If she did, it would be the first time she had since before Thanksgiving. "Let's get 'er going," she said. She moved her elbow across her front like she was ready to march. Teddy would have been mortified if Jasper weren't Jasper. In other words, this guy was as embarrassingly nerdy as his mom was, but maybe fifteen years younger.

Jasper reached a palm out to her for a high five, which she returned.

Her purse fell from her shoulder to her elbow. Jasper put his palm in Teddy's face next. He slapped it. He usually hated guys like this, guys who acted like they were massive dudes, like, ready to connect with kids on a deep and meaningful level. But something about Jasper just made him want to laugh. It had been the same with Milo.

"I'd take your coats, but we'll definitely look at the outdoor class-room," Jasper said. "Why don't you just unzip while we tour the indoor instructional spaces." Teddy watched Alice dutifully unzip her black coat, but he kept his ECSC warm-up jacket as it was.

"I'm comfortable," he said when Jasper eyed him.

"A man with his own ideas," Jasper said jovially. "I like it! Follow me."

Jasper started down the hallway to their right, and Teddy could hear classes of kids chatting and working. It was louder, for sure, than Elm Creek Junior High. "These are our primary rooms," he said. "You might know that Echo has been in existence since 2015. We began with K through 3, and we added a grade per year as we went. So the middle school started in 2017. We just opened the high school this fall, all four grades at once."

Teddy peeked into the classroom on his left and saw high schoolers sitting on the floor alongside kids littler than Aidy. "Cross-age-group partnerships," Jasper said when he saw Teddy looking. "Super important feature. The juniors are working with kindergartners to plan their winter herb garden."

Alice looked at the bulletin board in front of them with pictures of which crops to plant at which times for maximum harvest.

"The focus on gardening," Jasper was saying, "is definitely about awareness of the food system—big agriculture, environmental stress-ors, food deserts, and distribution—but it's also about the side benefits of diggin' in the dirt." He said this last part like he'd rehearsed it.

Teddy blinked at him and then glanced at his mom, who hated all yard work and didn't keep a garden. Her cheeks flushed a bit. Teddy

imagined she was hoping she wouldn't have to confess that she didn't like planting herb gardens, that she hired a service to take care of the lawn and flower beds in front of their house.

"Mental health benefits?" she asked tentatively.

"Yeah," Jasper said. "A lot of the moms come in knowing all about the benefits of gardening because of Michelle Obama. The White House garden? She loved talking about it. You a fan?"

Alice looked embarrassed. "I love Michelle." She awkwardly threw an arm over Teddy's shoulder. "Teddy knows that, right?"

He smiled. This was classic—his mom embarrassed by a random guy, in a tiny school, whom they'd maybe never see again. She'd try to impress him now, even though she didn't know why gardening was so great.

Jasper put his hand out and ticked off the benefits: "Better self-confidence, lower incidences of depression, lower cortisol, lowers the likelihood of dementia and Alzheimer's."

"Wow," Alice said. Teddy stepped away from her, and her arm fell to her side. Teddy waited for her follow-up questions, but before she could speak, he surprised himself by asking, "Can we see the gardens?"

"On our way, man," Jasper said. He led them slightly farther down the hallway and pointed out a large window. Teddy could see ten or twelve raised beds. Kids about his age were doing something with gardening tools and seeds.

Before Jasper could explain, Teddy broke in. "Are they planting winter wheat?"

Jasper's eyes brightened. "Dude!" He raised his hand again for another high five. Teddy couldn't help smiling as he gave it.

Before his mom could say anything stupid about nature therapy, Teddy asked, "Are they in science?"

"Caroline is our middle school science teacher." Jasper pointed at the woman in overalls and a bright yellow pom-pom hat who circulated among the kids. "But this is morning choice time."

"Choice?" Teddy watched the kids digging neat rows in the beds. They were laughing. He thought back to Tawna and her endless multiple-choice questions about comma placement with quotation marks. "You can meet with a particular teacher, and there are activities like this one. Or you can just do indoor or outdoor study hall or reading."

"Choice," Alice echoed. "You said morning choice. Is there afternoon choice, too?"

"Let me show you the middle school schedule," Jasper offered, walking on. "It's on the bulletin board up here, and I think you'll find it's pretty different from other schools."

FORTY-FIVE MINUTES LATER, Jasper led them back to the desk. Teddy snuck a look at Alice. Her face was still flushed. Did she mind it when Jasper said they didn't offer "advanced" anything, but rather valued inclusion in all subject areas?

"I can see you here, Teddy," Jasper said. Teddy turned his face up to Jasper's, noticing the way his stubble brushed the collar of his shirt. Mr. Whittaker's skin always looked pinched there against the top button. Jasper, obviously, had left his open. In fact, he'd left two buttons, revealing the green collar of a T-shirt underneath.

Teddy braced himself to ask the question he'd been avoiding, the one Alice had ignored when they'd first gotten in the car. "Do you have sports?" he blurted, and then he cringed. The answer, he knew, had to be no. He hadn't seen any trophy cases or any team pictures in the hallways. There hadn't been any cartoon mascots hanging in any of the classrooms. For the longest time, Teddy had envisioned himself in an Elm Creek jersey all the way through high school. The Elks had finished third in the state soccer tournament last year; the lacrosse team had been listed in the paper as one to watch.

Jasper smiled down at Teddy, and in that split second, he allowed

himself to hope. "We co-op, man." Teddy didn't know what that meant, but Jasper kept talking. "We have our sports with a bunch of other charters. Practice is usually at this campus. We're the Southside Stars."

Teddy's whole body relaxed. The Southside Stars hadn't made it to the state tournament, Teddy knew, but he had heard of the team.

Alice Sullivan

— — — —

E cho," Alice said to herself as she and Teddy got in the car.

"What?" Teddy looked back at the building, the bland 1970s exterior not at all reflecting the generative space they'd just found inside, literal seedlings sprouting in numerous classrooms.

Alice smiled as she pressed the ignition button. She wished, suddenly, that they'd sprung for the hybrid version of this car. One of the displays they'd seen inside had a bar graph made from construction paper showing the impact of hybrids on reduced emissions. "I was just thinking about how Nana and I would yell, 'Echo!' on our road trips. We'd find a tunnel or a valley or whatever, and we'd open the car windows." She felt her lips press together and gazed at the backup camera. "Echo," she said again.

Neither of them said anything for a bit, and then, to Alice's surprise, Teddy piped up. "I've heard of the Southside Stars."

"Yeah?" She worried that if she suggested he go there, that she call Jasper back when they got home and start the paperwork, he'd balk. But the truth was, she needed him to go back to some school. She couldn't work in the kitchen, hustling to keep a stray mudroom client here and there. She needed a to-the-studs LEED project in Minnevista, a hundred-thousand-dollar bathroom on Lake Wayzata. *What would Jasper think of those goals?* she wondered.

"I think it'd be better than online school," Teddy said quietly.

Alice's heart surged. If Echo could be his idea, if it could really be a fresh start, maybe they could all find a way to move forward. "You want some lunch?" Alice asked suddenly. They were near her office, near the sushi place she frequented. "You want some California rolls?"

Teddy flipped the Sirius radio to the Hits 1 channel. Alice could see a trace of his old smile, the one she associated with his second- or third-grade self, sucking orange slices after soccer practice. "You mean, like, to celebrate?" he asked.

"Celebrate?"

"Echo," Teddy said, and then laughed. She couldn't remember when she'd last heard his laugh, she realized.

She tipped her head from side to side, matching the beat of Maroon 5. "I guess?" she said. "Are you saying you want to go to Echo?"

"I don't want to go to online school." Teddy turned away from her. "And I think you're right about Elm Creek." He raised a hand to his earlobe and pulled, the same gesture that she and Patrick knew as a tell for exhaustion when he'd been a toddler.

"Okay, then." Alice turned right into her usual parking lot. She tensed a bit when she noticed Ramona's Mini Cooper in the next row. A second wave of uneasiness followed when she realized she and Teddy were making a decision about his future without letting Patrick weigh in. But, she reasoned, he'd agree. Teddy could go back to soccer; he could have a fresh start. "Let's celebrate," she said.

But Teddy was pointing at the parking garage wall in front of them, shaking with laughter. "Oh my God," he choked. "That's, like, above and beyond." Alice followed his gaze to the bright pink graffiti drawn even with her windshield.

"Teddy!" Alice's relief about Echo dissolved. "I swear to God, if I find out you're doing that, I'll straight-up kill you."

Teddy laughed harder. "Mom," he choked out. And then she was laughing, too. "You know I'm not doing that." He doubled over, consumed by giggles.

He isn't doing it. Suddenly, she was certain. His surprise and delight at the sight of this stupid and rudimentary penis drawing were genuine. After all, this was her usual parking spot. If he had known they were about to roll up to it, he would have been sitting next to her in smug anticipation. Instead he was incapacitated by laughter. "I'll straight-up kill you," she added for good measure, and then she kept laughing, too.

"Mom, no." Teddy shook his head and leaned back against the seat, still shaking. "Look, you didn't hear it from me, but I'm pretty sure it's the feminists."

Alice burst into giggles again, and Teddy caught them. "What?" she asked. She pointed at it. This one also had the hashtag that had so worried her. "What feminists are defacing public property with penises? And what's with that TT hashtag?"

Teddy lifted his chin toward the ceiling and let both of his arms hang at his sides as he laughed. Finally, when they'd caught their breath, he said, "Donovan told me it's the feminist club at the junior high. He thinks Mikaela Heffernan and her mom are the masterminds."

Alice had many more questions, but before she could ask them, Teddy interrupted. "I don't know any more about it. I don't have any apps, remember? All this stuff happens on Insta and Snapchat."

"Let's get lunch," Alice said. As soon as they'd settled into her favorite booth and ordered drinks—a Shirley Temple for Teddy, the first strings-free treat she'd gotten him since that first call from Jason Whittaker seven weeks ago—Ramona walked through the door.

Alice closed her eyes. *Of course,* she thought.

"Mom?" Teddy said.

Alice could hear Ramona asking for her takeout order in a faux-friendly tone—the one she used for delivery drivers and vendors. There was no way they'd avoid each other. The restaurant was too small, each table in full view of every other one. But perhaps, Alice thought, they'd both agree to pretend.

"Isn't that your boss?" Teddy grabbed his pint glass and drained half of the pink soda.

"Alice?" Ramona had reached their table, a takeout bag in her hand, receipt stapled to it.

"Hi, Ramona." She tried to smile, remembering her mother's admonishments about not setting a good example for Teddy. She'd show him, in this case at least, how to deal politely with a difficult person.

"Off school again?" She pointed at Teddy, as if he were inanimate.

Teddy smiled. "I've been doing online school, but we've just decided I'm starting at Echo."

She won't care, Alice thought.

"The environmental charter?" Ramona asked.

Alice cocked her head. "How do you know about Echo?"

Ramona shrugged. Her imperiousness dissolved, and suddenly she looked nervous.

"What?" Alice asked.

Ramona squinted over Alice's head at the back wall of the restaurant. Alice took a sip of her iced tea. "The Kerrigans' daughter goes there," she said finally. "The second grader. Bea told me."

Alice blinked. That explained the pristine Edible Schoolyard Pathway Jasper had shown them, as well as the custom commercial kitchen where kids worked with a professional chef to prepare their own lunches and snacks. Kerrigan funding.

"Could I ask you . . ." Ramona looked pointedly at Teddy, but Alice just blinked at her. Whatever it was she wanted to say, they could do it right here.

"Yes?" Alice prompted.

"Well, the thing is, I could use some help with the Kerrigan project. Bea, with her interest in environmentalism, is insistent on a LEED-certified renovation. I know you're thinking about disbanding our partnership, but . . ." She trailed off.

"But you need me." Alice took a sip of her iced tea and smiled.

"There's the *Elle Decor* shoot, too." Ramona bit her lip. "Maybe we could renegotiate the terms of that."

Alice pictured her Easter centerpiece, the beautiful, nestlike metal bowl she'd bought for the sideboard. "I'll call you," Alice said. As Ramona walked away, Alice smiled at Teddy. "A double celebration." They clinked their glasses, neither caring that Teddy's was almost empty.

Evelyn Brown

Evelyn put two fingers to her forehead and began massaging. "So sorry," Julienne had texted just a moment before. "I didn't realize the conflict."

And, Evelyn wanted to respond but didn't, *you didn't want to tell me about your tummy tuck.* She laughed out loud then. A tummy tuck? For a nature therapist?

Evelyn depressed the button on the electric kettle and grabbed a sachet of chamomile and a U of M mug from her cabinet. The cataract surgery, by all accounts, was routine, but she'd need someone to drive her. She hadn't even told Alice about the appointment. As she stood over her kettle, she pictured Alice chucking the Waterford at the siding, saw her stomping like a preteen toward her car, her red dress flaring out behind her. Even as a baby, Alice had always looked dynamite in red.

Evelyn surprised herself by laughing again. Alice breaking a hundred-dollar goblet on purpose at a family gathering? Evelyn never could have predicted it. Her daughter's temper had always manifested inwardly—her shoulders rounding, her chest heaving in long, gasping breaths when anger overcame her. There had been pages of journaling in scratchy, unreadable cursive. Nothing in Evelyn's house had ever been shattered, not even when Frank declined Alice's invitation to her high school graduation.

Evelyn placed a saucer over her mug and glanced at her watch. Alice always skipped this step—the steeping. Instead, she began sipping tea immediately after dropping the bag in. At least once a week in Evelyn's presence, Alice burned her tongue.

Evelyn picked up her phone again and opened her messages. It had been four days since she'd texted with Alice. They'd been just barely maintaining the lines of communication open in their post-Thanksgiving détente. But now, Evelyn needed her daughter.

"I'm having eye surgery tomorrow," Evelyn wrote. "Could you drive me?"

Alice's response came immediately. "You're having surgery? And you didn't tell me? What's wrong???"

Evelyn smiled again, picturing the same shocked expression that had taken over Alice's face when she'd first told her about Julienne. "It's just cataracts," Evelyn typed. "Left eye. Super routine." She thought about typing *Calm down*, but resisted.

"Of course I'll drive you," Alice said.

Evelyn felt mildly guilty. *Of course she'll drive me.* She'd decided at some point in the last few weeks that Alice was unreliable, different than she had been for her entire life. "Thanks," Evelyn said. "I'm supposed to be there at nine. Ok to leave Teddy?"

"He's fine," Alice typed back. "Or at least fine enough. And I've locked down the apps on his phone."

Good girl, Evelyn thought. She didn't know what to make of the next message that came in—"The feminists are doing the penises." But as she tried to decipher it, she started laughing again.

"Maybe you can tell me more tomorrow," she wrote.

ALICE TEXTED AT exactly eight forty-five the following morning, the time they'd agreed on pickup, from the driveway at Evelyn's building.

When Evelyn got into the car, she took quick stock of Alice's face. She'd put on a little mascara, she noticed. Her cheeks, while slightly hollow, had color in them. "Thanks for coming," she said tentatively.

"Of course." Alice didn't look at her as she put the car in drive. "Where are we going?"

"Take 35W," Evelyn said. She held up her phone where she'd put the address into Waze, the app Miguel had convinced her was superior to her regular Google Maps. "The office is right next to Abbott." That was the hospital where Teddy had been born. Evelyn remembered racing into the maternity ward, her heart bursting. She'd rounded the corner on Alice's room to see her daughter, her dark eyes serious and also dull with exhaustion, bent over a tiny squawking bundle. Alice had beamed when she'd seen Evelyn. She had lifted Teddy as if he were one of the art projects she'd made in grade school, her craftsmanship always a step ahead of her peers'.

Alice was quiet for a moment until she asked, "Why didn't you tell me about the surgery?"

"I was angry." Evelyn lowered her visor against the bright fall sun. It would snow soon, she knew. She imagined picking Aidy up from school, hauling the boots and mismatched mittens.

Alice accelerated down the freeway entrance ramp. "Were you planning on having Julienne drive you today?" Her voice had a steeliness to it.

"Yep." Evelyn kept hers level.

"But?" Alice turned to check her blind spot. Her curly ponytail whipped over her right shoulder. Evelyn felt an urge to tug on it, to tease her as she had when Alice was Aidy's age.

"But." Evelyn debated just for a few seconds, and then she spilled: "She's having a tummy tuck. She got the dates mixed up."

Evelyn reached toward the radio dial and turned up the volume on the pop playlist. She'd started bobbing her head to Aidy's favorite Ariana Grande. When she glanced over at Alice next, she had sucked her

lips in and held them between her teeth. Her shoulders had started to shake with laughter. In spite of herself, Evelyn started to laugh, too. She reached over and swatted Alice on her arm.

"Stop it," she said.

"Stop it?" Alice reached a hand up and wiped a tear from the corner of her eye. "Miss Perfect Anti-Pesticide is getting plastic surgery?" She guffawed then, mouth open.

Evelyn fought her smile. "I understand that after two pregnancies, you might have some extra skin . . ."

"Oh, Mom," Alice said. "You don't have to tell me about two pregnancies. That's what Spanx are made for."

After the eye surgery—routine, as Evelyn had promised, with no complications—Alice drove straight to the Sullivan house despite Evelyn's protestations. She ushered her mother into the living room and arranged the fuchsia pillows behind her head. "We'll order dinner," Alice said. And when Aidy came home, the little girl curled up around Evelyn's feet and read to her from her level G homework.

Meredith Yoshida

When Meredith got the email alerting her to Sadie's report card, she purposely ignored the live link until she finished her shift. She had been working on "staying present," an evergreen topic in *Thinking Mother*. And, for sure, Meredith felt she was more effective at everything when she was "in the moment." Although she might have seen five cases of diastasis recti in a single day at the clinic, she reminded herself that each new mother was experiencing the abdominal separation differently and acutely. To have your body rebel against you when you were trying to be the mother you always imagined? Meredith needed to access all of her compassion.

And she called on the same resources when she did finally click on Sadie's report card from the car pool line that afternoon. As Sadie had warned her, her science grade was an actual C. A C on the report card. Meredith flashed back to that ridiculous book club when Lacy Cushing had insisted that they read *The Scarlet Letter*. Meredith reached inside her jacket and touched the dry fit material of her work polo over her heart. She imagined a "C" branded there instead of Hester's "A." "C" for "commonplace." Middle-of-the-road. Average. Meredith drummed her chest, the tips of her fingers brushing against her jacket. On each tap, the weight of the C seemed to dissipate.

Finally, Meredith glanced at the clock on the dash—one minute until school dismissal. She picked up her phone and opened her texts.

Without thinking, she began a new message to Alice. "Sadie got a C," she wrote. "And the weird thing is, I think I'm okay."

Before she clicked send, she paused. She had heard from Nadia that Teddy would attend Echo. Alice was the last person Meredith would expect to enroll her son at the hippie school. In fact, Meredith thought they could probably discuss the ethics of charter schools at one of her parenting seminars. Was it right to segment the population into little pods by niche? Nadia had also told her about Donovan's theory that the feminist club was behind the graffiti.

She opened the NextDoor app to check for Shirley MacIntosh's latest indictment of the youth of Elm Creek. Sure enough, Grace Heffernan had commented on a picture from the parking garage near Alice's office. "I think we should start considering the larger political context of these tags." Meredith rolled her eyes. Of course, Grace would consider herself some kind of suburban Banksy.

The car in front of Meredith's inched ahead. Kids had started streaming from the front doors of the school. She saw Sadie's black ponytail, higher than usual, swinging. She walked with Mikaela, who put an arm around Sadie. They could be friends, Meredith thought, as long as Sadie didn't ask for one of those "This is what a feminist looks like" T-shirts. It wasn't that she didn't approve of feminism, but Meredith never wanted to see Officer Larson again. Radicalism wasn't on the Yoshida agenda.

When Sadie made eye contact with Meredith through the windshield, her smile immediately fell and she mouthed dramatically, *The C.* Meredith shrugged and put her phone back in the console without hitting send on the message to Alice. She'd be "in the moment" with Sadie on the drive home. Maybe they'd stop for a treat, celebrate a new mediocre frontier.

And then, Meredith would email Jason Whittaker and give him a tip for who to question about the graffiti.

Alice Sullivan

As soon as Patrick walked in the door the following Friday, Alice could see his relief.

"What?" she asked. She'd been prepared to hand him his to-do list: a litany of tasks related to Teddy joining the Southside Stars, as well as a waiver request for the Liston Heights Soccer Club for the winter indoor season. Rafael had emailed thanking her for the replacement Waterford she'd sent and offering to make an inquiry about spots on the Liston Heights 14U team. Patrick could make headway that weekend before they all got lost in the Christmas rush. Alice wasn't even remotely ready for another holiday.

Patrick kicked off his sneakers and dropped his duffel in a flourish. "The case settled!" He raised his arms. "It's over."

Alice gasped. A lightness filled her as she ran to Patrick and wrapped her arms around his chest. "It's over? No more Cincinnati?"

"Not only is it over," Patrick said into the top of her head, "but the deal is favorable and—you're not going to believe this—" He pushed her away from him and stared into her eyes. "Sachman says to take next week off."

Alice shook her head just as Aidy slid between them. Patrick let go of Alice and lifted their daughter, feigning strain at her weight. "Have you grown again?" Patrick said at the same time Alice shouted, *"The week off?"*

Patrick laughed. "Can you believe it?"

Alice shook her head and joined the hug. "I can't remember this ever happening. I mean, has this ever happened?"

"Has what ever happened?" Alice swiveled her head toward Teddy. His hair looked adorably messy, and she smiled at his new Echo T-shirt, the block letter "C" covered in ivy.

"Dad has a week off." Aidy stroked Alice's hair, a motherly gesture that made Alice giggle.

"Can I do a braid?" Aidy asked.

"Maybe after dinner." Alice extended her arm back toward Teddy. "Get in here," she said, definitive. *Will he?* She waited, and then after a second, she peeked at him. He'd stepped toward them, at least. She extended her fingers and grabbed the sleeve of his light green T-shirt, and he let himself be pulled.

PATRICK TOOK THE call from the Liston Heights 14U coach on January second. Evelyn had gone to Julienne's on Christmas Eve while Alice and Patrick had hosted Nadia, Ajay, and Donovan. The kids had opened the new Xbox, and all three played without incident after dinner. The following week, Alice had been working from home on some drawings for the Kerrigan bathroom, but stopped when she heard Patrick's excited tone. "Indoor, too?" Alice stood and leaned against the frame between the kitchen and the family room. "Oh, that's great." Patrick made a fist and lifted it as if in victory. "He'll be thrilled, and I appreciate so much your understanding. I'll look forward to the email. Yes. Thanks again."

When he hung up, he beamed at Alice. "He's in at Liston Heights. God bless Rafael!" Alice indulged her husband's campy high five and then turned back to her work. She thought of Julienne, recovered now from her surgery. Evelyn had suggested last week that the three of them go out for a glass of wine, but Alice had demurred. "Not yet," she'd told

her mother. But she planned to announce that week that she'd like to invite the Martíns for dinner to celebrate the soccer news. She'd include her mother as well.

Well, "*like* to invite" was perhaps a stretch, Alice thought. "Agreed that civility and graciousness were worthy aims" was more accurate. In the meantime, Teddy would go watch Miguel's soccer game that weekend. The two had been texting while Alice looked over Teddy's shoulder. Teddy showed Alice the full exchange with Miguel, and she'd worked hard not to flinch when she realized they referred to each other as "cuz." Teddy had shown her another message, too—one to Sadie. "I'm sorry," Teddy had written. Almost immediately, Sadie had typed back, "Me, too," and that was it.

Alice planned to discuss the new soccer opportunity and the apology with Nadia when the two of them went for their power walk on Sunday morning. It still felt weird to walk without Meredith, but Alice was getting used to it.

"It's okay," Nadia had said when Alice apologized for breaking up the friend group at the wine bar. "People become friends in all kinds of circumstances. For us, it was kindergarten round-up. But priorities change. People change." She had raised her glass to clink it with Alice's.

"But I don't want to be responsible for ending your friendship with Meredith," Alice had said.

Nadia had put her wineglass down and grabbed a bruschetta. "I make my own choices." She bit off half of the bread, and then, with her mouth full, said, "You don't have to worry about me."

When the two of them met at the Elm Creek Park trailhead on Sunday morning, Alice wordlessly pointed at Meredith's Jeep, which was already parked there. She felt tempted to leave, but Nadia shrugged and started on their usual path. The park staff had replaced the defaced sign, and Shirley MacIntosh had posted on NextDoor the article from the local paper that detailed the charges and fines incurred by Grace Heffernan and Elizabeth Hunt. "We regret the property dam-

age," Grace had told the reporter, "but we hope people remember our larger message about women's equality and the objectification of women's bodies."

Alice found it hard to believe that normally astute moms could have been so misguided. *If ever there were good candidates for Meredith's ethical parenting group,* she'd thought.

In the park, Alice jogged after Nadia to catch up. The two had discussed the Liston Heights soccer team and Donovan's plans to overwinter the pollinator garden when Alice saw Lacy Cushing and Meredith walking toward them. Alice stopped, just as she'd done the last time this had happened, but Meredith just smiled at them and waved as she passed. "Hey!" Lacy called breezily. And in a second, the encounter was over.

Teddy Sullivan

One Month Later

The Sullivans were leaving in fifteen minutes for Miguel's soccer game, and Teddy pulled on the U.S. Women's National Team T-shirt Nana had given him as a "back to school" present when he'd started at Echo. "I'm proud of you," she'd said as he opened the gift during one of their Tuesday night dinners.

His parents had said the same thing lately. They were proud of him, and as far as Teddy could tell, it didn't have much to do with soccer or grades. They didn't even get grades at Echo—just written evaluations. Teddy wasn't doing anything special. He just went to school. He continued therapy and nature group with Milo. His mom had taken to shoving a whole roll of poop bags into his pocket when he left with Weasley on their walks.

Teddy had started Liston Heights soccer, but much to his relief, his team didn't face Elm Creek Premier until midway through the indoor season. Teddy wasn't looking forward to seeing Landon and McCoy, and especially not Tane. But Milo had advised him to take one day, one game, one interaction at a time. It was getting so Teddy could predict Milo's advice. He'd told his mom about the therapist's suggestions, and then he also recommended that she herself see a counselor. Milo had encouraged him to do this, actually, but he didn't tell his mom

that part. It had come up because he'd told Milo she always seemed so stressed.

"Therapy is good, Mom," he'd said. "You're the one who told me it would be. You should try it." She hadn't answered him right then, but he had heard her on the phone with Nana later, asking for a recommendation.

Teddy thought his mom seemed tense, but not too hyper, as they drove to the Liston Heights soccer dome where Miguel's team would be playing. She kept skipping songs on her favorite Spotify playlist and finally handed the phone over to Aidy to play the *Hamilton* soundtrack. Teddy rolled his eyes. Aidy had been singing butchered lyrics to "My Shot" and "The Schuyler Sisters" for weeks. Once they'd parked next to Nana's car in the lot, Teddy led his family through the pressurized doorway of the dome and scanned the soccer fields. He saw Miguel right away, his green Liston Heights jersey glowing in the bright, artificial light.

Teddy jogged ahead and high-fived Laura as she ran past him toward Aidy. He looked over his shoulder, and Laura lifted his sister. "Aidy girl!" he heard her say. "I brought my old *Nate the Great*s for when we get bored!" Laura had been at their house three times that month, snuggling with Adrian on the couch during her reading homework time.

Teddy stopped jogging when he'd reached Nana, Raf, and Julienne. "Hey!" he said.

Rafael offered his fist for a bump and Julienne gave him a side hug. Nana pointed at his T-shirt. "Love it!" she said, and then walked back to greet his parents. When they all stood together, Teddy peered at his mom. Her shoulders seemed stiff, but she was smiling. A real smile, Teddy thought. She looked for Miguel on the field and gave a wave when they made eye contact, just like she always did when she arrived at Teddy's games.

Alice Sullivan

H ey," Alice typed to Bea Kerrigan. "After we finalize the tile, do you want to grab coffee on our way to the FSC?" As soon as she sent the text, she shook her head. If someone had told her three months ago that she'd be making time for the Family School Collective, Echo's version of the PTA, she would have laughed.

But when Jasper had called her at Bea Kerrigan's suggestion, she'd agreed almost immediately. They could use an expert in architecture, he'd told her. Her heart had swelled. He had mentioned *The Third Teacher*, a book that espoused the idea that an educational environment was as important as the people in the space. She'd read it, of course, as part of her training.

And, more important, she wanted to invest in her friendship with Bea. She liked the younger woman. The two of them had grabbed dinner after a couple of late-afternoon design meetings. Alice had introduced her to Nadia at the wine bar just the week before.

Bea sent back a thumbs-up as Alice started her car and headed out of the Elm Creek Elementary lot. At a follow-up conference for Aidy, Miss Miller had told Patrick and Alice that she was impressed by Adrian's quick progression from level E to G. "Even if we're not at M by the end of the year," the young woman had said, "I think she'll be more than ready for third grade. And she says she's being tutored by an older cousin?" Miss Miller showed them a drawing Aidy had made of herself and Laura, big smiles overtaking the majority of her figures' faces.

Alice nodded. Laura, Alice had to admit, was lovely. And she had her driver's license. Alice and Patrick had been happy to hire her as a babysitter after they'd discussed it at that dinner Alice had hosted. By the time the Martíns had made it to their house for Alice's go-to company lasagna, the custom paint job in the dining room had been finalized. A grasslike pattern wound up the walls, and a whimsical pair of bare feet hid in the corner. "Like earthing," Teddy had said to Julienne when he'd pointed it out. Laura's babysitting was a boon for Teddy, too. She marginally supervised when Alice and Patrick were both at their offices after school. Alice and Patrick hadn't told Miss Miller at the conference that they'd tentatively planned to enroll Adrian at Echo the following year. She'd be in the same class as Maisie Kerrigan, Bea's daughter. The learning specialist at Echo had done some preliminary testing with Adrian. "She'll be successful here," the woman said, despite her acknowledgment that there were some "quirks" in her reading and processing. Teddy had walked down to meet them after the testing, his knees dirty from his work in the outdoor classroom, and Alice agreed with the learning specialist. They'd all felt successful at Echo.

After a short drive, Alice pulled her Volvo into a parking spot at a nondescript office building. She glanced at the note she'd saved on her phone with the therapist's suite number. Rebecca D'Agostino, she said to herself as she zipped her jacket and headed inside. "Highly recommended," her mother had told her. After Teddy had suggested she try therapy, Alice felt her only choice was to do it. If nothing else, she'd be setting a good example and proving she cared about his opinions. But besides that, she still had the manila folder stuffed in her bookshelf, the legal paper on which her mother had written the names of her birth parents shoved inside. A bespectacled woman in her sixties emerged from an inner office just as Alice had taken a seat in the waiting room. "Alice?" she said. Alice nodded and followed her through the door. She said yes to Rebecca's offer of chamomile tea and glanced at the woman's bookshelf as she waited. Alice recognized many of the volumes

from her mother's library. She smiled when she found the spine of *Listen to Me*, the tome that had gotten Alice through the first days of Teddy's meltdown at Elm Creek Junior High.

"So," Rebecca said when she'd handed Alice a cerulean Le Creuset mug and sat in an adjacent chair. "What brings you in today?"

Acknowledgments

I can hardly believe I've been allowed to write another novel. My heartfelt thanks to those who've held my hand through this second finish line. Kerry Donovan, my brilliant editor, found the emotional truth of this story and also made the pages turn faster. I'm so grateful to continue our partnership. My agent, Joanna Mackenzie, read the earliest and most stilted drafts and still expressed faith in the effort. I don't think one's agent has to be a friend, but I'm happy and proud to consider Joanna that way.

I wrote most of this book in Nicole Kronzer's beautiful backyard Burrow. I could feel Molly Weasley's warmth and ferocity within those four walls, and in Nicole's steadfast friendship and whip-smart beta reading. She's magic. In fact, all of my early readers are extraordinary. Thank you to Jordan Cushing, Alison Hammer, Lee Heffernan, and Dan West, and to my mom, Miriam Williams. Mary McAdaragh and KK Neimann told me how the book should end, thank God. Anya DeNiro, Jessie Hennen, and Christine Utz axed a whole main character. The Toucans forced me to interrogate motivations and outcomes; Nigar Alam, Maureen Fischer, and Stacy Swearingen are equally gentle and exacting. Chadd Johnson has his finger on the pulse of seventh-grade boys and understands story (and dodgeball) like no one's business. My online writers' community, the Ink Tank, provides a daily source of friendship, comfort, and laughter. Thank you, thank you all.

Thank you also to the team at Berkley, including Diana Franco, Jessica Mangicaro, Mary Geren, Megha Jain, Amy J. Schneider, Craig

Burke, Jeanne-Marie Hudson, Claire Zion, and everyone else. You're unparalleled in skill and kindness, and I'm stunned by your unfailing support. Shout-out to Anthony Ramondo and Emily Osborne, who designed the perfect, striking cover, which I love so very much. I'm grateful, too, to the crew at Nelson Literary. I hope every writer feels as well cared for. And thank you to Mary Pender, Wayne Alexander, and Jenny Meyer for your good counsel and good cheer.

Many smart and generous people helped me nail down the details in this book. Anne Nervig explained synchronized skating (and the skaters' parents). Emily Hjelm picked the wallpaper, the furnishings, and the handbag. Laura Larson agreed that the Goyard was the perfect fit. Renee Corneille and Robin Ferguson told me how they might discipline seventh graders who make the mistakes I describe in this book. Stephanie O'Brien, my sister-in-law, advised me on physical therapy clinics and also fixed my back a few times at family parties. (Sorry, Steph.) Mary McAdaragh, who is my sister and also my favorite social worker, troubleshot the soccer, the therapy, and the HIPAA. If I made mistakes in these areas (or any others), they're 100 percent mine.

Thank you to the readers and booksellers who embraced me and expressed so much enthusiasm for my first book, *Minor Dramas & Other Catastrophes*. I felt so much love from book clubs, on Bookstagram, and from independent stores like Magers & Quinn, Excelsior Bay, Valley Booksellers, Scout & Morgan, Blue Willow, Anderson's, Madison Street, Lake Forest, and Belmont. Thank you for making me feel so welcome. I'm so hoping you'll like this sophomore effort—I owe you.

I have such good friends. Thanks to you all for the cocktails, the coffees, the texts, and the adventures. I love and appreciate you so much. I also love and appreciate my parents, my aunts and uncles and cousins, my siblings, my nieces and nephews, and my in-laws. This book is for you.

And, of course, the book is also for Dan and Shef and Mac, the best three anyone could ever have. Lucky, lucky me.

Praise for *Minor Dramas & Other Catastrophes*

"A wry, engaging debut."—*People*

"Just as good as Liane Moriarty's *Big Little Lies*."
—*Kirkus Reviews* (starred review)

"Fans of *Where'd You Go, Bernadette* will flip for this clever, drama-filled debut novel."—*Woman's World*

"A smart and delightful story of entitlement, friendship, and overparenting, with page-turning twists galore. West writes across lines of class and generation with grace and ease. A bighearted debut."
—Bruce Holsinger, author of *The Gifted School*

"As intriguing as it is timely. West provides a funny and shocking glimpse into American parenting through the lens of an out-of-control stage mother who has lost all sense of boundaries."
—Amy Poeppel, author of *Limelight*

"A cutting and witty examination of modern parenting that excels in suburban relatability, West's debut novel will pique the curiosity of fans of Maria Semple's *Where'd You Go, Bernadette*."—*Booklist*

"Helicopter parenting and high school politics at their worst—and funniest. A smart, fast-paced, and deliciously entertaining debut!"
—Meg Donohue, *USA Today* bestselling author of *You, Me, and the Sea*

D0350019

CH

DISCARD

Westminster Public Library
3705 W 112th Avenue
Westminster, CO 80031
westminsterlibrary.org